SPARROWHAWK ON THE HORIZON

By A. Scholte

First published in Great Britain 2017

© A. Scholte 2017

The right of A. Scholte to be identified as the author of this work has been
asserted in accordance with sections 77 and 78 of the Copyright Designs and
Patents Act 1988

Whilst the historical events upon which this book is based are true, it is a
work of fiction. Although it contains references to real people and real places,
these are used in a fictitious context. Other names, characters, places and
events are products of the author's imagination, and any resemblance to actual
events, places or persons, living or dead, is entirely coincidental.

ISBN Hardback: 978-1-9998282-1-9
Paperback: 978-1-9998282-0-2
e-book: 978-1-9998282-2-6

Typeset in Serif – Minion Pro by Action Graphics, Teddington
Printed and bound in Great Britain by Clays Ltd, St Ives plc

MIX
Paper from
responsible sources
FSC® C018072
www.fsc.org

www.1851cup.com

To

MY HUSBAND*

This Book

is

Affectionately Dedicated**

* we finally did it
** based on the words of Mark Twain

"*Most of us have seen the agitation which the appearance of a sparrowhawk in the horizon creates among a flock of woodpigeons or skylarks, when unsuspecting all danger, and engaged in airy fights or playing about over the fallows, they all at once come down to the ground and are rendered almost motionless by fear of the disagreeable visitor. Although the gentlemen whose business is on the waters of the Solent are neither woodpigeons nor skylarks, and although the America is not a sparrowhawk, the effect produced by her apparition off West Cowes among the yachtsmen seems to have been completely paralysing.*"

The London Times, 18 August 1851

Chapter 1

Above John's head, feet were moving about on deck; it was the purposeful sound of hard-working men going about their chores. He should get up; they probably expected him to be more involved by now. But the sea felt reasonably calm this morning, so hopefully they could do without him for a while longer. Staying where he was meant he didn't have to face the others just yet.

He looked up at the beams and breathed in the smell of the newly varnished wood. The rhythmic creaking of the boards was slowly becoming less unnerving. *How many of these planks had been through his hands?* Months of hard work had gone into this ship and now he was lying in a berth in the finished product somewhere out on the open ocean.

He ran his thumb over the scar on his left palm. It could have been a reminder of how physical the job had been over the winter months, but instead it was the result of a stupid incident when the wooden vessel surrounding him was only the ambitious idea of a few men. He recalled how he had been woken by screaming voices.

'Wake up, you lazy fool!'

John kept his eyes closed; he knew this wasn't meant for him. Someday his neighbours would come falling through the flimsy wall into his room, shouting at each other over his sleeping body. But today he was close to grateful that they had roused him, as he wanted to be at work on time. Shocked by the coldness of the floor, he was dressed and out the door in a matter of minutes. The icy air took his breath away and the freezing particles caused him to cough uncontrollably.

'Hey, steady boy!' Ole emerged from the darkness that hid his house across the alley.

'Sure, big fella, didn't expect you this early.' The broad-shouldered man was similarly wrapped in several layers of clothing. John liked Ole, and he enjoyed the tales of his native country as the two of them walked along 12th Street to the shipyard on the other side of Manhattan, on the shore of the East River. Even if he had to listen to the same story two or three times, at least this meant he didn't have to say much.

This morning's story was all about the winter days Ole had experienced as a child in his home town, in the far north of Norway. How from October the sun started to set earlier each afternoon until, at the end of November, it showed its rays for barely an hour. After this it would disappear behind the horizon until January, as if the curtains in the sky were drawn for the winter, only to be reopened in the new year for a first tantalizing half hour.

'But how do you work in the dark?'

'Polar twilight; the light that wins over darkness,' Ole said cryptically, raising his finger. 'Teaches you gratitude, and to keep faith; seeing the sun return would not be appreciated in the same way if not for the darkness.'

John smiled. Ole's story was new to him, and served as a reminder that this would be his first winter at the yard. The easygoing Norwegian had been the first to acknowledge John's presence at his new place of work. And when he'd needed another house some time afterwards, Ole had been the one to suggest he move into Gansevoort Street, close to where he lived himself. From the first morning John had left his new tenement, most journeys into work were spent in each other's company. By the time the men reached the gates, they were a group of four, having been joined by one of the workers from the blacksmith's shop and one of the plankers who was working on the vessel that was nearing completion down at the water's edge.

'I'll see you at twelve in the smithy,' Ole said in John's direction, 'to finish that game we started playing on Saturday. I've got a winning hand and there's nothing I like more than taking your money.'

John let out a short laugh and watched Ole disappear into the lumber store before heading to the mould loft. Mister George, the designer, was already present as he entered the room at the top of the stairs. He was in the company of some other men, one of whom was Mr Brown, the owner of the shipyard; the second was the master builder, Da Silva. John didn't recognise the third man but his expensive clothes stood out; they were more appropriate for a bank than a freezing cold shipyard. This man must have arrived in the carriage John had noticed at the gates, with horse and coachman waiting patiently for further instructions.

Could he be the one they were expecting today? John walked to the cupboard near the group of men. He was desperate to know what they were discussing as he searched for drawings he needed for that day's work.

'She looks splendid, gentlemen,' the visitor boomed.

'Thank you, Sir, she won't disappoint you. She will surely be the fastest one out there on the water, I can assure you of that!' replied George.

'She'd better be, George,' Brown remarked solemnly. 'The Commodore here has driven a hard bargain on this one; it could be the ruin of me.'

John tried not to smile. In the months he'd been working here, he had learned that each of the vessels that came out of the yard more than met expectations. According to Ole, Brown had acquired a considerable reputation in the shipbuilding community; together with George's qualities as a designer, it seemed that the two could do no wrong.

Was the man with the moustache the one they had been gossiping about; the Commodore of the New York Yacht Club who wanted to do business with Brown? John lingered by the cupboard, eager to find out what had been the object of the man's compliment.

'Oh, stop trying to fool me, Brown – there's good money for you in this one if she does what you and George have guaranteed.' The man they called Commodore directed his attention to something he was holding in his hands. 'She'd better, because I've got big plans for this lady.'

Finally, John glimpsed the piece of wood the Commodore was holding; he recognised it as a half model. He had learned enough about shipbuilding to know that these were carved in preparation for the build of a new vessel. So the rumour was true! Some members of the Yacht Club had commissioned a new ship. This implied more work for the yard – and maybe for John as well. He just hoped that another project could keep him distracted, as work was slowly losing its novelty. Making a cabinet for a ship hadn't turned out to be that different from making one for a home.

'Let's talk more about it in my office,' suggested Brown, guiding his guest towards the door. 'We need to get the men started as quickly as possible, as we'll have a very tight schedule.'

Once he was sure the men had gone, John walked over to the desk and carefully picked up the half model. The sharp line of the vessel's hull was remarkable; someone had put a lot of effort in carving that out of wood. He ran his hand along the side of it: narrow at the front and wider in the middle, with the section at the back tapering to slender once more. He recognised the beginnings of a fast ship, although it wasn't the usual: this was no steamship.

It explained the long hours George had been putting in over the last few weeks. He must have carved it at night while the others had gone home, because John had seen no evidence of this wooden model before. But why be so secretive about it?

'John, why are you still here?' Da Silva had come back to the loft. John was supposed to be completing the joinery in the galley of an almost finished vessel, but he didn't want to leave now.

'This new ship – what's it going to be?'

Da Silva hesitated. 'I suppose there's no harm in telling you, since the decision has been made. We will be building a ship that needs to be sailed across the Atlantic.' He made it sound as if this was a special feat, but John didn't follow; they regularly built ships that crossed oceans, so why should this be any different?

'However, she not only needs to be strong and seaworthy, she also needs to be race-worthy,' Da Silva continued. 'She is going to take part in an exhibition and she will show our British cousins just how far American shipbuilding has come in recent years.' He beamed with pride.

'Why does she need to be race-worthy if she's going to an exhibition? Who will sail her? When will this be?' John found it hard to contain his enthusiasm; his mind started to wander. *Could this ship hold clues for his future?*

'Hold your hosses! I've enough to do without answering all these questions. Aren't you supposed to be finishing off some joinery work?' Da Silva didn't wait for an answer; he collected the drawings and, with the half model under his arm, disappeared into Brown's office. The door closed resolutely behind him.

How John wished he could be in that room with the other men. Being excluded from what took place on the other side of the wall reminded him of his place at the yard. He shouldn't be delusional; the sole reason he was working here was because of the kindness of George's brother James. After the fire, when times were hard, James had taken pity on John and had helped him get a temporary job at the yard. Better not fool himself into thinking he had earned more work once his current job came to an end. But waiting for things to happen had proved in the past to have costly consequences; indecision had caused him to literally burn his fingers, and he had promised himself that he would never let that happen again. Angry that he hadn't asked Da Silva the right questions, he picked up his tools from the desk and only realised he had been gripping them too hard when a drop of blood landed on the paperwork in front of him.

'Damn it!' He dropped the tools and searched for a handkerchief, before quickly winding it around his left hand.

With worried anticipation he moved the papers to the edge of the table.

'Idiot!' he muttered to himself, dabbing at the blood on the stained document. The first two papers didn't seem that important, he noticed with a sense of relief. Just some scribbled notes and numbers. And the blood was hardly visible after he had blotted it up. The only other thing fouled was a newspaper. *It could have been worse.* Thinking about the drawings that had been on the desk earlier, he laughed nervously. As he placed the newspaper back he noticed the bold announcement written across the front page:

'England – London: Exhibition of the Industry of All Nations to be held in 1851. The preparations for the Great Exhibition, to be opened in May of next year, are progressing rapidly –'

He skimmed the page; it was an English newspaper, only a few weeks old, that mentioned the exhibition Da Silva had referred to.

'The operations in Hyde Park connected with the erection of the building which will house the Exhibition are being carried out with vigour.'

An exhibition centre in the middle of London? Were the men in the other room sure that the English were expecting boats to be sent over? John looked more closely at the drawing accompanying the piece; the building they were constructing was going to be made out of glass and iron. *Not one piece of wood*, he thought wryly. The structure appeared enormous; how would they get the building materials into the middle of a big city?

Wouldn't it be easier to build the damn thing near a river? This would make even more sense if their ship was indeed not the only one being built for the Exhibition. John imagined the hundreds of ladies, gentlemen and children parading through the corridors of glass, curious to see the inventions on display. And when they had strolled to their hearts' content, and were hot from being inside all day, they would saunter out to the River Thames to see the most striking sailing vessel they had ever seen, bobbing on the water, with the Stars and Stripes flying proudly in her mast. He could practically hear their adulation and feel the breeze on his face; a pang of urgency filled his whole being, and the throbbing pain in his hand was momentarily forgotten. He could be there.

A mere seven months later, the incident with the rusty nail had left nothing more than a crooked line of raised flesh and the unimaginable had become reality; he was now on his way from Manhattan to England.

Four days earlier, they had set sail. Although relieved to be on board, John was apprehensive at the same time. The first two days on the ship had been challenging for a lot of reasons, but what had affected his mood most was the fog that surrounded them. The world had dropped out of sight behind a suffocating wall that travelled with them. He was convinced that the disappearance of the horizon had contributed to him feeling sick only a short while into the journey.

The other men seemed unaffected and very much at home, which reminded him that he was one of only a few who had never been on a ship for more than a couple of hours. An ominous feeling had descended on him. *What if he felt like this for the whole journey? What if he wasn't cut out for sailing?* He'd always thought that if his brother had taken to it the way he had, he would be the same. There was no turning back. By convincing the Captain and the others to let him join this venture as the ship's carpenter, he had only himself to blame. He had to give it all he could. But that wasn't easy feeling as sick as he did.

He tried to ignore the redness of the scar. It had stopped being merely a memory of the day that had brought new opportunities. Instead, it had become more of a warning sign, highlighting his doubts, and his foolhardy decision to come along.

Lying on his back in the belly of the yacht, John stretched out his limbs as far as his berth allowed. He touched the wooden planks above his head. They had managed to make her in such a short space of time, he hoped they hadn't cut too many corners getting her finished.

Chapter 2

If Frank moved to the right and stretched out a little, he got a glimpse of the sea in between the buildings. An office with a 'sea view'. Not too dissimilar to his cottage on Creek Lane, 'delightfully situated on the edge of a picturesque creek', as they'd told him. All he'd found was a patch of soggy soil with a trickle of water seeping in or out, depending on the tide. Still, he had welcomed the sound of it: 'the edge' of a place, as far removed as possible from any interference. It was on the outer border of the village for sure, albeit not difficult to find as the smells of the coastal marshland were enough to guide you if you ever felt compelled to check out the cove for yourself.

Just like the ear-piercing sounds of the seagulls, the smells were a constant reminder of where he was: boggy and musty near his house, salty and fishy towards his work place. He had always intensely disliked the taste and smell of fish, and the irony didn't escape him; having avoided it for most of his adult life, he was now surrounded by its odour for twenty-four hours a day.

Luckily, he had his pipe to block it all out. He pulled his tobacco sachet from underneath a pile of papers. He preferred to smoke cigars, but he didn't want to get into another argument about smoking them in the office.

Where was his darn pipe? Finally he found it between some layers of old newspapers. One day he was going to set the place on fire if he wasn't more careful. He filled the bowl with tobacco and moved a lit match over the top; with a few puffs it was alight. He drew in the familiar taste of the tobacco, leaned back in his chair and closed his eyes. How quiet the office could be at times. However much he grumbled about being in a small-town office, he'd never before in his job enjoyed so much time to himself. Right from the beginning, he'd made it clear that he wouldn't be joining the others in their daily morning meeting. There was no point in him wasting his time sitting in a tiny office discussing the topics for the next edition and the stories they planned to run during the weeks to come. The team worked in such close proximity to one another that they could smell each other's breath, so making the editor feel important by having a meeting in his box room made no sense. He could say out loud what he wanted to see in print without the others having to move an inch from their desks. He got away with it. *The 'expert' from London*, he thought sneeringly. They seemed to have some sort of respect for that – but even if not, at least they left him alone.

Besides, there wasn't that much of importance to write about in this small town to justify such meetings. One day he ought to join them and point out that the world was bigger than the rows of cottages cramped between the hectares of empty ocean and the avalanche of rolling green fields: too much green, at this time of year.

Tipping back in his chair with his pipe in one hand, he gazed at the letters on his desk. This was a letter-writing nation indeed, and he'd discovered that in some villages the residents had more time on their hands than in others. Frank grumbled. Dividing the letters into some sort of order of relevance hadn't been very successful, as the stories were equally trivial. Should the announcement of the baking competition at the July fair appear in the same section as the accident with the cart whose horse had bolted after it lost a wheel?

The man who had told Frank the story had stopped him in the street when he was going for a drink the previous Sunday. The weather had persuaded him to go out; there was hardly any wind and it had been as quiet as it probably could get this close to the ocean. He had been on his way to a little inn just behind the main street, a place he had started to visit since he had considered himself ready to have another drink every now and then. In the beginning, venturing outdoors hadn't been a particularly relaxing experience. For several weeks after he'd arrived, he had felt like the fish he so detested. It was as if the locals could smell him coming down the cobbled streets; they stared and whispered as he passed. He would have preferred it if they'd said something to him – anything – but the only attention he got was the unashamed curiosity bestowed on a stranger who stuck out like a sore thumb. One of his old colleagues had warned him that he would never fit into a small town, and that he would be back in London in no time. But he'd had no choice and he had started to avoid being outside his cottage as much as he could. Given that he had arrived during the winter, he had been content with that. His cottage was a pleasant enough place in which to pass the time reading, once he got the fire going. Although small with cramped rooms, he had been grateful to discover that it came with a few practical pieces of furniture and one large comfortable armchair. Whilst it had seen better days, it had made all the difference as he didn't have the necessary funds to buy anything.

But one day, just like that, they'd stopped staring at him. It was as if they had become used to his presence when they realised he didn't pose a threat to their community – which meant that none of the rumours from London had made it through to them.

And now, after several months, they'd become almost too familiar, approaching him in the street with their so-called news stories, just like the man who had thrown himself at the runaway horse.

'You must have been afraid.' Whether or not he was worn out by these mundane stories, his naturally curious disposition made him put up with the more tedious members of public.

'Oh no, Sir, I'm used to 'orses, I work with 'em at Mr Richard's farm.'

'Yes, but you must have been surprised seeing that horse and broken cart coming hurtling down the street? Weren't you worried you'd be struck?' *Why was he still here speaking to this man when it was his day off?*

'I didn't 'ave no time to think, Sir, I did what I 'ad to do, just like the other day with the runaway 'orse.'

'Did you catch another one?' Frank looked at the man in surprise.

'Well, to be truthful, Sir, I didn't 'ave to catch this one, he was one of ours.'

'Right.' Frank's attention faltered; over the man's shoulder was the little lane that led to the inn, where a peaty malt awaited him.

'It 'ad been stolen from us the very day before,' the man continued, looking at Frank inquisitively. 'Didn't you 'ear about the robbery of the post office in the next village?'

The word 'robbery' brought Frank back to the cobbled street; this sounded unquestionably more interesting.

'No, I haven't. What happened?'

'Well, one morning 'bout two weeks ago, we found one of our 'orses missin', and there were signs it had been stolen.' The man paused for a moment.

Here we go, Frank thought: *another heroic citizen acting like the local bobby.*

'That afternoon, it came running back to its stables and we found out it 'ad been used by the thief.'

'Really? And how could you know that?'

The man roared with laughter. 'Ha ha, the 'orse ran back to the stables –' He slapped his thigh with delight and cried out, '– with the poor fellow still on it... and the loot in his 'ands! Guess who 'anded him over to the peelers?' With a big fist, he hit his own chest and then smacked Frank on the shoulder. 'Nah, what do you think of that story, hey?'

The unexpected ending caught Frank unawares and he smiled in appreciation.

'Well done. One day you catch a horse with a thief, the next day a horse with a cart.' Frank shook the man's hand. 'By the way, did you find out what happened to the coachman of the one-wheeled cart?'

'Ah, Mr Wrigglesworth's coachman? Poor soul, he got thrown

out of the cart and landed on his 'ead.'

'Did he? Well, is he all right?'

''Asn't woken up since.'

Frank moved the runaway cart story to one side of his desk, adding it to a new pile called 'Coroner's Inquests'. Drawing on his pipe, he decided to write the stolen horse story himself, and to embellish it with detail about how the thief had been tied to a sty full of hungry pigs until the police arrived.

He spread more letters on his desk. Selecting which ones would appear in the paper was part of his more senior role. He'd had to compose himself when McIlroy, the editor, had mentioned the 'senior' title and the importance of his role. How was he to pick between letters about fishing, the weather or harvesting?

Early harvesting. – On Friday 14 June 1850, a first cut of hay was carried out by Mr Terence TUMMON, at Meadow Farm.

One of the juniors had tried to explain the value of the farming news to the other farmers in the community, but Frank had quickly recognised that it was easier to stop questioning the local news and instead pass it on to one of the juniors to prepare.

EMIGRATION TO AMERICA: BOSTON AND LIVERPOOL PACKET SHIPS.
Sailing from Boston on the 5th and from Liverpool on the 20th of every month as follows.

Frank glossed over the details; he had never given them much thought. *Was it still an option?* If he picked up his few belongings from the cottage and headed for the Liverpool docks he could sail away from this windy and smelly place. To the New Country, to New York – or even better Chicago, further from the sea. All he had to do was to bear a few weeks on board a ship and then he could start a new life where nobody knew him.

Frank sighed; his pipe had run out of steam, just like himself. He felt old, too old to venture into something like that. He had barely managed to move the eighty miles from London and didn't have the energy to start again. *What was the point in starting a new life?* Undoubtedly in his case it would be an attempt to escape from the unavoidable – meaning himself. In any event, the thought of the passage was enough to make his stomach turn.

He pressed the tobacco further down in his pipe and tried to get the fire going, but to no avail. McIlroy's door was still closed. The atmosphere in that room had to be suffocating by now; perhaps they had passed out. *What was keeping them?* He picked up another letter from the endless pile.

'Dear Editor. The other day I came across an edition of your sister newspaper "The West Briton and Cornwall Advertiser" and was drawn to the following extremely unfortunate tale of loss of life. For reasons of compassion, I would like to share this tale with you and your readers in the hope that somewhere it can help bring to an end the relentless search of a grieving family for the truth. The article reads as follows: Bottle found – On Tuesday last, a sealed bottle was picked up in Falmouth inner harbour, containing a paper, of which the following is a copy: Brig "Camperdown", off the coast of Guiana, half-past eleven o'clock p.m. blowing a heavy gale of wind, leak in the vessel, working at pumps, not expecting to see land again, water gaining fast. Captain THOMAS, first mate JAMES, second mate RICHARDS. January 2, 1846.

After reading this tragic story, dear Editor, I hope you find reason to publish this account of misfortune for the public to read, such that they can help find the relatives of these ill-fated men. Yours sincerely, Mr Dedlock.

Suddenly the letter felt heavy: what a dramatic way to find out about the fate of a loved one. After years of waiting and speculating, they would finally discover what had happened by reading a brief message at the bottom of a newspaper page. The men had perished together with their sinking ship in the dark eve of a raging storm. Well, at least the families had an answer after years of agonising, which had to be better than no answer at all. Frank snorted. Not that he personally knew much about waiting for loved ones; there wasn't anybody waiting for him, and vice versa. The few relatives he had in London couldn't care less where he was and his 'fine' colleagues from the past were glad they were rid of him. His life, like the Captain's and his doomed crew, had eroded to a speck of sand washed up on the beach. He groaned; the self-pity was becoming tiresome, this wasn't about him. His thoughts flashed to the unopened box in his cottage; more than anybody else, he knew all about being reported missing and about grieving family members wanting to know where their relatives had vanished to.

He shook his head to do away with the images; at least the story was a good reminder why he'd never wanted to set foot aboard a ship. He got up; he needed some fresh air, even if it was of the salty variety.

'Frank, could you please come in for a moment?'

Frank nearly dropped the book he was holding; he had just returned from his unauthorised break and felt as if he'd been caught red-handed. What was he thinking? He was a forty-five-year-old man, not a seven-year-old boy caught stealing sweets in a shop.

'Yes, certainly,' he mumbled, picking up his pencil and notebook.

'We have had a discussion.' McIlroy sat broad-shouldered behind his desk, his back to Frank. Sometimes he conveyed the impression that Frank had been hired out of pity; the way one would feel sorry for a workhorse that was past its working days by giving it light jobs to do. The tone of his voice sounded hesitant today, and Frank didn't like what this might possibly allude to. In the five months he had been working there, he'd tried his best to make the transition from critical political writer to local newspaper writer. *Could they be tired of him already?*

'About what, may I ask?'

McIlroy spun around, with a grave look on his face. 'This.' He tapped with a heavy finger on a newspaper on his desk: it was the paper Frank used to work for.

'What about it?' Frank's suspicions arose. Why had McIlroy asked him into his office to talk about a newspaper he no longer had anything to do with?

'Well, it concerns that exhibition in London.' McIlroy turned the newspaper around for Frank to read it. In bold letters, it said: 'PREPARATIONS FOR GREAT EXHIBITION WELL UNDER WAY.'

'Since when do you have any interest in what is taking place in London?' Frank tried to sound light-hearted, hiding his concern about the reference to London.

'I have always had much interest,' McIlroy replied defensively. 'But as we can only incorporate a limited selection of news in our publication, I have to be somewhat discerning.'

'Are you pursuing a piece on the Great Exhibition for our paper?'

'There's no beating about the bush with you, is there Frank? Yes, I am considering it.' McIlroy folded the newspaper neatly in the middle and caressed the edges.

'Why now?'

'What do you mean? We've done pieces on it before; didn't you do some of them?'

'You mean those three-word contributions?'

'Was it worth more, then? The Queen's bored Consort coming up with a grander idea than educating his own children in the art of vegetable-growing?'

'You sound so sceptical,' said Frank with a laugh, satisfied now that their talk wasn't to do with his job. 'I thought that was my prerogative? Anyway, you should give that poor man some credit; he's conceived a plan for a world exhibition and people appear to be most enamoured by it, if I can believe what I've been reading in the other newspapers.' He emphasized the word 'other'.

'Since when do you feel empathy with members of the Royal Family? And the never-ending debates about who's going to finance the Exhibition, and where it's going to be held; didn't I hear you make unfavourable comments about them a few weeks ago?'

Frank let out another laugh. Whatever he thought about Prince Albert, one had to admire the man for finally finding himself a job to do. For so long he had been ignored and treated as 'that foreigner', someone not able to openly assist his wife in any political matter. Some members of Government were still suspicious of him because of his German background. 'Well, I can appreciate a chap's determination. He could have remained on the edge of the ballroom; instead he has come up with something that's being seen to be advantageous for the whole country. And it's not even his own country, but his adoptive home, I should add.'

'Oh, please, Frank, next you'll be telling me that inviting foreign manufacturers to display their products at a fair in England will encourage world peace.'

'Did you want to do a feature on it or not? By the way, I think you will find more people who will agonise over the fact that these foreign manufacturers will surpass our own efforts than those hoping more interaction between nations will lead to peace.'

'Do you not mean the other way around? How we are superior to whatever comes out of these foreign countries?' McIlroy mumbled. 'In any case, to encourage the submission of the most exciting products the Commission has decided to hand out awards.'

'Really, prizes, for what? Who can create the most innovative...' Frank paused for a moment, not sure exactly what the Exhibition was going to display, 'Farming implements? Weapons?' he added sarcastically.

'Oh no, they're thinking of excluding instruments of destruction from the Exhibition. To encourage peace, remember?'

'I see; the participating countries are going to meet, not in war, but in an amicable contest.'

'You almost sound as if you believe that yourself.'

'I just read it.' Frank pointed at the newspaper. 'But I do like an element of rivalry; we might learn something from others.'

'I thought you were too old for competition. Anyway, where were we?'

'You were going to explain to me why we're going to spend more time on it now.'

'Well, we've had criticism from the vicar.' McIlroy scratched his head. 'He accosted me last Sunday after service.'

'The vicar is interested in worldly goods?'

'I've never seen him so enthusiastic! He kept calling it the great Olympian festival of modern times.'

'Really? But what does he want from us?'

'He suggested that we assist in the promotion of the Great Exhibition.'

Frank raised his eyebrows.

'He's of the opinion that we haven't given enough attention to the call of the Royal Commission that any person wishing to exhibit next year should furnish details about themselves.'

'Such as?'

'Well, about the objects they propose to exhibit and the space required for exhibiting them.'

'What has that got to do with us?'

'He believes we should publish the appeal in our paper for everyone to read. We apparently have a local committee, and prospective exhibitors could make contact with it.'

Frank looked baffled. 'Does he really think we have potential exhibitors in our midst? In this town?'

'And that's when he became impatient with me; he told me in no uncertain terms that the Exhibition was intended for people from all pursuits and professions, and from all classes and callings of life.'

'So, you promised him an article? Why didn't you say so immediately? I'm sure it won't take that long to craft something on the Exhibition.'

'I know, but I was thinking that maybe we could make it a more regular feature – perhaps weekly or monthly. It will make our paper look more grown-up.'

Who was he fooling? A small provincial paper on the south coast of England; how many readers look beyond the advertisements?

'Anyway, I've made up my mind and this morning we've been discussing who might be the most suitable to do this and who could travel most easily to the capital if necessary. "From our own correspondent in London" sounds rather splendid, don't you think?'

For a moment Frank was taken aback. Did McIlroy mean one of them had to actually go to London? Frank thought about the city he had left all those months earlier; it had been cold and wet, a typical late winter's day. He had been ready to quit the place he had lived in all his life; he had outgrown it, in a sort of reverse manner, leaving the bigger town for a smaller one where nobody knew him. The metropolis had brought out his worst traits, especially after his arrest.

In this village only McIlroy knew him – or should he say, knew *of* him? Years ago, McIlroy had worked for a couple of months at the paper in Fleet Street; he didn't stay long, returning quickly home to his village on the south coast. Out of the blue, not long after Frank had made his decision to leave London, McIlroy had contacted him, explaining that he was now an editor and urgently needed a more experienced reporter in his office: did Frank know of anyone?

Frank hadn't asked any questions, including about how McIlroy knew he was available. He needed to work and he was in no position to be choosy about what was being offered.

Sitting in McIlroy's office now, he had to admit the months had passed more quickly than he'd expected, and without too much anguish. Was he settling into village life after all, leaving London to fade into the background?

'Who did you have in mind?' Frank asked the question

anyway.

'We were thinking of you.'

As if making it sound like a joint decision would make it more difficult for him to decline!

'And I've already told the others,' McIlroy added quickly.

'They can't have been too enamoured with that: last one in the office, first one to get to travel to the big city?' Frank remarked dryly, wondering if he still had a chance to get out of it.

'Well, I've made up my mind. In all honesty, you're the only one who could do it. We don't have excess funds, so I thought when you go back to visit relatives, you could remain a little longer and undertake your duties for the paper. That way we won't have any expenses for travel or lodgings.' McIlroy paused for a moment. 'So, what do you think?'

Frank sat quietly staring out the window, seeing only broad and noisy streets, overflowing with crowds of people and their insatiable desires. It was a bad idea to go back, but he couldn't come up with any good reasons to object. A seagull landed on the windowsill of a building across the narrow street; it had a shiny object in its beak – a small fish. The bird just sat there, not yet convinced that it was worth swallowing, while the little creature twisted and turned, desperate to escape.

Eat the damn thing, put it out of its misery. The bird bent its neck and then raised its head, ready for the final move. The sun caught the silvery creature wriggling vehemently until it managed to free itself. *What's the bloody point*, Frank sighed silently, watching the fish fall towards the cobbled street below.

'All right. I'll go.'

Chapter 3

The fog had lifted and then it had started to rain. The horizon, visible for a couple of hours, had disappeared once more, this time behind a solid curtain of water. Despite sitting with several men in a confined space, John had never felt so isolated. The absence of a view had added to his misery, causing him to feel sick all over again.

The pleasure that breakfast had given him the previous morning seemed incomprehensible now, as the thought of food made him gag. He watched the other men negotiate their way round the ship effortlessly; to them, the yacht was like any other place of work, no different to one ashore. But for him, the cold workshop back at the yard was preferable right now, despite the icy winds that had passed through it most of the winter. He was the odd one out, and he wouldn't get much sympathy for his suffering.

'John, give us a hand, will ya?' Nels Comstock shouted from before the mast.

He looked up, surprised to hear his name; this was the first time since they had set sail for England that he had heard it called. There hadn't been much opportunity before they'd left Manhattan to discuss what he was expected to do as the ship's carpenter, but he was ready for anything that was asked of him. He was sitting near the cockpit, waiting for instructions; he just wished he felt a bit better. He took a deep breath and slowly crossed the unsteady ship to help Comstock. *What had he been thinking, pursuing this trip so doggedly a month ago?*

'We're struggling to set our colours.' Nels handed John some lines. A few days earlier, they had watched an English brig set her colours in salute and when they had tried to reply, they hadn't been able to hoist theirs any further than halfway.

John held the lines while Comstock tried to work out why the flag had got stuck.

'Good we tried this before and didn't wait 'til we arrive in English waters.' Comstock's gaze remained focussed on higher up the mast. He looked just like his older brother, William, who was also on board. John had watched them work in unison without exchanging any words.

'I hope you're not superstitious like the others!' John said playfully, pleased that he had remembered at least one thing from Ole's humorous lesson about the long list of beliefs sailors held to make sure they avoided risks at sea.

Nels didn't look up from his work but snorted softly. 'If I was, I'd be more worried about the number of crew on this ship than a stuck flag.' He held his breath. 'Gotcha!' He managed to release one of the hooks of the line a few yards up the mast. 'I was gonna send you up there. But you're lucky today,' he added, emphasizing 'today'. He took the lines from John. 'Be careful when you walk back.'

John watched him walk to the bow, reflecting on the strange conversation. Like his brother, Nels appeared friendly, but John didn't like the tone of his voice. Had he been implying something? The thought struck him; as a late addition to the crew, was he the thirteenth member to come aboard? He counted the other men and, if he included the cook's assistant, he was indeed the extra roll in the baker's dozen. When he had climbed onto the ship on the day of departure, some of the other men had looked at him oddly, which he had interpreted as their disapproval of his lack of sailing experience. But he hadn't cared; all he wanted was to come along on this journey, and a few disgruntled men were not going to stop him.

John shivered; had Ole been serious? He had never been superstitious, but nevertheless, a powerful apprehension of something bad happening reared its ugly head – a feeling that he recognised from some time ago. He should have learned his lesson then not to be so impulsive. But it was too late; through the damp and salty air, the memory of the combined smell of intense heat and pungent sweat of his angst came rushing back, taking him back to that terrible evening more than a year ago.

The alarm had gone off. It was going to happen. Finally.

The crewmembers of Live Oak Engine Company No. 44 scrambled to get ready. An out-of-control fire off Goerck Street was the chilling message. His first big call-out, and this time it was for real, with lives at risk, possibly a lot of them. A four-storey tenement was their destination: living quarters, which meant families with children.

He buttoned up his uniform and straightened his gear. He was new to this, but it was what he had been preparing for and why he had joined the Engine Company. He was determined to demonstrate his abilities and his value as a member of the team. He knew his physical strength was going to be an advantage and they'd agreed he was going to go in first with James and Wilson.

Nothing had prepared him for the ferocity of the fire; fourteen men were confronted by a burning hell. He stood and looked in awe. Against the dark outline of the building, the dragon's breath burst out of the windows, through the roof, and any other gaps appearing in the structure, licking the walls with its flaming tongue. His father had told him about the intensity of the heat, but not about the noise that came from the burning materials, the screams of the people, and the overall chaos of their shadows running to and fro. One of these shadows came towards him, briefly illuminated against the glare of flames sprouting out of the building in the background. It gripped him hard by the shoulder; a man shouted in his face that there were women and children inside. With a jolt, he came to his senses; there was no time for any strategy, no time to think. Some of the top floors were alight. What chance did he have of finding people alive? Somebody turned him roughly around and pushed a hose into his hands. Above the noise, James shouted, 'Take the second door on the right, leave the first, no use, too late for them!'

He started running. His boots and uniform felt cumbersome, and the hose hung like a dead weight on his shoulder. He pulled the flexible tube with him as quickly as he possibly could, but it was clumsy and heavy and before he had reached the second door, he was out of breath. The heat was immense, brutal. There was no point in trying to fight this angry beast. Everything would be swallowed eventually – probably sooner rather than later. The only thing left for him to do was to get as many people out as possible.

Back at the engine, the others were struggling with the rest of the equipment. He was on his own. He opened the door to the building and then everything became silent. There was no sound on the narrow stairs towards the second floor, and none seemed to come from the corridor as he opened the door towards it. There was some smoke, but no flames yet. People would be able to get out of here. He decided to try the floor above. In the stairwell, thicker smoke greeted him and breathing became more difficult. Briefly, he thought about turning around, but at that very moment the world beyond his silent one kicked back into life; unrecognisable sounds reached him from behind the door he was about to open. *Were there people trapped on the other side?* Smoke streamed through the opening at the top and he remembered the warning about opening a door near where the fire was raging. The fresher air would give the flames a new lease of life, engulfing everything in the vicinity, including him. He hesitated, but a sudden cry made him reach out for the handle, luckily not yet hot to the touch. The door opened with difficulty but fortunately there was no backdraft. With a sigh of relief, he entered a hallway leading into a corridor; the top half was filled with so much billowing smoke that he had to crawl over the floor to breathe. It wouldn't be long before this part of the building would surrender to the flames as well.

He dragged himself towards the noises, not sure if they were being made by a person or if they were the cries of the building gradually submitting to the heat. As he needed one hand to guide him along the wall, his progress was painstakingly slow. A heap on the floor just ahead of him became visible: the shape of a person. John's heart jumped and his breathing quickened; inhaling the polluted air made him cough until he thought he would pass out.

There was movement; it was a man and to John's horror he was holding what seemed to be the lifeless body of a child in his arms.

'My wife, please...' The man's voice trailed off.

'Where? Where is she?' John tried to shout, but only managed a hoarse grunt. An arm lifted up and pointed into the darkness. No matter what the man asked him to do, John would have to bring him and the child to safety first. He attempted to pull the man towards the stairwell and then push him, but whatever he did, the man wouldn't cooperate. There was a faint, 'No, no – wife.'

John knew he wouldn't be able to do this without help; the motionless man was far too heavy. It occurred to him that he could perish on his first call-out along with this unknown person. Sensing the urgency, he barked angrily at the man, 'You need to get out!'

'My wife,' he grunted.

Perhaps the man was waiting for an answer. 'Go on, get out! And I'll look for your wife!' John lay down as low as possible; below the dense layer of suffocating smoke, he could see no more than a yard and a half in front of him. If he kept to the lines of the floorboards he would at least be going in a straight line. *How far should he venture into the darkness to find the wife? What the hell was taking his colleagues so long?*

The man near his feet was coughing, still cradling the lifeless body of the child. *What if he was wrong? What if he needed to try harder to get him out first? Or tell him to stay put, so he could find him on his way back? What about the child; ought he to take it out into the fresh air he desperately craved, and wait for his colleagues to help him with the father and his wife?* A debilitating panic rose; he had to make a decision he knew he couldn't make, and there was nobody to help him. The clocks stopped; time stood still. The only thing John could hear was his own breathing: oddly slow, but deliberate. His thoughts returned to the fresh air; he felt an invigorating breeze caress his forehead, and the happy shriek of a seagull passing by up high rang in his ears. Nature would come alive soon; the smell of the earth warming up in springtime entered his nostrils. He needed to rest. Maybe to shut his eyes. Silence had returned once more; no sounds came from the floor beside his feet. It took a moment before John understood what had happened; the man had stopped coughing and John watched the body of the child roll out of his arms. Reality hit him hard; the man had stopped breathing altogether.

Frantically, he removed the man's scarf to feel for a pulse, but he couldn't find one. He pulled up his sleeve to feel his wrist, tearing the fabric as he did so. But there was none; the man had died, just like that, while John was sitting an inch away. He had wasted valuable time deliberating. And now it was too late. It was imperative that he wasted no more time in finding the wife.

He crawled into the dark, away from the man and his only way out. He moved as quickly as he could, but crawling in his uniform was arduous. The destructive flames devouring anything in their way were nearing the floors above. There wasn't enough time to check each apartment and if the woman wasn't in the first one, he would leave; it was becoming too dangerous.

When he reached the door, he discovered it had become deformed from the heat and wouldn't give. The whole building was melting away around him and soon he was going to be engulfed by it, reduced to ashes, never to be found again.

He felt anger rising. For goodness' sake, he had volunteered for this job! And to get out of his predicament he was going to have to follow rules he had abandoned some time ago, left behind when he had decided to drop the water hose. To survive, he had to use his instinct, but he was no longer sure he could trust it, as his decision to join the Fire Department in the first place had been made without thought. *Or had it? Who had he been trying to please by aspiring to become the hero he wasn't?*

He took another breath and forced his whole body against the door. After the second try, it gave way enough for him to crawl through; inside it was as dark as outside, but he noticed that he could breathe a bit more easily. There was no time to inspect the room, so he shouted as loudly as he could. No reaction, only the cries of the building. And no reply meant getting the hell out of there. Just as he got back on his knees to turn around, he saw something move. On the other side of the room, a white cloth rose up like a swan slowly spreading its wings, preparing to take off. He was transfixed, captured by the delirium of a night fever. The cloth was flung into the air and standing in the midst of it was the figure of a woman.

'Get down!' he shouted. 'This way, quick!'

The memory of that fateful night was etched on his mind as if it had happened a week ago, instead of a long year. The terror in the woman's eyes had never left him, but over the weeks and months that had followed, he had found ways of blocking it out. But now fear had managed to find its way back to him, not as absolute and critical as when standing in a darkened space inside a crumbling building, but more like an accumulation of bad signs, warning that things could go wrong at any time if one made an impetuous decision. *That's probably how one ends up believing in superstition*, he thought wryly.

Carefully he made his way back to the stern; Comstock no longer needed his help. At least he was surrounded by water and not by flames.

'Ah, John, I see you're working on your sea legs,' said James, sitting in the cockpit near Captain Brown. The rain had ceased and the non-sailors were coming out of the woodwork.

'Yes, I'd better make myself useful.' John smiled at James's weathered face. He could be a sailor with that beard and those lines scored deeply into his face; even his tolerance of the moving ship was like that of an experienced boatman. Or that of a man determined to let nothing come in the way of his enjoyment of life, especially not an unsteady boat. The ability to forget easily probably helped. They had never spoken much about that night, except for when John had told the team he was going to leave the Fire Department. Briefly, James had tried to convince him he was an invaluable member of the team, but when John had showed his determination to leave, James had supported him without hesitation.

'What about you, Sir, are you enjoying being in the middle of the ocean?'

'I'm getting there. Better than my son – or my brother, for that matter.' James stroked the leather-bound notebook he was holding on his lap. 'Both sick as dogs.'

'How's the log-book coming along, Mister James?' Captain Brown's deep voice was easily heard above the wind in the sails.

'Very well, thank you, Captain. It's quite satisfying to record our progress. I think it's time to take some soundings and see how fast this lady is going today. I'm sure John here will be of assistance with that.'

'Yes, of course.' John welcomed the opportunity to be useful, and he took the log and the log line from James. He was glad James wasn't able to guess what he had been thinking about and how it still bothered him. He would probably tell him that he'd warned him from the beginning. When they'd met at the fire station, John was introduced to James as the 'woodman'. James had joked about how wood was both their friend and their foe, and how ending up at the one fire station carrying the name it did must have been fate. During their fire training, John found out that the bearded man with the unkempt eyebrows worked in shipbuilding, just like the other members, handling oak on a daily basis, not unlike John in the small furniture shop where he was employed.

'But boy, wait until it burns,' James had said. 'You'll see its destructive nature.'

John threw the log overboard; it disappeared into the dark water. One by one the knots slid through his hands, every one signalling they were one step closer to English shores, and one further away from the place he used to call home. They were moving fast.

Chapter 4

August 1850, London

'When did you arrive?'

'Yesterday.'

'I heard a rumour you were back working in London.'

'It's not quite like that, Bill.'

'Well, I took an hour for lunch, so go ahead and tell me why you're here.'

'Thanks for sparing the time, I appreciate it.'

Was Frank imagining it or did Bill sound guarded?

The two men were sat in a little tavern at the back of Fleet Street, not far from where Frank had spent the night in the shabby but familiar room at Mrs Jackson's residence. He had given it a lot of thought since yielding to McIlroy's 'suggestion' that he go to London every now and then. And however depressing it was that he'd ended up in the same damp room he'd found after being no longer welcome in his own home, it was all he could come up with – and afford, for that matter.

'What can I get you to eat?' As curious as he was about what had happened to the work left unfinished when he had departed in a hurry, he hadn't come to interrogate Bill about that. Bill probably didn't want to be reminded of Frank's behaviour in those last weeks in London, and he hadn't returned to reminisce about the old days. Besides, he was a different man now.

'I'll have the usual, the barmaid knows.' Bill gestured to her in the corner of the establishment.

Frank had been looking forward to a meal in this place; they sold a nourishing beef steak pie and, despite being on his own for some time now, he hadn't taken to cooking for himself.

'You're not coming back then?'

Bill sounded uneasy: not a demeanour Frank would have associated with his old colleague. They had met several years ago, when Frank had moved desks at the paper. Bill had been a few years his senior, and loved to share his experiences as a reporter. However questionable the quality of his written words was sometimes, he made up for it with his fearless and analytical attitude towards the people he wrote about. And no matter how serious the subject he was working on, he'd always had time for a joke or two. He'd changed slowly over the years he and Frank had worked together at the same paper – but even more so during the seven months since they had last met. His normally playful mood had become more thoughtful: something that Frank assumed came with more responsibilities at work. He looked different now, too – thinner in both body and hair. And when he wasn't holding his glass, he picked nervously at the flesh around his nails.

Was his presence making Bill tense? Or was it the possibility of his return?

'You remember McIlroy?' Frank looked at Bill through his glass of ale. 'You know, the young fellow who worked briefly for us, all those years ago, curly reddish hair?'

'Aidan?'

'Yes, Aidan McIlroy, that's the one.' Frank took a sip from his drink, savouring the smooth taste. 'I don't know how it happened, but he contacted me shortly after I decided to leave London and I've been working for him ever since my move down south.'

'Really?' Bill seemed indifferent to the apparent coincidence.

'He speaks highly of you,' Frank continued. 'Those months of tutoring must have made an impression.' He was beginning to question his decision to meet Bill; he couldn't work out his behaviour and wondered if he was the only one finding the situation awkward. His departure had been problematic, but what had happened in the past had nothing to do with Bill personally, and the man should know that. On the contrary, not only had Bill lent him a hand when things at the paper had become difficult, he'd also helped him move out of the marital home. But now his hope for renewed contact was fading; maybe he should stick to the work-related reason he'd come here for.

'I'm here to consult you, that's all.'

Bill's attention shifted; he looked away from the window and towards Frank.

'Should I feel flattered?' A quick smile flashed over Bill's face.

Frank recognised his old colleague's suppressed wit and relaxed. 'Yes, you should.'

'I can't imagine how I could be of any help to you.'

'What do you mean? You've helped me out often enough in the past.'

'That was different, covering your back because you turned up late.'

'Or not at all.' Frank hesitated for a second, sensing Bill's reluctance. 'Did I ever thank you for helping me out in the way you did?'

'Stop it, Frank, don't start with that. I'm sure you have and there's no need for it now, just tell me how you think I can help this time around.' He spoke resolutely and leaned back in his chair, which seemed to be how he felt most comfortable: giving out advice and being in control of the situation.

'I'll get straight to the point. The new gaffer wants a regular feature on the Great Exhibition and he wants me to do it.'

'So?'

'From London.'

'And you said you weren't coming back.' Bill looked concerned once more.

'I'm not. I'm supposed to be the correspondent in London while also visiting my relatives; that way it doesn't cost him anything.'

'What relatives?'

'Exactly. He doesn't know I've stopped travelling to London. Anyway, that's not really the point.' The barmaid came towards them with plates of steaming food; as the comforting smells reached Frank's nostrils, he realised how hungry he was. He attacked the pie impatiently with his fork. He could feel Bill's eyes on him while he took his first bite.

'I've just remembered this was your favourite haunt as well. Are they not feeding you down south?'

'Mmm. Just as I hoped it would be!' Frank groaned with pleasure. 'Too much fish; those scaly, reeking creatures have never been my thing. What was I saying?' He wiped his mouth with a cloth. 'My problem is that I've rather lost touch with what happens outside the village.' The last word came out sarcastically. 'And because I don't want to spend too much time here either, I thought you could give me some leads to help me approach the story: what the general feeling is about the Exhibition amongst Londoners, and so forth.'

'I see.' Bill moved his fork around his full plate.

'Don't worry, I'm not asking you to write my story. Not like you did for me on those occasions I wasn't capable. It's not like that,' Frank added quickly.

'I understand; you just want some ideas.' Bill put down his fork. 'Now, what kind of story are you pursuing? A positive, upbeat take on the progress of the Exhibition? Or do you feel like complaining, picking out the negatives?'

Frank laughed, remembering Bill's approach to some of the stories that landed on his desk; he would write two versions and then, depending on the mood he was in and how much he cared about the subject-matter, choose one based on the reaction he wanted from the reader.

'If you give me some viewpoints of the sentiments of Londoners, I'll decide later how to use them.'

'Let me see.' Bill took another sip of his drink. 'You're aware of all the problems they've had finding a suitable location for the Exhibition?'

'Yes, I've heard that the inhabitants of Knightsbridge and Kensington-gore have signed a petition objecting to building in Hyde Park, worrying what it would do to the 'lungs of the capital'.'

'Trust me, they didn't only complain about chopping down

some trees; they actually called it a partial destruction of the park. But they're just as worried about the negative effects of clogging up one of the most important thoroughfares of London with the transportation of building materials. And then again with the removal afterwards. They're very concerned about the prices of their houses, you see.'

Bill's pretend look of worry made Frank smile. 'I'm not sure if I can interest my readers in the very personal problems of rich homeowners. By the way, did you say removal? Of the building, that is?'

'Oh yes, didn't you know? It's going to be a temporary construction since, according to some obscure government decree, a permanent one isn't allowed in the park.'

'That sounds like a most expensive operation if you ask me.'

'Well, I won't bore you with that, or why other possible sites were ignored. They've made their decision: Hyde Park it will be. They didn't want to invite people from all over the world to an exhibition in London and then have to send them into the country in search of it.'

Frank took his last bite. How typical to see London, and especially certain privileged parts of it, as the centre of the Empire! And to regard anything outside it as the countryside, only worth travelling to if one owned a country home. Admittedly, he'd thought the same for practically the whole of his life; he'd been born in the capital, just like his parents, and the only journeys he had ever made out of the metropolis were trips to the seaside during his childhood, for the sake of his health.

'So, somebody has been brave enough to decide that a few rich individuals in the Hyde Park neighbourhood should suffer the inconvenience of an oversized Bartholomew Fair in their back garden?'

'Yes, they have been told they should surrender their own fancied comforts and the luxuries of air and recreation for a limited amount of time.' Bill let out a bellowing laugh. 'Now they're concerned that thousands of members of the lower classes

34

will travel to London and take the opportunity to pry around their well-maintained back gardens.'

'What; our lords and ladies are afraid that a curious vagrant might observe their riches through the fence?' Frank smiled.

'I'm not sure they have to worry; I doubt that the Exhibition will appeal to the masses.'

'You don't believe that it is meant to be a celebration of our working men and women? For everyone, by everyone? I actually thought it was a clever idea: to create a sentiment of unity by getting the people engaged in a national undertaking, not just something dreamt up by a prince or a government. And then have the public contribute the necessary funds.'

'I don't think the working man will spare his own money for such a frivolous idea.'

'Ah, you could be mistaken there. I've had some queries from villagers who were quite willing to donate their subscription of one shilling for the Exhibition.' Frank raised his hand in admission. 'I know, not a lot, but that's all they can afford. Besides, it will be a day out for them to see useful inventions, created by fellow workers from around the world.'

'You honestly believe the organisers will refrain from filling the enormous space with whimsical objects, suited to the wants of a few with sufficient wealth?' Bill sounded incredulous. 'While at the same time showing our superiority over foreign contributors?'

'All right, there may be an element of that,' Frank said defensively. At first, just like Bill and McIlroy, he too had assumed that the Exhibition would be an excuse for parading ostentatious, impractical items. But since the vicar had reminded them to appeal to their readers to come forth with goods, doubts had set in. Perhaps this gave the common man the opportunity to come up with something novel? An invention that could shake up the Establishment? That idea tantalized Frank the most; he could think of a few whose feathers desperately needed ruffling. 'I still believe the Exhibition will be of interest to all.'

'Maybe you're right.'

'Will the sacrifice of the residents at least be compensated by a rewarding view? I'm not even sure what the building is going to look like.'

'You don't know which design they've chosen?' Bill sounded surprised.

'No.' Frank pushed his plate aside. 'I've been distracted.'

'Ah, then you'll like this.' Bill moved his chair closer to the table and lowered his voice. 'They appointed a Building Committee who held a competition for the design of an edifice fit for the purpose. If anybody had any doubt about the interest of foreign nations in this project, this competition should be a good barometer. Do you know how many plans and drawings the Committee received from foreign architects?' He looked at Frank like a schoolteacher asking his favourite pupil a difficult question, but he wasn't willing to wait for an answer. 'Thirty-eight. All right, there were more than two hundred plans submitted in total, but do you know what was extremely interesting?' Another look of expectation crossed his face. 'Out of all the English contributors the Committee selected only three to include on their list for honorary distinction, while out of the thirty-eight competing foreigners they've recommended fifteen. Ha!' He raised his glass. 'Is that a sign of how well we're going to do as the host country, I wonder? Here's to losing the first battle of the international Exhibition which hasn't even started yet!'

His cheeks had turned red. Frank remembered how passionate Bill could be about causes he strongly believed in or was vehemently opposed to.

'I forgot how competitive you are. Are we not supposed to stay graceful in any possible defeat that could fall upon us?'

Bill groaned. 'Frank, think – not everybody in this country sees it as an innocent competition. There are some who anticipate that the British manufacturer and tradesman will suffer from the inventions of these foreign nations; they fear a duty-free admission of foreign goods.'

Frank examined the man who had looked for conflict all his life; he would sniff it out, form his opinion and write about it, no matter the consequences. And he had been a good mentor. 'Isn't it more important for our designers to be afforded the opportunity of studying other products? Surely that would be to our advantage in the long term?'

'Perhaps… I'm just more convinced it's a way to determine the true measure of our superiority.'

'Or our shortcomings,' Frank said with a raised eyebrow. 'You sound as if you already know what they're going to send our way.' He waved at the barmaid.

'No, not really, but I can confirm the general interest it has created among foreign nations.'

'Do tell me – but let me treat you to a pudding first. What would you like?'

'If you really want to hear me talk more, I will, but to make this clear, I'll pay for my own food. I can't believe your local newspaper salary will allow you to buy anything at all.' Bill told the barmaid to bring them some desserts.

'How's that different from you? Don't tell me you've stopped complaining about your salary after all these years?' Frank asked mockingly.

'Well…' Bill paused for a moment, busy folding the napkin on his lap. 'I got a promotion, and with it a modest raise.'

'Really? When? Promoted to what?' Frank was puzzled; he couldn't think of any jobs Bill could have been promoted to.

'Some time ago.' Bill caught Frank's stare. 'Must have been after you left.'

'Wonderful. Good for you,' Frank hastened to say. They both sat in silence for a while. In Frank's last weeks at the paper, they had met after work in a tavern and spent hours discussing their usual grievances about their employment. They'd complained about how they were going to be stuck doing the same work for the same salary for the rest of their lives. Frank had worked himself up to a similar position as Bill's, and the improbability of getting a raise used to bring both men's spirits right down. They had discussed ways to change their fortunes and had agreed they needed to find new opportunities to enhance their reputations. It was no longer sufficient to write well-balanced pieces about the state of world affairs; they needed to become more in-depth, even if it meant working outside the brief.

More often than not, their talks had been fuelled by alcohol, although from time to time Frank had wondered if he had been the only one getting intoxicated. Ever since he'd begun working on a new assignment in his own time, Frank had longed for ways to let off steam. On those evenings, he had refrained from confiding in Bill about the story he was working on; it was too early to trust anyone but himself. Instead he would bore Bill with rambling tales until long after midnight, before being reminded he had a wife to go back to. Frank had teased Bill a lot for not having married, but he had pointed out that at least he didn't have a wife to take care of while they were on their quest to progress their careers. During these get-togethers Frank had almost felt grateful that he hadn't had the children Agnes hankered after; this meant he could concentrate on his work and not worry about more mouths to feed.

The barmaid put the plates in front of them.

'These apple dumplings look absolutely delicious.' Bill broke the silence. 'You wanted to know about foreign contributions? I can give you an example of their standard. Any idea what the French are thinking of sending over?'

'You want me to guess?'

'Don't, because you won't be able to. They've been asked to send over to the Exhibition, for us all to admire, a male and female of an African tribe who are supposed to have tails. What do you think of that?'

'I hope you're joking.'

'That's what I thought.' Bill kept chewing on the warm dough. 'At least the Americans are taking the chance to exhibit extremely seriously. The American Minister has promised to send goods that will make us, as their noble ancestors, proud to have received them from their children on the other side of the water.'

'Still looking for parental approval then?'

'Oh yes, they want to make sure that in this mission for the civilization of mankind their role is worthy.'

'I wonder what they'll send to us.'

'They seem eager enough. They've already asked for extra space. I blame the Governor of New York who has announced free passage for objects that are intended for the Exhibition. They're probably going to send us every piece of farming equipment or other oddity they can think of.'

'Could be useful.' Frank watched Bill finish his dumplings. He had hardly touched his. He leaned back and closed his eyes for a moment. How had Bill managed to get a promotion not that long after his departure? When his work had started to get sloppy Bill had covered for his absences – but surely that was no reason for being rewarded. Besides, nobody else had known about it. Or had they? He tried to recognise the man sitting in front of him, but he couldn't; Bill felt like a stranger. Coming here was emotionally draining and he wondered whether his trip had been helpful or if it had only served to stir up memories he'd rather forget. He was going to leave with more questions than answers. If Bill had been promoted, he must have had a better relationship with Lewis, their editor, than Frank had realised.

'What's happened to Lewis?' Frank opened his eyes to find Bill looking at his pocket watch.

'What about him?'

'Where is he now?'

'I'm not sure what you're referring to.'

'Did he get another job somewhere?'

Bill looked at Frank evasively. 'No. What makes you think he took a job elsewhere?'

Bill's reply baffled Frank. 'I don't know...' He had always believed that Lewis had also left the paper. No matter what his opinion was of his old editor, he'd trusted him when he said he would take care of Frank's research. Moreover, the information he'd handed over would be too enticing for any reporter with a curious mind to let lie, especially Lewis. And as he'd never seen his story published, he had assumed Lewis had moved on.

'When he got his promotion,' said Bill, 'I got his job.'

'Promotion? They gave you Lewis's job?' Frank's voice trailed off, his thoughts racing. His faith that Lewis would be able to convince the owners to run the story had perhaps been as naive as his assumption that Lewis had left, disillusioned when nobody was willing to burn their fingers on it. Or maybe that he'd even been fired. How mistaken could he have been? Lewis was still there, sitting safe and sound behind his large mahogany desk, twirling his pen with his small white fingers and stroking his ridiculous moustache. *So, what had happened to his investigation?* Frank couldn't think straight; he shouldn't have had that one ale.

'Are you all right? Frank?'

Bill sounded as if he cared, but he was also shifting uncomfortably on his seat, as if ready to end their meeting. Frank tried to concentrate and to remember the events preceding his termination, but he couldn't. He got up. 'It's getting late. I've taken too much of your time already.' He put some money on the table. 'Thank you for seeing me, Bill.'

'I told you, I don't want your money. Here.' Bill handed the money back and held Frank's hand. 'You are most welcome, Frank.'

Frank took a few steps away, but then turned back to Bill. 'You still haven't told me what the building will look like. Which design did they go for in the end – one of the foreign ones?'

'No, at the last minute another English designer turned up with an idea.'

'So, they chose one of our own in the end?'

'Isn't that what we always do?'

Frank walked out as quickly as he could. *He shouldn't have left Lewis to deal with his research; he should have done it himself.*

Chapter 5

29 June 1851, Somewhere in the Atlantic

It had finally stopped raining and the early morning breeze had increased to a steady wind. The waves lapped soothingly against the yacht's hull and a gentle moaning had replaced the loud groaning of the previous days. John preferred the stronger wind; the yacht seemed to have come into her own, and the sickening swaying had stopped. With every nautical mile they gained, his delicately regained well-being improved.

He looked up at the taut sails; each of them was set to catch every breath of wind as they moved ever further from America.

As she ran smoothly through the water, an unexpected calm befell the yacht. Life on board had been reduced to moving through the water as efficiently as possible. Not much else seemed to matter. They existed in a cocoon created by the walls of rain, the screen of fog or the empty horizon in the distance, distorting any sense of time.

The crew was taking it easy; the stable ride meant that there was no need to hurry the jobs they were doing and, for the first time since their departure, there was time to appreciate their surroundings, and to quietly discuss the way the ship behaved under sail.

Out here at sea, the world was vast and empty, and the first ship they encountered had been far in the distance. Observing her big cross in her foretopsail, the crew realised to their satisfaction that they were catching her with ease. And it wasn't long before they passed more vessels with the same effortlessness. An air of anticipation hung around the small groups of men, and the Captain and Mister James were equally enthusiastic; their voices were increasingly animated as they gesticulated towards sails and hull. It was a promising start to their journey and John wished he had someone to share it with. He knew his brother would have loved to have joined him, given the chance. But perhaps more importantly, he would have encouraged John in his adventure and assured him he was up for the job. In his brother's eyes, nothing was ever impossible if one wanted it badly enough.

John wondered if he should put more effort in getting to know the other men; despite being together in a restricted space, they had ignored him most of the time. It was going to be a solitary crossing if he didn't do something about it.

It was not unlike his early days as a cabinet maker at the shipyard, where his presence had been acknowledged by the other men, although he presumed their interest was only in seeing him do his fair share of the work.

But Ole, the friendly Norwegian, had been different. One day the previous summer, some time before the visit of the Commodore, he had called John outside.

'Hey, new guy, come out and have a look at this!' The big man with the agreeable face had come into the workshop where John was working on some ship furniture. 'You can stop for a moment, really,' he added cheerfully.

Appreciatively, John put his tools down and followed Ole towards the quay.

'Watch this; I assume you've never seen it before.'

They were in a corner of the yard where a group of ship carpenters had assembled to watch the preparations for the launch of a large steam vessel. Above their heads, the seagulls screeched loudly as if joining in with the merry atmosphere. This was the part of the job John had looked forward to the most; no longer did he have to spend the whole of his days in a dark small joinery in a back street. His new work took him outside and, better still, onto ships which, once finished, would depart to sail all over the world. Looking around him, he found they were all there: Mr Brown, the yard owner, Mister George the designer, or 'superintendent' as some called him; even his brother James had turned up. Workmen were busying themselves around the ship and, higher up the quay, a number of people carrying colourful flags had gathered. All eyes were on the dock, where the gleaming new vessel was waiting for her water-birth. Above the jubilant sounds, loud noises rumbled from underneath the ship.

'What's that?' John called out.

'They're splitting out the keel blocks,' Ole shouted back. 'Won't be long before she moves!'

The wood groaned and snapped; it sounded menacing. The atmosphere intensified, unintelligible commands were yelled from one workman to the other, and then, after what seemed like an age, the vessel slowly shifted along the slip, pushing the water away with her hull. A cheer erupted along the shore; the crowd applauded happily and the men near the water shook hands. Brown and George congratulated one another on their latest success.

The uplifting mood in the yard took hold of John; he cheered just like the others, making a celebratory gesture to Mister James in the distance. He felt good about himself and he wanted to show his gratitude to the man who had made that possible, while secretly hoping there would be many more commissions to come.

'Mister! Hey, Mister!'

John didn't recognise the young boy who had appeared through the crowd. But, hearing the urgency in the boy's voice, he walked towards him, away from the festivities on the dock.

'What's the rush?'

The boy looked flustered. 'Mister, you need to go to the gate – there's someone asking for you.'

'Can't it wait?' Irritated, John looked back at the happy scene behind him; what could be important enough he had to walk away from that? The boy kept pointing impatiently in the direction of the entrance of the yard.

'She seemed in haste –' he added, out of breath.

She? A woman? Could it be his mother? But no, she lived a long distance away and was unable to travel. *Had something happened to her? Could it be his sister at the gate?* John racked his brains. He didn't know that many women, except for family members, but just like his mother and sister, they didn't live on Manhattan. Perhaps the woman was another visitor for the launch who had got lost – but why was she asking after him?

'Thanks,' he mumbled to the boy and walked past the outbuildings towards the entrance on 12th Street. His exhilaration had been replaced with trepidation. He quickened his step until he reached the corner of the blacksmith shop, from where the gate to the shipyard was visible. As his eyes skimmed the distance, he noticed a woman standing on the other side of it: a slight figure in a dark dress, with her back towards the yard. With a sense of relief, he realised she wasn't one of his family members; they were tall, heavy-boned women, nothing like this slender creature. He slowed down; despite being curious as to her identity, he was disappointed that he was going to miss the celebrations unfolding on the dock. A few yards before he reached her, the woman suddenly turned around as if she had heard him coming.

Those eyes: he would recognise them anywhere. John was looking into the face of the unknown woman who had become so awfully familiar to him, visiting him countless times at night. Mercilessly she would enter his unconscious thoughts after daylight had disappeared. And she wasn't on her own; with her she would bring the smells, the heat, and the screams. And then the deafening silence, more unsettling than any of the harrowing noises. In the complete paralysis of his dark dreams, her face with the pleading eyes would drift past his closed eyelids, together with those of her husband and her faceless child. And now, on this joyful day, she had chosen to enter his life unannounced. John looked at the woman in shock and stopped in his tracks.

Seeing him coming, she had started to walk cautiously in his direction through the open gate. 'I'm so sorry, I should have warned you somehow...' Her voice was soft and hesitant. 'I know you don't really know me, but I had to come here. I had to see you.'

John couldn't say a word; he stared at her in utter disbelief.

She ignored his silence. 'For months now I have been thinking about what you did for us, and I knew I had to thank you personally.'

John kept his eyes on the woman, not really seeing her, too distracted by his confusing thoughts.

'John?' She touched his arm lightly. 'That is your name, isn't it? I'm Elsie.'

John wasn't hearing anything she said.

'I didn't mean to...' Her voice trailed off. 'I shouldn't have come.'

John shook his head slowly and deliberately, trying to break out of his passive state. 'Sorry, what did you say?'

She had turned around, ready to leave.

'It's seeing you here... I didn't expect that.' He rubbed his face with his hands. 'How did you know where to find me?'

'I went to the fire station some time after the fire, and they told me about you: your name, where you worked, and so on.'

John didn't know how to react. What was he to say to this woman? Was he supposed to thank her for thanking him? How could he, after what had happened to her? She had lost everything in that fire.

She tilted her head, just as though she needed to make up her mind before she confided in him. 'Nathan's doing really well. Not even four years old but so resilient, aren't they, these little ones? As if that evening never happened, although he keeps talking about fire engines.' She moved her hands nervously along her dress.

John failed to understand whom she was referring to. His thoughts kept returning to that dreadful night. How he had dragged her over the floor along the hallway, wondering how he could prevent her from seeing her deceased husband and child when they passed them, worried that grief would stop her wanting to come outside with him. But for once the smoke had been on his side; it had obscured everything around them. He had guided her along the opposite wall and had pushed her towards the stairwell in the dark. Only when they arrived outside had he come across one of his colleagues about to enter the building. He recalled with clarity the anger with which he had hissed at the other man not to bother to go in as nobody else in there could have survived because of the smoke. He knew his colleague had heard his words, as he'd nodded, but he'd gone in regardless. He had pushed the woman out into the street and into the safe arms of another woman. He hadn't had the courage to stay while she learned of the horrible fate bestowed on her child and husband; he had no more emotions to give, and he'd walked away as quickly as he could.

John drew in a sharp breath; it pained him to think about it any further. Could it be that this Nathan she spoke about had been in the fire as well? 'Nathan?'

'Yes. My son?' She sounded puzzled. 'I'm sorry, I assumed you knew his name, how silly of me.'

'He– was – alive?' he stuttered. 'My god, your child is alive?!'

'Yes, yes! Heavens, you didn't know?'

'No, I had no idea…' John averted his eyes.

'Oh.' Quietly, she stepped back. 'I should leave you in peace now. I'm sorry I came.' But then she seemed to change her mind. 'No, I'm not, I'm glad I did and I should have come sooner and you would have known the good news about my son all along.'

'Good news about your son.' John only managed to repeat what she had said without looking at her; he wished she would leave. He felt her gaze expectantly on him: she was waiting to share her happiness and delight that not all had ended badly that night.

'Without you he wouldn't have a mother,' she said quietly. 'And I wouldn't have a son.'

He had to get to grips with the situation. 'I only wish I could have done more for your husband.'

'You did all you could have.' She sounded resolute. 'And I came here to thank you for that.' She extended her right hand. 'I want you to know that little Nathan and I are doing just fine.'

He couldn't ignore her any longer and, managing to regain his composure, he took her hand and held it briefly. He noticed that her big green eyes no longer stared at him in terror, but regarded him in a warm and grateful way. At the same time there was a determination there: it was the look of someone meaning to thank her rescuer. *If only she knew.* He shivered and hoped she wouldn't see it. He squeezed her hand gently, finally saying what he needed to. 'Thank you for coming here and for letting me know.'

They stood without moving. John sensed her incomprehension at his lack of gratitude. He let go of her hand and tried to make an effort to sound appreciative. 'If your Nathan ever wants to see a big boat...,' he said as sincerely as he could.

Elsie smiled back at him: an honest smile that made her eyes light up and the auburn curls along her face dance up and down.

'I'm sure he would love to see a real boat someday. It would be a welcoming change from fire engines.' She smiled again, slightly warily, nodded her head, and turned and walked away.

He watched her disappear; someone had rescued her child, but it hadn't been him. She had no idea her good news was simply adding to his sense of failure that night. Walking back into the yard, he heard his father's voice recounting tales of his numerous call-outs and the many people he had rescued. He was glad he was no longer alive to witness his own son's inadequacies. Past the crowds, he saw the launched vessel lying peacefully alongside the quay, ready to take her passengers aboard and leave these shores behind.

Chapter 6

Sometimes the people's voice was heard. With the help of some protesting letter-writers, an astute reporter and his supportive newspaper, the demanded result had been achieved: the trees had been saved. Not that long ago, Frank had also been able to accomplish such triumphs.

Inspecting the drawing more closely, he noticed the provision that had been made for the row of trees: a 108-foot transept in the middle of the building, covered by a semi-circular roof. The artist had drawn several specimens beneath it.

Was it an enchanted palace of glass or a monster balloon partially inflated? The large building being finished in Hyde Park ahead of the opening of the Exhibition had been described by some critics as a mammoth greenhouse. They were right: now that it had been decided to keep the trees, the building was not only going to look like a vast orangery, it was going to function like one as well.

'Trees protected against the rain.' *What were the visitors going to make of that?* It seemed quite outrageous.

Intriguingly, no bricks and mortar had been used in the building. Combining the most fragile and the strongest of building materials clearly had implications for the brightness; the rays of light would be able to enter without obstruction and the objects inside were going to be lit in the most intense way. Hopefully the summer of 1851 wasn't going to be terribly hot, because one could imagine the atmosphere inside if the sun were to come out in its full glory.

Although if this multi-tiered wedding cake was going to melt in the sun, at least the visitors could sit under the branch of a tree to protect themselves.

Frank extended his arms, still holding the newspaper; he would give it the benefit of the doubt. As long as the stability of the building wasn't going to be like that of a cake, this design could be an excellent test for future projects following the repeal of the tax on glass.

He pushed his chair back to give his legs more room; he could do with another editorial on the Exhibition, he had been negligent lately. Now the building was as good as ready to receive goods, he should prepare an extensive piece on Paxton's design and mention how one of the largest buildings ever made by human hands consisted mostly of glass, or how remarkably its assemblage had progressed without any scaffolding and with a silent speed.

He could see the heading: 'Nature as the Chief Engineer.' The glass roof, with its ridge and furrow design, reminded one of a rising and falling sea; surely the locals would appreciate the marine reference. He could include some testimonials from local residents, show them the final images and see if it changed their opinion of the building. There was no denying it had been an extraordinary feat of construction. He groaned: what a terribly dreary idea. Nobody seemed to be interested in a story of contentment nowadays; they wanted controversy, for this made their own lives look less bleak. Where had his critical mind gone? He needed to try harder.

The problem was that he was bored; he had learned more about the building than he wanted to, mostly thanks to the information Bill had kept sending him. He hadn't been back to London since they had met some time ago. There was no need for it; the necessary facts and figures kept appearing on his desk, almost as though Bill preferred him to stay out of town. McIlroy didn't seem to mind where the information came from; as long as Frank regularly did an entertaining piece, he was a happy man.

Frank glanced around the room at his colleagues working in silence. He had difficulties concentrating. There was no point in waiting for inspiration to arrive. He grabbed his coat. He needed a change of scenery.

He walked down the stairs and into the street; as he rounded the corner towards the beach, an agreeably cool wind greeted him. There was no need for the scarf he had left behind on his chair.

He had always found that a walk helped to order his mind.

After he'd met Bill in London and realised Lewis hadn't done anything with his investigation, he'd forced himself to walk up and down this stretch of beach numerous times until he was windswept and tired. It was essential that he kept himself busy and away from finding solace in the tavern.

Luckily, work had provided him with sufficient distraction. Shortly after his London trip, McIlroy had called him into the office for an assignment in Southampton. A banquet had been organised in the Town Hall by the Mayor, and reporters of the provincial press were allowed to attend. As the Exhibition was going to be an important topic of conversation, McIlroy thought it desirable to send one his reporters to witness the latest developments.

Frank had realised what a big affair it was going to be the moment he saw that the Town Hall was beautifully decorated with flowers. More than two hundred gentlemen sat down for dinner while the press was seated on the balcony, away from the diners. The guests were in jolly moods and numerous toasts were proposed that had them regularly laughing out loud. But Frank had to keep himself from nodding off; it had been heating up in the public gallery and he hadn't been sleeping well lately. Most of the toasts had been political, and when they finally mentioned the Exhibition it had been the same all over again; how it would prove a blessing not only to England but also to the 'World' by uniting all nations in one common brotherhood. Frank wondered if he should walk out; he'd had enough of all the peace talk. He gathered his belongings when he heard an invited Member of Parliament reel off a list of inventions: the new printing press which turned out 12,000 pages per hour, the Davy lamp that could be used in flammable atmospheres, and the electric telegraph, a wonderful new instrument of communication: all thought up by Englishmen over the last decades, and all examples of the high pre-eminence this country had attained in art and manufactures.

Frank looked over the balustrade to see who was speaking with such fervour. He saw the top of the speaker's head but couldn't make out who it was. The speaker went on to say that the Exhibition would not only demonstrate but also increase the authority already possessed by the English.

There you have it, Frank sat down again. The true nature and purpose of the Exhibition, just as McIlroy and Bill had maintained all along. Much the same as was on show in the arena below: gentlemen arrayed in waistcoats and top hats, having a sumptuous dinner laid down for them, discussing their excellence on the podium of the world, while the rest of them could merely look in on the richness of the gathering but not participate.

Frank was irritated; where had this arrogance come from? There had been a rumour that Greece was going to ask for less space than had been allocated to them. Surely it was an example of the danger of becoming too pleased with one's merits; a country that had created so much for mankind over the centuries now didn't have enough to fill their allocation? Was the exposition not supposed to be a reminder of how England was only a fraction of a much bigger arena in which other nations were extremely capable of teaching it a lesson? Moreover, didn't every nation at some point deserve to run the same splendid race of progress that elevated the dignity of their country and its people?

Agitated, Frank leaned further over the banister; he wished someone would come forward to speak up for the absent. A sudden urge came over him to shout down and tell the men to curtail their snobbery. They needed to give the other nations a chance rather than set them up to fail.

But he managed to contain himself; he didn't feel like getting arrested for an outburst that would probably sound like that of a lunatic. He grabbed his satchel and coat and made his way out of the viewing gallery, murmuring his apologies while stepping on a few toes. He found his way to the back entrance of the Town Hall and walked out onto the streets of Southampton. He didn't notice the crowds that had gathered at the front, nor the exquisitely gas-lit exterior of the building. He walked, heavy-booted and frustrated, in search of a horse bus, feeling disappointed not only by the event he had to write about but also by the reminder of the limitations of his job. How was he going to make known the needs of foreign participants when, in the past, he hadn't been able to give voice to the innocent girls that had gone missing? Maybe he should stick to more insignificant missions, like saving trees.

His trip to Southampton felt like a long time ago and whilst it should have given him material to write about, he struggled to put pen to paper. Although the opening of the Exhibition was still some time away, not even a walk during his unscheduled break could give him fresh ideas. He strolled further along the beach towards the water's edge. In the distance, the contours of the Isle of Wight were visible. The waves obscured the island with the rise and fall of the water. He watched them with anxiety. They were angry white where they hit the rocky beach, the sound of the rolling stones growing louder with each succeeding wave. They were out to get you and only needed one opportunity to catch you unawares.

Why someone would choose to spend time on those unpredictable seas was incomprehensible to Frank. Only a couple of weeks ago, deep down in the greedy water, eleven men had lost their lives while trying to rescue the crew of a barque in distress. They had been Worthing fishermen who'd sailed out into a winter storm to help people they'd never met. He'd decided to go out to Worthing to seek firsthand accounts for his piece, but he couldn't make himself do it the same day. He had waited several days and, although the unsettled weather was still hanging around, he'd found a group of villagers gathered in the street. They had told him they'd watched the incident unfold from the shore and had seen the fishing boat suddenly capsize before it had reached the ship they'd gone out to help.

Beyond them, near a row of fishermen's cottages, several women stood at the gate of one of the houses, engaged in passionate conversation. One of them had opened the white gate ready to walk to the front door when she noticed him.

She stopped and they all stared at him, a solitary figure in the middle of the cobbled road. It felt as if they were waiting for him to make the first move – probably preferably back in the direction he'd come from. These women were clearly in no mood to face a stranger on their streets. Frank gazed back, surprised by his hesitation. He used to have no qualms about approaching somebody for a story he'd planned to write.

The raw emotion of the women was etched on their faces, different stages of sorrow and grief staring back at him.

'What do you want?' a tall, strong-looking woman asked angrily.

'I, err...' Frank's voice faltered.

They kept glaring silently at him, the intruder who had walked into their private anguish.

'My name is Frank Grundy.' He didn't recognise the croaky voice as his own. 'I've come here to do a piece for my newspaper.' The last words had sounded like a question.

'You have come to do what?' The tall woman had turned her broad shoulders to face him and had put her hands on her hips, her head sarcastically dipped to one side.

For a moment Frank was rendered speechless. Whatever they were in the middle of was clearly most delicate as the hostility directed towards to him was most evident.

'If this is not the right time...?'

The woman let out a scornful growl and stepped towards him. 'I'll tell you when the time is right, Mister: after they've found all the bodies of our men, after we've had the chance to bury them and then mourn them, and after we've explained to our children that their fathers will not be coming home.' Her voice grew louder as she spoke, every word preceded by a trembling intake of heavy breath, until she was shouting. 'Now move on, Sir!'

Frank recoiled; the warm air coming out of her mouth was like the hot smoke rising from an angry steam engine. 'I'm sorry.'

'Mary, leave him,' one of the other women said gently. 'He's just doing his job, he's no different to the others that have come.'

'We should be left in peace, especially at this hour.' Mary was clearly distressed.

'I know, we know.' The other woman put her arm around Mary's waist and addressed Frank. 'You'd better go now – come back some other time if you have to.' She pulled Mary with her and the two of them walked back to the others.

'Yes, of course,' Frank muttered to their backs. From a safe distance, he observed them a little longer. One of them knocked on a door that was opened by a woman with a child holding onto her skirt. A brief conversation followed and suddenly a hair-raising scream tore down the street. The woman in the doorway threw her hands to her face and fell to her knees. Frank was desperate to leave the street and the village altogether. Turning around abruptly, he bumped into one of the villagers he'd spoken to earlier.

'Poor women,' the villager said, taking Frank by the arm. 'I heard them yell at you.'

'Yes, I understand now that this wasn't the time to come here,' Frank offered apologetically.

'You should know they found another body floating in the sea this morning,' the man added in a secretive voice. 'And they're not sure who it is.'

Frank instantly disliked the man who had invaded his personal space.

'You know, face been eaten away, impossible to identify.'

Frank didn't move, unsure where the man was going with his

tale.

'They think it's her husband.' The man nodded in the direction of the young woman at the door.

'Why?'

'One of the socks he was wearing had the initials "W.W." on it.' He paused for a moment and then clarified matters. 'That's her – Mrs William Wicks.'

Frank looked over at the group of women; somebody was crying loudly. He watched them disappear inside. Mrs Wicks had just been told the unavoidable truth that her husband was dead and her life had changed forever; from now on she would be on her own with her child, or maybe even several children, to take care of. And Frank had wanted some of their attention for a story. He felt awful. He'd returned home unable to get rid of the piercing scream in his ears. A few days later he'd found out that thirty-six children had been orphaned. In the small piece he had written, he'd made sure to appeal to the readers to subscribe to the donation fund that had been opened for the public. He'd sent a copy of the piece to Bill and asked him to do the same.

That same stretch of water and those same waves, which now almost rolled onto his shoes, had so cruelly taken some poor fishermen who, in spite of jeopardising their own lives, had sought to rescue people in danger at sea. He couldn't imagine the conversations those men had had with their loved ones before they had set out; how the women must have pleaded with them not to leave the safety of their cottages. But instead their men had chosen to risk all in service of a far bigger cause.

He glanced at the scene in front of him, just managing to avoid a rogue wave. A seagull came in from the sea; for a moment, it contained its speed and then it dived with a deadly accuracy towards the choppy water only to be swallowed up by the white crests of the waves. *Could seagulls drown?* Before Frank had time to think about it, the bird came fluttering triumphantly out of the water with a little fish in its beak. *No hesitation there: straight in, head first.*

'Damn!' A determined wave had succeeded in completely soaking both his feet and his trousers to the knees. He stood transfixed; it dawned on him that getting caught by a wave only meant getting wet feet, nothing more. He turned and walked towards the cobbled street. Rather than turning right at the corner, he walked decisively in the other direction, away from the office and towards his cottage. With every step, he was getting closer to the box that had sat unopened in the corner of his room for a year.

Chapter 7

Fourth of July 1851, somewhere in the Atlantic

'Nobody needs to do more than strictly necessary today.' The Captain bellowed across the ship. 'The fourth of July will be celebrated by all of us, no matter where we are.'

The day had started with a good breeze but the air had been thick and foggy. At the very moment the Captain spoke his words, the mist lifted and the sun came out. They could have done without the wind dying away completely, but it did mean that it was easier to follow up the order of limited labour as the yacht floated along like a lazy duck.

The bottle of gin handed out by the Captain was a welcome reward and it was accepted by the crew with gratitude and suppressed eagerness. 'Our Native Land – may it ever continue to be the abode of freedom, and the birthplace of heroes.' The Captain raised his glass and the men followed suit.

The first taste of alcohol after about two weeks caused John's head to spin and he was thankful for the Captain's orders. He lay down and closed his eyes, his thoughts drifting back to life in America, the country they were celebrating today.

He tried his hardest to imagine the land, the streets in his neighbourhood, and the concoction of smells emerging from the myriad of immigrants' kitchens, and from the nearby camphene distillery. But he couldn't. The ocean was overpowering; it created a dull uniformity and gave everything the same sticky odour. Instead his thoughts wandered to the same day exactly a year ago. The day he had met Nathan.

He had used the holiday to explore the neighbourhood close to his new apartment on Gansevoort Street, which he'd found with

Ole's help after he'd wanted to leave his previous dire living arrangements. It was difficult to pronounce the name of his new street, but he liked that it reminded him of the history of the place and of people more adventurous than him.

The room was in one of the newer townhouses and the walk to the shipyard took about forty-five minutes, taking him past the lumberyard and the distillery, and then along Greenwich Avenue and 11th Street. As nobody was waiting for him at home, the journey back from work was more leisurely and he had quickly started to get to know the area.

That particular day, he had strolled into the most westerly part of the neighbourhood where he was met by hordes of people celebrating along the quay by the Hudson River. He stopped near the water's edge and took in the view. How different the West side was to the East! No shipyards, but nevertheless a lot of different ships moored alongside it: packet steamers and large sailing ships transporting goods all over the world.

As he was admiring the scene, a woman's voice just to the side of him drew his attention.

'Don't you ever tire of seeing boats?'

Unsure if the woman was addressing him, he'd turned and, startled, recognised Elsie standing a bit further along, holding the hand of a little boy with a lot of fair curls. If she had been surprised to see him there, she definitely didn't show it.

'Hello, Elsie.' He'd remained where he was, not knowing what to do. He stared at the child by her side, who stared back at him with big eyes: not green like his mother's, but a striking hazel brown. The limp bundle of cloth and bone the dead man had been holding so tightly was this slight child, very much alive, albeit a bit shy. The boy shifted nearer to his mother's skirts and John realised that he was scaring the boy with his gaze.

'Is he coming?' a tiny voice asked.

'Nathan, please, this very kind man is called Mister John and no, he is not coming to the park with us.' Elsie gave John an apologetic look, and then a more intent one. 'Or would you like to?'

He was momentarily taken aback by her request. 'Where are you going?'

'There's a park on Abingdon Square near Hudson and Troy Street.' She pointed to her left and started walking without waiting for an answer. 'I guess you don't know it.'

'No, I don't, but I haven't been in this area for very long.' *Did she expect him to follow them?*

'We haven't been living here that long either.' She stopped walking and glanced over to John. 'What a coincidence we meet again.'

Her cheerful demeanour made it hard to say no to her; she effortlessly made him feel at ease. 'I'd better start investigating the sights, so let me join you.'

Together they walked further along the quay, Elsie holding firmly onto her son's hand, with their attention on the bustling scenes of men at work unloading ships. John couldn't keep his eyes off the little boy who had been quietly toddling along, stealing a glance at John every so often, until he was distracted by something in the distance. Whatever it was among the busy wharves, it made him so happy that he started to jump up and down.

'Over there, his favourite ship,' Elsie said. 'It took me a while before I'd figured it out; what he likes are the flags.'

In between the masts, one ship stood out due to the series of colourful flags that were hung from its mastheads and tied to the taffrail. It was clear to see why the boy was attracted to them as they waved happily in the wind.

Nathan stopped with a satisfied expression on his face. 'Boat has a party,' he stated with conviction.

'He thinks they are having a party there every day,' Elsie explained.

'Well, I can understand him thinking that.' John took another look at the ship and smiled as well.

'Look at you two grinning. Am I missing something? Just like another little boy – do you men ever grow up?' teased Elsie.

'Some of us never do.' What he really wanted to say was that he was glad the boy had been given a chance to grow up at all. He knelt down so he was on the same level as the boy. 'Nathan, do you like those pretty flags?'

The boy waved his arm and squealed with delight, 'Flags, pretty flags!'

'Just like a party, don't you think?'

'Oh, please, John, don't encourage him even more.'

'Nathan, you can tell your mother you are right; they are having a party.' Mischievously, he looked up at Elsie, who slowly shook her head.

Nathan watched John's face intently; his hushed voice drew his small face closer as he leaned his body against John's knee. The simple gesture of this little child took his breath away; his throat tightened and his eyes started to sting alarmingly. He swallowed hard and pointed at one string of flags. 'Because if you look closely, the ones on the right spell the word "birthday" from top to bottom.'

The boy stared at the flags; a frown appeared, crinkling up the skin of his smooth forehead.

'And if you look at the flags on the left,' said John, watching how the boy followed his finger, 'they spell "happy". But you already knew that, didn't you, you clever boy?' He ruffled the boy's curls intuitively.

Nathan didn't move but kept staring at the flags, not quite understanding what John was talking about. When John got up and turned to Elsie, he saw she had the same expression on her face.

'Like mother, like son.' It was John's time to tease.

'I never knew that,' she admitted. 'I've always thought they were just for decoration.'

'That, too, of course,' John continued. 'In this case anyway.'

'Do they teach you these things at the yard?'

'Yes, amongst other things.'

They locked eyes briefly; John noticed the tiny irregular freckles on the bridge of her small but straight nose, she even had some on her eyelids, behind the thick curled-up eyelashes. The corners of her perfectly formed mouth turned up and a warm smile crossed her face, reassuring him. A small voice broke the spell. 'The boat has his birthday?'

Both Elsie and John started laughing.

'You could say that.'

'Like me!'

'Really? Is it your birthday?' John looked from the boy to his mother.

She knelt down and took Nathan's hands in hers. 'Not yet, honey. Do you remember I told you your birthday is the day after that other one with lots of celebrations? Your party is tomorrow.'

'Will you come to my birthday?' Nathan asked, looking up at John.

He didn't know what to say; it had been such a plain question, asked without any hesitation by a young child not yet burdened by times past. The little boy kept looking up at him expectantly. An unforeseen sense of duty towards this innocent being overcame him, surpassing even the deep-rooted feelings of guilt. 'Yes, of course, I would love to, if…' Apologetically, he looked at Elsie, instantly regretting expressing the willingness he had momentarily felt to join them.

'What a good idea to invite John, sweetie.'

That year, Nathan had turned four years old.

Tomorrow he would be five, and John was going to miss that birthday. He drank the last bit of gin; why was it that the very last sip always tasted more bitter? He stared at the bottom of his mug as if to make sure it was really empty. Maybe he should get rid of the bitter taste by asking for some more.

Chapter 8

February 1851, the south coast of England

A distinct squidgy noise came from Frank's wet shoes whenever he took a step along the cobbled lane. How could he have been so stupid? He should have known not to stand too close to the water; the unexpected wave always struck when you felt most at ease. He needed to get into some dry socks.

As he walked determinedly back towards the creek, the brief thought that he ought to warn his McIlroy he was taking the afternoon off was soon forgotten. He needed to concentrate on where he was walking. The slippery shoes on the irregular pavement had caused him to slip a few times, and he had just about managed to keep himself upright. Near the small row of identical white cottages, he passed a few women who'd watched him steady himself and he was convinced they were talking behind his back, no doubt thinking he was intoxicated.

Making it to his front door without any mishaps, Frank quickly let himself in and changed into a new pair of trousers and dry socks. Within the thick walls of the cottage it was damp and nippy and he hesitated briefly, undecided as to whether he should light a fire in the living room or get himself a hot drink. How his life had changed. He was now quite capable of doing the basic household tasks, but he detested having to carry them out. He didn't see the point of tedious odd jobs that took too much time and kept reoccurring. Certain chores weren't worth doing too frequently as he never had guests to check upon them, anyway, but he had tried other things over and over again during the last year, and he still couldn't get them right.

As he poured water into the kettle, he imagined Agnes in their marital home in London – or, more appropriately, her house, since he'd given it all up. He watched the old kettle on the fire; the water stirred in its dented belly. He had found it at the back of one of the kitchen cabinets and it had become his most reliable friend. Hours of drinking copious amounts of coffee had helped him onto the right path – or should he say, had prevented him from heading off down an alcohol-fuelled road to oblivion?

He opened the coffee pot and the strong smell of the beans triggered another memory. Every morning without fail, Agnes used to prepare them a pot of tea whilst he was dressing. She would get out the special cups with the pink and golden roses, and wait for him before pouring the boiled water on the leaves. He had always assumed this morning ritual was there for her own pleasure and he had never dared to tell her he would have preferred a strong coffee instead. But now he knew it was far more than that; for her, it had been a moment to enjoy together.

He felt a sharp pain in his chest; he had walked out on this beautiful woman, although leaving hadn't been his choice. He tried to picture her making a tea for herself, maybe still in her nightdress, because mornings weren't 'her thing'. But the overriding image was that of her face, after she had learned of his arrest in the company of prostitutes. He wasn't sure who had told her and if it had been the police knocking on her door, but he would never forget the pained look in her eyes when he'd come home late after his release. Not being able to explain had been one of his biggest regrets.

The water was now boiling angrily, but Frank didn't notice. He looked at the limp wet socks hanging over the back of the other chair, wilted and lifeless. He hoped her life hadn't taken a similar path to his.

Somewhere in the mostly empty cabinets was a bottle of brandy: once his reliable companion in difficult times, a soother of negative thoughts and pains in his body. Just after the move he'd unwrapped it and stored it there, standing by in case of need.

'Aahrgh!' Frank dropped the kettle back on the stove. 'You idiot!' Distracted, he'd tried to pick up the kettle and burned his fingers on its hot handle. The pain in his hand and the stupidity of what he'd tried to do made him even more annoyed, but there was no time to keep his hand under the cold running water; he had some long overdue unpacking of a box to do. The bottle of brandy could wait.

Frank pulled the wooden crate from his bedroom and sat it near the fire in the living room. The wood had become damp over the period it had been hidden in the corner behind the other crates, and with difficulty he managed to pry off the lid. The smell of the paper and ink, now mixed with the musty smell of decay, greeted him.

He slowly arranged the paperwork in neat piles on the floor in front of him, being careful not to damage the thin paper clippings. On one pile, he put the files containing the names of the girls he had met and the ones he had planned to see. Some of them he'd interviewed, although you could hardly call them interviews. He would find them and pay them a visit, sometimes in the middle of the night, and convince them to talk to him, but they were wary, not understanding what he wanted from them. He had felt dreadful after such nights: the way these prostitutes lived, the work they had to do, and how young some of them looked. Usually he felt embarrassed to be a man and on some of those evenings he would meet up with Bill and drink too much.

On the second pile, he put any articles containing background information: material on the girls, but also on how they got paid and by whom. And the third pile contained background information on their clients: the type of man that would pay for their services, the ones who would have their ways with them and, once done, leave them behind in the filth and squalor. The fourth pile was small: some paperwork he'd managed to grab from the drawer in his desk after they had fired him, personal files and some knick-knacks. And then there was the fifth pile.

Frank sat back and leaned against the heavy armchair behind him, the papers silently accusing him of incompetence. Five irregular heaps of documents: a diverse collection of letters forming words on pieces of browned, and now crumbling, paper. From where he was sitting, they seemed to hold no value. But read together, they would form an image of the collector: some seedy-minded individual with an unhealthy interest in prostitutes and in the sordid sex life of men in a big city. It didn't look good. Not least to his wife.

But it wasn't about the women mentioned in those first piles, no matter how sad he felt for the way they lived their lives. It was about the names mentioned in the fifth pile, only a few sheets high, but the one he'd spent months of his life collecting. It contained the names of a few girls he hadn't been able to find.

Frank got up from the floor; it was getting chilly and his limbs were stiffening. He should rekindle the fire.

With a fresh coffee and a blazing fire, he sat down in the large armchair, picked up the smallest pile and placed it on his lap. Amongst the papers were a few newspaper clippings.

Left her home on Wednesday evening, wearing a dark cape and a red shawl.
A girl of twelve, by the name of Lisa.
Anybody with information on her whereabouts, please contact Mr Possett, Totton Street, East London.

And from a couple of weeks later another one, mentioning a girl with the name of Mary H., followed by a third, this time a girl named Margaret. And then several more.

All advertisements were placed discreetly near the job applications and he hadn't been the one who had found them initially. It had been Agnes. On lazy Sunday mornings, she would take several pages from his newspaper and read out loud the most curious advertisements she could find. She knew to stay away from political or social features, as she didn't like him to become agitated, so she stuck to advertisements that were innocent enough, deriving pleasure in finding the most fascinating ones. 'Poisonous lotions as cure for minor ailments, colognes to generate beards and plant extracts to reduce grey hairs.' She would jokingly threaten to use all of them on him.

One morning, she suddenly went quiet.

'If something happens to me, would you come and find me?'

'Excuse me?'

'If I didn't come home one day, would you start looking for me?'

'Agnes, what kind of question is that?'

'Well, I could get knocked over by an omnibus in the street and nobody would know who I was or where I was going or where I live, would they?'

'Maybe, but –?'

'You would come home and I wouldn't be there. What would you do?'

'Oh please, Agnes, what makes you think about such things?'

'Would you be able to describe me? Know what I'd been wearing that day?

'Agnes!'

'Well?'

She threw him momentarily; was it wiser to play along or tell her straight away to stop being silly? Over the last few months, he'd noticed how her mood would change suddenly, very often after she'd questioned him on what at first seemed like random topics. Then he'd figured out it revolved around growing old together, just the two of them, without children. But this was different; this was about her disappearing.

'Agnes, what are you talking about? I hope you're not planning to walk out on me?' He had surprised her with that; she opened her mouth to say something and then changed her mind.

'No, of course not, I didn't mean to suggest anything like that, sorry – it's just that I read this.' She put the newspaper in front of him, her finger on the advertisement about a missing girl. 'I was thinking how odd and sad it would be to go missing and have nobody come to find you.'

He had to read the few lines a couple of times.

'These young persons sometimes have troubles at home.'

'Frank, she's only twelve. Where would she go?'

'Mmm. Anyway, you're wrong; she has somebody looking for her.'

'What kind of unsolvable problem could a young child like that have, to decide to walk away? I couldn't believe a child of mine would ever feel the need to do that, especially not a young daughter. What do you think happened? Poor child, alone on the streets of London.'

'I don't know. Please don't worry about it, I'm sure she has already been found. And I'm convinced these things are very rare. I've never seen such a personal ad before.'

How wrong he had been; the following week Agnes found another one in a similar spot in the paper, causing her to go quiet. After that he made sure he read the paper first and took out the page with the distressing announcements; he couldn't bear to witness what they did to Agnes. He would hide the page between his paperwork in a small bedroom at the back of the house that was more like a box room. When they had first moved into the house, he promised Agnes he'd decorate and prepare it for the day their family extended. But after a while he had started to use it for abandoned objects, cast aside to be dealt with at a later date. Although it was too small for a maid, Agnes had started to call it the maid's room, as if giving it that name could thwart the negative spirits from taking up residence in there. Because of the mess, it had been a good place to put his work out of sight where nobody would check it.

One Sunday morning, whilst sifting through the pile on his desk at home, he realised he'd gathered evidence of five disappearances: Lisa P., Mary H., Margaret B., Gladys P. and Victoria T. He spoke their names out loud and from that moment on, they wouldn't leave him alone. They started to call out to him, recognising that only readers of a caring nature deserved their cries for attention. They'd decided to put their trust in him, as would a child in their father after a favourite toy had broken. He had no duty towards these daughters of strangers, but he felt a moral obligation towards Agnes to make up for the things he had failed to give her.

At the same time, his heart had started to beat faster and with it came the familiar rush of blood to his head. His reporter's instinct was telling him that this was the story he had been waiting for. Who were these girls, and where had they gone?

Frank stared at the fifth pile; following his decision to look into these advertisements not much had been added. How heart-breaking that the only thing he had managed to do for the lost girls was to add a few pages to a pile.

The day he had finally confided in Lewis, as he needed assistance with his research, hadn't started well.

'You've been doing what?' The editor's voice roared through the office as he shook his head in disbelief. 'That explains some of your behaviour, I must say.' Lewis threw his arms up in despair, 'You've been getting in late, you've been missing your deadlines and your stories are often in a less than perfect state – I even wonder if you wrote them at all.' He leaned forward, fists on his desk, face close to Frank's. 'And now you're telling me you've been working on a story of your own!'

'Well…'

'And it involves ladies of the night? Not a topic our newspaper would like to take up, is it?' Lewis snarled the last words.

'But this is different.' Frank struggled to get some words in.

'Different? What can be different? Women who get paid for intimacy with men and perform their acts in little back rooms in parts of the capital you and I wouldn't, or shouldn't, venture into? May I remind you, Frank, that that particular exploit has been going on since long before you and I arrived on this earth and it will continue long after we've passed on. And what could you possibly want from me?' Lewis slumped back into his chair.

Frank cleared his throat. The only things he knew for sure were that he couldn't continue to research in his spare time any longer and that he owed Lewis an explanation for his unreliable behaviour of late. In addition, he wanted to share his ideas with him, especially after his latest discoveries.

'I would like you to read this.' Frank put the heavy box that stood next to his feet on top of Lewis's desk. 'It will hopefully better explain why we should give this our attention, especially since it involves young girls and it implicates men of repute.'

'What men?'

'Don't know for sure. Yet. But I am reliably informed that the police are involved.'

Lewis raised his eyebrows at those last words. 'Are you saying this is not about prostitutes, but about girls?'

'Missing girls.'

'Missing girls?'

He had ended up giving Lewis all the material he'd discovered thus far and then, for several days, everything had gone quiet. One morning he'd arrived at his desk and the box he had lent to Lewis was there along with a scrawled note saying: *Two more months to finish the research and depending on the result we will discuss publication – or not. PS. Where is the evidence? We need facts! Find a girl!*

He'd managed to work another month on it, day and night, but he never got to the second month. One night, before he'd unearthed all the necessary information, the police had caught him whilst carrying out a big swoop in the East End. Their actions were part of a clamp down on an area known for immoral behaviour, including prostitution. He'd walked straight into the part they were busy cleaning up and he knew now that he would have been better off if he'd been inside one of the rooms, as some of the prostitutes had been left alone.

The events that followed had been disastrous. News had travelled fast; it hadn't just been his colleagues who immediately discovered he'd been arrested in the company of prostitutes, but the owner of the newspaper was informed as well. And also, worst of all, his wife. He'd wanted the opportunity to talk to her, but he didn't get it; her parents were called in and had shielded her from him. He had been furious, demanding that he be allowed to explain, but he'd only made matters worse and instead they'd disappeared, taking their daughter with them.

In desperation, he had turned to Lewis, pleading with him to help clarify his absences and to testify that his arrest had been a misunderstanding.

But Lewis had been evasive.

'Frank, listen to me, I've tried to explain it to the owner as well as I could. I told him you were onto a story of considerable importance, but when I said what it was about, he became extremely angry and unwilling to hear any more.'

'But did you tell him it was a significant discovery? That the paper was going to benefit from it immensely once I'd finished my work?'

'He kept telling me over and over again that he has his reputation to think about. Believe me, I tried to defend you, but in all honesty, you had only given me so much I could pass on to him, which wasn't very convincing. And, I shall be straight with you, you are dispensable, which goes not only for you but for many other reporters. Unlike his good name.'

'But it's a compelling story...' The last energy drained out of Frank. 'And it's one that needs to be told; those girls need a voice.'

'That may well be, but you've no concrete evidence for some of the things you claim. I regret to say, Frank, that you've angered the owner and you know his displeasure for anyone who does that to him.'

They sat in silence until Lewis told Frank it was no longer sustainable to keep him on. Frank had stopped listening; he knew he had no chance to retain his job, but he still had a chance to save his marriage. 'I have one last request. My wife. I need you to talk to my wife.'

A quizzical look crossed Lewis's face.

'I need you to explain things to her, about my arrest…' Frank's voice weakened.

'I see. What makes you so sure she'll talk to me?'

'I do not know, but we have to try.' Frank couldn't hide the desperation in his voice.

'Where will I be able to find her?'

'I'm not sure about that either; her parents collected her from our house soon after and I haven't spoken to her since.'

Lewis put his hand on Frank's arm. 'I will talk to her.'

He had agreed to try to find Agnes, but nothing had happened. It had been impossible to tie Lewis down and eventually even Bill had started to avoid Frank. In a last attempt to reach her, he had written numerous letters, sometimes one per day. But they had been returned to him untouched: another failed editorial.

It was then when it struck him; all his working life he had prided himself on expressing views in solid, well-written pieces for people to read. Not just his own opinions, but those of others, often vulnerable citizens of society with no voice of their own. And now he had gained firsthand experience of what it meant to have that voice taken away, because the people who should care had stopped listening. Without his words, he'd become nothing more than a bystander observing the passage of his own petty life.

Frank laid the sheets on the small dining table in the corner of the living room. He picked up the contents of his old office drawer from the organised mess on the floor; surely there was no reason to keep any of it. He flicked through the files: old bills, a novel Christmas card, some newspaper clippings of pieces he had done, some old envelopes with notes. He pulled one out that contained a crisp-looking letter: his letter of dismissal. He couldn't really remember receiving it. He pulled it a few inches from the envelope and recognised his own name at the top in prominent letters. Had Lewis given it to him? He recalled their conversation;

it had stuck in his mind how the word *sustainable* had distracted him and how he'd forgotten to listen to what else Lewis had to say.

Whatever it had meant, it hadn't prevented him from getting the job he was in right now, which meant the contents couldn't have been too bad. Or that not everyone knew he had been arrested.

He gazed with interest at the large envelope, suddenly curious as to what the reason for his dismissal had been. Pulling out the letter in its entirety, he skimmed over the neat handwriting, which mentioned what he assumed were the usual words for letters like these: *'We regret to inform you that your employment with us is terminated – for reasons of company reorganisation –'*

Ha, Frank thought, nothing was mentioned about poor performance for showing up late, and, on the odd occasion, under the influence of alcohol.

'Please vacate the premise immediately with only your personal possessions –'

He remembered how peculiar it had felt when they'd guided him out of the building. He'd only been able to take the few personal belongings from his desk, no more. His colleagues had already started to avoid him, seemingly afraid that his deteriorating performance could be contagious, like an illness, but their stares that day had made him feel like a criminal. He'd almost felt sorry for Bill, who'd shown his support to Frank in those fragile weeks, but on the day of his departure even Bill didn't know what to say or where to look.

Still, it was as if he'd had a premonition that day would come; he'd taken most of the paperwork on his research home, in case he felt like consulting it during one of his sleepless nights. He'd hidden it together with the advertisements in the maid's room.

And then it had followed him to the south coast.

The dismissal letter had been signed by two people, but Lewis's name wasn't one of them. Frank recognised one name as that of the owner, but he didn't know the other. Lewis had told him he had been instructed to fire him and thus Frank's fate had been decided by men he had never met and who likely had no idea of his abilities as a reporter. He looked again at the other name.

'Darlingden-Frence.' He spoke the unusual, but not unfamiliar, name out loud. *Had they perhaps met in the office at some point? Or had he seen him somewhere else?* His investigative heart skipped a beat, and his thoughts became lucid for a split second: had he seen the name somewhere in those papers? He glanced at the stacks on the floor and was aware of his breathing becoming shallow. Could he have seen it in his own notes? Impatiently, he picked up one paper after the other, the neat piles dissolving in the process, hankering to make sense of his old notes, but unsure what he was looking for.

Chapter 9

The days became interchangeable: the same view, the same routines, the same men for company. In truth, life at sea had started to echo the one ashore. But John wasn't going to grumble; at least he was outside, and he was grateful for the wind in his face.

There were some variations to each day, such as the strength of the wind, the size of the waves or the speed of the yacht.

But the one development John had welcomed the most was his body getting used to the rocking of the ship. The same couldn't be said of Mister George, or little George, James's son; neither of them had shown their faces very often.

James was the lucky one of the family, although even he had been unhappy the previous day. It had been foggy once more and the wind had been light, which had changed the boat back into a rocking horse. But the heavy rain, coming over the yacht in successive curtains of water, had been the worst; it had drenched everything and all of them. James had come out of the cabin cursing about how a bucket of water had entered while he was trying to write his diary. He had added in dismay that his son was still vomiting and his brother was not much better, and he had mumbled that, should he live to get back home, this was the last sea trip he would make.

Hearing James complain vehemently, a little smile had crossed the Captain's face and he'd commented dryly that being wet was dismal, but not as miserable as continuing seasickness, before adding supportively that it was almost dinnertime and that would sort everything out.

The Captain was right; James's appetite hadn't at any stage been affected by the weather and now, with the misery of yesterday's rain forgotten, James was as chirpy as ever.

'John, can you give me a hand? I'd like to copper the starboard rail to keep the jib sheets from chafing on it.'

'Yes Sir.' John jumped up, grabbed his tool bag and followed James to the bow of the yacht. It had been a problem over the last few days; every time they trimmed the jib, the rope attached to the sail would get caught on the railing, which not only impeded the action but was also slowly fraying the line. It didn't take long before they were immersed in their work. Finally, the sun had come out for the first time and, as the men took advantage of its warming rays, the yacht soon became a hive of activity. The crew busied themselves drying everything out and cleaning the yacht.

'How's it going?'

John and James looked up to see George. His face looked awfully grey, and was matched by his ruffled hair and creased clothes.

'Hey, brother, good to see you!'

'Yes, I thought I should show my face at least once this trip.' The sarcasm in George's voice was obvious.

'And a pretty face it is; how are you feeling?' James teased.

'Please don't ask. I took another dose of calomel – no idea if I should have, but by now I'll do anything to make me feel better. Actually, it has worked a bit. What about you – not been sick at all?'

John and James looked at each other, wondering whether the truth was called for in front of this poor man.

'I'm feeling better now,' John offered.

'Same with me,' James chipped in with a guilty look on his face. They both knew it was a blatant lie, as every day he ate his own weight in boiled hams, plum puddings and custard, washing it all down with brandy.

'So, what are you two doing here?'

'We're modifying the railing to make sure the jib sheet doesn't get caught.'

'How is she doing?' George sounded like the worried parent of an unruly child.

'I say it's the best sea boat that ever went out of the Hook. You should see the way we've passed every vessel we have encountered 'til now.'

'Good, I'm glad to hear it. Lying horizontally in a bed certainly doesn't give the best impression of her performance.'

'Well, you're back in the land of the living, so you can find out for yourself. Just look at how she glides through the waves like a Portuguese Man of War, taking on very little water.'

The two of them continued to discuss the running of the yacht and other possible modifications they could make during the rest of the journey. Watching the men interact with good humour, John thought about his brother Joe. It had been a couple of years since they were last together.

John glided his hand along the new sheet of copper; it was as smooth as silk. How he wished his younger brother could see him; he would have never guessed what he had ended up doing. Definitely not imagined him crossing an ocean. He wondered if the speed they were doing compared with the pilot boats Joe used to work on.

'There, over that way! Have a look!' George indicated towards a position on lee bow further out to sea. 'There's something floating – it's big!'

They followed his agitated finger but the sea was heavy, with a slow and large swell that made focusing on anything particularly difficult. In the distance was a large, rounded shape, low in the water. Whatever it was, it didn't appear to have any structure on it, so it couldn't be a boat – or could it?

Similarly alarmed, James said, 'What the hell is it? That had better not be…' His voice faded and John knew he was thinking the same. *Were they looking at the smooth hull of an upturned ship?*

Some of the other men had heard the commotion and joined them at the bow. 'Let's run down to see what it is,' suggested

Harkness, the first mate. They adjusted their course and advanced slowly towards the mysterious object. Apart from the wind and the water slapping their hull, there was no sound; the men had stopped talking and were watching the grim shape come closer, wave by wave.

What they would do if it turned out to be what they dreaded most? The thought of a ship upside down in the middle of the ocean filled John with horror. Not once had he considered that a fate like that could be bestowed upon them, although of all people he should have known better. For he had visualized it often enough, contemplating how dark it would be in the water underneath an upturned hull, wondering whether there would be any pockets of air.

'My goodness, it's enormous!'

'Look at it!'

'It's the size of a small house!'

The colossal form drifted closer to the yacht and, with a collective sigh of relief, they realised they were looking at the shiny and puffed-up body of a dead whale. It was about the size of a small yacht and the men agreed it was the largest they had ever seen.

'Look at the fat on that; that must be about a foot thick if not more.'

'How long do you think it has been in the water?'

'I guess some time, judging by how bloated it is.'

'We'd better leave it, before it explodes on us.'

'Nice thought, Comstock.'

'Sorry about that! Let's be glad we didn't encounter it in the dark.'

'That doesn't bear thinking about!'

What would happen if a yacht their size accidently hit such a large structure, dead or alive? Would it crack the hull, letting in water instantly, giving the crew no chance to get out as the entire ship was swallowed up, leaving no trace behind as it sank straight to the bottom? Could that have happened to his brother on the day his ship hadn't returned?

The memory of his own, more adventurous, brother rose to the foreground. He had been three years younger and had always been more intrigued by his father's stories of their ancestors' ocean travels. No matter how much his father tried to convince Joe their journey was born out of necessity rather than adventure, this hadn't stopped him developing a passion for the water. Without telling anybody, Joe would sometimes join a friend on one of the fishing boats down at the harbour. And when his father suspected his time spent away from the house had been on the water, Joe would tell him he was helping with repairs to the boat. He'd even roped in his older brother to help him cover his back. One day, Joe couldn't hide it any longer and admitted that sometimes he went out fishing with a friend. Their father had been disappointed and angry with Joe but had ended up pleading with him, warning him about the destructive nature of the sea, and recounting the chances of getting injured or, even worse, dying, as did a great number of fishermen per year.

But it was to no avail. After a couple of months, Joe had laid down his tools and, after a brief period on a fishing boat, he had taken up the opportunity to join a pilot boat a little further up the coast.

John had long thought that his parents had been right to consider Joe foolish and irresponsible; sailing should be left to others.

He remembered Ole asking him about it one day, shortly after the visit from the Commodore.

'Ever thought of becoming a sailor?' Ole spoke with his mouth full of cold meat. The men were sitting in John's workshop having a break.

'No, never.' But John immediately knew his answer wasn't completely true. Experiencing life at sea was something both he and his brother had dreamt of ever since they had been small boys, although unlike his brother, John had never considered sailing to be a way to earn a living. He had visited the docks with Joe, but these visits were mostly done in secret, because John had never openly dared to go against his father's will.

'What did your father do?'

'He was a carpenter.'

'Probably safer.'

'I think he liked to get his excitement from his occasional work as a fireman which he was good at.'

'Didn't you do that as well?'

'Yes, for a short while.'

'Risky job.'

'Sometimes, but I guess being a mariner is even more so. That's why my father kept us from it. What about you?'

'It never appealed to me. I prefer sturdy soil under my feet. The only experience of ocean-faring in our family is from the grandparents who came over on a ship. I like to keep it that way.'

'You sound like my father,' John mumbled, wiping some soup out of his stubble. 'The ocean takes too many lives he always warned us. He made it clear he had other plans for his sons, and they didn't involve the sea – he told us not to waste the opportunities our forefathers had given us.'

'He must have done a good job scaring you off! Didn't you say your brother is a carpenter as well?'

'He was a carpenter, just like me and our father, but only at first.'

'Your father taught you the trade, then?' Ole was curious, and when this happened it wasn't easy to evade his questioning.

'From a very young age, to stop me carving useless figurines from leftover wood.' John smiled at the thought of the countless dogs, birds and boats he had carved before his father found out he was handy enough to use tools without cutting himself and had put him to work.

'Cabinet-making is what he made sure I was good at.'

'How did you end up here?'

'One of the brothers suggested it.' John got up, signalling his break was over.

Ole looked surprised. 'Mister George? Do you know the designer?'

'No, his brother James. But I don't really know him,' John hastened to add.

'Go on.' Ole's curiosity was awakened and John could tell he wasn't going to let go.

'It's a long story.'

'I have time.' With a grin, Ole showed John his unfinished lunch box. 'Go ahead, I'm listening.'

'All right then, I'll give you the short version. About half a year ago there was a big fire in an alley off Georck Street. It was out of control, but I managed to rescue this lady from the burning building and –'

'Oh my god, that must have been something.' Ole had stopped eating.

'Yes, it was awful.'

'But you must be proud – you rescued people!' Ole exclaimed.

'I don't know…' John hesitated. *What could he explain about that night? He still couldn't make sense of it himself.* 'I didn't manage to rescue her husband,' he added faintly. 'The father of the child. For a while I didn't even know that the child had survived.'

Ole frowned and then his eyebrows shot up. 'The woman at the gate!' He couldn't suppress the delight at his own perceptiveness.

John nodded. 'After that fire, I wasn't sure the volunteering was for me.'

'But what has James got to do with that?'

'We were both with the same fire-engine company. And we talked a bit just after the incident.'

'I never knew that.' Ole nodded appreciatively. 'Who would have thought people like that would volunteer for such things?'

'Well, we all have our reasons, don't we? Protection of the shipyards in the vicinity was probably as good as any.'

'Perhaps. You said you had a carpentry job – why leave that?'

'I got restless.' John dithered. He wasn't prepared to tell Ole about the bad dreams he had started to get every night, or how he would wake up in a sweat, dreading the day ahead. The fear of not being able to escape. James's passionate account of how an image on a drawing would slowly come alive on the quay, until finally she was set free in the water, ready to set sail, had reawakened childhood dreams.

'I liked the idea of being closer to the water and I knew that James was part of this shipyard.'

'You asked him for a job?'

'He couldn't guarantee exactly what kind of carpentry job, or for how long, but I told him I didn't mind.'

'Well, lucky for you the yard is expected to stay busy in the coming months thanks to the new commission from the Yacht Club,' Ole said as he stood up.

John followed him outside and watched as he walked over to some of the men working at the quay. He heard their laughs as they shared a joke. It was as if he was observing his younger brother and his buddies engaged in passionate conversation about ships.

Thinking about Joe, it was now clear: when his brother had decided to sail, he hadn't been the careless one. On the contrary, he had been the one with the courage to go against what was asked of him and had answered the vast ocean's invitation to travel, *despite* its sirens.

He, on the other hand, had appeased his father by staying away from the water's edge for as long as he had. It was time he stopped denying his own desires. He had to find a way to get on board the new yacht.

Chapter 10

February 1851, the south coast of England

'An experienced naval architect of New York is now constructing a yacht schooner, of about 150 tons, which will be present on the Thames during the Exhibition of next year. He has carte blanche from the gentlemen to whom she will belong; and is so confident of rendering her the model of perfection which they wish for, that he contracts to build her without charge, if she do not prove to be faster than any other which may be brought forward in competition.'

How could Frank have missed that article before?

He had come in late that morning, feeling exhausted. He had been tempted not to come in at all because he had a splitting headache, but he was worried that his colleagues might start to wonder what had happened to him since he had disappeared the previous afternoon. He wouldn't want them to come looking for him, so he'd dragged himself out of the house.

He had been awake most of the night, sifting through endless notes, some of which were more readable than others. What state had he been in when he'd written down some of this stuff? When he'd woken up that morning, he was still sitting in his chair in his clothes, feeling clammy and worn-out. He'd had a feverish dream about being aboard a ship being wrecked in high seas. He couldn't remember any details except for the desperation he'd felt watching a child float away on a piece of wreckage in choppy water. Instead of being its saviour, he had let it go, left behind on a lifeboat that he didn't know how to sail. Ignoring his pounding head and the doubts that he was going to be of use to anybody today, he'd managed to haul himself into the office.

He flopped down on his chair that groaned under the sudden

movement and weight. *How good we are at ignoring emotionally charged matters!* Frank peeked at Harold through the disorder on his desk. Harold hadn't batted an eyelid to acknowledge that Frank was back in the office; he just kept his head down, pretending to be working.

Frank's desk was a mess: piles of newspapers and clippings, mostly about the Great Exhibition, which Bill kept sending. When he had asked Bill for help, he hadn't expected him to be this dedicated; it was as if Bill owed him something. Perhaps he should tell him to call it a day? Apparently, the organisation was running smoothly and criticism of the whole project had started to wane; either people were happy with how it was going or they'd stopped caring about it – just like him. For some time now, he'd been stuck for ideas, but could today be the day to solve that problem?

Frank turned the article over; it was dated December 3, 1850, and it came from a newspaper in New York, which meant that the announcement was a couple of months old. *Were the Americans of the opinion they had made technical advances in shipbuilding?*

'Ha!' Frank chuckled. What a gutsy idea of the Yankees to send over a yacht and show her to the old Mother Country, the greatest maritime nation of the world. This Exhibition was starting to sound like a proper competition, not merely an amicable contest. *Were they planning to show off their own maritime designs at the Great Exhibition?* Frank wasn't sure; he looked across the table at the tall, slender frame of Harold, who did most of the naval intelligence and shipping news.

'Harold, will we be sending a boat to the Great Exhibition?'

'I beg your pardon?' Harold looked at him quizzically, pushing his tiny spectacles back to the top of his nose. 'I thought you were the specialist on the Great Exhibition?'

'Perhaps, but you're the boat specialist, so please help me out, will you?'

Harold smiled with self-satisfaction, clearly pleased to hear Frank's recognition of his knowledge and contacts.

'Don't you go out with these sailing toffs every summer

weekend? Surely you talk constantly about boats, don't you?' Frank said.

Harold sighed and shook his head. 'Maybe you should come with us one day. It might cure you of your fear of water as well,' he added sarcastically.

Frank knew it had been a mistake to tell Harold about that; trying to be sociable and share facts about yourself when meeting people for the first time always came back to haunt you. At the time, it had seemed quite funny and a good way to break the ice, admitting to a dislike of water and especially the sea after getting a job at a newspaper on the south coast.

'No, as far as I'm aware, we're not sending any vessel to the Exhibition. We probably haven't felt the need to do so. Why are you asking?'

'I've just read in an article here that the Americans will take the opportunity in May to show us a novel boat design.'

Harold snorted. 'What an insult! Does the pupil think he can educate the teacher?'

His cheeks flushed a bright pink and the pitch of his voice went up: the first signs he was starting to care about a topic. Despite his seemingly meek demeanour and the dull appearance Frank had judged him on at first, Harold wasn't afraid to show a fiery spirit and an ability to quickly analyse complicated matters. The warning his father had given him as a young man crossed Frank's mind. That being judgemental was a lazy trait for a man to have and hindered human interaction. "Start asking the right questions instead, and you'll find the motivation for a person's behaviour, and maybe friendship along the way", he used to say. Frank was still learning.

'You could call it arrogance, but don't you think they are showing courage in believing that they can beat us on our own territory?' Frank retorted.

'I thought you said the Exhibition wasn't a competition?'

'There will be prizes for effort, if that's what you mean.' Frank winked at Harold. 'But who needs a piece of metal when the biggest reward is having motivated your pupil to do better than you?'

'No, I don't see the honour in that.' Harold spoke the last words with disdain. 'Are you sure they're not referring to a model of a yacht? Anyway, how do you expect them to prove to us that their ship is better than any of ours? Sailing a ship over to England and mooring it on the Thames somewhere doesn't quite do that. Do we even know what they intend to send?'

'I'm not sure; the piece talks about a yacht schooner. Why?' Frank looked at the man behind the other desk who was pretending not to be interested but whose curiosity was clearly aroused, judging by the way he unnecessarily pushed his glasses further up his nose.

'Well, if the Americans are intent on sending a yacht over to show the world that their design surpasses any of ours, they would have to sail her in a race with other yachts, preferably of the same type.'

'I see… of course.' Frank scratched his head. 'I can't believe I'm talking about sailing boats with you,' he mumbled.

'And that implies that the Americans will have to build an ocean-worthy yacht that would also be fast in a race around the shores of England.'

Frank opened his mouth to say something, but quickly closed it again; what did he know? 'Is that unusual?'

'It requires different design features, although pilot boats probably come closest to meeting those different demands –'

Frank had stopped listening; while Harold went on about the differences between several designs, his mind drifted away. The previous night was starting to take its toll, as was the fear that his old research would resurface and interfere with his daily work. Maybe this American boat-thing could keep him occupied over the coming weeks. A proper fight between the Old World and the New; he applauded the audacity of that plan. He smiled; there could be a good story in this and he was ready for one. The only thing he needed to do was to get over the fact that there were boats and water involved.

'And they'd better start building her, otherwise they won't make it in time for the Exhibition.'

Harold's voice brought Frank back to the present.

'You mean the American ship, or an English one? Because the Americans might be finished already.' Frank tried not to sound hopeful. 'This newspaper article is a couple of months old. I'll think of a way to get some more information on this. Which reminds me, can't you introduce me to one of your sailing friends?'

'They're called "my friends" now?'

'Don't make me beg you, Harold.' Frank sounded earnest.

'All right, I will see what I can do, but you'll be in my debt for this.' Harold took off his glasses and cleaned them with his handkerchief, taking his time to finish his sentence. 'You're in luck; this weekend our sailing club is coming together for our first meet of the season. Even the members from the Isle of Wight will attend and they're normally the ones with the latest gossip.'

'Isle of Wight?' Frank's eyes grew larger.

'Yes, we became a club long before we moved away to different places. Some of our members live over there.' He nodded in the direction of the office window.

'And where did you say you're going to meet again?'

Harold laughed, a sound Frank had never heard before: oafish and too loud, but pleasingly revealing. 'Don't you worry, Frank, we're meeting this side of the Solent, in a public house in Gosport.'

Frank tried to imagine Harold amongst a group of keen sailors; although Harold had the slim physique of an athlete, it was difficult to imagine him hoisting up sails or doing any strong physical labour. 'And how did you get involved in sailing? Or is a better question to ask what you're doing here, on a junior desk at a provincial newspaper? Couldn't one of Papa's friends get you a proper job in London?'

'Too far from the sea,' Harold replied tersely.

'I see. Thanks for the offer; I'd appreciate the opportunity to meet your friends,' Frank added, feeling guilty for being cynical about his favourite pastime.

'Good,' said Harold. 'A bow won't be necessary, but I'll teach you the secret handshake.'

Frank had to bend his head slightly to get through the door of the tavern. The atmosphere was heavy with the smells of tobacco and stale beer and the thick smoke brought tears to his eyes. He remained near the entrance and observed the social interaction, while searching for the familiar face of Harold in the crowd. *Why had they decided to meet here?* It was going to be difficult to hear the person in front of him, let alone to attempt a conversation with several people.

Gradually he managed to get closer to the bar. Judging by the number of weathered faces and chunky sweaters, most of the men present that evening were fishermen. He'd seen some of them before in the village and when he moved amongst them, he was greeted by a few.

He hesitated over his order, but decided that a pint of lovely golden ale would do him no harm. When he turned away from the bar, he saw Harold walking to the rear of the inn and disappearing into a room at the back. In a small, dimly lit area, separated from the main bar, a group of men jovially welcomed each other: a lot of shoulder patting, accompanied by brisk handshakes and broad grins. Frank hovered near the doorway, feeling silly for making derogatory remarks about Harold's sailing chums. Their comradeship was apparent; how wonderful to be part of a club of men who shared a passion for sailing and also a competitive nature! There hadn't been many tight friendships for him when he had been younger; his health had always interfered. Whenever he had been poorly, it had been his mother who had taken him out of the house to 'clean out his lungs'. And when he had grown older, and his lungs stronger, he'd become used to his own company.

'Evening, Sir, can we be of any assistance?' Someone had

noticed him near the entrance; it was the pleasant voice of a man with authority.

Before Frank could answer, Harold stepped forward and announced loudly, 'Men, I would like to introduce you to my colleague Frank Grundy. He asked if he could join us tonight because he has developed an interest in sailing and we could always do with a new member.' Harold gently nudged Frank's arm, encouraging him to come nearer, but Frank merely opened his mouth in protest at Harold's remark. Just in time, he saw Harold wink.

The twelve men seemed unconcerned by the sudden arrival of a stranger in their midst and they murmured approvingly.

'I see we all have a drink. I suggest we pull up our chairs and start the meeting promptly.' The pleasant voice belonged to a young man with a neatly trimmed beard and dark glistening eyes.

They organized themselves around a few small tables and one of them got out some papers. Very efficiently, the men discussed their plans and ideas for the coming season. From the way they spoke, it became apparent that some, although not all, were from well-to-do families.

The meeting went smoothly: everyone had something to say, but the rest listened attentively. Frank thought about the chaos in his old office just before a new edition of the paper was due: a verbal tussle between men trying to outsmart each other. After what seemed like a short session, they had a break and a few members left the room to get some more drinks.

'Are you a sailor?'

The manner in which the question was asked made Frank think he'd given the game away; was it his appearance or the way he spoke?

'I do apologise, I haven't introduced myself properly. I'm Robert Underwood.' The man with the neat beard offered his hand.

Frank took it and said defensively, 'No, I'm not a sailor. One day, maybe, I would love to…' He immediately regretted this. It was a blatant lie; he would never contemplate voluntarily setting foot on a ship. 'But I'm very interested in sailing and shipbuilding and I'm thinking of doing an article. I have a lot of questions that need answering, hence Harold's idea to bring me here.' He hoped he wasn't letting Harold down. 'He suggested that I consult with you because of the amount of knowledge in this group; I hope you don't mind. He's a good colleague,' he added quickly.

'Yes, he's a good man. And I'm sure we would love to answer your questions, if we can.' Robert turned around to the others. 'May I have your attention everybody. Frank here has some questions for us, and if you answer them well, you might get your name in the paper.'

'Right, yes.' Frank scratched his chin. 'First of all, I would like to thank you for allowing me to be present at your meeting here tonight.'

The group nodded happily.

'And although I could think of thousands of questions to ask you about sailing, I don't want you to have to put up with my ignorance for too long, so I'll keep it limited. Can any of you can share any information about an American plan to send over a ship, probably a yacht, which is being built especially for the Great Exhibition?' He paused a moment. 'And if we are doing the same? That is, building a yacht to show off our nautical skills at the Exhibition?'

The men started to talk amongst each other, until one of them said loudly, 'Hey Isaac, you're somewhat of a yacht builder yourself – heard anything about an English yacht?'

'No, nothing's come to my attention.'

Isaac came into Frank's vision; he was the most delicate-looking of all the men present.

'Personally, I'm not sure if we've felt the need to do so.'

'Hear, hear.' The room filled itself with heartfelt laughter.

'What about our ears and eyes of the Island?' They turned simultaneously to face a club member with windswept hair and a little moustache, who had been sitting in the corner with a drink in his hand, quietly watching the proceedings.

'Archie's one of the Islanders who loves his old sailing club so much that he comes over especially for our get-togethers,' Robert explained. 'And more importantly, he has some friends in high places at the Royal Yacht Squadron in Cowes, so if there's anything of significance being planned, he'll know.'

Archie got up from his seat and bowed his head as if receiving the audience's applause on stage. 'Thank you, gentlemen.' He raised his hand for attention and took a sip from his drink to clear his throat.

'You will be pleased to know that there is a rumour circulating in Cowes…' He swallowed another mouthful of his beer and took his time to enjoy it.

'Come on, don't keep us in suspense.' Someone poked him roughly in the back.

'All right, I've heard that the Commodore of the Squadron has invited his counterpart from the New York Yacht Club to the Clubhouse in Cowes during their stay in England.'

'What are you saying?'

'That the Americans are coming over to England this summer and that they're bringing a yacht. And that we – that is, the Royal Yacht Squadron – are politely offering them a place to stay.'

'Did you just say the Commodore of the New York Yacht Club?'

'Yes, apparently he and his noble friends are the ones bringing over the new yacht.'

Frank smiled at the confirmation of the news in the article; the owners were apparently connected to a well-known yacht club in New York.

'Does that mean the sailing club in Cowes is going to organise a race for them as well?' Frank was keen to know.

'I haven't heard anything about that. Good luck to the Yankees if they do, because the Squadron's fleet is made for these waters; they'll win easily. And I drink to that!' Archie raised his glass again and downed the rest of his drink in one. Clearly, he'd come a long way, so he was making sure he would have a good time.

The other men joined him, clinking their glasses and raising their spirits.

Frank admired the men's unshakable belief in the skills of the people around them; together with their love of sailing, they exuded an air of unlimited possibilities. He didn't want to criticize these men for their confidence, but he believed strongly that others should be given a chance to show what they were worth. For now, he felt satisfied; at least he had a good story to look forward to. He picked up his beer to toast Archie. 'Thanks, Archie, you've been a big help.'

'*New American Yacht –*

'*A new American yacht is currently being built for members of the New York Yacht Club who intend to sail her to England to participate in the Great Exhibition that is opening in London in eight weeks' time. Whilst here, they want to demonstrate her sailing qualities by competing against the yachts of the Royal Yacht Squadron at Cowes. The American builder is said to be so assured of her ability to successfully compete against anything here, that he's willing to receive no payment if she is not the fastest.*"

Frank sat back and studied what he'd written thus far. It was the first thing he'd done when he'd arrived home; he felt invigorated and unable to sleep, mulling over the possible consequences of such a race for the sea-faring nations involved.

Although strictly speaking he had no reliable source to confirm that the Yankees were intent on a contest, he was convinced that that was what needed to happen, assuming they wanted to show the English what they were made of.

He stretched his stiff limbs and through the window he noticed the welcoming signs of a new morning; he wasn't in the least bit tired, as the thrill of knowing he had found a story worthwhile pursuing was keeping him awake. The desperation he had felt the previous night, when he had realised that his entire research into the missing girls had been indecipherable and fruitless, was slowly disappearing with the increasingly pink sky. For the moment, he had perhaps returned to back the competitor least likely to win, but this time he was determined to make his voice count and to help the Americans' cause along by giving them a platform to speak from.

Chapter 11

December 1850, Manhattan

Ole's prediction that the yard would be busier than ever hadn't been an exaggeration. Straight after the Commodore's visit, the men had sprung into action and started with the construction of a stage on which the new yacht was going to be built near the river. John watched them enviously through the small window of his workshop.

The weather was bad and progress was slow; the men outside had barely worked for more than a couple of days when Da Silva's assistant came into John's workshop and told him he was needed in the mould loft.

John followed the other man up the stairs to the loft where several others were already present, amongst them the yard owner, as well as George and Da Silva. Not one of them acknowledged his arrival and he was worried that he had misheard and wasn't expected after all. He waited at the door; the men were discussing numbers, and comparing them with a plan on the wall. Some of them were on their hands and knees on the floor and on a table nearby was the half model John had admired once before. He understood that it was supposed to give one an idea of what the finished ship would look like, but how it translated into the full-size version was beyond him. He remained awkwardly in a corner of the loft, not knowing what to do, until George noticed him.

'Da Silva, is that the one you've called for?' George pointed in John's direction with a piece of chalk in his hand.

'Ah yes, John, please.' Da Silva gestured for him to come closer.

Crossing the length of the room, John took care to avoid the chalk lines that the men had been applying to the floor.

'He's a cabinet maker and accurate in his work; that's why I asked for him. He used to work at Hutchings furniture makers,' Da Silva explained to George.

'I guess we don't have much choice.' George scarcely looked at John. 'But you're responsible for him.'

'Yes, of course, Sir.' Da Silva took John by the arm. 'I'll explain what I want you to do and you'd better listen carefully.' He pulled him towards the line drawing on the wall, in the shape of the yacht. 'The lines are taken from the half model. It's what we call a sheer plan. We're going to use it to draw the yacht in real scale on the floor. I want you to –'

John had stopped listening; what Da Silva was trying to explain was complex material and he was rapidly feeling out of his depth.

'John?' Da Silva's stern voice made him jump.

'Sorry Sir,' he said, sounding apologetic. 'I was just wondering how a full-size drawing of the yacht would fit on this floor. And why would you want the drawing on the floor?' The moment he had said it, he regretted it; he saw Da Silva was getting impatient.

'There's no need for you to fully understand it.' Da Silva handed John a piece of chalk.

George stepped closer and John realised that he had overheard everything.

'All I want you to remember is that the very essence of a ship's temperament is to be found in the form of the hull.' George rested one hand on the half model. 'It will decide what she will be: how fast, how ocean-worthy and how race-worthy, her stability, her limits of safety and her comfort. Everything.' He ran his other hand along the shape of the hull. 'What Da Silva is trying to tell you is that the wooden frames that make up the hull need to be an exact replica of this model; that's why we have put the measurements on this sheer plan and then we'll multiply them to create a full-size body plan on the floor.'

John began to understand what the chalk lines were for – they were a bigger version of the plan on the wall – but it still mystified him as to why they kept talking about drawing a full-size yacht when anybody could see that the mould loft was far too short.

'That way we will end up with frames in the right sizes drawn on the floor, after which we will cut moulds made of thin pine wood into an exact copy.'

'And those moulds will be used by the joiner to cut out the definite frames. Which means it's of the utmost importance to get the measurements right; Mister George here has worked long and hard to get her outline perfect.' Da Silva called John to the middle of the loft. 'We've drawn the horizontal waterlines and this line represents the top of the keel. We now have to draw all the vertical lines for every point where a frame will be positioned. So, let's get started.'

As Da Silva called out the number of the so-called frame-stations, John drew a vertical line along the loft floor. He worked his way from the centre of the room towards what was to be the stern of the vessel, while the other men did the same towards the bow. Slowly, a grid pattern was revealed: an arrangement of lines crossing at right angles. Once all the vertical lines were put down, George calculated the location of the stern and keel after which they marked them as well.

Because of the scale, it wasn't possible to get a good overview of the yacht now drawn on the floor, but John could distinguish the front and the back of the yacht, which seemed too close together somehow. *Was this how short the yacht was going to be?* He couldn't afford to make any mistakes. *Should he say something about it?*

George and Da Silva were too occupied to notice his confusion. The other men were taking a break, waiting for the next instructions. *Should he go over and ask them?* John didn't feel like approaching them as they had kept mostly to themselves all morning. His panic grew; a sudden vision crossed his mind of an oddly short vessel revealing itself on the slip outside and George full of rage wanting to know who had messed up the calculations.

'Sir, may I talk to you for a moment?' John plucked up all his courage and tapped on Da Silva's shoulder. 'I'm so sorry to disturb you, but the yacht…' He hesitated for a second. 'It seems short – too short.'

Da Silva stared at him and then at the floor. John's face burned; he was warm and sweaty. Expecting to be scowled at, he prepared himself to make a quick exit, but then George started to laugh out loud. Unable to stop expressing his amusement, he slapped Da Silva on his shoulder. 'Your boy has a good pair of eyes in his head,' he chuckled.

Da Silva didn't appear similarly pleased: 'You'd better leave the real work to us, John,' he said in a disapproving voice.

'Oh come on, at least he had the guts to ask us the question.' George turned to John; 'As the whole yacht doesn't fit in the loft, we don't reproduce the midsection of the vessel on the floor since no change of hull shape occurs in that part.' He walked away, still grinning.

Time in the mould loft flew by and, much to his relief, John picked up the work with ease. Each night after work, rather than going straight back to his workshop to continue his assignment, he ventured towards the river where the platform was progressing. All of the keel blocks had been placed in position and equipment for lifting had been added. From the length of the platform, it was easy to see that the yacht was going to be a size somewhat bigger than the loft floor. He felt embarrassed; he had made a fool of himself. He should have known that it wasn't possible to draw a yacht in real scale. But the shame he had felt was slowly being overshadowed by his feelings of guilt for letting Nathan down once again by being late.

'I'm so sorry I wasn't there the other evening.' John watched Elsie's back. *Again*, he should have added. After a long day in the mould loft, the relative warmth of his workshop made it difficult to keep his eyes open. Once more he had woken up in the middle of the workshop, although this time not too late to come around and offer his apologies.

'That's all right, John, I understand.' Elsie continued scrubbing the potatoes she was preparing for his late dinner.

She lived only two blocks away and since he'd joined them for Nathan's birthday in the summer, they had met up a few times. At first, he had been hesitant to accept her invitations; the birthday celebration had been a pleasant change to his normal routine, as was being in her company, but he couldn't help wondering if his presence was as untroubling as she led him to believe. *Did she feel obliged to invite him to express gratitude for rescuing her?* It was impossible to know what she was thinking; she kept her emotions to herself. But what he did know for certain was the effort it took him to ignore certain distressing thoughts. They came to him unexpectedly. Like on the day of Nathan's birthday; how things could have been different if had he managed to do more for the boy's father, who would have been there to celebrate with his son.

When the days became colder and shorter, Elsie would invite him for dinner, a few times on Sundays and sometimes during the week. John had accepted the invitations selfishly; he was no cook and the sight of Nathan's little face beaming whenever he came through the door managed to dull his guilty conscience.

'They've given me different work to do. To be more precise, they've given me *more* work. And I'm sorry I'm late this evening.'

Nathan had fallen asleep on some blankets in the corner of the room. They had already eaten and it was past the boy's bedtime.

'Stop saying sorry, I'm pleased you've made it. And you've already explained, several times. I understand that you like your sleep above anything else.'

John opened his mouth to object but realised she was mocking him. He couldn't see her face, but he imagined the delight in her eyes. He tried not to laugh for fear of waking Nathan. She kept surprising him and although she had quickly dispelled his concern that she would be leading a cheerless life after all that she had lost in the fire, her carefree sense of humour still caught him unawares.

'You'd better help me cut up these carrots.' Elsie handed John a knife, holding onto it longer than necessary. 'Really, I'm fine with it. But this isn't just about me – he was looking forward to your company.' She glanced at Nathan stretched out on the floor.

Every day he started to look less like his mother; his curls had become more chocolate-brown than chestnut and his eyes were almost black.

'Yes, I understand. I'll make it up to him; I'll take you both to the yard on a Sunday and he can see the ships and the workshop.'

'That's a nice idea.' Elsie lowered a potato into a pan of water. 'We'll have to see what the weather is like as it will be a long trip for him.'

'Of course.'

'Did you say they gave you another job? Does that mean you're no longer employed as a cabinet maker?'

'No, I still am.' He smiled. 'It's just that the yard received an important commission for a yacht, which needs to be finished in a couple of months.'

'Building a ship – isn't that very complicated?'

'Tell me something!' He thought about what happened in the mould loft. 'But I'm learning quickly.'

'But are you all right with the change? What is it they make you do?'

'I've mainly helped with sizing up the frames in the mould loft.' The more he told her, the more animated he became, trying to explain about the function of the half model and the puzzle of transferring the lines.

'You'd better keep your promise and take us there, because you make it sound very exciting.'

He must have rambled on. 'Sorry, I must be boring you.'

'Not at all, I'm not sure if I've seen you this enthusiastic before.'

She was right. He felt energised, which was odd considering that he had worked so hard over the last period.

He watched her vigorously stirring the pot on the stove; locks of curly hair that had escaped what must have been a tidy bun danced along her neck. Looks could deceive and, in her case, they did; she appeared delicate and vulnerable, but he knew there was a steely determination beneath her small frame. She was one of those people who somehow managed to find a solution for every problem that they encountered and being in her company it was easy to make the mistake to think she never needed any help herself.

'How have you been?'

'We're getting there. I've even met some other women in the same position.'

Elsie was dependent on help with Nathan to get any work. 'Don't you have any family nearby?' John was still chopping the carrots.

'No, my family is in Vermont. We moved here some time before Nathan was born, for more work opportunities for my husband.' Elsie added some onion to the broth. 'And his family, well, we just don't see each other much since the accident.'

She hardly ever mentioned the fire, but it hung around her and the little boy like an invisible cloth.

'Oh, John, what were you thinking?' She turned around to have a look at his work; he had absentmindedly cut the carrots into a lot of tiny pieces. 'You should probably stick to boat building and stop dissecting my vegetables.'

'Perhaps I should,' John grinned broadly, although deep down he knew his ambition lay beyond the finished vessel.

Chapter 12

March 1851, Southampton

With a spring in his step Frank walked towards Orchard Place. He was back in Southampton, but this time he was looking forward to his visit.

When he'd left the pub after meeting Harold's sailing friends, he had asked Archie whom he could approach for more information on the American yacht and the men behind the plan. Archie had pointed at Harold, remarking that his father was a merchant who did business with the Americans on a daily business, receiving goods carried on ships built in Manhattan. Archie had seemed surprised that Frank didn't know this already, before stipulating with a smile that if he discovered anything about the yacht being built, he owed their sailing club the information.

Harold had appeared unhappy when Frank had asked him for help and he remembered too late that Harold's relationship with his father was rather fragile. Nevertheless, he was kind enough to set up a meeting and to Frank's relief his journey took him relatively close to home.

It didn't take Frank long to find the house although Harold's description of it didn't do it justice. It was far grander than he had made it out to be.

Frank looked up at the elegant Regency house; there were several large bay windows on the first floor and, at ground level, a few steps led to a large gleaming door. *Papa was doing well in life; clearly his son had not chosen to follow in his father's footsteps.*

The sound made by the heavy door knocker seemed to reverberate throughout the house and the servant who opened the door looked at Frank disapprovingly. He followed the man to the morning room where two men were present, engaged in animated conversation about trade.

One of them strode towards him with an outstretched hand.

'You must be Frank Grundy. How wonderful to meet a colleague of my son. I wish he could have joined you. But he seems to think the journey to our house is longer than mine to his.' Mr Hayes shook Frank's hand enthusiastically and then gestured towards the other man. 'Mr Grundy, you are in luck today; we have the pleasure of the company of Mr Croskey, who knows all there is to know about steamships made in Manhattan.'

The other man rose from his seat and nodded, while a smile played around his lips. 'Now, Cornelius, let's not exaggerate.'

Frank smiled back at the statuesque man with the faint moustache. He tried to hide his frustration; he hadn't come to talk about steamships or discuss their line of business. But he didn't want to appear ungrateful, he recognised the man's name and the accent confirmed his guess; he was the American Consul at Southampton.

'Mr Grundy, ignore what Mr Croskey says, he's being modest. He's been in the steam shipping business for years, whereas I merely take goods from him and transport them through England by road.' Mr Hayes signalled to the maid to pour his newly arrived guest a drink.

'Harold told me you wanted to talk about the shipyards in Manhattan?'

'Yes, I do, but I'm actually interested in a specific vessel: a yacht to be precise.'

There was a silence in the room, until the Consul explained. 'Then I'm afraid I can't help you. The shipyards I'm familiar with on Manhattan hardly make small sailing vessels anymore, sorry. Their yards are mainly set up for constructing merchant vessels of large dimensions – most of them steam.'

Mr Hayes looked from his friend to Frank and sighed loudly. 'Typical of Harold. Tries to help, but messes things up. Croskey, I do apologise for asking you to come over, I thought this was about steamships.' He shrugged his shoulders defiantly.

'Perhaps Mr Croskey can tell me something in general terms about the builders on the other side of the Atlantic.' Frank couldn't let Harold down. 'I'm interested in the men behind a plan to bring over an American yacht. It has been said the builder is willing to take substantial risks building her. And if I understand Mr Croskey's information correctly, the low demand for such sailing vessels makes the builder's willingness to take those risks even more intriguing.'

'Ah, you see, Mr Grundy, never underestimate the entrepreneurial spirit of the American people. For whom did you say the yacht is being built?'

'Supposedly for some members of the New York Yacht Club.'

Croskey let out a hearty laugh. 'You should have said so straight away; that's William Brown's yard. Brown is well known for his American enterprise. He's the only one who won't let a full order book get in the way of his love for yachting.'

Cornelius looked surprised at his friend's words. 'Since when do you know about yachting? I thought you didn't have much time for people who waste their hard-earned cash on frivolous pastimes like sailing small boats for pleasure?'

'One can't avoid it around here, and nor can I. I've been reminded about that often enough during my time on the Isle of Wight. The Royal Yacht Squadron has feted me over the years and it's hard not to get infected by their enthusiasm.'

'I see.' Cornelius shook his head in disbelief. 'It's perhaps better you show some interest if it's true they are coming this way with a yacht; you'll probably end up having to entertain them.'

'Of course, it's part of my job. In any event, Commodore Wilton of the Squadron has already invited them to enjoy the hospitality of their clubhouse in Cowes. But you're right, I have let the members of the New York Yacht Club know they shouldn't hesitate to ask for assistance from the Consulate once they've arrived in these waters.'

'Does that mean you know the men who will own her?' Frank

moved to the end of his seat. *Maybe Consul Croskey was more useful after all?*

'Yes, I do. The yard owner and the designer who works with him have done work for the American Commodore in the past. I guess Stevens liked what they built for him. Unfortunately, I don't know much about what it is they're building now. It seems they're not willing to share much about their plan, not even with their Consul.' Croskey smiled apologetically. 'I've heard rumours that they're trying to keep the details of the build and the model of the vessel to themselves. They must be concerned someone is going to steal their design.'

'Tell them they don't need to worry; as far as I know we won't be stealing any ideas as nothing is being built on these shores,' Frank remarked wryly.

'Well, let's wait and see what will happen. It's not certain she will turn up in England, anyway.' The Consul sat back in his chair, complimenting Cornelius on his whisky.

What an odd thing to say. Was the Consul implying she might not make it across the Atlantic? 'Why is that?'

'When I asked them when they could be expected in England, they advised that the yacht being built by Brown still needed to be faster than any other yacht in America before they would sail her over.'

Cornelius tutted. 'What kind of deal is that? Who is paying for this yacht that is perhaps going nowhere?'

The Consul grinned once more. 'I told you about the willingness of the American entrepreneur to take a risk for profit? Brown has offered to build the yacht and only expects to be paid if she turns out to be the fastest in America.'

'What a daring thing to suggest.'

'That's how confident he is. And a sportsman, I wish I could say that of all of the other members of the Yacht Club.'

'Which yacht club would that be, my dear friend Croskey?'

'Don't you worry, I would never speak ill of your beloved countrymen. I was referring to our club founded in New York.

Some of them are ardent yachtsmen, others are just keen to make up for times gone by and to find an opportunity to unseat the British naval power.'

'No love lost.'

'I can think of one member in particular, a certain Colonel Hamilton, who's a veteran of the War of 1812 and dreams of giving the Brits another beating. Sorry Cornelius, that's how it is.'

Cornelius turned to Frank. 'Mr Grundy, it seems your questions have led to a lot of fighting talk. I'm not sure if that's been of any help.'

'Gentlemen, you have been extremely helpful. I'm all for a spirited interaction and a good battle.' Going against the Establishment appealed to Frank, as long as the opponent was given a fighting chance. Contrary to what had happened to Lisa P. or Mary H. Or even to Scarlet.

Chapter 13

December 1850, Manhattan

Silence had descended on the mould loft; the men worked without saying more than necessary. Occasionally, someone commented on the unusual line of the novel yacht. Nothing more than a whisper, as if it needed to remain confidential, even though there were no strangers in the room. A sense of wonder at the invention they were creating was clearly noticeable amongst the men.

It had taken them several days to transfer the lofted lines from the floor to the moulds and John had lost count of the number of moulds he had helped cut out of thin wood. Once a complete set of frame moulds was bundled up, it was taken to the mill building, where the moulds were cut from oak, which was the timber used for the ship.

Outside, the yard was alive; men were walking up and down with steely determination, concentrating on the task at hand, covered up in their warmest clothes, cheeks red from the cold and intensive labour.

John was helping with the last set of moulds when Da Silva entered the mill announcing they were going to start laying the keel. He pointed at a few men and told them to report to the foreman, Max.

Before John had a chance to put himself forward, the group had left and joined a crew outside who were arranging different sizes of timber near the framing stage. John saw them gathering around a sturdy beam. Ole was watching them as well and, despite his disappointment, John joined him near the slip, curious as to what was about to happen.

'They'll be laying the keel. That beam will run from the bow to the stern of the ship.'

'That was one mighty old tree.' John admired the solid piece of wood lying parallel to the slip.

'It will be the backbone to the whole structure - placed in the middle of the platform and then the frames will be fastened to it by the gangs. Only the best tree will do; that's how the owner likes it. But first we have to await the ceremony.'

Another group of men had come nearer to the platform. Among them was Mister James together with a younger version of himself. A man who looked vaguely familiar stood next to the yard owner.

'Thank you for inviting me here today, Brown. My brother and the other members of the syndicate send their greetings.'

'Thank you, Mr Stevens, I'm sorry to hear the Commodore couldn't make it, but I'm glad you're here to witness this special occasion on behalf of the syndicate.'

'I agree, it's important that we mark the start of the creation of this special yacht, and, more importantly, mark our position amongst boat-building nations. Show them it's not just our packets that are unbeatable.'

'I apologise for interrupting, gentlemen, but let me introduce to you another important contributor to our momentous undertaking.' In George's company was a tall man with a strong build and piercing blue eyes above an oblong beard.

'William Brown, meet Captain Brown.'

The visitor shook the hand of the yard owner and smiled. 'We've met before; it's good to see you again.' He then turned to Commodore Stevens's brother and introduced himself as Richard Brown.

'Our Captain,' George added. 'The best Sandy Hook pilot there is – but you already know that.'

'I think it's time we start, before we freeze solid.' The yard owner signalled to Max and the framing crew started to move the large beam into the construction cradle.

'What do you think of the ceremonial beginnings of a yacht?' Da Silva had joined Ole and John to watch the events unfolding near the platform. 'There's much to do around the building of a ship.' He sounded cynical; he probably preferred a good day's work.

'I never knew the laying of the keel had its own ceremony.'

'There are lots of traditions in shipbuilding; if you work here long enough you'll get to see them all. Isn't that so, Ole?

Ole grinned. 'Some might call them superstitions, Sir.'

'Who's the tall man with the bushy beard?' John wanted to know.

'That's the Captain.'

'Captain of what?'

'He captains pilot boats.'

'Why is he here?'

'The "Mary Taylor" he pilots is one of the fastest around. George was also involved in the design of that.'

'Will this be like a pilot boat?' John nodded towards the framing stage, where the keel was slowly being laid in place.

'To a certain extent. We are after the qualities of a pilot boat if we want to cross the Atlantic and then race her in England. Stable enough to withstand heavy seas as well as fast in getting to the ships that need guiding before the other pilot boats do. Except her interior will be nothing like that of an ordinary pilot boat, of course.'

John gazed at the man with the stocky build and friendly demeanour; his brother Joe had worked for a man like that. It wasn't difficult to imagine him at the helm of a ship on rough seas. He wondered how he himself would fare in a fight with Nature.

'Did you say he'll captain the finished yacht?'

'It looks like it.' Da Silva pointed towards the slip. 'They're finishing.'

The Commodore's brother, Edwin, walked towards the keel and wrote something on the large beam with a piece of chalk.

'Fare thee well, *America*,' he said out loud and then he raised his arms towards the small group of spectators and added with a joyous voice, 'The keel has been truly and fairly laid.'

'And then they placed a coin in the beam and wished her a safe journey, after which they shook hands and applauded.' John put the cup back on the table. 'A group of grown men, talking to a piece of wood,' he added with disbelief. For a change, he had made it to Elsie's in time. After the ceremony, there hadn't been much daylight left and thus they were allowed to retire early.

'Who was present at this ceremony?' Elsie sat opposite John at the table.

'Most of them. Sometimes they invite family members of the builders and crew along to this, but I don't think there is a crew yet.'

'Why are they making such a big out of it? You said they haven't even started building,' commented Elsie. Nathan climbed onto her lap; he had been playing on the floor when John came in. He curled up against her, his eyes sleepy.

'I've been told it's one of the most important ceremonies in the life of a ship; I think it has something to do with attracting good luck, not only for the process of building her but also throughout her life.'

'Her – life?' She drawled her words mockingly.

'Apparently another one of those customs: mariners with their love of the ocean who spend all their time out at sea end up giving their ship a name, normally after the women they love.' He made fun of the traditions, but secretly he was beginning to appreciate the practices that existed amongst this particular group of men. To them their ceremonies were of special significance; they had been passed on through generations of sailors and shipwrights for safekeeping. And just by watching them perform their ritual that day, John had felt as if he'd been part of a secret rite of passage: as if knowing the tradition was enough to become part of it.

'So, she's like a woman.' Elsie took a little sip of her tea, looking at John over the rim of her cup. 'Should I be jealous when you go to work, spending so much time with this other lady?'

Briefly, he was taken aback by her joke about another woman; in the time that they had seen each other neither of them had ever referred to feelings stronger than friendship. Although naturally, he could only speak for himself; he had never let it cross his mind, as the idea seemed inconceivable. *Had he missed something? Not recognised the signs?*

He sneaked a glance at her; Elsie had placed her head on her son's and was gently kissing his hair, while looking directly at John. He enjoyed her company; she was a beautiful and witty woman and once he had found ways to banish certain thoughts to the back of his mind, he had even let her make him feel at ease, something that didn't happen to him readily. But he hadn't allowed himself to think of anything further. *That was not possible. Or was it?*

Encouraged by the twinkle in her eyes he said impulsively, 'Well, maybe you should come one day and check her out.'

'I thought there was nothing to see yet.'

'You're right – at this moment she's a large pile of wood, waiting for someone to put her together. So far, she's more of a "mysterious woman"; who knows what she'll be like?'

'Maybe she isn't your type after all.'

'We'll have to wait and see.'

'You're asking me to be patient? Tell me, what's my competition called; does she at least have a name?' Elsie clearly didn't mind playing the game of the spurned lover.

'To tell you the truth, I don't know for sure. I think it could be "America".'

'She's called "America" – are you telling me I'm competing against the whole of the United States?'

'It sounds like that.'

'Somebody must love this country a lot and have a lot of faith in her.'

They looked at each other and laughed at the same time. The shaking of Elsie's body woke Nathan. 'Poor little one, I had to wake him very early this morning to drop him off at Jane's.'

'How's the new job going?' John knew the cleaning jobs she had decided to take on were tiring her out, but she had told him how lucky she was that she'd finally found a woman who could take care of Nathan when she was away.

'Yes, we're doing all right, thanks. Hopefully we can fend for ourselves again soon. Another cup?'

'Will we see the boat?' Nathan sat on Elsie's chair while she heated up the tea; he was drowsy and barely able to sit up straight.

'We'll go sometime soon. The weather is still too cold, Nathan, and we have to build her first.' He hadn't told Elsie about his frustration of being back doing his old job, working on the interior of a steamship. She had other things on her mind.

He moved closer to Nathan. 'I'll know what we'll do; I'll make you a drawing of how we are putting the boat together. You just sit here quietly.'

The boy watched him draw the yacht, his eyes getting heavy; by the time John was finished, he was asleep again. John moved him quietly to the bed and Elsie tucked him in.

John could do with a bed himself. While getting ready for the chilly night outside, he got some money out of his wallet and put it on the table. It was clear that Elsie didn't receive any help from family and he had been taking advantage of her hospitality numerous times now; the least he could do was to contribute in some way.

'What did you do that for?' An angry voice reverberated through the room; she had seen him put down the money.

There were many reasons why he'd done it, but he couldn't come up with an answer quickly enough.

'I don't want your money. Don't think you are obliged in any way to pay me; the food I provide you with is leftovers, anyway.'

The last sentence sounded out of character and unnecessarily harsh, as if John had been a mere passer-by, simply hungry for something to eat. Is that what she thought of him: somebody she felt duty-bound to feed?

'You can pay me back. See it as a loan.' Her angry demeanour had thrown him, but just before she had angrily turned around, pursing her lips in disapproval, her vulnerability behind the feigned tough exterior had become visible. Unlike the rest of her face, her eyes were filled with despair and something that looked like relief; they were undoubtedly telling him she wasn't just in need of financial support. He took her by the shoulders and made her face him, but she kept her eyes lowered to the ground.

'Until things get easier for you, I make enough for myself, for now anyway.'

Finally, her eyes met his; her usual grit had returned. She let out a loud sigh: 'All right, then, a loan, but I'll pay you back as soon as I can.'

John left her house confronted by emotions he had ignored until now: not only his own, but hers as well. Her anger had confused him. He was torn between his affection for her and his intentions to keep her at a safe distance. *He should tread more carefully.*

John thought about the drawing he had made for Nathan that evening when he sat on a dry log with his back against the timber shed and looked at the progress they had made over the winter months. The drawing had been relatively correct in detail, but he couldn't have guessed how long it was going to take to get to the different stages of the build.

It had taken the gangs weeks to assemble the frames on the framing platform and fasten them to the keel; to place the numerous pieces of timber into one cohesive frame that would be able to withstand the pressures at sea had been like assembling the pieces of an enormous puzzle and for some time she had resembled the ribcage of a decomposed whale. The winter months had stayed unrelentingly cold but, despite that, John would find any excuse to go outside and observe the work being done. Progress had seemed slow until, as the air had started to warm up, the yacht had suddenly advanced from being a skeleton to a mastless hull.

Those hadn't been the only developments; time had caught up with them. John had overheard some tense conversations between Da Silva and the foreman about finishing before a certain date. The increasing pressure put on the men on the slip was met with resistance. Hearing them complain, John wished he could do the hard work himself.

One morning, Da Silva called them together in the timber shed; he sounded grave.

'Can I have your attention, please? I've been instructed to relay the following message. As you might be aware, the agreement that was made between the syndicate that commissioned this ship and the yard owner contains a delivery date for the vessel of April the first.'

An immediate murmur rose up.

'But that's impossible,' one of the men said out loud, 'with all the weather delays we've had.'

'I know, believe me, there's no point in explaining the obvious.' Da Silva sounded impatient. 'This meeting is for me to tell you what will happen in the next few weeks – just in case you were wondering about that date, as it's about two weeks away.' He picked up a document from the table in front of him.

'We will continue to work as hard as we have been; I trust you all understand the risks Mr Brown has taken to have this yacht built for the syndicate and thus our obligation to continue our best efforts.' He stopped for a moment. 'This means that in the next few weeks we will finish her joinery, while the masts are being placed and her rigging and sails received. Any questions?'

Disappointed, John wondered why Da Silva had asked him to be present, as this didn't concern him.

One of the carpenters raised his hand. 'But what if we don't make it and the syndicate keeps Mr Brown to the agreement?'

'And they no longer want the yacht?' another carpenter added.

'I'm confident that the men in charge will come to a solution. It is not up to us to question any of their decisions nor to speculate about them.' He emphasized the last sentence with a bang of his hand on the table. 'Now back to work!'

John walked out with the others. So that explained the frequent talks Mr Brown and Mister George had been conducting lately, very often in the presence of George's brother James: hushed conversations in corners, worried looks.

Concerned, he walked back to the workshop. Turning the corner, he almost bumped into Captain Brown who was standing at the entrance. Since the day they'd laid the keel, Captain Brown had been around more often, paying his friend George a visit, or occasionally just standing there, out of everyone's way, watching over the quay as if to keep an eye on the build.

'Good morning, Captain.'

'Good morning. You must be John.'

'Correct, Captain.'

'I've just had a look at the joinery work for the cabins of the steamship; it's coming along nicely.'

'Thank you, I'm happy with the way it's turning out.' John had to bite his lip and hide his displeasure that he was still doing the same work. But the meeting was foremost in his mind.

'Captain, what will you do if she isn't going to sail?'

A quizzical look crossed the Captain's face. 'What do you mean?'

'Da Silva had a chat with us about the deadline for *America*. Which we're not going to make,' he added regretfully.

'Ah, that…' Captain Brown scratched his beard. 'I don't think you need to worry about it. Both parties in this venture are eager for a good outcome. Don't forget the yard owner will do anything to prevent suffering the loss of building a ship that doesn't get to sail. And, just like the syndicate, he wants to prove his skills. These men share their passion for sailing and nothing will interfere with their plan to sail to England, mark my words.'

The Captain was right, John was worried, but not about the lack of a few men's longing for acknowledgement. What troubled him most was that the opportunity of a journey could pass him by.

The Captain returned his attention to the furniture. 'What's this?'

'That will be a water closet.'

'Really?' he mumbled disapprovingly. 'What's wrong with the side of the boat?'

John laughed at the Captain who exited the workshop at the same time as Da Silva entered.

'John, I want you to have a look at this.' He handed John some paperwork. 'Set all other work aside – this needs to be given priority. Your meticulous work in the mould loft got you this job; you'd better not disappoint me.'

John opened the first document. It contained the plans of the interior of a yacht. Written at the top, in elegant lettering, was the word 'America'.

Chapter 14

It had started with a name. Scarlet was supposedly the one Frank needed to speak to. He knew it wasn't much to go on, but it was all he had. Why had a name like that not surprised him? When the father of one of the missing girls had mentioned her as a possible link to the disappearance of his daughter, Frank had asked him sarcastically how difficult it could be to find a prostitute with red hair and that name, but the father had retorted tersely that he hadn't managed, although he had tried.

The man's story had been similar to the four others he heard that day at different addresses across the east of London.

One Saturday, on a damp autumn morning, he had stayed in bed, pretending to be ill, when he knew Agnes was going to visit her sister at their parents' house. It worried him that he had lied to her by faking an illness, but he kept reminding himself it was for a good cause. She had been concerned, but luckily not enough to stay with him.

Before she left the house, she had berated him for working too hard. He knew he'd been distracted lately, often disappearing into the little room after work, telling her he didn't want to be disturbed. But he had chosen to ignore her rising irritation in the hope she would eventually give up. The accusation had lingered in the air when she had closed the door behind her. He realised he should be more careful.

He had waited until the closing of the front door confirmed her departure before he had dressed and slipped out quietly in search of a neighbourhood he had not been in before.

It reminded him of just how lucky he and Agnes were; although his salary wasn't enough to allow them any luxuries, the financial help Agnes had received from her father permitted them to live in a modest but lovely area, nothing like the dirty and poor place he had ventured into that day.

He hadn't been looking forward to the trip, but the visits to the first few addresses on his list had gone unexpectedly smoothly, if one could call it that. Each time a mother would appear reluctantly from behind a door of an overcrowded house in a filthy street. Raised voices could be heard behind the crumbling walls: adults yelling at invisible children in no uncertain terms to 'clear orf'. He would come face to face with a woman, prematurely aged, looking tired and lifeless. And when he'd tell her he wanted to ask some questions about her missing daughter, she would be shocked, but at the same time she would express a glimmer of hope. He should have known better than to give them the impression he knew more about the whereabouts of their daughters than he did.

At the second address he had resorted to giving a vague explanation as to who he was; he didn't want to tell them he was merely a reporter intrigued by some advertisements he'd found in the paper. It seemed enough to give their plight some attention by saying he was involved in the investigation of the disappearance of their daughter.

Somehow, the fact that there were several other girls missing, making him suspect a link between them, resulted in an apparent willingness to share some details with him. Such as how the bobbies hadn't done much after they had reported their daughters missing. He had told them the police got things wrong all the time and that's why he did what he did: *if the authorities fail to protect our children, we need to take things into our own hands.* He had come to help.

Although he had been aware that perhaps he was giving them false hope.

It had spurred the women on to tell him of the lies the police had told them about their girls. The fact that their pretty young daughters were going out more often, and sometimes not coming back for hours, was enough for the police to think they had ended up in prostitution, especially when they'd been seen in the company of men.

When Frank had suggested that their daughters had perhaps found suitors instead, one of the mothers had furiously reminded him her child was only twelve. Besides, her husband had followed her one day and had seen her meeting up with an older man, whom the daughter had later explained was the father of a friend. The fact that this man had been far too well-dressed to be who she said he was hadn't concerned them at the time and they had left it alone. That was until the day she hadn't come home. Just like all the other girls. According to the police, they were too ashamed to do so because they were selling their bodies to men.

That's when they had decided to put an advertisement in the paper, often with the financial help of another relative as they couldn't continue to wander the streets in the vain hope of finding their girl.

On the face of it their story had sounded like a sad, but not uncommon, tale of poverty, in itself not extraordinary enough to roam the streets in pursuit of a story.

Had the girls been looking for a way out and stumbled naively into another dark and dingy world? Or had someone persuaded them to go elsewhere with the promise of a better life? Looking around him, Frank couldn't blame them; what were these children supposed to make of their lives if this dark and foul street was all they had to look forward to?

A familiar feeling came over him – the rush of blood brought a moment of lucidity; a pattern was emerging and he had been long enough in the business to know that, to solve a problem, one had to recognise this first.

If the girls really had ended up in prostitution, would their families have been left completely in the dark? Would they have broken all contact with them, even the mothers? How certain were they that the girls had vanished of their own accord? His intuition told him that there were other, more complicated reasons behind the disappearances and somebody somewhere knew more about them. He didn't dare to answer his own question about how many parents were out there who didn't even have the money for an advertisement.

He had looked for an excuse for a quick departure; these people had laid bare their emotions, thinking he would solve the mystery of their daughters' whereabouts, but the truth was he had nothing to give in return. He had mumbled a promise to do his utmost to get to the bottom of this. At least these poor bastards still clearly cared about what happened to their children, but he doubted he would be able to give these despairing parents good news any time soon. Like them, he couldn't wander around in search of the girls. But then one of the fathers had come out of the house and told him about Scarlet. After a couple of days of looking for his daughter, he'd managed to find some prostitutes who said they remembered seeing their daughter with a prostitute called Scarlet – although nobody seemed to know where she was supposed to work. Perhaps trying to find her was a start.

The next few weeks were unproductive as Frank tried to figure out how he was going to track her down; he couldn't start knocking on people's doors in broad daylight, asking for a girl called Scarlet. To have any hope of success, most of his work would have to be done under the cover of night, which complicated matters.

For a short while he'd contemplated confiding in Bill, but in the end he hadn't dared. He would have to explain too much and he was concerned he'd start a rumour with lots of untruths in it. What if it got back to Agnes? He decided he had to be as discreet as possible.

And then one day he had come across a report written by a colleague about a major operation the police had carried out in the streets around Soho. It said something about the number of vagrants and prostitutes they'd arrested and the brothels they'd searched and, under the pretence that he was writing about a new plan for social housing, he had asked the colleague about it. It was true when they said the first lie was the most difficult; after that they would come out as easily as slippery eels escaping their traps.

His colleague had been flattered and more than willing to tell him where the arrests had been made. He couldn't stop bragging about the important contact he had within the police force and had offered to arrange for Frank to visit the underbelly of society. But he had declined; he couldn't risk his colleague finding out what the real research was about.

Instead he had bought the cheapest London map he could find to plan his approach. He had highlighted the area where one of the fathers had seen his daughter talking to an older gentleman and had then added the information given to the colleague by his policeman-friend. Based on the description of the older man's attire, it was possible that Scarlet was a high-class prostitute, but probing around Mayfair was out of the question, so the starting point had to be the main area in Soho, helpfully pointed out by the police officer.

From the day Frank had made his decision as to where to go, he visited the area as often as he could, normally straight after work, warning Agnes he was going to be late. At first she had seemed more than happy with his longer working hours.

Going from tavern to tavern in grimy back streets, he would encounter the low life his colleague had told him about. He had felt like a fish out of water while sitting in stinking pubs waiting for something to happen. But the alternative was to walk the streets until he saw a red-haired woman. She probably didn't even appear outside at this time of the day. And then he was reminded of the possible biggest hurdle: his assumption she had red hair. He had no idea what she looked like and the fact that he expected her hair to have that colour was just another wild guess.

He was approached by enough of her colleagues during his trips, discreetly declining their offers of business at first, until he realised he would have to engage with them if he was to have any hope of progressing his flimsy plan given he had so little to go by.

Then he was sent Rose. For some reason, her Madam had decided that he was after someone like her. Sitting in yet another tavern, he had been so transfixed by a pretty girl with striking honey-blonde hair and full cerise-pink lips that he hadn't realised he'd been joined at the table by another girl: Rose. She had appeared suddenly, a small girl in a dusky pink dress, smiling shyly. She looked as if she shouldn't be in a public house, but instead at home, playing with her sisters.

Seen from up close, she looked older than he'd thought at first, the layer of powder clear to see on her face. And the unexpectedly adult voice asking him if he had brought cash reminded him of the business she was in. There was no time for dithering.

He had cursed himself for not having thought about what he should do once he actually talked to a prostitute and, as she led him away from the tavern to the nearby brothel, he had wanted several times to stop Rose and tell her he hadn't come for what she thought. But his curiosity had surpassed his feelings of shame. Moreover, he had come with a mission.

So, when they'd finally stopped outside a nondescript house in a secluded back street in an unrecognisable part of London, he had urged himself to tell her he didn't want what she expected. With worry in her voice she had queried if it was because he wasn't satisfied with the way she looked.

She meant not looking young enough. Her remark shouldn't have come as a surprise; hadn't she merely confirmed his suspicion, the reason he was there? The missing girls as sexual objects, wandering around somewhere in the world of prostitution? He still couldn't believe they would choose this above a world of just being poor. He had so many questions.

He ended up paying Rose to talk, although she had already answered most of his questions: the way she looked and behaved, her assumption that his preference had been for a young girl. Her lot was evidently to satisfy the men who were looking for a woman who looked like one.

But what about the girls who actually were young? He had been too shocked to ask. But there had been no need; she had volunteered by telling him that if he had wanted another girl he should have said so straight away as her Madam could have sent him elsewhere, adding, 'cause we don't do things like that'.

Eager to find out where these girls could be found, he had made up a story that he was looking for a daughter who had walked away from home. Who wouldn't want to be found by people who cared for you? Rose must have wanted that at one stage. But it wasn't good enough; she was no longer willing to cooperate, warning him he was wasting his time trying to find her there.

She had showed him the door. When he walked past her, she slid her hand into her dress and took out the money he'd given her. She had put it in his hand and before she had closed the door she'd said, 'You want to find Scarlet, she can tell you more.'

The name Scarlet had started to dominate his thoughts and it wasn't just his peace of mind that suffered because of it. Agnes's was suffering as well.

She had tried to tell him in different ways that he was working too hard. At first she pleaded with him to come home earlier, telling him he looked tired, bringing him freshly brewed cups of tea and coffee, clumsily fluffing up the cushions behind his back. She didn't know that most of the time he was dying for a good glass of brandy, neat, the way he preferred it.

She had assumed he'd been given other work to do, judging by his longer working hours. She had wisely chosen not to mention the evenings he'd come back home in the middle of the night and spent what was left of them in the maid's room.

Hoping she would leave him alone, he explained impatiently that a new assignment meant he had to interview people after working hours, but that it would stop soon. In all likelihood, he would never be able to tell Agnes about the work he was doing on his own initiative; she would get too upset about it. But he had brushed that complication aside; it was a problem he was going to deal with at a later stage, when he really had to.

One evening, she had pulled the curtains behind his back so violently that he could hear the pelmet flap and smell the dust falling out of it. Her worry had changed to annoyance. She failed to understand why he had to perform such tasks as a reporter and, because of it, she was angry with Lewis for making him do his dirty work.

He'd never heard her speak words like that before, nor in that tone. Then, suddenly, she had stopped asking him about the story he was working on. This had him worried even more. Her anger had been replaced by resentment that his irregular work hours were playing havoc with her social calendar as she had to decline numerous dinner invitations from their dear friends.

When the Harrisons had asked them for the third time in a row, he had to disappoint her again. She hadn't waited for him to finish his sentence; with all the energy and anger she could muster she'd turned on her heels, and disappeared through the door, her skirt narrowly missing being trapped by the slamming door. The house had trembled.

Finally, after yet another cancelled social evening and when he had arrived home late in an intoxicated state, her displeasure and anger had been replaced by something new altogether; she simply became withdrawn. Progressively, he and Agnes had started to be rarely in the same place at the same time and one morning she'd told him coldly that she was going to spend a couple of days at her parents' house to help her mother with preparing for her yearly charity dinner. Just before she walked out of the door she had announced that Bill had paid a visit to their house one evening.

The way she said it had made him sit up straight; he didn't like the sound of the two of them talking about him. She had noticed his apprehension and had carried on to reveal that they'd had an interesting conversation about his work. She had added how Bill was a 'charming man'. She hadn't waited for Frank's reaction and had abruptly left the room.

He was left behind not knowing what to think; his wife was undoubtedly trying to provoke him, but he felt vulnerable as he couldn't be sure what they'd talked about. Would Bill have discussed his behaviour of late with her? He would tell Bill not to drop by like that again; anything he needed to discuss with Frank he could do at work.

He had watched his wife get in a carriage and sighed with relief. With her away for a couple of days, it meant he could go out in the evenings without having to worry about her. He was eager to go on his investigative trips as up until now he had not been getting any nearer to locating Scarlet. On the contrary, he felt as if he was getting further away from her. At first, he had been pleased to have a name, but he was no longer convinced it was a good thing. Every time he had gone out to locate her, he would get different reactions, although none of them seemed to lead him anywhere. His working method had been the same each time; he would visit the public houses of interest and wait for the moment he would be approached by a woman. Then, at a suitable moment, he would mention her name: Scarlet. But he would never know to what effect. The other women would react with different degrees of indifference. '*If you want her, why come here.*' '*Don't know her.*' Other responses were more pronounced, ranging from a clear instant dislike of him to some even looking scared. But the outcome was similar; he would get no further with his search and he would arrive home late, too late, smelling of smoke and alcohol. The latter was rapidly becoming his friend: a dangerous companion.

'Brandy, please.' He leaned against the bar and tried to concentrate on how he presented himself, making sure he stood upright and didn't slur his words. Agnes being away, he could have one more: the last of the evening. He looked around the establishment; he'd been there before, some weeks ago. He hadn't stayed long; as a matter of fact, he'd been in and out quickly. The place was miserable, tatty and soiled, where the few regulars, sitting passively at the bar and on the seats along the wall, came to drink themselves into oblivion. A perfect place for him this evening, although tonight it was different; it felt more alive. The regulars were still there, but Frank noted another breed of man, much better dressed, as if they'd taken a wrong turn coming from Mayfair or Regent Street. They probably looked more like him, he realised, or perhaps a smarter version.

He also noticed that there were no women to be seen. Another fruitless trip, if one didn't count the grapes in the numerous glasses of wine he had already had. He laughed out loud at his own joke, realising too late that somebody was watching him. A man, positioned on the other side of the bar, dressed in tails as if he'd come from an evening at the theatre, was studying him over the rim of his glass. He nodded when he saw Frank had noticed him and walked over.

'New here?'

The question confused Frank; it implied the other man came here more often, which seemed inconceivable for a man of his class.

'Yes, first time.' Not quite the truth, but who cared. 'And probably the last,' he mumbled to himself.

'Not your thing?'

He wasn't sure if there was sarcasm in the man's voice, but he chose to ignore his provocation.

'Just not what I expected.'

'Well, around here, this tavern is as good as any, perhaps far better. Are you on your own?'

'Yes.' He wished the man would leave him alone; he wanted to enjoy his last drink in peace and then go.

'Are you looking for company?'

Frank glanced sideways at the man, slightly thrown by the question. The other man's appearance was immaculate; his clothes matched his well-groomed moustache and short beard. Even his eyebrows seemed trimmed: two high arches above light grey eyes, creating a permanent expression of disdain. His lips were curled at the ends like a court jester, but now pinched into a narrow line, waiting for an answer.

Frank ignored him but he could feel the tension rising. He felt intimidated: a feeling not helped by the piercing gaze of a second, younger, man on the other side of the bar, with the same sharp suit and attention to detail evident in his facial hair. He shouldn't drink to the point where he wasn't able to judge things properly. He ought to take another failure in his stride, go home, lay his head on a pillow and end the day. He picked up his glass, but a firm hand on his arm prevented him from putting it to his mouth.

'You haven't answered my question yet.' The grip eased, but the hand remained, now resting lightly on his wrist, working its way slowly down to his hand. The voice had changed as well: more soothing and inviting.

Frank stared at the man's hand fully enclosing his own, when it dawned on him that he wasn't offering female company at all. Was he offering himself? Frank was stunned. He was told by one of the women he'd met on a previous run he should visit this public house and he was now unsure if he'd understood her correctly. Or had it been a strange way of getting back at him, as he hadn't showed interest in her services?

Adrenaline rushed through Frank's body, awakening him from his drowsy state. 'No, I haven't. I am looking for company.' He freed himself from the other man's grip and drank the last of his drink in one swig. 'But I've an acquired taste, so to speak.'

'Male or female?'

'Female.'

'As I said before, you've come to the right place, especially for gentlemen with exquisite taste.' He signalled to the landlord to refill both of their glasses. The stranger picked up his and raised it. 'And, more importantly, you have come to the right person.' He carefully took a sip of his red wine, letting the liquid sit in his mouth, before swallowing it with an expression of delight, all with his eyes closed. 'Magnifique. Very good indeed.'

Now was the time to leave; escape from this overbearing man and this unsavoury place. Nobody would notice it, especially not the man next to him with his eyes still closed. But Frank couldn't move. Transfixed, he watched this man's public display of pleasure that felt as if he had walked into a room where people were being intimate, embarrassing but spellbinding at the same time.

The man finally opened his eyes as if he suddenly remembered he'd been having a conversation with somebody and looked directly at Frank: 'You said you were looking for what?'

Frank said cautiously, 'Remind me, what is on offer?'

An ice-cold look was thrown into his direction. 'Surely, a man knows his own preferences?' His voice dripped with contempt.

'Yes, sure, but today just seemed a good day for, erm, a change.'

'A good day for a change.' He slowly repeated Frank's words and with a deep sense of drama he added, 'I wish that's how it worked.' Those last words were directed to the young man at the other side of the bar, who hadn't moved and was still watching the two of them. 'Anyway, it's female company you're after. There are a lot of ladies available tonight, so help me out here; you could at least tell me what kind of age, colouring, able-bodied or not – I could go on, which means we'll be here all night and you'll go home dissatisfied.'

Frank processed what the man had said; he had confirmed he was some sort of a Madam, in charge of renting out ladies of the night to men who were looking for intimacy. And, he assumed, renting out men to other men. He tried his best not to look appalled by his remark about the choice of able-bodied or not; it raised so many questions, questions he wouldn't see answered tonight.

'Young.'

'How young?'

'How young do you have?'

'As young as you like, but I have to warn you, tonight isn't a good night for that. So, what about a young-looking girl?'

'If you say that's good.'

'Well, I wouldn't know personally.' He let out a fake laugh. 'But, trust me, she is one of the best.' He signalled to the young man. 'Take this gentleman here to see Scarlet.'

Frank could have kicked himself; on the one night he was being taken to the woman he had been looking for all that time, his head was fuddled.

Before he knew it, they'd arrived at a four-storey building in a back alley somewhere in Soho. He suspected that the young man had deliberately taken him on a zigzagging route, to prevent him from returning by himself at a later date.

'You wait here.' The young man disappeared into the house and left Frank standing in the dingy street. He looked up, and he could see some lights flickering behind the darkened windows; he hadn't thought it through. He hoped the young man wouldn't stick around and wait for him; he feared what might happen if he found out he had come for information. If these men were part of the wrongdoing he suspected was occurring, they obviously wouldn't want him to pry and ask questions. Before Frank could think of a possible escape plan, the young man had returned.

'She's ready for you: top floor, the room at the end of the corridor. It's important you get the room right; the other rooms are strictly out of bounds.' He stood with his arms folded.

'Right, top floor.'

'Good. I'll be waiting for you right here.'

'Really?'

The other man's expression changed from pompous to haughty. 'We're in your time now, suit yourself if you want to waste it discussing such matters with me.'

Frank walked past him without saying anything more and closed the front door behind him a little more loudly than was necessary. He hoped there was a back door.

Hesitantly he proceeded up the stairs, past rooms emitting a variation of hushed tones, grunts and uncontrolled cries of gratification and, more disturbingly, sounds of suffering. The landing on the top floor was small: a few rooms tucked away from sight and out of earshot, Frank realised.

He knocked on the last door and waited, his heart beating in his throat. It didn't take long before the door was opened slightly. And then nothing happened.

'Hello? Can I come in?'

He heard a giggle and then a voice say, 'Yes, please, why don't you come in my room to play?'

Frank didn't move; the voice was something he hadn't prepared himself for. It was that of a small girl who, he guessed, could be anything under ten years old. He started to feel sick in his stomach and he wasn't certain whether it was because of the amount of alcohol he'd consumed or that he finally had come close to what he'd feared he would find.

He pushed the door open and stepped into the dimly lit room: it was large and covered most of the attic. Like the other rooms he'd been in, it was furnished with some practical pieces like a wooden desk, a chair and a folding screen, but here he spotted some dolls and other girls' toys dotted around. The colours and textiles used were more elegant and delicate: fluffy and comfortable cushions and curtains in soft pinks and creams. In the middle of the area were full-length pieces of fabric suspended from the ceiling, separating the space in two parts.

'Have a seat. And close the door.'

He couldn't see Scarlet, just a shadow moving about behind the flowing drapes. He walked up and down anxiously.

'It's all right, just sit down and relax.'

He almost laughed; the idea of a young girl telling him to unwind was ridiculous. There was some more movement behind the curtains.

'All done and ready for you.' At once she pulled the curtains to the side to reveal a large bed and, more importantly, herself.

Frank gawked shamelessly at her from top to bottom; in front of him stood the slight figure of a girl, not yet 5 feet tall, dressed in soft pinks with one fresh white rose in her hair. He'd never seen hair like that before: thick wavy strands of an intense burnt-orange colour, cascading freely from the crown of her head down to her shoulders, caressing the top of her arms and falling gently onto her chest. The weak light in the room intensified the exceptional colour and made the rose and the alabaster skin of her face and neck contrast sharply with it. A memory sprang to mind of the first time he'd tasted a piece of an orange; how he'd carefully bitten into the soft flesh of a segment which burst open between his teeth to reveal a sweet, yet tangy juice: a thirst-quenching sensation he'd never experienced before. Looking at this exquisite creature was like tasting the fruit; he averted his eyes. She *was* a forbidden fruit.

She showed no reaction to his overt gaping; instead she extended her hand. She was holding a brush.

'Would you like to?' She tilted her head to one side and offered him the brush.

Frank didn't know what to say or do; he was spellbound and tried to avoid her eyes.

'Or do you prefer to watch me do it?' She held out her other hand and took his. 'Let's sit over here, it's more comfortable.' She gently pulled him through the space in the curtains and onto the bed. She sat herself down with her back turned towards him and carefully pulled the rose from her hair and started to brush it.

Frank didn't move and instead stared at the back of her neck and her small shoulders; every now and then she rotated her face a little, so he could see her profile. Her full lips were stained a bright red and they were almost too much for her delicate features, not unlike her ears that were protruding slightly through her hair. He caught a glimpse of her eyes; he guessed they were of a smoky hazel-green colour; like her lips they seemed too large for her face. All the features put together resulted in this exotic-looking living thing, a strange mix of the vulnerability and cuteness of a dormouse curled up in its nest and the fierce look of an Iberian lynx. She was bewitching.

Being this close, she resembled a little child wearing a little too much make-up. But Frank could see the lines on her face and the pores of her skin coming through the powder. And the hands holding her brush were those of someone older. Frank was fascinated. He assumed Scarlet was used to this kind of attention from men; she kept babbling on without him saying a thing back, which gave him the opportunity to explore her without being watched. The other week Rose had looked like a very young woman, maybe even an older girl, but compared to Scarlet, she had looked mature. Scarlet, on the other hand, not only looked but also sounded like a girl: a child who should be interested in playing with a doll's house, instead of entertaining an old man.

Frank shivered; he remembered he wasn't looking at a curiosity, but a real person, who, for whatever reason, had ended up in this house for the pleasure of men with unusual fixations. Men who were willing to pay the extra money to perform acts on a woman that looked like their young daughter. And more disturbing, because the real thing hadn't been available when they'd wanted it. Images of what these men would do to her crossed his mind and made him shudder with disgust. He knew he had to leave his emotions out of it while he was here; his task was to find out more about the girls who were mentioned by the man in the bar – girls who hadn't been accessible tonight but clearly existed somewhere.

He was dependent on Scarlet's help, but how was he going to gain her trust? He had to convince her to help him uncover the truth about the business of these demonic acts with minors. As a woman herself, someone who one day would have a daughter of her own, she should understand his reasoning. And if empathy couldn't persuade her, perhaps her business sense could, because in the end, achieving his aim meant she would benefit from receiving more clients as the men could no longer access the real thing.

He was surprised with his calculated way of thinking; the effects of the alcohol must be wearing off.

'You're new here, I gather?'

Her tiny but melodious voice cut through his thoughts, which were now running through his mind.

'Yes.' He assumed she worked for the man in the bar; he had acted as an agent, directing potential clients to the place of their fixation. Was she aware he was offering the services of small children? Even if she didn't, he was about to tell her she supplied services to men who should be locked up. Anyway, it meant he could get into trouble with her as well as with several others. He thought about the man waiting for him downstairs.

'You can unwind now, you're quite safe here.'

He must have appeared all fidgety, Frank realised, not saying anything and not making any advances either. But he wasn't sure why she'd felt the need to say something about his safety.

'Sorry, I'm not sure what you mean?'

'I thought you might be worried about the arrests they've been making in recent weeks; but they never come here, the police always leave us alone, so you can start to enjoy your time with me now.' She giggled like a happy child, which was in odd contrast to the words she spoke. She flicked her hair over her right shoulder, touched his face briefly, and moved her back closer to him. He felt her lean her body against his and the effect she had on him was momentarily bewildering. He tried his hardest to understand what she had said; he knew about the raids that had been going on for some time now as part of the clamp down on immoral behaviour, but what she suggested had entirely new implications; did she suggest the police played a role here?

Chapter 15

'I think we should go and visit the yard this Sunday.'

'Why now, is it finished?' Elsie was folding clothes.

'Oh, no, there's still a lot to do, but the weather is getting a bit better and she's starting to look like a proper yacht.' John had thought about it a lot; what if the syndicate called the whole venture off when they realised the ship wasn't going to be ready in time? He'd better show the ship to Nathan now, before it was too late. Besides, he had been preoccupied lately and it seemed like a good opportunity to show Nathan something special.

'You call this better weather? Those months of working out there in the elements, you must have gotten immune to the freezing temperatures.' Elsie got up to put the clothes into a set of drawers. 'I've never understood why you don't work under some sort of covering to keep yourselves and the boat sheltered.'

'I don't know, no workshop on our stretch of the river seems to.'

'At least it would save you having to dig the boat out of the snow every time we have a whiteout.' She lingered at the dresser, staring at the top drawer. Neatly folded amongst the clothes was a woollen jumper; she pulled it out gently.

'Here, it's still cold out there.' She turned around and handed him the dark green garment.

He immediately understood whom it had belonged to. He didn't know what to say and made no move to take it from her.

'Take it, I would hate to see the moths get to it.'

'Are you sure, you know, somebody wearing this?' He couldn't remember if he ever had said his name.

'Yes, I think so. Anyway, you're not "somebody", are you?' She swiftly turned away and said resolutely, 'Come here, Nathan, John has something exciting to tell you.'

Protected by several layers of clothing, they had gone out that Sunday morning. Nathan had walked alongside John with the biggest steps he could muster, wanting to know all about the ship they were going to see.

John had put Nathan on his shoulders and pretended to be a ship on rough seas with Nathan the Captain at the helm. The journey had gone quickly and the little boy cheered with delight whenever he skipped up and down to avoid an imaginary wave.

John had to assure Elsie that their presence in the yard would cause no problem as a lot of people had already shown their interest and had paid visits. Moreover, he expected nobody would be around this Sunday.

'Who have been the other notable visitors, do you know?' Elsie patted her son on his knee for being a good boy.

'Well, one day we had a gentleman visiting us who turned out to be the British Ambassador.'

'Really?' Elsie sounded impressed. 'Why did he come over?'

'I don't know but,' whispered John, moving his face closer to hers, 'the rumour is he came over to spy on her for the English, to check out the competition.'

'Really?' For a moment she fell for it, but when he started to laugh out loud she thumped him on the arm. 'Stop teasing me, you nasty man!' She pushed a red curl out of her face. 'I'll get you back some day.'

'I'm very afraid, brrr.'

'Brrr.' A little voice from high up echoed John.

The adults laughed and Nathan joined in, happy to be happy.

'On several occasions, we've had members of the syndicate come by in their carriages – you know, the ones who commissioned the yacht. Actually, one of them has been coming most days of the week; he just stands there and watches us work.'

'What dedication! Don't they have jobs to go to? Who are these men?'

'They are the founding members of the Yacht Club of New York.'

'All sailors themselves, then?'

'Not necessarily.'

Elsie looked surprised.

'Into boats, but not always into sailing.' John grinned before he added, 'But enough money to spend.'

'Who is going to sail her to England, then?'

'They haven't mentioned a crew yet, but I have seen the man who will captain her.'

'Me! Captain Nate, I am Captain Nate.' The boy started humming.

'You are a bit young for that, sweetie,' said Elsie, smiling, 'and I couldn't be without you for that long.'

'Ay, Captain Nate, we are there!' John opened the gate. The first thing he noticed was the stillness of the place. No caulkers banging their mallets and irons on the hull of the ship. No carpenters hitting their nails or using their saws. No gangs shouting orders at each other, encouraging one another to work faster than the other gang. It was almost peaceful, apart from the shrieking of the gulls. They walked past the abandoned blacksmith's shop and the mill building towards the quay.

'There she is.' John pointed in the direction of the river, towards the ship on the pier.

'Where?' Nathan stood between his mother and John, his voice shrill with anticipation.

'There, can't you see her?' John was surprised that the keen little boy hadn't spotted her yet. He bent down to Nathan's level and showed him where to look.

Nathan followed the direction of his finger; his eyes widened for a moment, but then a deep frown ensued. 'That's no ship,' he declared disappointedly.

'It is, Nathan, that's the ship I told you about.'

'That's no ship,' he repeated more angrily, kicking with his foot on the firm soil.

'It still needs some paint and other things, but really, Nathan...'

'Sweetie, don't be angry, we don't understand.' Elsie tried to calm her son down.

'There are no flags.' He exhaled noisily, the sound of a tear rising in his breath.

Elsie and John looked at one another; they tried their best not to laugh.

'Let me show you why that is; we'll get a bit closer.'

They walked towards the yacht. Although the yacht wasn't finished yet, enough had been done to get a good impression of her elegant shape. All the internal and exterior planking had been fitted, together with the decks. They were in the process of sealing the joints between the planks which the caulkers did in complete harmony. One man would lay one or more threads of cotton between the seams of the planks and another would come behind him with a mallet to drive the thread just far enough into it to make the ship watertight.

'Does Captain Nathan know what those big beams lying on the floor are?' A sudden cold wind drifted in from the river, making it difficult for John to be heard.

The young boy had turned suddenly and clutched his mother's skirt.

'We need to hang our flags from somewhere, don't we?'

'How else are we going to catch this lively wind?' A deep strong voice had blended with John's.

The three of them turned around in surprise.

'I do apologise, I didn't mean to startle you.'

John looked into the friendly face of Captain Brown. 'Good day, Captain, I didn't expect you here.' He thought about their conversation the other day; he must be more interested in the project than he'd made out, coming here on a Sunday with nobody else around.

'I was passing through, and what about you, my friend?' He

turned to face Elsie and Nathan. 'And your lovely company; out here in the cold weather?'

'We decided to come this way to show little Nathan here the yacht.' John put his hand on the boy's head.

'Captain Nathan.' A tiny voice corrected him, still sounding annoyed.

'Aha, so this is Captain Nathan?'

Nathan pressed his body closer to his mother's, clearly impressed by the tall big man with the low voice.

'Well, I am Captain Brown.' He stuck his hand out. 'Nice to meet you, Captain Nathan. Maybe your father can bring you back here when they hoist the masts on the yacht and set the flags; it's very exciting to watch.'

Nathan's small fingers disappeared in Brown's large hand.

'And this lovely lady?'

'Sorry, let me introduce you; Captain Brown, this is Mrs Elsie Tucker, Nathan's mother and my…,' for a split second he hesitated, '…acquaintance.'

'Nice meeting you.' Captain Brown gave a little nod with his head. 'I could have guessed with a beautiful child like that.'

Elsie started to blush; John had never seen her do that before. She looked even prettier, the red flushed cheeks setting off the green of her eyes.

'You'd better take them out of the cold,' said Captain Brown to John. Before walking away, he turned towards Elsie. 'I'm sure we'll meet again.'

'Is he the Captain you spoke about before? What a charming man.'

'I could see that.'

'What do you mean?'

'That you found him charming.'

'Don't be silly.' Elsie blushed again.

John was glad he had taken Nathan that Sunday; not long after, rumours had started going around the yard that she would never sail to England because they were not going to make the contractual deadline as they had feared. Morale had gone right down, but before it had crushed their work spirit completely, the foreman had gathered them around once more. He had explained something about another contract that had been negotiated with a new delivery date, now for the first of May, and, with everybody pulling their weight, they would manage to get her ready for that launch on time – albeit without the usual celebrations.

John wasn't paying attention; his mind was on a conversation he had just overheard between two carpenters. They had talked about the trials *America* was supposed to have in a few weeks' time against some other American yachts shortly after her launch.

A stocky carpenter called Tom had described to the other man how the vessels were going to be towed out to Bedloe's Island, where they would compete against one another.

Asked why those trials were needed, Tom had explained that in the contract it was stipulated that the buyer was under no obligation to buy her if she lost those races, adding that the yard owner could end up with one expensive racing yacht and their hard work could still be for nothing.

The other man had whistled disbelievingly and had marvelled at the idea of people willing to take gambles like that.

But what had caught John's attention most was Tom's concern that Captain Brown wouldn't be available to skipper her during those races in May; he stated the importance of having her sailed properly. The men had joked about which one of them would make the better skipper to take Brown's place or at least help to crew her.

A hunch told John he needed to stay close to Tom, as he seemed to know more than most about the upcoming trials and, more importantly, who was going to crew her.

'I count on you to keep up your commitment to the cause.' The foreman's voice was unusually shrill. 'Da Silva and I expect a lot from you. Now, let's get back to work!'

The group broke up and John quickly grabbed Tom's arm.

'Tom, could I talk to you for a second?'

'Sure, what's up?'

'I heard you talking earlier about the trials in May; do you know anything about who is going to race her?'

Tom looked at John inquisitively. 'You mean here at home?'

'Yes, that too.'

'No idea. I know Captain Brown is going to England with her, but for the rest I wouldn't know. What's with all the questions? Do you have ambitions yourself – want to hoist some sails in choppy waters?' Tom was mocking him.

'No, of course not.'

'Well, if you do get that idea in your head, join the queue.'

Before he could ask what he meant by that, Tom walked off.

'John, can I have a word?' Da Silva had walked up to him. 'I need you to come in earlier, just like the others; the syndicate has requested some modifications to the cabinets in the stateroom. I assume that won't be a problem?'

'Not at all.' He watched Tom disappear out of sight. 'I'll be here before anybody else.'

'Damn it, I'm late!' John grabbed his clothes from the chair. *What a bad start to the day.* He had no idea how much he'd managed to sleep, but it couldn't have been a lot. The previous night he had gone to Elsie after work to tell her about the longer working hours. He thought he saw some disappointment in her eyes, but he didn't have time to dwell on it as Nathan had woken up and wanted to play. When Elsie had pulled Nathan onto her lap to have something to eat, he had whimpered. At that point, they'd realised he had a fever and Elsie had quickly carried him to bed.

'I know some of the children around here have been ill, so maybe he's caught something.' Elsie sounded self-assured, but she looked worried. He quickly finished his food.

'Let me sit with him while you get some cold water so we can cool him down.'

Nathan groaned as he tossed and turned.

'You will be all right, little one, just lie still.' John touched his face and felt that his skin was burning. To see this helpless little person in such pain was upsetting; he was powerless to do anything. A horribly familiar sensation of doom stirred in his stomach. He wondered what kept Elsie. He put his hands on Nathan's shoulders to stop him twisting his body about deliriously as he groaned more loudly and gasped for air.

'Hot, hot,' he panted. 'Fire, papa, here.'

Shocked, John looked down at the feverish child; he was having a frightening dream about a fire and that could only mean one thing.

Elsie returned with a wet cloth and put it tenderly on Nathan's glowing face and chest. Nathan opened his eyes briefly, watching his mother like a wounded animal.

'Sweetie, I'll make you feel better, I promise.'

The little boy closed his eyes again and let out a sigh. She had calmed him down, her healing hands reassuring her sick son instantaneously, but the worried frown on her face remained.

They sat like that for some time: John on a chair he'd pulled closer to the bed and Elsie on the bed with her son, fanning him with a small paper fan she had made.

When John finally left them, the boy's sleep had seemed more peaceful. He said his goodbyes to Elsie, but she'd hardly paid attention to him leaving.

With one hand, he tried to pull up his trousers, while with the other he managed to get a shirt over his head. He realised he wasn't going to be able to make up the lost time. The knot in his stomach was still there; *should he have stayed the night to make sure the boy was going to be all right?* He struggled to make a decision; if he hurried now, he would only be a bit late for work, and maybe nobody would notice. But if he went via Elsie's place, it would make him more than an hour late. He hesitated and then snatched his satchel and overcoat and hurried out of the door.

No reaction.

John banged the door a bit louder; they had to be in. He held his breath and listened for any sounds on the other side of the door. There were enough noises in the building made by people getting ready for work, and children running down the stairs. But only silence came from Elsie's place.

Where could they be? Could they have gone out? Thinking about the state the boy had been in the previous night, he couldn't believe she would have done so. *What if they were both ill, lying in there?*

He stared at the closed door. There was no use asking any of the neighbours on this floor; as far as he knew Elsie didn't have much contact with them. And he didn't know where the woman lived who took Nathan in when Elsie went to work; somewhere in this block, that's all he knew. *Should he kick down the door?*

He squatted down, back against the wall. He couldn't think straight; he was hungry and the lack of sleep didn't help either. He put his head in his hands; thoughts of that disastrous night flashed through his mind, when his instinct had deserted him. He thumped on the door one more time, but there was still no reply. He couldn't stay any longer. He needed to get to work; he had to believe they were all right.

John climbed aboard the yacht via the staging frame. He'd tried to get there without being noticed, but Max had seen him arrive with his tools, although he hadn't said a word. John was angry with himself; he wanted to show Da Silva that he could rely on him, but he had failed to deliver.

What was more unsettling, however, was the possibility that something had happened to Elsie and Nathan: something that he should have prevented.

He pushed the mahogany dressing cabinet into position; the deep shiny velvety surface of the wood exuded luxury and wealth. The material was a pleasure to work with and the furniture had come along nicely, but today it vexed him. He thought about Elsie's place and his own; they both lived in small cheap rooms with thin walls, through which every word the neighbours said could be heard and the food they ate could be smelled. The drafts and coldness of Elsie's house in wintertime could easily have made Nathan ill. And here he was, making opulent items for a ship destined to be shown off by people with more money than sense. To make matters worse, it wasn't even certain that this ship was going anywhere.

Yet he had to admit that the cabinet looked beautiful next to the other pieces. At some point, the entire living quarters of the ship would be filled with furniture like this: chairs and velvet sofas next to paintings on the walls, and crystal in the cupboards. He knew Da Silva liked John's creations; he just hoped that his work would get to be seen by more people in the world than just the ones working at the yard.

The footsteps above his head intensified; they were getting ready to mast the yacht. When he had arrived that morning, he saw that everything had been done in preparation for the proceedings. The riggers had completed the construction to lift the two masts on board, and this morning the masts were hauled to a position alongside the schooner.

He had seen the Oregon pine logs arrive at the yard some time ago, with the bark still attached, and had watched how they were transformed into smooth round masts by being given straight angles to begin with. They were then cut into eight-sided poles, after which the corners were removed to make them sixteen-sided. One more step had made them perfectly round, while still allowing for the mast's narrowing at the top. John had marvelled at the idea that one could end up with one shape by starting off with something so different.

The noises outside increased, commands were shouted as the tension rose; any time now they were going to lift the first mast into position. John realised that he'd forgotten to tell Nathan what would be happening today. He hoped he was all right. He gathered up his tools; he would come back for the finishing touches.

'It never ceases to remind you how much can go wrong.' Tom had come up to John.

'Is that why so many have come out; to see something go wrong?' It seemed as if everyone had left their work and collected around the dock, hardly making a sound, afraid they would distract the riggers.

'Perhaps.' Tom grinned, before adding derisively, 'Or to put some money under the mast.'

'Money? I thought they did that when they're laying the keel.'

'Yes, as well. All for good luck.'

'Those sailors are one bunch of superstitious people,' John mused. 'Surely we won't be needing good luck if we build her right.'

'Very instinctive people, I would say. If you get it wrong, they don't want you on board in case you mess it up for them,' Tom replied.

A loud cry came from the direction of the yacht. The riggers had started to raise one of the masts. It looked like an impossible task to lift the long heavy piece of wood high enough to clear the schooner's rail, but somehow they managed to keep it away from the hull.

John watched the operation, holding his breath; one mast to go and then nothing should come between her and the water. But one mistake could set them back several weeks, maybe even several months, and the failure of their venture would be unavoidable.

'It won't be long before we can launch her,' Tom said, reading John's thoughts.

'We have to, don't we; the new delivery date is only two weeks away.'

'Yes, someone mentioned the third of May,' Tom replied. 'By the way, I also heard they have a crew for the trials.'

The men were getting ready for the second mast, but John was no longer interested. 'Really, who are they?'

'Some men Captain Brown knows – apparently local sailors, plus one of the boys here from the yard.'

John's breathing quickened. 'Someone from the yard?'

'Yes, Da Silva came in first thing this morning; they have decided they want another carpenter on board to England and the trials will give him a chance to get used to sailing.'

'This morning?'

'Yep, Da Silva came and picked out that young lad, what's his name, started working here roughly the same time as you?'

'Sid?' John had seen him around, but he'd never spoken to him directly.

'Yes, that's the one. I think most of us were glad he was keen and volunteered straight away.' Tom grinned. 'Saved me the embarrassment of saying no. You know, seasickness and the rest, but mostly an angry wife.' He turned to John. 'How come you weren't around, I thought you were interested in such a trip?'

John couldn't believe what he was hearing; he could have kicked himself.

He quickened his step. It was late; it had been a long and emotional day. At times, he had completely forgotten about Nathan and Elsie; there had been too much going on at the yard and Tom's news about the carpenter had distracted him. He should have been there when Da Silva had picked a carpenter.

One more block before he was at his destination; he could feel the knot return to his stomach. He shivered and pulled up the collar of his coat. The wind had started up again; spring seemed to come and go, definitely not keeping its promise. Just like he had failed to fulfil his promise to start making the right decisions – or any decision, for that matter.

He ran up the stairs two at a time to Elsie's door. He knocked on it, more loudly than he intended to. There were noises behind the door and to his relief Elsie opened it.

'I'm so glad to see you.' John stepped inside. 'How's Nathan?

Where is he?'

'Quiet, John, please, he's asleep. Come and sit over here, you can look in on him later.'

'But what happened, where were you?' He didn't sit down, but stared at Elsie. 'Are you all right?'

'I'm fine. Is something wrong?'

'I came here this morning, but you didn't answer the door.' John paced the small area between the table and the sink.

'Please sit down, John, you're making me nervous.'

'I was so worried, I thought you were both ill!' He stopped and turned to face her, his hands on the back of the wooden chair in front of him, demanding an explanation.

'He was much better this morning.' Elsie sounded apologetic. 'Jane promised to keep an eye on him, so I went to work.'

John dropped down on the chair.

'I'm so sorry if it worried you.' She touched his arm lightly. 'Small children recover quickly sometimes. This morning he even talked about the boat you're building and how she will be decorated with flags once the masts are on, especially for him.'

She had smiled. He'd felt like a fool; conscious that he might have overreacted to Nathan's illness.

That night when he'd said goodbye, he had caught her troubled eyes; had she picked up on the reasons behind his response? It had reminded him that he could never be completely honest with her. And then the thought had hit him: of all people she deserved a happy, carefree period in her life without a constant reminder of her suffering. And that wasn't meant to be if he was the one by her side.

He had walked out thinking that there was no need for the naked truth and the unnecessary pain that came with it. There never would be. He'd heard his mother reminding him to show one's love every day. He didn't agree with her; it was far easier not to get involved, as loving one person less meant one less chance of getting hurt.

John tried his hardest to picture Elsie's pretty face, but he couldn't. The memory of her was leaving him with every nautical mile they sailed.

James's angry voice rose above the violent flapping of the sails - crossing the Atlantic was taking longer than he would have liked. 'First, we thought we were going to arrive in fourteen days; yesterday, you told us that if we had several days of good wind we would make land in three days' time and today, you tell me it may be another week?' James sounded highly irritated as he tried to make himself heard. 'I've got a brother who is mostly on his back, sick as a pig, and now, on top of that, he's heavy-hearted and longing for home. How much longer will we be?' He sounded desperate, uncertain who to turn to and blame.

The Captain kept his eyes on the sails, worried that the gusty wind could tear them into pieces. 'I'm sorry to hear Mister George is still unwell,' he said calmly, 'but the lack of wind has been against us and we can't change Mother Nature.'

James sat down and pulled an apologetic face. 'I know there's nothing you can do about it. It's just disappointing, especially for someone who is desperate to get both feet on solid ground.'

John had to agree; the novelty of the trip had worn off and boredom had set in. During the empty hours of insufficient wind there had been little to do and he understood why thoughts were being drawn to life ashore. However he felt blessed that his own recollections of home passed swiftly by, carried away by the numerous waves as they glided along the smooth hull of the yacht. It wouldn't be long before everything would be left behind, leaving only the restlessness.

Just like James and his brother, John was eager to reach land again.

Chapter 16

July 1851, the south coast of England

'Frank, how many months now have you been writing articles and letters and God knows what else about it?'

'Just because I write about an audacious plan doesn't mean I have to be excited about the activity itself.'

'Oh come on, admit it; after writing numerous articles about yacht building, you must be getting excited about sailing yourself?'

'Harold, don't tell me you've never written something that didn't have your full personal interest? May I remind you about Mrs Dimbleson's tea parties? And that's just one example.'

'Perhaps. But I can't remember I've ever given her tea parties as much devotion and attention to detail as you've given this mysterious Yankee ship. Nor approached any of my subject matters in the zealous way you have this. The way, for example, you've been taunting the Establishment by explaining the advantages of the American packet ships and their greater speed, and the fact that this new ship is based on the same principles, thereby warning them about the danger soon coming through the waves of the Atlantic Ocean. I thought you must have a compelling reason to do so, which has led me to presume your infatuation with the subject matter.'

'Taunting? What did I do for you to call it that?'

'You have led the yachtsmen around the Solent to believe that the yacht they can expect is being built according to the latest innovations in American shipbuilding. And that the finished article will come over with the sole purpose of showing her off in a daring contest on the waters along these shores.'

'*If* she comes over. First, she has to compete in some trials back home that I told you about, don't you remember?' Frank thought back to what the Consul had told him. If she didn't win those, it would end the Americans' venture before it had even started – as it would the main reason for his interest in the Great Exhibition.

The excitement of the Exhibition had been building to a crescendo over the last few months and the closer in time they came to the opening on the first of May, the more McIlroy had expected of his contributions. He'd been working harder than ever before, resulting in little time for anything else.

He contemplated attending the preview they'd organised for the public to see the interior of the Crystal Palace before the grand opening, but he realised too late Bill had given him an incorrect date; like the rest of the public, he had to wait until the official opening. He couldn't be angry with Bill because he kept supplying him with information on the latest developments, to the extent that he didn't even have to go to London when the Exhibition was finally opened to great success. Thanks to Bill he had no difficulties trying to picture the arrangements of the articles from behind his desk. The productions of the United Kingdom and British Colonies on one side of the central transept and the rest of the world spread out on the opposite side. He had enthralled his readers with his creative writing and infected them with a similar sense of wonder, although not always to his own benefit as the pile of incoming letters had quadrupled. In particular his pieces representing the worries of some readers with regards to where all the visitors would stay while in London, and who was going to feed them and do their laundry, had been met by additional letters from readers concerned about the lack of water closets and the awful sight of beggars in the streets. Each letter he dealt with resulted in at least four more.

As a trip to London could wait, he decided to make another trip to Southampton as he knew the American yacht had been launched on the third of May. Frank was dying to find out about the trials.

**

'There's good news and bad news.' The Consul greeted Frank as warmly as an old friend, but his message was ominous.

'*America* has run her trials, but she wasn't the clear winner. I'm not sure what you'll make of that?'

Did the Consul wonder where his loyalties lay? Should he explain that he was looking forward to a tussle with the American yacht, despite being English?

'What happened?'

'Well, they had three trials and, depending on whose analysis one hears, *America* won one or two or none.'

'How is that possible?'

'I guess different interests in the outcome?' Croskey smiled broadly. 'We don't need you to divide us; we're fully capable of doing that ourselves. Let me get you a drink before I tell you about it.'

The men made themselves comfortable before the Consul explained that newspapers in New York had reported that, in the trials against the sloop *Maria*, *America* had won two races.

'Shortly after publication, they stood corrected by letters from the Commodore himself and from Mr Schuyler, one of the other syndicate members. According to them, the accounts given were apparently so wide of the truth, that they felt compelled to let the public know that, in the first race, *Maria* had run aground and, in the second race, a guest on board had inadvertently changed the position of the centreboard, causing her to lose again. The third race was won by *Maria*; they obviously didn't contest that.' Croskey took a sip from his drink and continued. 'You'll be interested to know that *Maria* is one of Commodore Stevens's own sloops and that one of the umpires during the trials was Mr Schuyler – the same one who was still in the process of purchasing the yacht from Brown on behalf of the syndicate.'

Frank had to get his mind around what all of this meant for the Americans' plan. He had to suppress his disappointment. 'What will happen now?'

'They decided on one final trial, to determine the question of speed once and for all.'

'Has that been raced yet?' Frank sat back in his chair; *why were they taking so long? The Exhibition was in full flow.*

'Here's the good news. Although not perhaps for the yard-owner. The syndicate waived the condition requiring a positive outcome of the trials and decided to buy the yacht outright. For a reduced price. Seems like she'll be coming over after all.'

'So, someone is willing to take a loss.'

'Yes, William Brown – of ten thousand dollars.'

'Although the syndicate is now putting up with an inferior yacht?' Frank wondered why, if the other yacht had been faster, they didn't sail that one over instead.

'Or they have an excuse for when they lose here in England; it's because they haven't brought their fastest boat.'

Frank looked at Croskey in surprise, but before he could think he was serious, he chuckled. 'May the best yacht win.'

'Harold, your father sends his love.' When he had exited the Consul's residence, he had encountered Mr Hayes, who had pressed him to give his greetings to his son, adding the warning that, if he didn't visit his old father soon, he would come to find him.

But Harold ignored him, not showing the slightest interest in Frank's visit to his father's hometown. Frank expected that his curiosity about the American yacht would soon prevail.

'I thought you would like to know that confirmation has been received the yacht will come over.'

'Really?' Harold kept his head down.

'We're just not sure exactly when.'

'Well, I am.'

Without looking up, Frank was still able to visualise Harold's smug face. The man sounded pleased to have outsmarted a friend of his father's.

'Come on, Harold, tell me!'

'That elusive yacht of yours – Archie told me to tell you she looks amazing.'

'How does he know? Where is she?' Frank was beginning to get annoyed by Harold's teasing.

'She's in France. And she's fast; apparently when she glides through the water, there's almost no bow water detectable. Wait until you see her, Frank.'

'How does Archie know all of this?'

'Papa isn't the only one with useful friends.' Suddenly Harold sounded like a little child. 'Some of Archie's friends are pilots, just like the other chap, Robert – you remember? One of them told him what she looked like.'

'I still don't understand, I thought you said she was in France?' Frank felt envious.

'That's correct; she's in Le Havre where she'll be prepared before being sailed to the Island. But she came through British waters and took on an English pilot near the Scilly Islands to guide her through the Channel.'

'I see.'

'And he had a good look while he was on board.' Harold grinned mischievously. 'She's a two-master, painted in a dark grey colour, rigged as a schooner. Which means her foremast is shorter than the mainmast.' Outlining the American yacht with two hands, he sounded as enthusiastic as Frank felt.

'But it was the angle of her masts that made her look different; they're raked with a distinctive tilt aft – sorry, set at a sloping angle backwards. And she's pretty, with a beautifully carved tiller and clear decks and a golden eagle at the transom with an enormous wingspan.'

'That's wonderful, but tell me again about her speed?' Frank was eager to know.

'Ah, apparently she made so little fuss in the water that Archie's friend asked to heave the log himself, because he couldn't believe they were doing twelve knots.'

That sounded promising, Frank thought expectantly.

'Is the news getting out she is swift?' A frown appeared on his forehead as doubt set in. 'Could that have consequences for a possible race? What if nobody dares to take her on?'

'What makes you say that?'

'If she's made out to be too fast, perhaps no member of any of the English clubs will be interested in placing a bet. And no bet, no race.'

'Listen to yourself; you're starting to sound like a proper connoisseur of sailing.' Harold saluted Frank teasingly. 'There's always the possibility of entering a regatta for a piece of silver. In any case, perhaps you should be careful what you write about her.'

Frank appreciated the irony of the situation; he, who feared the water and anything on it, was now slowly getting absorbed in a possible sailing match between the Yankees and the English. 'Before I forget, I appreciate your patience with me when it comes to sailing, thank you.'

'My pleasure. I'll ask Archie and Robert to keep an eye on what is coming from the Squadron.'

'Even if they don't see the need for a race?' Frank asked provocatively.

'Being confident in one's own abilities doesn't mean being too arrogant to race. They're no cowards either; on the contrary, they're sportsmen. They love a challenge.'

Had he touched a nerve with Harold?

'Excellent; I'm glad to hear that.' Frank felt excited. This was what he'd been waiting for: the imminent arrival of the American yacht. Soon the battle could begin.

He thought about Harold's warning about what to write. It wouldn't be the first time his journalistic work had not benefitted the people whose cause he had tried to fight. This time he needed to get it right; if he said too much about the yacht, he might ruin the chances of a race altogether. He needed to tread more carefully and spend enough time figuring out the best way of conveying his message to his readers. His first step would be to learn more about the plans of the Americans coming over for the Great Exhibition.

Chapter 17

No longer was he convinced that he was cut out to be a sailor. Twenty days on the water had taken its toll. And it wasn't because of the seasickness he had suffered, as that had ceased some time ago. Nor was it because of a lack of work; there had been enough to do on board, helping James and George with fine-tuning the yacht. It was about being on a small vessel with nowhere else to go. It made life beyond being at sea difficult to imagine and he had started to question his decision to come.

It was hard to believe now how disappointed he had been when the yacht was finished and the prospect of an adventure out at sea had vanished before his eyes.

When she was finally launched, he should have been enthusiastic, more than with any of the other launches he had witnessed, but he had avoided the simple celebrations of that day. There had been a pang of regret that he hadn't told Elsie and Nathan about the launch; the little boy would probably have had the best time of his life, but he had forced the thought to the back of his mind. As for Nathan, there was always a new ship that would come along. John knew the time had come to prepare him for that.

When the dates for the trials were announced, he had watched Sid's excitable face with envy. He had tried to ignore the reports that came back with detailed information on how the yacht had fared out in the Bay, close to Bedloe Island, but it had been impossible not to sense the worry amongst the men at the yard as apparently she hadn't done as well as expected.

Nevertheless, just as Captain Brown had predicted, the men involved were eager enough to make the arrangement work and they had renegotiated the contract once more. No more trials: instead, a sale against a reduced price. John had recognised their desperation to make the venture work; it hadn't been unlike his own desire to sail. Or that of Sid.

But as the trials had progressed, Sid had discovered that sailing wasn't for him. During the last day on the water, he hadn't been able to move for seasickness and the syndicate had decided to find a replacement at the last minute. Someone who would have to leave everything behind in a short space of time and sail to England for a couple of weeks, or perhaps months.

His meticulous work had paid off, so Da Silva had told him; George liked it and for some reason the Captain had suggested him as well. Would he like to sail?

He had thrown himself at the opportunity of a lifetime; there was nothing that kept him in Manhattan and, no, he never got seasick.

His departure had been sudden, although Ole had managed to give him a long list of instructions on how to behave like a proper mariner. He had been grateful for this, and full of expectations.

But now, after several weeks, he wondered how these genuine sailors coped with being at sea for long periods at a time. He was suffering from not being able to move around freely; he was desperate for a change of scenery.

He should have been more pleased to feel the sturdy soil under his feet again, but neither his body nor his mind was quite ready for the experience.

That morning they'd finally arrived in the French port of Le Havre and he'd filled his nostrils with the scent of the green fields beyond the shore. He felt drunk, even though the dizziness wasn't unpleasant.

There was no time to acclimatize to their new surroundings or to explore the harbour town as the yacht was hauled into the dry dock for preparations for the last part of the trip. Mister George had left instructions with the Captain before he and his brother James had left for a quick visit to Paris, and the Captain was adamant they should make a good start before their return.

It didn't take long before the overpowering smell of the paint had blended with the salty odour of the harbour water and the whiffs of dried earth from further afield.

John looked up at the hull; they had spent hours cleaning it, removing algae and other deposits picked up during their voyage before they could prepare it for painting. She was going to be black with a gold stripe along the top.

'I see our Captain has got his hand on the gold while we weren't watching.' Mister George had arrived back from his trip and was standing on the quay in his work clothes, observing the activities around the yacht, ready to get his own hands dirty.

'One day soon we will, Sir,' Captain Brown replied optimistically. 'But it will be the real thing!' He stopped painting the golden eagle that decorated the horizontal beam at the ship's stern. It was an impressive bird with a nine-foot wingspan holding a shield adorned with the Stars and Stripes. Just before her launch in May, the Captain had joked with John that if they couldn't tell from the innovative lines she was an American ship, they would have no doubt after seeing her stern while being passed.

'I'm glad to hear you're confident, Captain Brown, unfortunately not everybody thinks the same.'

'Sir, who is spreading rumours?'

'Well, I've just bumped into one of the owners and he spoke to a few people while he was in Paris.'

'Jealous French folk, that is.' The Captain plunged his brush back into the pot of paint.

'No, not French, but some of our own.' George paused for a moment. 'Apparently, we've been urged by several of our countrymen not to sail her to the Island for a race, because it is certain we will be defeated by the English.'

'Unbelievable,' Captain Brown grunted. 'They don't know what they are talking about.'

'Wait, that wasn't all; one of them warned us by stating that we, as a country, should expect even more abuse if we get beaten. It has something to do with the Exhibition in London; the goods we're displaying there are being criticised heavily. And now that "the eyes of the world" are on us, he even said not to return home to America if we lose.'

Hearing this Captain Brown let out a disapproving grunt. 'I hope the Commodore put them in their place.'

John couldn't believe what George was saying; they didn't believe in their venture? And the threat of not being able to return home?

'Let these idiots talk, we know what she's capable of.' Captain Brown daubed a final splash of golden paint on the bird's beak. 'That's you done.'

'Well, let's see it in a positive light; at least there seems to be a keen interest in our venture. Gentlemen, there's only one thing we can do now, and that is to make her as fast as possible!' George pointed to John. 'Get your tools – let's get to work on her hull.'

They climbed over the scaffolding to the rudder and the keel and George explained what he wanted to change to improve her speed.

John struggled to concentrate; he was distracted by the negative news from Paris and he couldn't get over the fact that it didn't seem to bother George. He had to be worried just like the others, as it was his creation they were doubting.

'Sir, have you always wanted to make ships?'

They had been working for over an hour in silence, their tools making the only noise. George put down his plane. 'You could say that. I grew up with it; boatbuilding has been in my family for some time.' He leaned against the yacht, relaxing for a moment. 'My father was a shipwright and after he emigrated to America he continued to work as one. I guess it was easy to follow in his footsteps. Although I might leave out the "easy"; I would have never become who I am today if my first boat hadn't been deliberately destroyed.' George grinned at the memory.

'Destroyed?' John wondered whether he had heard correctly.

'Yes, demolished. I was a child when I built my first boat; I'd put all my energy and knowledge into it – at least so I thought – but it sailed like a soap box and leaked like a colander. I didn't care; I could always improve it. However, my older brothers thought otherwise…' He paused for a moment and moved closer to John, speaking in a whisper. 'They took her apart.'

'James did?' John asked disbelievingly.

'Yes, together with our brother, and you know what for? They were convinced it would go to the bottom of the ocean and they were afraid that their little brother would go with it.'

'Was it that bad?' The thought that George had made a leaky boat was quite amusing.

'It probably was.' George smiled too. 'For a while I was very angry though. But what better encouragement could I have than to show older brothers and a critical father I could do better? And here we are.' His hand touched the hull lovingly. 'More importantly, I have a lot of faith in this lady.'

John admired George's confidence in the ship; he hoped it would be justified.

'Strange to think that, in a couple of days, I'll be back in the country that my father sailed away from all those years ago.' George closed his eyes and lifted his face to the sun. 'He came from the South of England, not far from where we will sail to.'

'Why did the family travel to America?'

'I believe my father left England for similar reasons as many had in those days, and still do: in pursuit of a dream. I don't think he left because of acute hardship, but I wouldn't know for sure, I never asked him.'

'Not that different from the reasons behind this trip, I guess.'

'You're probably right, although I would like to think this is no longer just a dream; that stage was passed a long time ago. I would like to call it a well-rehearsed plan, although I could have done with more time to prepare. What about you – are you chasing a dream?'

'Me? I guess it's more like escaping one.' John thought about his own father and brother. The sight of the lonely figure of his father waiting on the harbour docks was etched in his memory, as if someone had engraved it on the inside of his eyes. Every day for weeks he had stood there hoping for some news about his son. John's brother had vanished after setting out with a seven-man crew; he'd been just twenty-three. Before long, his father had started to scour the neighbouring beaches for any evidence of debris, but no piece was ever found. The guilt that accompanied that vision – that John had let his brother pursue his dream of sailing without telling his father – had remained as raw as ever. He should have prevented his brother's death. And that of his father. Six months after his brother had disappeared, his father had died in his bed of a heart attack. The loss of his youngest son had broken his heart.

John had never felt so lonely, left behind by the two men he had looked up to. Nothing lasted forever. And the knowledge had hit him hard.

As soon as his sister had married and could take care of their increasingly frail mother, he had packed a bag and closed his father's workshop. He had left the life he associated with loss and that had left him with a fear of losing. There was no point in looking back.

'I see.' George glanced out to sea; if he had noticed John's anguish, he didn't show it. 'I've been looking forward to coming to England, although I will never again cross the Atlantic on such a small boat,' he added wryly.

It was a shame that George hadn't enjoyed the journey on his own yacht.

'I heard that for some people there is no escape from seasickness; it could last the whole journey. Apparently it happens to the most experienced sailors. Although I did see the Captain and some of the crew take Seidlitz powders when we set off, so maybe we missed a trick.'

'Are you telling me they kept a secret from us? Damn sailors.' George grinned. 'Luckily James managed to open the box with rum to sooth my misery.'

Did George know they had finished all the liquor they had brought on board for the journey? On one of the last days, James had decided to open one of the boxes of alcohol from the Commodore's store. He'd justified it because it was meant as a medicine for his brother's belly-ache. He remembered what James had said: that he had no intention of starving in a marketplace. They had all laughed about that, including Captain Brown.

'Is it true we're not sure yet if we are going to race her in England?' The conversation with George didn't manage to dispel the dark cloud hanging above their yacht.

'Right, the race. Indeed, the Commodore needs to work on that some more once we arrive in England.'

'But I thought that was the sole reason for bringing her over all this way?' John asked quizzically.

'Yes, it was. But we haven't entered into an agreement of the sort as yet. Although months ago, before we had even finished her, the English Yacht Squadron did invite us to visit their clubhouse while we are over for the summer.'

'To race?'

'Ah, that's the interesting part. Their invitation suspiciously avoided mentioning the possibility of such a contest.' George's face turned into a grimace. 'For that reason, the Commodore turned their invitation to visit into an invitation for a contest and wrote back that we would love to graciously take any thrashing we were likely to get on their waters by their more skilful yachtsmen.' He paused for a second and added thoughtfully, 'I think Commodore Stevens always counted on the English not letting the opportunity pass by to show off their proficiency on the water.'

John lifted an eyebrow. 'And what if he's wrong?'

'It's a gamble. Not unlike the gambling the syndicate will have to do to make this trip profitable. But rest assured, nobody here is interested in the possibilities of defeat.' George got up and stretched out before picking up his tools. 'I just hope it won't lead to a hastened decision that any contest will do, because for a fair comparison we should only compete against yachts of a similar size. I don't want to end up throwing my reputation away because of a bad decision.'

'Gentlemen, look at this!'

Down towards the quay stood James, surrounded by wooden crates.

'The finishing touches have arrived, and I don't just mean the fancy furniture!' He was grinning from ear to ear, and holding a newly bought bottle of wine in his hands as if it were a trophy.

'Don't drop it,' George warned his brother. 'We can't have more liquor spillage.' The irony wasn't lost on James.

'No, little brother, I won't ever let it go to waste, you know that. Who is in charge of putting all of this in its proper place?' He pointed at the boxes alongside him.

'I'll get you some men; I think it's better that we load the goods straight away. We wouldn't want anything happening to them.'

John recognised some of the crates; he had seen them on the quay in New York. In the narrow boxes were paintings, while some of the other bigger boxes contained china, silverware, crystal and numerous other items that had had travelled to Europe on the steamship *Humboldt* with the Commodore and others, including Henry, another of James's sons. Once on the yacht, the contents would make her interior resemble that of a stately home.

There was still much to do before the yacht was ready to sail to England. They had yet to set the racing trim they had brought along and also to finish giving the mastheads, the main boom and bulwarks another coat of white paint. They had some French mechanics helping them out but they were more precise than George was and were taking a long time. Irritated, John wondered how much longer their departure to England was going to be delayed.

'Men, can I have your attention, please.' Captain Brown's voice carried through the early morning air. 'You'll be pleased to hear that this morning we'll set sail for the last stretch of our journey to England.'

Over several days they had continuously worked on the yacht's modifications and were eager to get the yacht to her final destination.

'The only thing left to do is to wait for the Commodore to come aboard.'

The men exchanged glances; they had got used to each other's company over the last long month and the fact that George and James and his son had to make way for members of the syndicate didn't feel right. John questioned the decision not to allow them to be present on the yacht during their arrival in Cowes; shouldn't George be there when the English saw his boat for the first time? But the Captain had insisted it was because of a lack of space. The brothers had left the previous morning to go to London by steamship, and would travel from there to the Isle of Wight; the arrival of the new guests who would take their place was met with apprehension. The men were all aware that the brothers had been more like them.

'Things are going to be somewhat different and I expect you to adjust your behaviour accordingly, if necessary. For some of you it means less swearing. For others, it means accepting the fact that they are the owners of this wonderful yacht.' Several of the men let out suppressed laughs.

John was convinced that the Captain meant himself by that and he smiled. He believed things had already changed. The yacht no longer looked like the racing machine she was supposed to be; now she had been decorated. And it wasn't just the transformation of the yacht. Since the departure of the brothers the atmosphere had altered, as if the ship's ballast had shifted to one side.

The moment the Captain said it, a group of visitors arrived at the dock; amongst them were Commodore Stevens, his brother Edwin and another member of the syndicate called James Hamilton. They had brought several others along with them and the crowd looked in admiration at the yacht.

'She looks absolutely beautiful.' Hamilton confirmed everybody's thoughts. 'I can't wait to see her sail off. Unfortunately, the French cook hasn't arrived yet, so I'm afraid we'll have to delay our departure a bit longer.'

Commodore Stevens turned to his colleague. 'Are you telling me you hired a cook who can't be on time?'

'Seems like it.' Hamilton looked as annoyed as Stevens. 'The man agreed to the pay he was offered and signed all the necessary papers, so I assume he's interested in coming along to Cowes.'

'Maybe he didn't understand your French, Hamilton.'

'The French-speaking steward you brought along from New York did all the translations, so I assume that isn't the problem.'

John remembered the black man who had turned up at the docks with the Commodore when they had arrived in Le Havre. He had wondered if he was one of the sailors, but now he understood he was a translator for the Commodore. Translators, an extra cook, paintings? It was evident this exploit wasn't just about sailing; the syndicate was intent on entertaining their guests in the most sumptuous manner.

When they were finally towed by steamer out to sea at about ten in the morning, it took the men no time to settle back into their routine on board. After two weeks on land, they were glad to be back at sea. John didn't share their sentiment entirely, but he was just as keen as they were to cross the Channel and get closer to their ultimate goal: the shores of England.

Their aim was the Royal Yacht Squadron's anchorage off the village of Cowes, but they had left Le Havre with a light breeze and the fog and tide were against them. It was dark when the Captain decided to lay anchor several miles outside Cowes. John was disappointed, as if it was a final test of their patience; they were so close that they could sense England but not see it.

At daybreak, John got his first clear view of the Island; there it was emerging from the jade-coloured water, covered with lush green woods and, in the distance, slightly higher in between the trees, a stately home was visible.

'Osborne House.' The Captain nodded in the direction of the large sand-coloured building. 'Queen Victoria's summer house. I've heard her husband teaches their children how to grow vegetables in the gardens. And there, over to the other side: England's mainland.' He pointed in the other direction. 'With the town of Portsmouth and about eighty miles to the north, the city of London.'

That's how close England is, John thought. The men were quietly observing their end destination, while waiting for the tide to turn and the wind to pick up. In the early morning sun, the Isle of Wight spread amongst the sparkling water like a beacon, ready to guide and welcome them to the shores of the land holding the key to their hopes and ambitions.

Whatever John thought about the crossing, he could look forward to what lay ahead of them; he hoped it was going to be the land of their glory.

The Commodore must have had the same thought on his mind. 'Edwin, we need to talk to the Captain about racing.' They joined the Captain in the cockpit.

'We've had another look at the chart of the race course which the Squadron normally uses for their annual races: it's too close to the shore of the island. I think the conditions are not right for us. What do you think, Captain? You have sailed her across the Atlantic and through the Channel, so we would appreciate your opinion.'

'Sir, she performs at her best if she can run on longer sections of water with a certain amount of breeze.' Captain Brown looked at the coastline and then back out to the open water. 'If we have a choice,' he said thoughtfully, 'we should sail her from the east coast of the Island, out into the Channel and back again.'

'That's what we thought.' The Commodore leaned back against his seat, looking pleased with himself. 'Much better than those narrow sections of the race course. Another benefit is that we won't need a pilot to get us through unknown tidal waters, isn't that correct, Captain?'

'Yes, Sir, unless you've heard differently.'

'No, I haven't, but I was wondering about those boats over there; are they pilots?' The Commodore pointed to a few small yachts nearing from the mainland.

'Or what about that one?' John gestured towards a yacht coming from the direction of the Island.

'Nah, that's not a pilot either,' Captain Brown grumbled. 'I think it's more of a welcoming party.'

An English cutter drew near to them and the Captain raised his arm to salute the other boat. It was clear the tide had finally turned.

'I guess not just a welcome,' the Commodore said thoughtfully. 'I think someone wants to assess our qualities before we have even reached England. You'd better get us ready for departure; I think they're out to get a little race.'

'Sir, what if they just want to escort us to Cowes?' The Captain didn't seem eager to play along. 'Isn't it better to wait before testing her against one of our hosts?'

'Oh, come on, look at the other yacht, they've probably sent out their fastest cutter and that's no coincidence, for sure.' The Commodore got up. 'Weigh the anchor and give them what they want!'

Chapter 18

'Tell me what this is about,' Frank demanded to know. Together with Harold, he was standing near the seafront at a godforsaken early hour of the morning.

Harold had kept his promise and had continued to inform Frank about developments in the sailing world. He had arranged a meeting with Archie who happened to be on the mainland, because they were desperate to show him something special.

He had resisted at first; he'd never been one for surprises, but no matter how he'd insisted on an explanation for their get-together, Harold wouldn't give anything away. He had assured Frank he was going to appreciate it, because it had something to do with the American yacht.

'Harold told us you were keen, but I didn't realise to what extent.' Archie shook Frank's hand. 'Good to see you again, especially at this time of the day.'

'Yes, he told me you had some interesting news about the sailing, so I've come prepared.' Frank pointed at the notebook under his arm.

'The infamous notebook; is it true you have been writing those stories about the American yacht?'

'Which ones are you referring to?'

'For example, the one about how she's as comfortable as our British yachts, but built for racing? And that they managed to finish her within six months?'

'Ah, those ones – yes, I did. Are you telling me you've read them?'

'How could I not? Someone on the Island talked about them

and suddenly several copies were to be found, and not only with the newspaper boy. Which meant that the news spread like wildfire and created a bit of a stir amongst the yachtsmen; you have some of the sailing clubs wondering what to expect. I would even say that some are getting a bit nervous.'

'Really?' Frank liked what he was hearing. 'I was only trying to attract more visitors to your beautiful Island. Have you seen her yet?'

'No, I heard she will be in Cowes soon, won't she, Harold?'

Harold wasn't paying much attention to the conversation; he seemed more interested in what was happening in the little harbour they'd arrived at. A buzz of excitement floated overhead as people walked down to the different boats moored at the quay. Absentmindedly he nodded his head.

'I've been told one of your friends has already seen her, though.' Frank followed Harold's gaze towards the water where some men were about to board a ship. There were lots of loud voices, something Frank realised now was a part of life on the water; one needed to shout to be heard above the noise of crashing waves, flapping sails and whistling winds. He could hear American accents.

'I'll be back shortly.' Harold patted both men on their arms. 'I forgot something.' And off he went. Curious, Frank watched him walk hastily to the group of men who were about to board a boat.

'I wonder what story you were told.' Archie's voice drew Frank's attention back to the conversation. 'Because the story I read in your paper about the English pilot boarding the American yacht to spy on the ship wasn't how I recall it.'

'Are you suggesting there was no English pilot?'

'Oh no, an English pilot did get on board and saw her up close, but he wasn't hired by some English sailors as an informant who was going to report back on her speed and other clever inventions.'

'May I remind you that he did come back with information on how fast she was and how good she looked?'

Archie seemed peeved and Frank added quickly, 'All right, I used my artistic licence to a small degree. To tell you the truth, I thought it was time this venture of the Americans received more awareness amongst the yachting enthusiasts, and I thought that giving publicity to her prowess would start a little controversy. But I've been reminded of the opposite effect: that it could put people off a race.'

Archie shrugged. 'Of course there will be a race. One should never underestimate the superb skills of our yachtsmen; there's a long history of our proficiency on the water and the unlikely chance of a faster yacht won't put them off. Anyway, the Squadron is more open to a race then you think; they already decided more than a month ago that during the Club's regatta in August they will offer a Cup of One Hundred Sovereigns for a race which will be open to yachts from all nations.'

Frank was surprised. 'Have they created a race especially for the Americans?'

'We'll be there shortly.' Archie waved at Harold to say he should stay where he was. 'Not quite. It's rather that they're allowing other yachts to enter; normally Squadron races are open to their own yachts only, with just a few exceptions in the past.'

'Maybe your sailing club could enter?' Frank said with a mischievous smile.

'We're the sailing club without a clubhouse, so I doubt it, and more importantly, as you can see, our yacht is probably not quite up for it.' He pointed at a small boat that was moored down at the quay: a pretty wooden yacht with one mast. Frank recognised a few of the men who were busying themselves on deck and before he could give in to a rising feeling of unease, he felt a tap on his shoulder and heard Harold say, 'Here take this, although you hopefully won't need it.' Harold pushed something in his hands.

'What is it?' Frank didn't recognise what he was holding.

'It's the latest invention in floating devices, a swimming belt made by a clever chap called Frederick Ayckbourn.'

Frank looked at it more carefully and it slowly dawned on him that he was supposed to wear it. And that could only mean one thing. Before he could open his mouth, the two men gently pushed him towards the moored ships.

'It won't be long before *America* will be arriving from France and we are going to get the best view available.' Harold grinned from ear to ear. 'From the water, that is.'

Frank felt his knees weakening; he could no longer move, worried he'd make a fool of himself.

'You always say the best reporters will do anything necessary to get every angle on the story; well, here's your chance.'

'Did you say the "America"?' Frank didn't recognise his own voice, which sounded curious yet was trembling with terror.

'Yes, that's her name according to those Americans down there.' Harold pointed to the boat that was about to sail out of the harbour. 'And they should know, because one of them introduced his brother as the one who designed her.'

Frank watched the boat set her second sail and then slowly gather speed. He tried to distinguish the figures on deck; one of the men now disappearing across the water was responsible for creating this supposedly majestic ship. If he acted now he could meet them both. Harold's and Archie's expectant eyes were on him; the time had come to make a decision.

'Let's do this then.'

'Just keep your eyes on the horizon and concentrate on something still; it will help prevent you feeling nauseous.'

The blood had drained out of Frank's face some time ago. But he didn't feel queasy, not yet at least; he just couldn't stop looking at the dark water surrounding the small yacht. *What if they capsized?* The fact that he was wearing something that should prevent him from drowning wasn't reassuring at all. *What if a freakish wave or gust of wind surprised the skipper and the main sail caught all the wind and flattened the ship?*

He'd seen this happen before, on a lovely but blustery summer's day, on one of his childhood trips to the coast. He'd watched a small sailing boat leave the protected surroundings of a harbour in a lively fishing village. Steadily it had sailed past some of the fishing boats moored along the harbour wall and just before it had reached open water, he had felt a gust of wind travelling from the hill behind the village. It had hit his body with a thud and shaken his trouser legs; just in time he'd managed to rescue the blanket on his lap before it flew away. The gust had travelled past the moored boats, leaving them swaying and with clanging ropes and sails, on to the unsuspecting sailing boat. The crew had just tightened the main sail and before any of the men knew what had hit them, the main sail caught the full blast of it directly in her taut canvas; in an instant, the force pushed the boat onto her side and the crew had had to hold on for dear life. A few of them tumbled over the deck, arms flailing, before finding something to cling to.

Frank's heart had skipped a few beats while he watched the boat right itself and the skipper scramble to his feet, just in time to steer the boat into the wind to prevent a second blast hitting the sail in full. The boat lost most of its speed while the men worked hard to adjust the sails. Before he could settle his rapid breathing, they had been on their way again, as if nothing had happened. He was convinced he'd watched them nearly drown.

And now, contrary to what he'd assured himself that day, he had left the solid ground underneath his feet.

The boat rocked calmly on the water; there was hardly any wind this early in the morning and his immediate state of panic started to subside a little.

Instead, he felt anger rise; *how dare they bring him along under false pretences!* They knew how he hated the sea. They'd given him no choice; they'd convinced him to get out of bed unnecessarily early to join them on a beach, and without further explanation they'd tricked him into getting on the boat. He couldn't remember now why he'd agreed to meet them in the first place.

Frank felt the direction of his anger change towards himself; he could have insisted on staying on dry land, but no, there he was, the only one wearing some foolish jacket that was supposed to keep him afloat if the boat sank. He wasn't sure if he should blame his impudent curiosity or the promise he had made to himself not that long ago to spend more time figuring out how to be a better reporter whose stories mattered. Learning more about the plans of the Americans by following the boat carrying the designer of the American yacht seemed suddenly like a ridiculous idea.

Why was the man who had such a big part in the American venture not on the yacht himself? There were more questions he could ask himself, but for now they were secondary to the wish that he hadn't eaten his breakfast with haste.

Excitement coming from the front of the ship gave some distraction; Harold, Archie and one of the other boys were at the bow, and Frank knew the only way of finding out what was happening was to get up from his favoured position close to the cabin door. He gathered courage and got up, wondering how best to cross the ship.

'There she is.' The skipper pointed in the same direction as the others. 'The Yankees must have anchored her there last night, or perhaps early this morning.'

Frank stretched his neck; in between the bobbing of the ship he could make out several other small yachts, but still no American ship.

'If you walk along the boom to the bow, you can hold onto the rigging. I'll keep her steady.'

'Thanks.' Embarrassed, he climbed on deck, stepping over a rail and under an arrangement of lines. Slowly, he walked to the others and, finally, after he found some tight ropes against which he could position himself tentatively, he dared to look up. For the first time that morning he had a good view of his surroundings. Alongside them more boats had assembled; they all seemed to be going in one direction.

'Frank,' said Harold, sounding pleased, 'you're looking much better.'

'Flattery won't get you anywhere, Harold, you both owe me an apology.' Frank glanced at Archie, who, like Harold, looked rather guilty.

'I'm sorry for dragging you out here, but any moment now and you'll be thanking us forever.' Archie and Harold grinned at each other like two naughty schoolboys.

'This had better be good, otherwise –' Frank stopped mid-sentence; over the shoulders of the men he'd spotted what they'd come to see, some hundred yards in front of them. Gently moving up and down on the water lay two enormous masts. What was attached to the masts was more difficult to see: a yacht lying extremely low in the water. There was no doubt about it, this was the American ship, the red, blue and white flag waving lightly at the stern, contrasting strongly with the black hull. A ray of the morning sun caught the water and Frank saw the sea being reflected in the yacht's shiny exterior; for a moment, she seemed to become one with the water. The whole ship sparkled; the varnished timber and polished brass gleamed in the bright light.

'How to make a first impression,' Frank mumbled. His eyes moved from the wider stern, along the burnished hull towards the elegant narrow bow of the ship. He had learned about ship designs over the last months, but she looked different.

Slowly, the yacht turned around her anchor and her stern became visible to the men. Positioned at the back of the yacht was an enormous golden eagle carved from wood, holding what looked like a green olive branch in its claw, with its wings stretched out as if to greet them. *Or was she telling them to keep a distance?*

'A bird of beauty and courage,' he said out loud.

'And that from a man who can't stand boats, but you're right; courage is what she is going to need.'

'Look at that sharp bow and those raked masts; like her hair has come undone in the wind.' Frank stared at her with admiration. 'But why is she anchored here?'

'Remember the fog last night? Cowes must have been

impossible to reach with the changing tides. I assume they decided to anchor here.'

'And there hasn't been a lot of wind this morning; that's why she's still here.' Harold added.

'Do you think they were pleasantly surprised as well then?' Frank pointed at the small yacht that sailed out in front of them. 'I wonder if the designer has stayed on the mainland somewhere.'

'I've heard that the owners joined the crew in France. It must have been too crowded.'

'The owners kicked the designer off? He came all the way from New York to be evicted at the very end; why would he put up with that?'

'He must have had his reasons to come along. Those three weeks crossing the Atlantic were a unique chance for him to see what the yacht's strengths and weaknesses are,' Archie mused. 'Just like you, Frank; to give your readers your best work you need to immerse yourself in the world of your subjects. Remember, that's why you came sailing today?'

Frank grinned back at him; he was starting to feel much better and he'd almost forgotten he was surrounded by water.

'See over there?' Archie pointed to a ship. 'That's Captain Williams's cutter *Lavrock* from the Royal Yacht Squadron; they must have come from Cowes to greet the Yankees and guide her onto her anchorage.'

The ship coming towards them indicated that the tide had changed.

'It's more likely they couldn't contain their curiosity and wanted a closer look.' Frank commented. 'They've definitely managed to get a reaction from the Americans – look how busy they are.'

The men aboard *America* started to unfurl the sails, while *Lavrock* passed alongside her, close enough for the skippers to exchange some words. Whatever the brief conversation was, they heard the stocky American bellow some commands to his crew and the men quickly took up their positions on the yacht. With slow but steady movements, the mainsail was hoisted; a large canvas opened up, so clear and bright that it lit up the water surrounding the boat.

'That's their racing trim, it must be brand new.' Isaac had joined them.

'Do all sails start off so taut?' Frank inquired.

'Yes, but unfortunately, they start to slacken after several uses…' Archie paused for a moment, looking more intently at the large canvas. 'Theirs seems to have been made from a different material than our flax sails. Interesting.'

The sound of clanking carried over the water.

'They're raising their anchor.' Harold pointed to the bow of the American yacht.

'Look at *Lavrock*; she must be challenging *America*.'

Lavrock had stayed close and encircled the other yacht twice, but the moment the anchor was raised, she started to come alongside and when *America* made her first move, she eagerly led the way.

The wind found the canvas of both yachts. *America*'s hull moaned and groaned with the initial movement, but not in a complaining way, more like the contented sigh of a dog stretching out its legs after a long snooze, ready to be taken outdoors for the long walk it had been dreaming about just before.

They sailed quickly out of sight; it was impossible to see who was ahead.

'I bet you they're testing her, before she's even made it into an English harbour.'

'Archie's right,' Harold agreed. 'There was a reason to send *Lavrock*; she's one of the most suitable yachts to measure against her if you consider her design.'

'You're both starting to sound suspicious; I hope it has nothing to do with me.' Frank looked at the other men.

'Let's see what the outcome of this little race is,' Archie said.

'I suggest we do that with the mainland under our feet.' Frank was sure his face looked grey; the wind had started to rock their

172

boat and he was instantly reminded of his precarious situation.

Harold put a hand on Frank's arm. 'I never thought you'd come along. Well done, my friend.'

'This morning a mysterious-looking vessel could be observed from the mainland, laid for anchor mid-channel, abreast Osborne House. A closer inspection by our own correspondent has confirmed that "the America" has finally arrived in our waters. With great splendour, she has emerged silently from the fog, flaunting her features as they have not been seen before. Her sails are taut, and her bow is sharp. She cuts through the water like a knife through butter. Her stern is delicately rounded, curved like the hind legs of a strong race horse.

She seems to be a novel work of naval architecture, her lines unfamiliar to our own experienced mariner's eyes, but it has been said she is a fine specimen of racing craft, ready to measure her swiftness with the speed of a choice of English yachts.

For the time being, she will be a guest to the Royal Yacht Squadron in Cowes and any person visiting the Great Exhibition and with an interest in nautical affairs is called upon to pay a visit and come and see this beautiful example of advancement in shipbuilding for themselves.

For now, her acclaimed speed will remain a mystery as, in trials with an American yacht earlier this year back in New York, she has already been beaten whereas, on the day of her arrival in England, she demonstrated her racing abilities in a little tussle with the cutter "Lavrock" by quickly showing her the way to Cowes. Although, for good measure, our reporter would like to clarify that the "Lavrock" was towing her longboat.'

Frank examined the text in front of him, being careful not to smudge the wet ink. Coming off the boat after they'd arrived back had left him not only extremely relieved but exhilarated at the same time. The first sighting of *America* had left a big impression on all of them. When he returned to the office, the words had flowed. He knew exactly what he wanted to say. But now looking at his piece he wasn't certain how to proceed. First of all, he wasn't sure how much he should write about the encounter with *Lavrock*. It was true that *America* had quickly worked her way ahead of *Lavrock*, but as a result of their first small triumph a rumour had started to spread only a few hours after her anchoring at Cowes.

Whispers were heard about how unlikely it was that any of the existing schooners, and probably cutters, of any of the sailing clubs around the Solent could beat the American yacht to windward in a moderate breeze. Because *Lavrock* had been classed as a match for a schooner not larger than *America*, her early defeat had blighted the Squadron's faith in the untouchable sailing qualities of their own yachts.

Should he start to doubt Archie's conviction there would be a race no matter what?

'An indication of the American belief in the qualities of their yacht speaks from the American willingness to place a bet. From a reliable source it has come to the attention of our reporter that back in the United States several American sailing enthusiasts have authorised the owners to take a bet on their behalf, if, on the part of the owners of a European Yacht, a proposal was being made to match that vessel against the "America", the total sum of which apparently runs into several thousands of dollars.'

Maybe it was better to leave that out as well? He wouldn't want to tempt anybody into paying an unwarranted visit to the yacht in search of some cash. Frank sat back, holding his sheet of paper at arm's length.

He needed to find a way to create interest in the yacht. The more people wanting to see an official skirmish between the English and Americans, the more likely it was that it would happen. The 'voice of the people': he knew how it worked.

It meant that he had to convince the men in the street to come out and admire her, not just the sailing gentry who could choose to ignore a challenge. But could he entice the working men and women to come to the seaside and watch a rich man's sport? Perhaps they would love to see the Establishment being challenged. They had come out in their thousands to visit the Exhibition in Hyde Park against the predictions of some sceptical elitists.

Frank grunted and tossed the crumpled piece of paper into the paper basket. He knew the weak spot in his plan. The public hadn't been impressed by the American presence. Their display at the Exhibition had received extremely negative reviews; it had been judged as the poorest and least appealing of all foreign countries, and the public had lost interest.

How was he going to get them to be favourable to an American cause?

He folded his hands behind his head and stretched his back; perhaps the time had come for another visit to London. Not just to attend the Great Exhibition; he'd already decided he would combine it with some other long overdue visits.

Chapter 19

Another waiting game had started, and at times John forgot what they were waiting for. Lately he wondered why they had come at all, because nobody seemed to be expecting anything of them, apart from that they behave like grateful guests.

When they'd finally arrived in Cowes, there had been a warm welcome from the crowds who were happy to see them, just like the members of the Squadron. But apart from the niceties, the invitations to dinner offered to some of the members of the syndicate, and the constant stream of visitors with their endless conversations about sailing, nothing much had happened.

Officially, they weren't participating in any contest. Unofficially, they went out on the water every now and then, which only served to further demonstrate their quality as one of the fastest yachts around. All the while the English showed no interest in verifying how well she performed; it was as if the *America*'s speed, or lack of it, was merely a topic of conversation, not a matter for any public records.

Time passed at a snail's pace and the men sat around being idle. John felt worse than on the windless days during their crossing; at least then, while slowly progressing to England, there had been something to look forward to once they arrived, or so he'd thought. More and more, he started to loathe the empty hours between sweeping the deck and polishing the copper; there was too much free time and to prevent his mind from wandering, he would venture ashore whenever he could. But not even the lively town or the pretty countryside could lift his spirit.

The moment he heard of an opportunity to take a trip to see

the Exhibition, he seized it, even if it meant he had to help carry stuff back for the Commodore and his brother.

They had been discussing a trip to London with James, who had been himself with George before they had come to the Island, and had mentioned their intention to bring back some souvenirs. When James suggested they would need an assistant, he proposed they take John. And as nobody else seemed interested or willing to pay for the fare to the mainland and back again, they were happy to take him.

Early in the morning, a ferry sailed them from Cowes to Southampton, from where they caught a train to London. The Commodore and his brother were too busy with their own affairs to engage John in any conversation, so all he needed to do was sit back and watch the English countryside go by. Gentle hills rolled past his window, and dotted between green hedges were quaint brick farmhouses with livestock grazing happily on the adjoining meadows; away from the yacht, he was at last able to enjoy his surroundings.

His contentment was further enhanced when he saw the Crystal Palace for the first time. But arriving at the American display, his exhilaration turned quickly to a more sombre mood. It was easy to see why they felt unfairly treated; it was tucked away in the furthest corner of the building – definitely not an area that would be happened upon by chance. At least their space was large, although they didn't seem to make good use of it.

John walked around the exhibits; compared with the opulence displayed by some countries, the variety of mostly practical goods laid in front of the visitor required a certain amount of imagination. Farming equipment, however valuable in use, probably wasn't the most appealing object to look at.

He watched a young American girl behind a sewing machine for a while, away from the others who were discussing the manner in which they were being judged by the English. The American delegation member was extremely agitated; his arms were moving in the same rhythm as the heavy eyebrows above his small eyes and the motions of the needle in the sewing machine.

Most words that were being said were unintelligible, but John heard enough to feel uncomfortable; how many more people were listening to this angry man's rhetoric that their location in the building was as if their contribution to this World Fair had been discarded.

John scanned the crowd that had gathered around the American stand. These were people who had come for a good day out, to be entertained and surprised by the things creative minds had come up with, not to hear an American being angry about the nation that was hosting this magnificent exhibition.

Fortunately, nobody seemed to take notice of the three men preoccupied in their worldly affairs, except for a boy standing at the edge of the crowd and an older man, standing slightly behind him.

The child was slender with thick brown hair and John wondered why he had caught his eye since he had blended perfectly into his surroundings; he was ordinary-looking, and was wearing the same drab clothes as lots of people present. It was when he turned around to face the harsh voices behind him that John noticed the big eyes; they were of a deep brown colour, shining like varnished mahogany, a bit droopy and sad-looking. But it was the expression on his face that struck John the most; clearly he had overheard something of the conversation, which had resulted in a frown that had rippled the skin of his forehead from the bridge of his nose to the hairline. The boy had tilted his head slightly to one side and was observing the three arguing Americans with a serious and intense look, a curious expression that John recognised as worry. Instantly he knew; he was looking at Nathan, albeit an older version of Elsie's son. The boy's slight frame had fooled him for an instant, but not his mannerisms; the frown was identical to Nathan's when he was pondering something that bothered him.

This was just like Nathan had done shortly before John's departure, when he'd visited him unannounced at the house of

Elsie's friend Jane, because he knew Elsie was at work. John had retrieved a little wooden sailing boat from his sack; it had been one of two items he'd taken from his father's workshop when he'd closed it up for good. He'd found it in a drawer, together with an identical second one; at first, he wasn't sure if his father had made them, but the delicate manner in which they had been cut out of one piece of wood, with raised sails on thin masts, showed the hand of the skilful woodworker he was. Each boat had the letter 'J' on its side: one of them engraved in simple and straight lines, and the other in smaller, curvier grooves. Surprised his father had made such objects, he realised at once who they had been made for. When John had given one to Nathan and told him to keep it, he had frowned. John wasn't sure if he'd understood when he'd told him to take care of it because he was going away for a long time on a similar ship, but he couldn't find a better way to explain his sudden departure to the little boy. When he'd left Jane's house and had turned around one last time, he saw Nathan running around the room with the boat in his hand, humming 'Captain Nate, I am Captain Nate'.

That goodbye felt like a lifetime ago: a feeling exacerbated by the insular life they led around the boat. It surprised John how easy it had been to forget what he had left behind, as if the constant movement of the yacht, however slow some days, meant one never looked backwards, only forward. The only looking back was done when he had tossed the log off the stern of the yacht and had counted the knots passing through his hands, but that was to determine how quickly they were moving forward, ever closer to their destination. There had been no time for reflection and the memory of Nathan's brown eyes, the same soft and smart eyes as Elsie, was unexpected, just like the sun appearing from behind a cloud on a windy day, instantly warming one's body to the core. How he longed to see them again, even for just a moment. The acute sense of belonging struck him without warning, and at an odd time and place; an inauspicious bit of America in the middle of London. The irony wasn't lost on him:

no matter how much travelling he had done, he hadn't escaped the place he had set off from.

'John? John?'

The sun that had briefly warmed his core disappeared once more. Commodore Stevens's voice sounded more cheerful; the three men were smiling and shaking each other's hands.

'If Mr Riddle here decides to come and visit us on the Isle of Wight, will you be so kind to tell George to give him a tour of our yacht?' Commodore Stevens beckoned John to come closer. 'This is John, our master ship's carpenter,' he added.

'Yes, of course, Sir, I will make sure he does.'

'We have told Mr Riddle that although our personal contribution to this event would probably have fitted inside this hall, we prefer to show it to the world in the place it was built for: on the water! So he needs to come to the Island, where he can admire her.'

After some more polite exchanges, Commodore Stevens turned around purposefully and viewed the long corridor.

'Come on, Edwin, let's explore while we are here!'

Edwin Stevens had a scowl on his face. 'Brother, you should have told him the truth. They're putting an excessive responsibility on our shoulders, as if we alone can save our dented honour, but how can we if the English don't seem very keen to take on the challenge of racing her?'

'Edwin, you're such a pessimist, just like Commissioner Riddle. Don't you worry, before we left I reminded our friends at the Royal Yacht Squadron by formal letter of our intentions and proposed a race against any number of schooners belonging to any of the yacht squadrons of the Kingdom.'

'They keep saying we've come here to challenge the world; it does worry me.'

'Regard it as a compliment. It means that they consider our young republic capable of doing so. For what it's worth, I refuse to believe that they'll let a chance pass by to show us their fastest yachts; their sense of rivalry will overcome any fear they might have.'

'I hope you're right, I'd hate to think we've come all this way in vain.'

John turned around to see if the boy was still there but he had disappeared in the masses, together with the remainder of cheerfulness with which he had arrived that morning. The chance of fulfilling their sole purpose for crossing the Atlantic was fading rapidly, leaving him to deal with his own nagging doubts about his intention for coming. What was the point of the trip if they were being denied the reward they all hoped for?

'Gentlemen, let's leave this godforsaken corner.'

In the dark, the lines of the ship were just visible in the distance; the masts were moving gently up and down with the rhythm of the currents around the Island. He stood on the quay in Cowes, hands in his pockets, looking over the stretch of water between the Island and the mainland which he had left a couple of hours before. Even in the now almost complete darkness, he could see the swan-like beauty of the yacht; you didn't have to sail her to understand that she was made to race, with her excessively raked masts and her empty deck.

John wasn't surprised to see the little rowing boat bobbing up and down near one of the stairways leading to the quay; the men liked to enjoy a nightcap or two before retiring to their berths. He sighed; after the long and tiring trip to London, he was longing for a good night's sleep. He desperately wanted the day to end, and to silence the turmoil in his head by surrendering to a world of sleep. He had no interest in joining the rest of the crew socialising in a pub somewhere. All he could do was to wait for the first two men to come back.

He walked along the harbour walls. Plenty of people were still strolling around the area, and the music floating from the public places in the back streets blended with the voices and laughter of the passers-by.

Since their arrival more than a week earlier, celebrations had been ongoing for the Island's yearly sailing regattas. People had come over from the mainland to be entertained by the festivities surrounding the events. Different sailing clubs had their own regattas and participating boats would race for cups.

John thought back to the jewellers displaying their silver and gold wares at the Exhibition; he remembered seeing these kinds of trophies amongst the goods: elaborately decorated tableaus of hunting scenes or racehorses next to tall cups, all meant to end up in the hands of the winner of whatever race had been run.

Edwin had pointed out wryly that it wouldn't make their trip very profitable if that was the only thing on offer: not even if you were to melt it down and make use of the silver. The Commodore had reassured him that his intention was to go home with more than a piece of silver. Honour is nice, he'd stated, but he preferred to keep score in other ways.

John walked away from the lively atmosphere, towards the castle. It was situated at one end of the promenade, prominently positioned alongside the water. It had been made as a defence fort, constructed out of big limestone blocks, and if you took the path around the structure, you could see the big squat round tower on the other side.

He walked past several tall flagpoles that, in the daytime, bore huge British flags and a few small wooden boats that had been put on the quay.

'Nice evening, Sir, don't you think?'

Near one of the upturned rowing boats, a man was sitting on a low stool holding the end of a large fishing net.

'Yes, indeed.' Truthfully, John hadn't noticed the cool summer breeze or the white light of the moon that made the sea sparkle like diamonds and gave the quay its soft muted tones.

'Is that still used for defence?' John nodded towards the castle that was lit up by the moonlight.

The man followed John's gaze. 'Oh no, that was modified a while ago; it's now the residency of the Marquess of Anglesey.'

That didn't surprise John at all; he had deemed the house fit for a Royal, and someone with a title like Marquess didn't seem far off that. The name sounded familiar.

'What does this Marquess do?'

The man looked up at John. 'Not much nowadays but he's passionate about sailing and a member of the Royal Yacht Squadron. And a famous war hero, too. Did you know he fought with the Duke of Wellington at the Battle for Waterloo and lost his leg?'

Then John remembered the gentleman who had climbed aboard *America* shortly after they'd arrived in Cowes more than a week ago. Several Englishmen had paid them a visit, amongst them a man of advanced age but with a spring in his step. The thought of that made John laugh now.

'You have a long and colourful history to look back at,' he said appreciatively, marvelling at the man's attempt to repair the large net in the low light.

'Perhaps. But we ought to take away the lessons it gives us.'

'What makes you say that?'

The fisherman was an older man with a white bushy beard and rough hands which competently pushed a thread through the holes in the net.

'I'll give you a good example.' He nodded in the direction of the anchorage of *America*. 'The lines of that yacht? If only our shipbuilders had done something with the idea of a certain English naval architect, people wouldn't have been this surprised by it.'

John recalled the Marquess's eager questions about the design of the yacht. He had been especially curious about the lines of the boat, querying why they seemed to be in reverse: narrow and sharp at the bow and broad at the stern instead of the other way around. The gentleman had wondered out loud if he had been sailing his cutter backwards for all that time. They'd all agreed that the eccentric man had a lovely sense of humour, and John could tell Mister George had been pleased that he'd surprised some Brits with his design. Was this fisherman implying that the novel design had been previously thought up by an Englishman? But before he had a chance to ask, the man continued.

'But sometimes we need the help of others to point out to us what we already know.' The man hadn't stopped searching the net for what John thought must be another hole. 'Because sometimes we're too close to a problem to see the solution.' He got up and shook the net violently, spreading it out on the ground around him. 'Not unlike mending a net. There it is! Gotcha.' He grabbed the area that contained the hole and pulled it closer for repair.

'I see.' *Was the man alluding to fishing?* John was too tired to think clearly. He turned around and muttered, 'Thanks for the advice.'

He peered through the window of the pub; it was full of people having a good time. It took him a while before he spotted the others in the crowd, the tall posture of the Captain giving the group away. *First time lucky*, John thought; *this place is clearly their favourite.*

He entered and slowly made his way towards the back of the bar; he could see from their faces and the glasses spread around them that they had been there for some time. He was surprised to see the Captain amongst them; during the journey, he seemed to appreciate time to himself, however difficult it had been on the ship.

The Captain was having an animated conversation with a few local boatmen and his hearty laugh could be heard over the noise. John felt like a stranger at a family party. He considered quietly asking one of his shipmates to row him over to the yacht, but before he had the chance, Captain Brown noticed him hovering nearby.

'Hey, John, you're back!' He raised his hand in a salute. 'Come, join us, I could do with your help here!' He put his big hand on the shoulder of the Englishman next to him. 'Meet my new friend Edward; he knows a lot about sailing, so he thinks, but nothing about American science or our culture for that matter. I need you to explain a few things to him.' The Englishman didn't seem to mind the insult and touched the Captain's glass with his while letting out a happy 'Cheers'.

To see the Captain in such a playful spirit lifted John's mood. 'Not sure if I can be of any assistance, but I need a beer first.'

'I hope you'll have success with that boat of yours, because I've heard your contribution to the World Fair won't win you any prizes,' mused Edward the Englishman in a loud voice.

'Have you been over to see it yourself?' the Captain wanted to know.

'Not yet,' Edward mumbled. 'But I don't need to go, I've read all about it in the newspaper. Apparently you're trying to entertain the rest of the world with cured meat, preserved peaches and lots of other cheap goods. Oh, and a buck-eyed stuffed squirrel?'

'John, help us out, what is this man talking about?'

The first sip of the lukewarm bitter made John slightly lightheaded; he couldn't remember seeing the animal.

'You probably didn't see it because it was hidden behind the jar of maple sugar.' The Englishman laughed at his own joke.

The man was right, their display hadn't been convincing, but John wasn't going to admit to it. 'You know us Americans, we like to focus our efforts on creating and perfecting goods that bring about convenience to the lives of larger groups of people, not just a privileged few.'

'Like that machine that helps you turn your sheet music while you play the piano,' Edward said teasingly, turning to the Captain. 'Let's raise our glasses to you visiting our country – and getting the opportunity to learn how things should be done.'

Captain Brown stopped his glass in mid-air, just avoiding touching Edward's; he stared at the Englishman without saying a word. There was tension in the air and John wondered if the man had pushed the Captain enough to be angry.

The Captain leaned closer to the Englishman and said in a deep voice, 'Your country's wealth and luxury goods may well exceed ours right now, but I warn you, we're coming after you as fast as a greyhound chasing a hare – you'll soon be caught.' He tilted his head back and let out a roaring laugh, slapping Edward on his shoulder a little too forcefully.

Edward mumbled a few appreciative remarks about the American sense of humour and how it must have derived from the British. The men were a good match for each other and would probably continue their banter for the rest of the evening; but John was tired.

'John, tell this man that our best entry to the Fair lies just outside these doors and that we look forward to racing her.'

'Don't tell me you really think you could win a race against a British yacht?' Edward suddenly sounded serious.

'If that sounds so fanciful, how come no one has taken up our offer for a race yet?'

Edward didn't react, seemingly embarrassed by the reluctance of his sea-faring countrymen. 'I've just thought of it; you have at least one Englishman on your side.'

'What do you mean?'

'One of the reporters on the mainland; he's been writing articles urging the gentlemen of the sailing community to offer you a race.'

'Really? That's good to hear, but it's had no effect yet.'

'Maybe you need to give it some more time.'

'Time is what we don't have a lot of.' The Captain offered Edward another beer. 'Which reminds me, how well do you know the waters around here?'

'Rather well; why, do you want to come fishing with me?' Edward looked surprised.

'No thanks.' A smile flashed across the Captain's face. 'I have to plan for the eventuality that none of these cowards will agree to a challenge. That will leave us to enter for one of the Cups. And those races are run around the Island – water I'm not familiar with, and neither is my crew. We'll need a British pilot to guide us through.'

Did the Captain not know about George's concern with having

to race under unfavourable circumstances?

'What do you think, John? Edward here wants to know what the crew thinks about employing some Englishmen to help us race the yacht.'

This was the first time Captain Brown had talked about asking English sailors to join them.

'Being on an American ship, based on an American design, commanded by an American skipper – surely that makes them honorary Americans?' John suggested.

'Wise man. Let's keep the skipper happy and get him another beer!' Brown said loudly.

'Please let me do the honour.' The Englishman took their empty glasses and walked to the bar.

With Edward out of earshot, the Captain turned to John and hissed, 'We were always going to need a larger crew for racing. And whatever race that will be, we need to prepare for it if we want to win. I'm not going to sit here and wait until the syndicate make up their mind. I'll do whatever it takes, even hire English sailors.'

John looked in amazement at Captain Brown's outburst; he hadn't seen him this agitated before. He wasn't the only one frustrated at how the trip was turning out. To see both the Commodore's brother and the Captain lose their temper in one day didn't bode well.

Chapter 20

They'd warned Frank that the streets were going to be busy, especially around Hyde Park. In the first few weeks after the Exhibition had opened, the roads near the Crystal Palace had been blocked daily with carriages: reason enough to walk from the lodging house to Kensington High Street. He knew it would take some time, but there was no use trying to fight the crowds.

The caution hadn't been an exaggeration; hundreds of people were cramming the streets. It was easy to recognise the other visitors: extended families with children of all ages being tugged along by their mothers, babies being carried by their fathers along with baskets full of provisions. It had to be the result of dropping the entrance fee to one shilling, thus encouraging even more people to visit. Some must have come with the excursion trains to London, making use of the cheap-ticket days for the common people, just as he'd done. A wry smile crossed his face; at least the organisers could pride themselves on having persuaded all layers of society to come out for the chance of a lifetime and to use every penny they had to see the triumphs of man.

Walking through Green Park, he watched the visitors picnicking on the grass, resting their tired feet. Some had come a long way; the rough, gritty sound of the Liverpool folk and the rolling 'r's' of the Cornish were easily identifiable. There were people dressed in their finest garments: women in bright coloured bonnets and polka jackets, men wearing their best coats. Others were dressed in simple cotton shirts or crumpled jackets: red-cheeked countrymen, the dust collected during their travels still on the shoulders of their shirts. But all displayed an air of infectious excitement, the children revelling in a rare day out with their parents and the adults drawn to the big city by the Wonders of the World.

Were these the people the locals had worried about causing unrest while visiting London? The ones who would misbehave and relieve themselves in their gardens? Frank shook his head at the thought; these people had made a significant effort to come to London, and not just financially. All they wanted was to be entertained by promised treasures from abroad, not to provoke unrest.

Amongst the sightseers were men and women wearing foreign national dress: hats with feathers worn by men with big moustaches, and by their women wearing short cotton dresses. It was true that 'People of all Nations' were drawn to the Exhibition; it had indeed created an opportunity for distant countries to become more acquainted with each other.

Frank pulled out of his top pocket a leaflet he'd been given earlier by a merchant who had developed a special Exhibition coffee: a blend of 'the finest coffees of all Nations'. Frank smiled; someone else was profiting from uniting the best ingredients these countries had to offer. Perhaps he should get McIlroy some beans as a souvenir for letting him come up to London. He could do with a good cup now.

He quickened his step; he was getting nearer to Carriage Drive. Carefully crossing the road, he followed the ever-increasing masses.

There it was: a multi-layered structure shimmering in the sun. He could make out the dome in the centre of the building with the tiered sides spreading out like the beams of a cross. It was as if an enormous bird of prey had laid herself down on the ground, with her wings spread out, protecting the treasures beneath. Rows of flags adorned the building and as he got closer he could hear the sound they made in the breeze.

Hemmed in by the crowds, Frank slowly made his way to the door; gradually he was funnelled through the entrance passage and before he realised it, he was inside, standing in the middle of the avenue that ran the whole length of the building.

He looked to his right and left, wondering where to go first, dazzled by the scene before him. A gigantic crystal fountain was erected in the centre, covered by the dome-shaped roof, next to enormous trees and a row of sculptures arranged on each side. Every surface, from the ceiling to the walls and the floor, was decorated by the most astounding objects in brilliant colours, all of them competing for his attention.

The heartfelt sigh he heard next to him could have been his own. A young lad with curly hair stood transfixed, soaking up the atmosphere; his face was lifted upwards to the roof and his mouth open.

Frank watched him close his eyes and laughed. 'Isn't that something?'

'It's, it's so – pretty!'

Large brown eyes looked up at Frank and another sigh followed. He saw the rest of the family over the boy's head; most of them were equally in awe of their surroundings. A woman smiled down at the boy and gently pulled his arm. 'Come on, son, we don't have all day,' she said with a playful voice.

'A day isn't nearly enough; we need several, don't you think, boy? Well, enjoy your time here.' Frank saluted the boy and nodded to the lady.

One didn't need to spend a long time inside to realise it contained a truly remarkable exposition of productions from around the globe; passing the different displays was like a proper circumnavigation of the world. And not just any world, but one filled with wealth and sumptuous splendour, objects brought in to show off the skill of the maker.

The delicacy of the Italian mosaics was astounding, just like the rich embroideries and laces in the Spanish display. But the splendid frontage of articles of France with heavy silks and tapestries, jewellery and porcelains, were the most exquisite. This was like an Aladdin's cave; there was no doubt about it.

Frank wondered where the objects of utility were exhibited;

the beauty of the finery he witnessed was extraordinary but he was more interested in industrial objects, like the famous printing press he kept hearing about. He wasn't the only one following the sign that said 'passage to machinery'. He hadn't expected that it would draw such large groups of people. Not just labourers and other folks who used their hands on a daily basis but school children and women joined the rows of people intent on seeing the moving objects, all equally dedicated to learn about the newest inventions.

He agreed; the printing press that could turn out 5,000 copies of an illustrated newspaper per hour was extremely exciting. *Imagine the implications of such a machine!* To be able to reach larger groups of people in the country faster; what would that mean for spreading news? But he had no time to dwell on impending changes to his job, he had only one day to see what he had come for and his guidebook told him that the American display was situated at the far end of the Eastern side of the building. It struck him as a bit odd, as if someone had purposely reversed the geographical order of the world.

As he walked through the central transept and along the main corridor towards the end of the eastern nave, his gaze was automatically drawn towards the ceiling. High up there, with wings outstretched, was an enormous eagle, towering over an organ and holding a drapery of the Stars and Stripes not too dissimilar to the eagle on the transom of the American yacht. There was no doubt where he was.

The first thing he noticed was the amount of open space; unlike in some of the other displays, where the volume of goods made it difficult to concentrate on anything in particular, here objects stood out. And for the first time that day it was possible to walk around freely between the displays: no need to look over people's shoulders or to wait patiently for them to move away.

On the tables in front of him were lots of small items like locks and clocks, pyramids of soap and jars of pickle and honey. Next to a sign saying 'formidable revolving charge pistols' he spotted some firearms. He heard a man praising the maker, a Mr Samuel Colt, and pointing out how decorative they were. Frank shook his head; the Peace Society's appeal not to allow any lethal weapons had clearly been rejected by the organisers. Unfortunately, it would have taken more than that to deny an American his arms.

Hardly any of the exhibits managed to generate the excitement he'd felt earlier that morning and it was beyond him why they'd been brought over all this way. It wasn't obvious how they were connected with the United States' industry, nor with their art for that matter. Although there were some bigger pieces, like the double grand piano that allowed four performers to play at a time, and a reaping machine, the collection as a total was an incoherent assortment of objects and clearly very disappointing. And he wasn't alone in his disenchantment; judging by some angry voices behind him, others were openly unhappy about something.

He turned around and searched for the source of the loud voices; some excitable American men stood a couple of yards away. They seemed to be having an argument, unconcerned that anybody else was able to listen in. It was impossible not to hear snippets of what was being said and Frank noticed that he wasn't the only one. Slightly away from them stood the young lad he'd seen earlier that morning with his mother. Like Frank, he was taking notice of the heated conversation, his head slightly tilted and his big brown eyes fixed on the men in front of him, a concerned frown on his forehead. Frank smiled; the lad wasn't at all worried if someone caught him eavesdropping.

The men were discussing their displeasure with their hosts. *Why would you have that conversation here?* thought Frank, his reporter's instinct prompting him to move closer.

One of the Americans complained about their space in the exhibition hall. Another man in the group seemed to reassure him, after which the first man raised his voice.

'I hope you realise that turning back is no longer an option; you have to race her and you'd better win that race! American honour needs to be saved.'

The American with the reassuring voice answered resolutely, 'We have every confidence in her speed and her ability to sail faster than any English yacht. Our packet ships have been outrunning theirs for some time now and this yacht will do exactly the same.'

The men moved away, still heatedly discussing matters, but it was no longer possible to understand what was being said. Another man had joined the group and the last thing Frank heard was one of Americans extending an invitation to travel to the Isle of Wight to admire the yacht.

Frank couldn't believe he had stumbled across this conversation. They had been talking about the American yacht at anchor off Cowes. And they had reminded him of how much the Americans had relied on a successful exhibition for a share of the appreciation from the rest of the world for their young Republic.

Unfortunately for them, the critics were right; theirs was an uninspiring performance. Too many simple products in a space too large to be filled properly. He remembered Bill telling him that the Americans had asked for more space; had it been their arrogance? Perhaps this was all they had to offer.

At least there's enough room to eat my sandwich, Frank thought with scorn. One corner had been assigned to allow tired visitors to rest their weary feet. Deflated, he found himself a place next to a family. He unwrapped the sausage roll he'd bought earlier from its greasy wrapping paper, but not even the smell of the sausage and mustard could bring the usual contentment. He knew he had a problem; he had come to Hyde Park in the hope he would find inspiration, perhaps from an American object overlooked by everybody else. Instead, he was going to leave empty-handed.

Nevertheless, it felt good to take the weight off his feet for a while. He ate his sausage roll and watched a group that had gathered around the reaping machine; farmers and some men in suits were discussing the ugly and cumbersome piece of equipment. They seemed to be impressed by its qualities, praising the machine loudly. Of all the goods present, one could never have guessed that it was going to be the object that justified so much attention.

One of the men came over and sat down next to Frank.

'What's so special about that machine?'

'Sir, that Mr McCormick has created one of the best grain reapers around.' The man removed his cap, put it on his lap and laid upon it a squashed package, which contained some pieces of ham and a chunk of bread, yellow with oozing mustard.

'Is that so?'

'Sir, believe me, that invention is the most valuable I've seen today.'

'And why is that?'

'Well, for a start, it would make my life much easier.' He stuffed a piece of ham into his mouth. 'It not only cuts the straw about thirty times faster than my sickle, but also much nearer to the soil. It beggars belief we haven't seen it before!'

It was time to leave; the farmer's excessive contentment irritated Frank. The Exhibition had nothing more to offer.

He walked away, past the other seated visitors and a model of what looked like a church floating on water. But a group of people positioned near the opening of a red velvet canopy hindered his departure; they were huddled together in the middle of the pathway, waiting their turn to see what was sheltered inside the little tent.

Was it a clever ploy to attract people or was there something exciting in there after all?

He couldn't help his own curiosity and moved towards the queue, wondering what they were looking at. Once close enough, he saw the life-size statue of a young woman, the white marble standing out against the deep red of her shelter. Her nudity was a shock at first; Frank didn't expect to see a naked young woman, standing on a plinth for everyone to gaze at. He noticed that her hands were bound by a chain and he spotted a little crucifix attached to it. There she stood, exposed, awaiting her fate, her gaze averted away from the onlookers. He followed the slender curves of her body, the young pointy breasts and soft stomach. Frank felt shame for her nakedness.

'*The Greek slave*', the description in his guide said. '*A Greek girl stripped of her clothes by her Turkish captors so she could be displayed and sold for money.*' He wondered why the Americans had sent an example of a white slave of the Greek revolution and not a black slave as was still the case over there. They must have had their reasons to want to remind the world that slaves came in different shapes, sizes and colours? And ages?

Of course, there she was! The girl he hadn't been able to find; she stood right in front of him. Sold to men for their pleasure and sent abroad. Suddenly it dawned on him that, like the girl in stone, the girls he had been looking for had perhaps vanished to foreign parts, never to be seen again. He stared at the sculpture until he was pushed aside by some disgruntled visitors who also wanted a look.

What if these girls were no longer in England; how was he ever going to find the truth? Did anybody care, apart from a few desperate family members?

He headed for the exit; seeing the others stare at this young vulnerable girl in marble flesh brought to life her helplessness. Despite her dignified face cut out in stone, she suffered and she needed to be rescued. She needed him. *They* needed him – Mary H., Margaret B., Lisa P., Victoria T., Gladys P.: the missing children whose rescue he had become responsible for.

A sense of urgency overcame him, and along with it a moment of clarity: to get what he wanted he needed to adjust his focus and change his plans for that day. He needed to organise an extra visit.

Chapter 21

11 August 1851, Cowes

'He is sending us out like errand boys?'

'Please, James, leave it.'

'That's exactly the sort of behaviour that is making me want to go home.' James snorted loudly. 'Not once during these last weeks has he acknowledged the sacrifices we've made to be here. We both left our businesses and our employees behind in America. Not to mention the personal labours we put in to get the boat in as fit a condition as possible. But he has no qualms using us as his messengers.'

'At least he's acknowledged that we are the best people to judge what we need for the flying jib boom he wants.'

'That's another thing – does she really need that to go faster? You know Captain Brown isn't very happy with the fact he has to sail with it, God willing.'

'Well, if you feel we should head for home, then it's even more important that we ensure the Captain gets the best materials to work with once we're gone. What's more, hopefully we can come to a beneficial arrangement with the sparmaker, surely that'll appeal to you.'

'If all that we will be getting on a race is the flying jib boom and a sail, I still don't see the point in us hanging around,' James complained. 'I've lost enough money as it is – I need to go back to work.'

They were on their way into Cowes to get a jib boom and new sail and James had told John to come along, together with Henry, one of his sons. The brothers were walking in front, and James made no attempt to hide his disregard for the Commodore. It surprised John they were talking about leaving.

'By the way, I've told him what I think of him.' James sounded complacent.

'You did what?' George stopped in the middle of the narrow high street.

'After Henry and little George found the stateroom door locked again, which meant, as you know, they couldn't get into bed, I confronted him and told him he was a damned old hog.'

'Oh no, you didn't!' George raised his hands in exasperation.

'Well, I did. He was basically accusing us of thieving – why did he have to lock the door otherwise?'

'How did he react?'

'He told me he'd locked the room because he had some things in it and he was afraid some of the men would take them.'

'He's probably wondering where his wine is disappearing to. May I remind you that we have indeed been taking some of that?'

'Well, if he'd only treated us to some as a thank you for our hard and enduring work, we wouldn't have felt the need to take it ourselves, would we? And as long as we're here, I'm not going to hand the key to the wine locker back.' James walked on, adding loudly, 'And if he says anything about it to either of us, he'll get hell, or something worse.'

John sneaked a glance at Henry but he didn't seem to be bothered by his father's outburst; he was probably used to his candour.

They continued to weave through the winding streets of Cowes, encountering the numerous passengers who had just disembarked from the steam-packet that had recently arrived from Southampton.

'Who are we going to meet?' John asked Henry.

'Michael Ratsey. He's part of a family of shipbuilders. My uncle and papa met him yesterday. Hopefully he can make the spar for us.'

They arrived at a shipbuilding yard, just off the main street. As he entered, it was the smell of the wood that John noticed first;

freshly cut planks were lying near the saw mill, ready for use in a new ship. It wasn't simply the familiar smell, there were the noises as well: the hammering and the sawing, together with the seagulls flying overhead. None of them anything special, but together they triggered a strong sensation. John closed his eyes: he was back home on the East river. He hadn't set foot in a shipyard for almost two months yet it was as if he had never left.

'Mr Ratsey, good to see you again. Thank you for making time for us at such short notice.'

John felt embarrassed as the other men greeted each other; he was glad that they hadn't noticed him daydreaming.

'You're most welcome. I'm honoured you have chosen our yard to do the work.'

'Well, you convinced us at dinner. The food was marvellous. And you know we've been seeing more of your brother-in-law Underwood lately, as he'll probably be doing some work for us as a pilot. You'll be pleased to hear he's been very complimentary about the quality of your work,' James said teasingly.

'He had better be.' Mr Ratsey grinned.

'We're hoping we can achieve a good deal on this jib boom.' James was ready to do business.

'Let me show you what we have first. Gentlemen, please follow me into the saw mill.'

George and Henry followed him across the yard, but James held back and turned to John. 'No need to come inside; perhaps you'd like to have a look around and see how ships are built in England.'

Appreciatively, John watched James disappear into the building. James would never let a chance slip by to make sure he stayed ahead of the competition. Was he supposed to spy on the English shipbuilders? He couldn't believe James thought they could learn anything new from the English, but he was happy enough to stay away from any negotiations conducted by James.

It was a lovely day and John strolled around the yard, which was much smaller than William Brown's back home. But because of the lack of space, the buildings were efficiently arranged around the site.

A boat was being built near the water's edge and to John's surprise a roof had been constructed to protect the workers from the weather. He couldn't believe there was a lot of snowfall on the island, but perhaps rain forced them to seek shelter. He looked with envy at the men who could work protected against the elements, remembering Elsie asking him about it once, suggesting that they would save much time every winter morning if they didn't have to remove the snow.

There was no time to let his thoughts drift as James's voice boomed down the yard. 'At least you are more into betting than the rest of them.'

'How could I not be? I wouldn't be a good shipbuilder if I weren't naturally curious about innovative designs. I would love to see your yacht race.'

'I'm pleased to hear you agree with my brother's proposal. We'll bet you the price of the boom that we can beat any boat you can name if we have a race.'

'All right, I nominate the schooner *Beatrice*.'

'Not one of your own?'

'*Aurora*? No, too small, I'll stick with *Beatrice*. Which reminds me about something I've been meaning to ask you about your yacht.'

'Please, go ahead.'

'Most of the yachts around here have been built so that whoever sails them for longer periods of time can do so in comfort. How did you manage to spend three weeks in her?'

'You mean she looks uncomfortable?'

'I would say economical?'

George laughed. 'Despite the way she looks, she has ample space below decks and is extremely pleasant to live in. John here is the skilful master of utilising space – ask him if you want to know how he did it.' He shook Ratsey's hand. 'I insist you visit and see her for yourself.'

'Maybe I will.'

'Let's visit the sail-maker straight away; I suggest we place a similar bet with him,' said George enthusiastically as he led the men out of the yard. The brothers were clearly in better spirits than when they'd arrived; perhaps their threat to leave England had been just that, a threat.

Chapter 22

Frank felt he could sleep for days; the excursion to London had drained him of all energy. The visit to the Crystal Palace had been tiring but it wasn't the main cause for the turmoil he'd experienced following his return; the visits after leaving the Exhibition were mostly to blame.

However, he had no time to dwell on them now. He had to direct his attention to more current matters, such as the forthcoming trip Harold had alluded to the moment he had set foot in the office.

Harold had explained that McIlroy had been remarkably excited about Frank's work of late and had promised to give them some time off to go on another trip. According to McIlroy, Frank's articles were gaining momentum, especially since one had made it all the way into a New York paper. Harold repeated McIlroy's stipulation that the focus should be on the American yacht from now on, instead of the Exhibition, because this race could become the story of the decade – just as Frank had been doing all along, Harold added quickly. He concluded by saying that, while Frank had been away in London, he'd been asked by McIlroy to use his sailing connections and he was pleased to say that he'd obtained an invitation to a dinner with the American designer of the yacht.

Before Frank had a chance to ask how Harold had managed that, Harold threw in the last bit of news: that they would be taking a ferry on Monday to the Isle of Wight. Frank couldn't get a word in as Harold rambled on, explaining how they could use their time on the Island well since the regattas were about to start, and how perhaps they could visit the American yacht as a lot of people seemed to have done already.

He completely ignored Frank's fragile relationship with boats, and brushed away Frank's concern that they were unlikely to get any lodgings at this late hour; Harold had pulled some more strings and had found them a neat little place not far from Cowes.

'Then I can see no reason for not going.' Frank tried to sound as sincere as possible.

Against all expectations, the boat journey wasn't the disaster Frank had predicted it would be. And when he admitted it, Harold was glad to take the glory. 'I'm pleased I helped you to get over your fear of water.'

'Don't get ahead of yourself; I still wouldn't venture out of my own accord.'

'Well, you don't have to for the next few days. I think you'll enjoy your visit to the Island. At least there's no cooking to be done this week; I heard our landlady is an excellent cook. We're here.'

They'd arrived at a quaint little cottage, slightly up a hill to the southwest of Cowes. It was strangely quiet and peaceful considering the town was so close. They walked through the decorative gate onto the path leading to a freshly painted black front door. Around the door, red roses crept up the wall and along it, purple lavender bushes were interspersed with white daisies.

'Very nice,' Frank mumbled, admiring the idyllic setting.

At the same moment, a little girl opened the front door, gave the men one look, and yelled, 'Aunt Alexandra, they're here!'

They heard a hushed voice of a woman and the little girl opened the door wider. 'Would you please come in, gentlemen?' The words were clearly whispered in her ear and the men had to suppress a laugh.

'Please, if we may, young lady.' Harold touched his hat and bowed to the girl, who started to giggle.

The men entered a fresh-smelling hallway where a woman stood waiting for them, smiling pleasantly.

'I'm teaching my niece here the art of welcoming guests.' The woman put her hand on the girl's shoulder. 'We're not quite there yet. Welcome to Rose Cottage, gentlemen. I'm Ms Alexandra Davies, and we are glad you've arrived safely at our home.' She gently nudged her niece's back. 'And this is my niece – Abigail?'

The girl performed a quick curtsey and spoke in a tiny voice. 'May I show you to the garden for a fresh cup of tea?' She looked nervously up at her aunt, who discreetly raised one eyebrow. 'Gentlemen, please?' the girl quickly added.

'We could definitely do with a refreshment, couldn't we, Frank?'

'If you would like to follow Abigail to the garden, I'll make sure your luggage is placed in your rooms.'

Frank and Harold followed the girl through the hallway to the back of the house and through some tall doors onto a paved seating area in the garden. The garden was of a modest size but contained a vast array of different plants. *That couldn't have been an easy feat*, Frank thought; although the area was sheltered from the worst of the sea winds, there was no escaping the salty air.

They sat down at a table on which a tea service was arranged together with a bowl of fruit and several plates covered with a cloth.

'Tea will be with you shortly.' Abigail turned on her heel and disappeared into the house.

'Charming,' Frank said appreciatively. 'How did you manage this, considering how busy it is?'

'Archie recommended it; apparently the owner has just started to rent out some rooms, so we could well be her first guests.'

'I see. Well, so far so good.' He got up and walked to the end of the sloped garden; if he stood on his toes he could just peer over the hedge and see the sea in the distance. He was slowly coming to terms with the fact that the ocean was always nearby in this part of England.

He walked past the flowerbeds and admired the arrangements of colours and textures. He took a deep breath; the sweetness of the flowers combined with the smell of fresh grass under his feet made him feel light-headed and sleepy; he was looking forward to the clean sheets of his new bed. He looked back longingly at the house. Viewed from the garden, the cottage was much bigger than one's first impression from the lane. He counted what must be several rooms on the first floor. He had been somewhat worried that he'd have to share a room with Harold, especially when it seemed the landlady had family staying as well, but now he felt assured he wouldn't have to. The sound of the rattling of a teapot reminded him of the strong cup of tea awaiting him. At the table, he saw an unfamiliar woman pour the tea and uncover the serving dishes to reveal a cake and a plate of scones. She was explaining to Harold what was on the table and, from Harold's reaction, Frank gathered she must be an attractive lady. When she turned around to look for him, Frank stopped in his tracks: not only a pretty face, but also a familiar one. Where had he seen her before? He couldn't place her and just in time he realised it must seem odd for him to be staring at her like that.

'Frank, come over, don't let your tea get cold. You won't believe the size of these wonderful scones. By the way, this is Abigail's mother, Ms Josephine Wicks; may I introduce my colleague Frank Grundy?'

'Nice to meet you, Sir. I understand you have met my daughter; I hope she hasn't been too impudent.'

'She's been a delight and takes her role very seriously.'

'Ah yes, my sister is teaching her some etiquette – at least it keeps her occupied.' She collected the dish covers. 'I'll be in the kitchen if there is anything else I can do for you.'

'Thank you, it looks delicious.'

The moment that Josephine was out of sight, Harold turned to Frank. 'What was that about, you staring at her like that? You almost scared her.'

'Did I? I didn't mean to, I've seen her before, but I can't remember exactly when – it gave me a little jolt.'

'Really? Not a fluttering butterfly?' Harold said mockingly. 'She didn't seem to recognise you, so it can't have been a momentous occasion for her, unless she'd a reason to hide it.' He winked.

'Don't be a fool.'

'Anyway, clearly not as memorable as these scones. Tuck in, my friend.'

It bothered him he couldn't remember where he had seen her before; he prided himself on having a good memory for faces and names. But it was as if his recollection of the events from the last tumultuous years was becoming increasingly imprecise.

Although he hadn't forgotten what Scarlet looked like; his recent visit to her had reminded him of her beauty.

He had turned up without warning. First, he'd watched the house from across the alley and after he saw some clients leave, he had slipped in. Listening to the sounds behind her closed door, he'd made sure she was on her own before he let himself in. He expected her to be displeased with his sudden appearance but she didn't look surprised to see him.

'Excuse me for a moment.' She spoke softly, but this time not with the childlike voice. She turned her back to him, pulling the cotton gown more tightly around her naked body.

'Of course.' He stood in the corner of the room, watching her disappear behind a screen. 'Do you want me to come back later?' He asked the question but wasn't genuinely interested in her answer; he wasn't going to leave the room.

'No, just give me a moment.'

If she had been worried about his presence, she didn't let it show. The only concern she had was whether anybody had seen him come in. What amazed him even more was that she instantly knew who he was; their last contact had been more than eighteen months ago.

He looked at the elongated shadows she created on the wall; an arm rose above the screen, followed by its silhouette on the wall. The candlelight gave her soft pale skin a gentle glow and he imagined the strands of her hair sticking to the slightly moist skin. He felt weak at his knees; the hot room didn't help and he had to sit down. He found a rickety chair near the door and watched the play of shadows from there. Pieces of fabric were carefully pulled off the top of the screen. She adjusted her hair; two elbows rising above the screen, busy fingers taming the hair into a messy bun. He recognised her little routine, but this was the first time he didn't feel in a hurry to get out; he wasn't going to leave without some answers.

'I'm glad you're still here.' Frank sounded hoarse; he needed to stay alert, persuade her to cooperate.

She let out a haughty laugh. 'I thought you'd wish me to be somewhere else.'

'Of course.' He added apologetically, 'I meant I'm pleased to see you looking well. Are you?'

'What do you think?' She sounded sharp.

'Sorry, I...' He hesitated for a moment, not knowing what to say. 'How are the other girls in the house?'

'They're fine, the usual. Some go, some new ones arrive, but most of us are still here.' She appeared from behind the screen, wearing a striking green dress. He couldn't stop himself from looking her over; she'd changed from the last time he'd seen her. Gone was the child-like creature, and instead a slightly older girl – or should he say a seductive young woman – stood in front of him, with a soft and more voluptuous body instead of the flat chest of a child. It was still difficult to guess her age, even though her young girl alter-ego seemed to have disappeared.

He wondered if she ever showed herself like this to her regular clientele, the ones that came to her for her childlikeness. Or had things changed and had she grown out of it?

'Should I ask you why you're here, since you've come without an invitation?'

'Last time I was here, I asked you about my daughter and her friend.'

She looked at him compassionately; just as she had on previous occasions. Could she really have no knowledge of young girls doing the same work as she did? It seemed terribly unlikely

– unless his hunch that they'd left the country had something to do with it.

When they had met before, he had told Scarlet a similar story as the one he'd told Rose: how he was looking for a young daughter and a friend of hers. And how somebody had suggested they might have ended up in Scarlet's neighbourhood and were too ashamed to come home. He had left out his presumption that they were being held against their free will. Scarlet had told him then that the names didn't mean anything to her, as girls would come and go and they hardly ever kept their own name in the business, anyway.

'Yes, I remember; did you find them?'

'No, that's why I'm here – to ask you some more questions.'

'I'm sorry, I don't have time for this. My next customer will be here shortly and if all you want to do is ask me some more questions, I have to ask you to leave, before anybody sees you here.' Her voice had changed - harsher and impatient, and her delicate features had hardened. He had been naive to think a teary story about a missing young daughter would win her over.

He felt a pang of guilt; he had a suspicion that she was reluctant to say anything out of fear for her own safety. The man in the bar, who seemed to be her agent, was probably connected somehow to the young girls and Frank didn't want to get her in any kind of trouble. But he was mindful that, if he didn't convince her this time to help him, he stood no chance of ever finding out the truth. He hadn't come to find out how much she knew or how deeply she was involved.

He glanced over at her; she was still standing on the same spot, but she was no longer upright. Instead, with eyes willing him to leave, she had put one arm on a chair to support herself. She looked tired and concerned, lost in her own thoughts.

He reminded himself of the promise he'd made to one of the mothers: to give a voice to her daughter, because she could not speak for herself. And when his eyes had adjusted themselves to the darkness of the velvet tent, and he'd realised he was looking at one of the girls, he knew it was his job to give it his best and perhaps last shot.

Scarlet had to understand that, by helping him, he was helping her. He had arrived too late to save the child she'd once been, but he was in a position to defend the innocence of many nameless others who would be forced to follow in her footsteps after she could no longer satisfy the needs of a perverted few.

'I cannot leave, I need your help. It's important and considering the condition you're in, it should be of interest to you as well.'

'Why would I wish to hear anything you have to say?' She sat down at her dressing table and started fiddling with her boots, showing disregard for his presence.

'Because the girls I mentioned to you weren't rebellious silly young women or desperately poor – no, these girls were loved by their parents and some of them were not even eleven years of age when they went missing.'

'And this has occupied you for all that time? I'm sorry, I just don't see why you should bother about a few cases. Besides, are you sure these so-called grieving parents don't know where their darling daughters have ended up?'

She seemed oddly cold and strangely indifferent to what he'd just revealed. Her last remark confused him. He had seen the advertisements and the anguish of the parents. Why would she say such a thing? Frank was getting impatient. 'Did you not hear what I said? These girls were like infants, much younger than you. They didn't have a choice like you.' He had said it without thinking.

She reacted furiously. 'Where do you think I started out?' Her eyes sparked. 'I was as young as they were. My only good fortune was that I continued to look young, so they kept me here instead of –' She stopped abruptly.

The words "good fortune" dripped with such scorn that Frank thought he could taste it in his mouth. Distracted, he almost missed her reference to how she was kept. His mind was racing;

what was her role in this? Did she know more? He wiped his brow with his handkerchief, he was hot. And worried that if he confronted her, he would definitely leave empty-handed.

'I'm sorry, Scarlet, that was very inconsiderate of me, I didn't realise. What I was trying to say is that I worry that these girls were taken against their own free will and sold to men abroad.'

She avoided looking at him while she spoke. 'Are you sure about that? I've heard that some of them are being sold by their parents, so I'd look into those tears if I were you.'

Frank tried not to look shocked by that. Perhaps she did know more about who lured the young girls to wherever they ended up, but clearly she wasn't going to share that with him. And without finding a girl, he had one last option.

'I came here today hoping you could tell me more about the men who choose to visit them.' He held the back of his chair to steady himself; his head was spinning. 'It could very well be that you, Scarlet, are one of the few to have seen these men up close.'

'I don't see why I would have encountered these men.' She sounded sullen and evasive.

Frank watched her face; something in her eyes convinced him that she knew more about the arrangements, and her failure to help started to annoy him. 'For goodness' sake, woman, you dress up like a child! And that's what these men are after: a particular kind of girl, a child. And if these girls are not available, the men are sent to you or to Rose. She told me you worked together for a while. Come on, Scarlet, this can't come as a surprise to you.' He almost shouted the last words, suddenly doubtful that the information would touch her in any way; perhaps her work had left her heartless.

'Did you talk to Rose?'

'Yes, and she told me I reminded her of some men who had visited you both a few times. Because of the similar way we spoke and dressed. I want you to think back; what do you remember about them? Where did they come from? What were their names?' He knew he was holding onto a thread, but it was the only option left to him: having her clients lead him to the men grooming the girls.

'I want to stay out of it, I have to think of my own safety. For all I know I'm already in trouble because of you being here.' Her voice was unnaturally low with a tremor in it.

'Don't worry, nobody saw me come in. Just like the last time I came to visit you. I did so on my own initiative.' He didn't dare to tell her there had been another time after that; it had been the day he got arrested before he'd set foot in her door, but this was not the time to bring that up.

'I know you've been let down by a lot of people when you were younger, and unfortunately I can't change that, but you know as well as I do that it won't be long before you won't be able to do what you do right now, because even you can't stop time and remain young forever. And you know there will be a young girl somewhere who will be forced to take your place. Or worse, she'll be taken abroad. That child could be my daughter, or yours. She needs help – our help.'

Frank saw Scarlet's face blush a deep red and he thought he saw a tear well up in her eyes. She managed to contain herself and with a tremble in her voice she said, 'You need to promise me you'll never mention you've met me.'

'Whatever you tell me will stay between these walls, I promise.'

'What is it you want from me?'

'Rose told me there was something odd about the men who visited you.'

'I'm sorry, I don't recall much about them.' She started to pace up and down. 'Perhaps Rose meant to say they were not like our usual customers.'

'Why was that?'

'Just like she said – better-dressed and eloquent, but also young and arrogant. Ones who would ordinarily choose to go to Mayfair rather than Soho.'

'Go on, anything else you remember?'

'Not much, apart from them being a welcome change. They

said they were planning to talk to our agent, because they were looking for beautiful girls like Rose and me to take on their travels. We joked about them, that they would be our princes on white horses who would finally rescue us from this dreadful place.' She sighed. 'We talked for hours about where we were going to live, the four of us, after our liberation. Somewhere on the coast, in a small cottage with pink roses around the front door.' She shook her head, looking embarrassed. 'I know, it was silly to think that. Of course, after a while we never saw them again. They must have found their girls elsewhere,' she added despondently.

Frank didn't know what to say; *how could she be so naïve?* 'I'm sorry things didn't work out the way you wanted them to.' He realised too late what a stupid remark it was, but he couldn't help feeling sad for her and the loss of the different life she'd envisaged.

'They never do. Things are changing anyway. As you said, I'm getting older.'

Frank hadn't thought it through; what would happen if she lost her usual clientele? But he shouldn't let himself get distracted. 'Did these men know each other?'

'They arrived on the same day and at the same time and after their time spent in here, they would leave together. We would watch them meet up in the street below before they disappeared out of view. The short, skinny guy would visit Rose, and I would get the smooth talker, the arrogant young one with floppy hair – of course!'

She jumped up suddenly. Startled, Frank watched her cross the room with long strides, her hair, now completely undone, flowed behind her like the bushy tail of a cat in pursuit of its prey. A faint smell of powder drifted towards Frank as she opened a set of drawers along the back wall of the room. She picked up a trinket box and started to rummage through its contents.

'Mine gave me a card, which I saved.' Embarrassed, she added, 'Because one never knows.' Impatiently she turned the box upside down. 'Somewhere in here,' she murmured with irritation.

Frank came closer. *Could there be a card with a name?*

'Here it is!' Triumphantly she held up a calling card and they both peered eagerly at the small piece of paper. 'No name.'

'Just some initials, several of them.'

'No address – what's the point?' she complained. 'Why did I keep it?'

She handed it over to Frank with a disapproving look on her face. 'You have it, I don't want it.'

He heard the disillusionment in her voice; the card had meant more to her than it was actually worth. Angrily she threw the other bits back into the box.

'All the same,' she mumbled. 'No difference between the ones with fancy clothes or the ones in rags, the ones with posh double-barrelled names or the ones called John Smith; all of them full of promises, never to be kept.' She slammed the box into the corner.

'He wasn't called John Smith then?' The moment he said it, he regretted it; it wasn't the time for frivolity. 'Sorry, I didn't mean to make light of the situation, I know you are upset.'

Scarlet stared at him with big eyes and wide-open mouth; Frank was ready for a torrent of abuse, but instead she exclaimed, 'Of course, now I remember, a double-barrelled name!'

'Are you sure?'

'Yes, these rich men; they both had double-barrelled names.'

'Do you remember what they were?'

'Not exactly.' She frowned. 'But I do remember we joked about it.'

'Who? About what?'

'Rose and me. Whenever they would leave together, we could hear them say their goodbyes outside in the little lane, with their plummy voices.' Scarlet tried her most upper-class voice and said, 'Darling friend. Farewell weakling.'

Frank looked at her in confusion. 'Those are not names, I presume?'

'No, of course not, but they sounded like that and we turned them into – never mind, I can't recall them precisely, sorry, but I hope this will help you, I really do.'

Frank didn't have the heart to tell her how many people carried double-barrelled names and how many of these were quite similar.

'I hope so too.' He faltered for a moment, looking at the young woman in front of him, her cheeks flushed red and her eyes bright and alive with passion. 'Can I ask you one more thing?'

'Yes.'

'What is your real name?'

'Rebecca.'

'That's beautiful. Rebecca, don't ever doubt whether you've made the right decision today to help me; you have. Not only for yourself, but also for a lot of young girls – some not even born yet, like the child you're carrying. I'll try my very best not to let any of you down.'

Her eyes grew large but he didn't wait for her reaction. Without further delay he walked out of the room, hoping with all his heart he could keep his promise to her and her unborn child and to those grieving parents.

Chapter 23

'The Captain will be going.'

'Really, are you sure about that?' John looked in surprise at Harkness, the first mate.

'They said it's a fete for everybody.'

'Hosted by the Queen? I can't believe that's the case.'

'Well, you'd better start believing it because we're all going,' Comstock added, shrugging his shoulders. 'Are you coming or not?'

It was intriguing how people dealt differently with unsatisfactory situations. John had learned that August the twenty-fourth was the last day of sailing for most of the gentry, after which they would retreat to their estates in the country for the start of the hunting season. And as it was now almost the middle of August, their chance of racing one of the English yachts was diminishing by the day.

But some people just kept on going, regardless how desperate the circumstances appeared to be. Like the Captain, he hadn't stopped preparing for a race. They'd gone out for informal pursuits, chasing down and passing unsuspecting sailing boats, testing the new racing sails.

For others, it was too much to bear. Only a few days ago, John had returned from running an errand ashore to find the state room locked again, meaning that the crew quarters were out of bounds. It had been happening more often, much to James's chagrin, and John was glad there was only Harkness to witness it. He had joked that the Commodore preferred to lock himself in to count the liquor and his betting-money, which was going to take some time as all the money was still there. While John had hovered at the door, he heard some heated voices on the other side. Hamilton was clearly unhappy about something.

'I went to the Club last night and again nothing was said about a match. I'm bored of the dinners and fed up with their lack of candour!'

'I've been assured by their Commodore that our challenges have been received and our message has been sent out to other clubs, but it takes time.' Stevens tried to calm Hamilton down.

'I hope you've told them our period of visit is limited?' Hamilton sounded impatient and added, 'You know they're playing a game with us? They will pretend there isn't enough time to gather a schooner fleet to race against us in the English Channel because, actually, they have nothing suitable. And you know why that is, don't you?' There was a short pause, after which Hamilton spurted out, 'Because their boats are made for seasick-prone owners with no real taste for the sea, who hardly ever lift their anchor and if they do it's to make a short trip to Hurst Castle or to stay even closer to the Island!'

He stopped to catch his breath and continued with a final push. 'We will *not* enter her for one of the Cups in a race around the Island, because that's what they want us to do and everyone knows the course is notoriously unfair to strangers!'

'Don't forget that some of the gentlemen of our party want to make their expenses after coming so far.'

'I'm sure these Brits are willing to give us thousands of pounds as long as we would go off about our business.'

Stevens laughed at Hamilton's remark.

'I wouldn't laugh if I were you; I'm quite certain that if they do give us a race for a Cup it won't be accompanied by a bet. I suggest we go home.' Hamilton said angrily. A long silence ensued.

'Come on, Colonel, you should know better than anybody that the more we are tested, the more we triumph; it's in our nature. Besides, I've already let the yacht club in Ryde know we would like to enter for their race around the Island unless we get our latest challenge accepted.'

'I wouldn't rely on our latest challenge bringing us what we're hoping for. I'm afraid that our proposal to run *America* against all kind of yachts, not just schooners, will only attract undesirables. I heard a Squadron member has come forward who is willing to race us in his enormous iron schooner.' Hamilton's contempt was obvious.

'Yes, the owner of *Titania* has accepted our challenge for a match race.'

'Why? She stands no chance of winning against us! If the owner is doing it to save the reputation of the other members of the Squadron, he needs to be told there is no point as beating her would be no proof of our superiority.'

'I'm worried there won't be many more offers; I think our willingness to bet £10,000 hasn't done us any favours. It has left the majority of Englishmen astonished, I heard, and we've probably given them even more reason to be so evasive.'

There was a silence after which Stevens suggested hesitatingly. 'I know you don't want this, nor do the rest of us, but perhaps we should consider joining the Squadron regatta, in addition to the one at Ryde. I know it isn't always the best test of the merits of vessels engaged in it, but if that's the only way to get an official record of us beating them, so be it.'

'You are right about one thing; the fact as to whether they can beat us, or we them, ought to be a matter of public record, not a private opinion. Nevertheless, it should be on fairer ground.'

'I agree, but we no longer have the luxury of being critical, so I've taken the liberty of preparing ourselves for such a course. I have had our dear Consul Croskey find us an English pilot to guide us safely through the tides and shoals. I'm also looking into supplementing our crew with some extra hands on deck.'

'Do you think we can trust an English pilot? Shouldn't we get a second one to oversee him? By the way, I regret to say our crew is not infused with any sort of order. The fact is that some of them are too much chums of the Captain and George. And the latter and his brother James seem to consider themselves visitors.'

'Leave that to me, I'll have to have a talk to them anyway about the flying jib they have arranged for us.'

Without any explanation to the crew, the syndicate pulled out of the race they were supposed to compete in at Ryde. The sudden decision left the men baffled and added to their restlessness. But they weren't the only ones dissatisfied with the state of affairs. A day after their discussion, word was circulating that Mister George and James were arranging for their return to New York by steamship. It was said they were no longer prepared to wait for a possible English offer for a suitable race. But John knew that George didn't want to stay to witness his yacht being tested in tidal waters around the Island and in lighter winds, as he'd told him that the qualities of the hull should be tested, not the skill of the pilot.

Someone suggested that the reason behind their departure was their deteriorating relationship with the Commodore, but whatever it was the atmosphere on board the yacht had sunk to a new low. Their rumoured departure sounded the death knell for any remaining hope of seeing a fulfilling end to their venture.

Even the Captain's mood had changed noticeably; he couldn't conceal his displeasure with the decisions made by the syndicate and he was heard mumbling how they didn't need a wretched flying jib. He chose to completely ignore the possible departure of his friends.

Perhaps an evening of light entertainment was the only sensible thing left to do, especially if the invitation was sent out by the Royal Family.

John sat back in the cockpit, wondering who else was going.

'Have you made up your mind; are you coming or not?'

Comstock had scrubbed up well for the party, just like the rest of the crew, but John was still not in the mood.

'If not, can you row us over and pick us up later?'

'Sure. What about George and James?' It seemed unlikely the

brothers were going to show their faces at a party. James would be a liability; he could never keep quiet about what he felt was a gross injustice.

'They have their own dinner somewhere in Cowes, I believe, but will be staying in their hotel.'

'I see.' It was possibly one of their last dinners on the Island before an eventual return home. John still didn't think it could be true; he saw George as a role model. He had seen him as a sturdy oak tree amongst the fraternity of shipbuilders; standing strong and tall while watching over the horizons in the distance, wondering what lay beyond and which boat would get there first. John remembered how George had told him in France never to be afraid to take risks, which included designing at least one leaky boat. For all this time, he had believed that George didn't fear taking a wrong turn, but now it seemed he was trying to stay clear of a possible defeat. As if he was afraid of being damaged by an oncoming storm.

But how could he walk away now? However small the chance, there was still the prospect of glory. John had set his hopes on it.

Perhaps I'm cut from a different wood than George, John thought wryly. *More flexible, and therefore easily guided by the wind.*

Or could it be that, whilst they were both on the move, George was the only one who knew where he was heading?

Chapter 24

14 August 1851, Cowes

Frank now remembered where he had seen Josephine before! Harold had teased him mercilessly, but it had been Archie who had come to his rescue.

They had been visiting Cowes where the quay had been covered with a sea of people; the bustle of the place was reminiscent of that of a busy port.

Along the waterfront, people were parading in the warm summer sun. However, the principal spectacle was taking place out at sea. Bobbing on the water, just outside the harbour, were countless boats: steam packets, private yachts and every other type of vessel, the flags in the masts adding to the feeling of festivity. Small rowing boats filled with men and women were being rowed to and from the moored ships.

They had been admiring *America* in all her splendour from a distance when Harold had spotted Archie in the crowds.

'You've arrived!' Archie greeted them warmly. 'Are you enjoying yourself thus far?'

'Yes, surprisingly so. Harold was just trying to explain to me who some of the owners of those yachts are.' Frank pointed to the scene in front of them. 'Rich gentlemen with a keen interest in sailing who live on the south coast or in London and come down to their yachts a few weekends in the summer.'

'Not quite like that. Some spend rather more time on their yachts,' Archie corrected Frank.

'Yes, while being anchored in the safety of the harbour, like a floating lodging house.' Even with his fear of water, Frank found the idea of having a boat built to store it in the safety of a harbour somewhat peculiar. 'I assume one doesn't have to be able to sail to become a member of the Squadron, just have a good crew and enough money.'

Archie opened his mouth to say something, but Harold beat him to it. 'What an excellent find, old chap, the lodging house you recommended.' He slapped Archie appreciatively on the shoulder. 'I think we've met most of the family by now, lots of children, but luckily well behaved.'

'Yes, unexpectedly quiet,' Frank concurred. 'How do you know them and how come we haven't seen any husbands?'

'There are no husbands,' Archie replied. 'Alexandra Davies is the spinster sister of Josephine Wicks and our families are acquainted. The children are all Josephine's who became a widow about a year ago.'

'How tragic.'

'Yes, sad story indeed, not easy to forget. It happened last November – you'll remember that storm on the coast? And those fishermen who died trying to rescue passengers on a boat that got stranded in the bad weather?'

Harold nodded slowly, but Frank exclaimed, 'That's her, of course!'

Both men looked at Frank in surprise. 'What do you mean?'

'I told you she looked familiar, didn't I?' But before he could explain further, their attention was drawn to some commotion on the water.

'What's all that about?' Bursts of laughter and snippets of lively conversations drifted in over the water. They watched the activity near the hull of *America* with interest; visitors were arriving and being picked up in a constant stream. It seemed she had turned into a fairground attraction.

'How bored the crew must be, having to clean the deck every day for all those visitors,' Frank commented.

'Not as bored as you think; I've heard that the American crew is enjoying themselves by telling anybody who comes along there's a secret compartment in the yacht they're not allowed to open.

They're doing nothing to dispel the rumour that they have been hiding some sort of propeller beneath the hull.'

Frank laughed. 'I suppose it's hard to believe her speed is being aided by just the wind. Perhaps we should check it out ourselves, tell them we're important reporters from a small but keen newspaper in the South of England?'

'You won't be the first ones,' Archie answered. 'The American designer is becoming a bit of a public figure. People are eager to know more about his design, and some prefer to talk to him instead of the owner.'

'That can't sit well with Commodore Stevens,' Frank mused.

'You can ask the designer all about his relationship with the syndicate at dinner tomorrow, but first things first, gentlemen. I'm thirsty – what about a drink somewhere? I've found out where the crew get their drinks, which from a journalistic point of view must be of interest to you.'

'I'm sure Harold will join you, Archie, but I was more thinking about my bed in the cottage.'

On his way back to the cottage, he thought about what Archie had told them about Josephine. After the disaster in Worthing, the Benevolent Society had received an extraordinary amount of money from people all over the country, given with strict instructions to help out the widows of the courageous fishermen. Josephine had apparently used her share to come over to the Island to be near her sister and together they decided to start taking in guests.

He remembered his visit to the village clearly and how useless he had felt afterwards. He had resorted to writing an emotional piece on how he'd been witness to the grief bestowed on the wives and the children, left behind to fend for themselves, describing in detail how the screams of their profound loss had cut through the oppressive atmosphere in the street.

After his request to donate money had been printed in their local paper, he'd contacted Bill and suggested he'd do the same to reach a larger audience. He hadn't been hopeful about the outcome of his appeal, but it seemed that he'd been wrong.

The sleep that had followed that night was peaceful; Frank felt rejuvenated and ready for the dinner Archie had organised for him and Harold. The decision the previous evening not to follow Harold and Archie to a pub had been the right one. He was clear-headed and relaxed, which couldn't be said of Harold.

'That must have been quite an afternoon and evening; I haven't seen much of you today. You're one dark horse, Harold.'

'I don't know how it happened. I didn't think I had that much to drink.' He touched his head as if to check if it was still there.

'Don't know or can't remember?'

'Oh, I do remember… some things,' Harold added.

Frank laughed out loud. 'Who kept buying you these drinks you really didn't want?'

'Archie decided to take me to this watering hole where the boatmen of Cowes go to quench their thirst.'

'A proper sailor's booze up.'

'Indeed; I should have known better. My god, these men can drink.'

'It sounds like I missed a great evening.'

'Doubtful,' Harold said with regret. 'Although you would have found the last pub interesting; there were some English sailors who have been hired by the Americans to crew for them.'

'An English crew?' Frank looked puzzled.

'Yes, for racing they need more men than they brought over, so there will be a partly English crew to help them out. They've even hired an English pilot – in fact someone you met at our club night.'

'But I thought the Americans only wanted to race out in the channel?'

'I think the Americans are slowly starting to realise their conditions for a race are not going to be met.'

'Who told you that?'

'One of the men there last night. Furthermore, they keep adjusting their challenge. The latest one has abandoned the idea of only wanting to sail their schooner against a similar vessel. I think they're finally coming to their senses. There's no use trying to pressurise members of the Royal Yacht Squadron into a race they don't want to run. I predict it won't be long before the Yankees yield to the pressure and agree to whatever is offered to them.'

'Who knows what course the parties involved will decide on? I'm starting to get the impression they are both trying to avoid a confrontation.'

The men made their way through the crowds of another busy evening on the Island. Once more it had been a beautiful day for sailing and it was easy to identify those who had been out on the water; their faces were glowing and their tussles with the wind were being described with gusto, captivating not just the sailing crowds.

'I don't expect everybody tonight to be as happy as them,' Frank said deflatedly, worried about the mood they were going to find the Americans in. 'Who'll be there this evening?' he asked as they neared the tavern.

'Archie's old school friend Stanley along with a few other friends of his who have come over for the sailing. And, hopefully, the American designer and his brother.'

'Sounds like mixed company. How did he manage to organise it? The Americans must be in demand.'

'You know how it works; this island is like a village. Stanley's sister is married into one of the Ratsey families who did some work for the Americans here on the Island. He helped arrange it and should be here as well.' Harold opened the heavy door to the Union Inn. 'And as for the Americans being busy – they get wined and dined by their English peers, but I understand the invitations don't always include the designer of the yacht.'

'The owners get invited, but George needs to entertain himself?'

'You heard Archie the other day. No need to feel sorry for him, he's been getting enough attention.'

Once inside, they were greeted by the landlord and immediately shown to several large tables at the back of the establishment. Everybody seemed to be there except the Americans.

'Are you sure they're coming? You did tell them this was going to be a social occasion, not an official interview?' One of Stanley's friends gave Frank and Harold a sideways glance before continuing. 'Because I can imagine they won't be in the mood for any English reporters.'

'Why is that?' David Ratsey came closer.

'Well, while the Americans have been waiting for someone to take up their challenge to race them somewhere in the Channel, they decided to participate in one of the races of the Ryde regatta – the one around the Island. And the Royal Victoria Yacht Club refused them entry.'

'Why?'

'Because of their rule requiring entrants to have only one owner. Unlike *America*, which is owned by a syndicate. But what a lot of people didn't know was that the Americans withdrew from it at the same time.'

'That doesn't make sense. Did they or didn't they want a race?'

'Of course they wanted to race, but preferably not in a regatta in the notorious waters around the Island, which the Ryde regatta is as well. Here it gets complicated: in the days before that race, the Americans had sent out a new challenge and stipulated it should be taken up before the seventeenth of August, which was supposedly the end of their stay in England.'

'And nobody's reacted to that.'

'Correct. As it got closer to the Ryde regatta, they decided to withdraw, saying they were still waiting for an answer on their latest challenge. And now some reporter has ignored the Club's refusal and has focussed instead on the American withdrawal, calling it a dodging excuse for trying to escape the course round the Island. Because of it, the tide seems to be turning; people are starting to call them cowards for trying to avoid a race altogether.'

'Didn't they race at Ryde informally? And were fastest again?' Harold seemed confused. 'Doesn't that prove a point?'

'That we have nothing – that is, no cutter, schooner or anything alike that could sail against *America*?' Frank listened to the men with curiosity. 'Is it true that we don't have anything suitable? I thought the Squadron had announced back in May there would be a race open to yachts belonging to the Clubs of all Nations.'

The men turned to Frank and started to talk at once. A heated exchange followed, with some arguing that they should have been better prepared.

'I know refitting of some yachts of the Squadron has taken place recently; rigs have been altered and new sails ordered,' David Ratsey volunteered.

'That sounds like a last-minute attempt to give a racehorse a new saddle, whereas they should have trained a new jockey. Or better still, bred a new horse,' Frank grumbled.

'I don't think anybody expected to build something new for the Squadron Regatta. As I understood it, that race wasn't even created with an American participating ship in mind, but more for yachts from a Russian and a Dutch yacht club. And once the Americans arrived at the end of July, they had to work with the horses they had in the stable, so to speak.' David gave Frank a half-smile.

But Frank wasn't ready to join in any jokes.

'The American Government already appealed more than a year ago to send modes of sailing and steam vessels to the Exhibition. And that same year they announced that a very fast yacht schooner was being constructed in New York to be present here in this country during the fair. Surely we had clues as to what was coming? With the reputation of New York pilot boats?' Frank raised his voice and the other men fell silent. 'And what did we do – sew a new sail? Sorry, no offence.' Frank nodded in David's direction. 'I now understand the importance of a good sail, but what it comes down to is that we, although forewarned, were blinded by our arrogance and didn't take it seriously. We never expected our poorer cousins to come up with something so new and innovative.' In a deep, trembling voice, he added, 'And now we don't even have the courage to admit our defeat; only because nobody has the backbone or moral fibre to come forward. I say, if England chooses not to fight, let her be beaten.' And with that he slammed his glass on the table.

The table had gone quiet.

'Whose side are you on?' one of Stanley's friends finally wanted to know.

Harold put his hand on Frank's shoulder. 'I'll tell my friends to be better prepared next time and start building that new yacht early enough.' He patted Frank a few times on his back. 'Now, we'd better cheer up, here they come.'

The Americans had arrived at the tavern. Frank hoped their guests hadn't heard any of his outburst. The two men walked towards them and Frank recognised the younger one as the designer George Steers, which meant the larger man with the lined face had to be his older brother James. They all moved around the table so the men could fit in while Stanley did the introductions.

'I'm extremely pleased you could make it.' He spoke in an official voice. 'I understand you went out sailing again today, so you must be feeling tired from all the wind.'

'Maybe tired, but also hungry. Since I've been able to eat normally again, my appetite has been growing.' George grinned apologetically. 'I'm looking forward to this supper and I would like to take this opportunity to thank you for inviting my brother and me. When it comes to pleasing our stomachs, you have been treating your guests very well.'

The men started laughing, but Frank thought he could detect some sarcasm in George's voice; it was going to be a long evening if nobody was going to discuss the obvious problem there was in the room. He didn't have to worry for long; various conversations were swiftly started up around the table. Stanley and George discussed the different sails being used by the Americans and the English, and animatedly compared the shipbuilding business on the Island and Manhattan. James was entertaining the other men with stories of being on board *America*: how the brothers had never made a crossing like that on a ship before, but how they'd felt secure in the hands of their Captain.

'I see you didn't bring your Captain, the much-admired Richard Brown.' Stanley poured some more wine into James's glass.

'Admired or feared?' James uttered a chortle. 'He sends his apologies. He went to some fete given by your delightful Queen for all sorts of folk.'

'I've heard it's a jolly event; I hope he'll enjoy himself.'

'Yes, I wish him the same – it seems it's the only enjoyment he will be getting.' James's face turned sour.

'James, please.' George's eyes flashed towards his brother. 'Not now.'

'George, why not? Look around the table – these are our friends. I'm sure they would want to hear the true story.'

Did Frank detect the speech of a drunken man?

'And some of these men are reporters working for the finest newspapers in England; maybe they can help us rectify a few misunderstandings printed earlier this week by some of their colleagues.'

'We've come to enjoy ourselves, nobody is interested in hearing you moan, James.'

'Come on, George, I'm sure it's the only reason we're here – to talk about sailing. And besides, in a few days' time we will be on our way home. Do you honestly think I care any longer about the possible impression I leave behind? They can write what they want, but not until I've said what I'd like to say about this catastrophe.' He slammed his fist on the table.

'James!' George's voice sounded firmer and more exasperated.

'It's all right, George, we all know what James is referring to – the unresolved matter.' Stanley tried to calm things down, but James objected to his choice of words.

'Unresolved matter? Hah, nice way of putting it.' James looked provocatively around the table.

'Did you say you're leaving?' Frank cut through the silence.

James looked at George sheepishly. George cleared his throat. 'It's time for us to go back home, to our families and our business. The men working in our shipyard have been without us long enough. We'll leave in a few days, on the seventeenth, to catch a crossing from Liverpool.'

Another silence descended around the table, as each of them tried to take in the implications of what had just been said.

'My dear brother is trying to say we're fed up with waiting. The Commodore can't make up his mind and now we're running out of time.'

'James is right. I've made enough sacrifices to build that yacht, thinking we would be given a fair chance to show off our work. And all we seem to have encountered is opposition.' George shrugged his shoulders.

'We could have predicted resistance from English sailing clubs – but Commodore Stevens! That mean old pig.'

'James! Be quiet now.' George looked warningly at his brother. 'I do apologise, the only thing my brother is guilty of is surrendering to the gloomy moods of most of us on board *America* as well as the people back home.

'So you're giving in?' Frank knew the question was on the minds of most men there.

'You can interpret it in any way you like.' George looked straight at Frank. 'I've been fully committed to this cause and I've created this wonderful yacht as if she were my own child. We've made her out of the best wood and put her together with love, piece by piece; I've celebrated her first steps into the wide world and have even joined her on her first overseas adventure. Do you have children, Mr Grundy?'

'Erm, no, I don't.' Frank looked puzzled.

'Well, let me tell you that there comes a point when you need to stand aside and watch your child go their own way.' He smiled knowingly. 'She's now in the hands of the Commodore and the syndicate.'

'But why leave without seeing her race?' What Frank wanted to say in response was that he would never leave a child to fend for itself, but he knew it wasn't truthful. 'The Squadron's last day of racing is the twenty-second; why not stay for that and race her?'

'Ah, I didn't build her for that, and I have no desire to witness such a contest.' George planted his fork resolutely on the table. 'This is one of the last meals we'll have here, so let's enjoy it, gentlemen.'

The men at the table agreed and the rest of the evening was spent talking as best as they could about neutral topics. The more wine and food arrived at their table, the jollier the atmosphere became and when it was time to go, the men said farewell cheerfully. The Englishmen wished the Americans a good journey back home and the brothers thanked them in return for their hospitality.

Frank shook George's hand and, at the risk of spoiling his good mood, he said softly, 'Tell your Commodore that if he's willing to take his chances to sail her anywhere, he needs to take action promptly, because tomorrow is the last day of registration for the £100 Cup race.'

'Thanks, I'll tell him.' George held his hand firmly. 'You're not a sailor, are you?'

'No, I'm not. To tell you the truth, I very much dislike the sea.'

'Why are you so interested in all of this, then?'

Frank wondered for a moment if they'd heard his outburst after all. 'I used to recognise a good cause when I saw one. I'm convinced you've been treated unfairly and I have the opportunity to do something about it – to write about it.' He realised too late that he'd spoken in the past tense. *Had he made any sense?*

George raised his eyebrows, and a little smile played on his lips. 'The first boat I ever designed sank. It only made me more determined. I guess for some of us it takes longer to discover when something is worth pursuing.' He let go of Frank's hand. 'As for your dislike of the sea, don't waste your time trying to get away from the ocean. It won't let you. It's in the rolling of the waves that our subconscious recognises the cycles of life. Fearing it is like fearing life passing by. Start counting yourself lucky to be near this endless immensity instead. I wish you all the best.'

Frank and Harold's journey back to the cottage was mostly spent in silence. Frank couldn't get George's words out of his head about recognising which causes were worth pursuing. Had he failed to recognise such a cause in the past? Or had he been blinded by one? He had never stopped feeling convinced that he needed to find out what had happened to the missing girls. The injustice done to these vulnerable children was too grave to close one's eyes to. But perhaps the battle had been too big for him? Perhaps it had been one he couldn't win on his own? And by abandoning his research, he'd ended up deserting not only the girls, he'd also walked out on their parents and Agnes, losing himself in the process. Maybe he should have never started the fight.

At the cottage, Frank said goodnight to Harold and retired promptly to his room. But too much food and drink meant that he couldn't fall asleep straight away. He sat down behind the small table he had put into service as his desk and poured himself a glass of water. He watched it swirl against the sides. He thought about George's leaky boat; George believed it was better to start and fail a plan than not to start at all. One needed to persevere to be able to change. Not unlike water that seemingly surrenders to its surroundings, but with time could wear away stone. This wasn't about choosing the wrong fight; it was about not daring to start one.

He got out his pen and ink and laid an empty piece of paper in front of him.

'If England does not choose to fight, let her be beaten.'

His hand hovered above the inkpot; he felt ambiguous about writing 'England'. He could probably substitute it with 'America'.

The memory of the Exhibition crossed Frank's mind; had America already fought and lost? He thought about the farmer and his admiration for the reaping machine. Had he dismissed that too readily? Considering the large fields around his village, such an invention might be enormously valuable to farming. The unsightly device had been overlooked, not only by several of his colleagues, but also by himself. Could it be even more useful than he had thought – perhaps providing the missing link between the Americans' failure and their success?

He smiled broadly while envisaging his next two large editorials, one introducing the most beneficial invention for overworked farmers in the whole of England, handed to them by the Americans, and one shortly after, about why their American brothers and sisters deserved more respect from the public, especially for their latest venture bobbing on the water just outside Cowes.

He thought of another heading for his second article.

'The "America": last minute entry into the battle of the Old against the New World.' Or: *'The yacht as saviour of American national pride.'*

Perhaps it was a gamble on his conviction that most people appreciated a good match and a sense of sportsmanship, but he had to give it a try.

Chapter 25

17 August 1851, Cowes

Harold arrived at breakfast with a big smirk on his face.

'I've just heard from Archie that they've entered!'

When Harold grinned like that he looked even younger than his twenty-eight years.

'Exactly as you told them to do: their last chance!'

Frank raised his fist playfully to demonstrate his delight; finally, the Americans had decided to participate in the last race of the season. He had worried the Americans had missed the registration deadline as there had been so little time. But Archie's informant at the Royal Yacht Squadron had seen Commodore Stevens's letter requesting their participation. At last, it seemed that a race was going to happen.

'The American Commodore has finally admitted defeat considering he will be up against numerous boats all built for sailing inside the waters round the Island.'

Frank had to bite his lip; he was tempted to correct his younger colleague on his one-sighted usage of the word 'defeat', but he didn't feel like debating whose it might be.

'Could still be exciting though,' Harold added optimistically. 'It's a shame I won't be here to witness it.'

'Where are you going?'

'I can't stay until Friday; I promised I would be back by Wednesday.'

Neither of them had mentioned when they'd planned on returning home and if that was the agreement with McIlroy, he would be going home too. Frank felt disappointed.

'I promised my wife. I'm sure McIlroy won't mind you staying longer to cover the race. Let me check with Miss Davies if you can keep your room for the rest of the week.'

'Don't worry, Harold, I'll do it myself, you have your breakfast.' He got up from his chair and wandered into the house. Noises came from the kitchen and through the half-opened door he saw they were all in there, sitting around a large wooden kitchen table: all except for Josephine, whom he found in the garden.

'I didn't realise the house had a vegetable garden.' Frank sounded casual, but he startled her nevertheless. She had been on her knees attending to some weeds. On hearing his voice, she got up as quickly as she could, but her shoe caught the inside seam of one of her skirts and she almost lost her balance. Frank managed to grab one of her arms tightly enough for her not to fall into the vegetable beds and for a moment she stood there breathing heavily, her body leaning against his.

Frank was the first to step back. 'I apologise, I didn't mean to surprise you like that.'

Josephine stared at him with wide eyes, trying to regain her composure while beating her skirts absentmindedly.

'It's all right, I didn't expect anybody out here. I'm just clumsy falling over like that.' Her eyes flashed towards the plants. 'I'm glad you caught me, it would have been a pity to flatten the onions.'

Frank heard a smile in her voice. 'I'm relieved you didn't, although I've no idea which bit of greenery are the onions.'

'As long as you can distinguish between weeds and vegetables, it'll be just fine.' She pointed at the basket on the ground. 'We're making a special dish for your Sunday meal as you'll be leaving in a couple of days – freshly picked by me.'

'Ah, that's one of the reasons I came out here; I was wondering if I could keep my room a few days longer. My colleague will be leaving as planned, but my work here isn't finished yet.'

'I see.'

'I hope it's not inconvenient?'

'Oh no, not at all.' A warm smile spread across her face and for a moment he forgot that she would be like this with all guests. 'But you'd better talk to my sister; she organises the bookings of the rooms.'

'I will.' He wavered, wondering if it was appropriate to stay around a bit longer. 'If you need any help around the garden this week, please let me know. I don't need to work all day, and I would love to help.' The moment he said it he knew it sounded presumptuous. 'Only if you don't mind,' he added quickly. 'I could do with some lessons about onions and carrots.'

'Why, are you planning to grow your own vegetables?'

'Well, perhaps.' Frank thought about the piece of land around his house; he wasn't even sure how big it was, as overgrown as it was. 'Anyway, I'm never too old to learn.'

When he came down for breakfast early Wednesday morning, Harold was waiting in a chair in the hallway, his packed bags at his feet.

'Accompany me to the ferry? There's a special delivery waiting for you. If, that is, I can prise you away from the sister of the proprietor.'

'Don't be a fool, Harold, I'm far too old for her.'

Before he could embarrass Frank even more, Harold got to his feet.

The ferry moved slowly into the harbour; every space on deck was filled with people.

'Look at the amount of people coming this way. I don't think I'll have any problems getting back to Portsmouth Harbour. Don't forget to get that copy; it's an extra edition of our paper. Something you wrote after our dinner with the Americans?'

'Did McIlroy manage to print it already? Even he can get things done quickly if he wants to.'

'Yes, you've got him eating out of your hand nowadays. The papers should be delivered on the quay somewhere for the newspaper boy to collect.'

'Harold?' Frank grabbed the elbow of his colleague before he walked off. 'Thanks again – you've been a great help, together with those sailing chums of yours. I know I've been critical about their clubs, so I haven't been easy company.'

'Don't worry; they say you're all right. Maybe a bit stubborn, but what's new? Anyway, you know where to find them. I'd better get to that ferry.'

They shook hands and Harold walked down the path on the embankment. 'See you in the office!' he shouted to Frank before disappearing into the hustle and bustle on the dock.

Frank raised his hand in a salute; he decided to wait until the arriving crowd had thinned out and the porters had moved the suitcases out of the way. He found himself a wooden bench to sit on, slightly higher, overlooking the jetty. There was something evocative about watching people arrive and depart. Every now and then he would visit Southampton Port on his day off, just as he used to loiter around Waterloo Station after it had opened. It was like leaving without having to leave: "secondary travel", as he called it – not to foreign places, but into other people's lives.

It was something he had mastered while confined to a chair for hours as a child. In the worst periods, when his breathing had become laborious, and his parents had sent him away for a change of air, he would watch the visitors to the seaside town walk past the lawn they had moved him onto. As soon as his breathing improved and he'd started to get bored with the constant sea breeze, he had kept himself occupied with the stories unfolding in front of him. All he had to do was watch carefully and he'd obtain a brief glimpse into these strangers' existences. Some seemed happy to arrive, others sorrowful to leave.

He quickly learned that these travellers were one and the same; they seemed not only to share the desire for a better place, but also the intent not to stay – as if their destination would inevitably turn into the one they were leaving behind.

It was easy to see that most of the people getting off the ferry had come for a few pleasurable days away; happy faces streamed past and lively chats could be heard. These people expected a good time on the Island, and were hoping for some nice weather, a comfortable bed and decent food. He wondered how many of them had been tempted to visit because of his writing.

Frank thought about the next few days. He needed to find out more about the final race. Perhaps Archie could tell him where to go for the best view of it.

Nothing beat the feeling of contentment of a plan coming together and the thought of having to return to the cottage at the end of the day made him feel even more satisfied. He was looking forward to spending time at the homely place and he was secretly hoping that some of it would be in company of Josephine.

Now was the right time to go down to collect the newspaper; the ferry had almost been emptied. Amidst some late arrivals Frank spotted Harold; he was about to board, but had stopped to talk to some visitors. It didn't take Frank long to recognise the tall figure with the unkempt hair: it was Bill. *Did he and Harold know each other?* He couldn't remember Harold having ever talked about Bill. *Had he come to the Island to report on the sailing? Surely that wouldn't be a job for him but more for one of his juniors?*

When Frank got to his feet, he noticed there were other people in Bill's party: some men in fine suits, their faces turned away. Talking to them was a woman.

Agnes. Just as Harold shook Bill's hand and walked away to the ferry, the face of the woman who was standing at the back of the group caught the sun. *What was she doing here? She must have come with Bill; of course; how he could be such an idiot.*

Frank thought back to the last visit he had made during his London trip. After seeing Scarlet, he had gone to his old house. His decision to go there had been an impulsive one. *Or had it?* The feeling of annoyance over unfinished business and his guilt had been strong driving forces. Every time he thought about her, alone in their house, he blamed himself. He knew she had family nearby, but the house must have been eerily quiet.

**

236

As he had watched his old house from across the street, a rush of familiarity had come back to him; nothing much had changed. They had lived in the house for at least ten years. It had taken him some time to get used to it, but that had more to do with the fact that Agnes had turned to her father for what she called a 'long-term loan'. Frank had felt the pressure of needing to increase his salary to be able to pay it back some day.

Standing in the shadow of the house opposite, he had no difficulties in visualising the interior of their old home: where their bedroom was, and his favourite armchair. But picturing Agnes was a different matter. He hadn't seen her for almost two years. He had met up with her father once or twice, and after that had mainly exchanged letters with him via his solicitor, but he'd never had the chance to look directly into her eyes. He had no idea as to how she had coped.

Sadness had overcome him while he stood there: ten years of a reasonably good marriage gone to waste. He knew things hadn't been perfect and Agnes had been frequently upset about not getting pregnant – something he'd felt terribly helpless about. *But had she blamed him for not fulfilling her dream of being a mother?* He wasn't sure. Although he had begun to ask himself that question more often, especially when she'd started to make comments at dinner with friends on how he could be an old bore, which happened if one married an older man. He had dismissed it as a joke, but as time went on, he was no longer confident it had been. Lately, it had crossed his mind that perhaps his swift departure had come as a relief to her, instead of merely a shock.

For a while, he had watched people walk past his old house, like the pendulum of a grandfather clock, continuously and reassuringly calming. He hadn't been certain what he wanted from her; he wasn't even sure if she was home. But when he'd made himself knock on the door, things had gone quickly. After she had regained her composure, he had pleaded with her to let him in so he could talk to her.

Following her into the house he knew so well had been

awkward and he had noticed a few things had changed; there were some new pictures on the wall, and his old chair had been replaced by two new chairs in front of the fireplace.

When he had told her he had come to finally explain things, a harsh voice had intervened, the one she had resorted to at the end of their relationship: cold and direct, not allowing any interruption.

After that, most of their meeting had been a blur.

What he remembered was that she was convinced he had been with these other women because he hadn't been satisfied with her. His explanation that he had been involved in research for the paper had brought sarcastic laughter. Sarcasm was something she'd never done very well, but now she sounded like someone who was used to being lied to.

What she had alluded to next was something he couldn't forget: how she had been warned that that would be his excuse, but why would he have been fired after his arrest if his work had been for the paper? That made no sense; he was telling one big lie.

Somebody had warned her? It sounded as if neither Lewis nor Bill had ever talked to her. Worse, somebody had been telling lies about him. His head had exploded; who had done this, and why?

He had looked at the unfamiliar woman standing opposite him and knew his chances of convincing her of his innocence had disappeared completely.

When Agnes had calmed down, she had told him it no longer mattered as she had learned to take care of herself. She looked well, better than he remembered, slightly fuller in her face and eyes glowing.

A pipe and other objects dotted around the room had indicated the presence of a man in the house. Had she managed to keep the house by taking in a lodger? Did Papa approve of a male lodger in his daughter's house? It had surprised him that her father hadn't come to her rescue. But it was no longer his place to criticise her and the cold look on her face had warned him she wanted him gone.

When the door had closed behind him, he had been too weak to walk; exhausted, he sat down on some steps to a basement across the road. With his head in his hands, he had cried a silent cry. His life with the woman he'd once loved had undeniably and very definitely ended, just like the chance of telling her the truth.

When he realised people were looking at him, he had left, giving his old house one last glance. Just in time to see Agnes open the door to a man, whom she seemed to pull into the house very quickly.

Bill? Frank stopped in his tracks; there was no doubt about it, he had just seen another face from the past. His old colleague and friend Bill. He had never mentioned Agnes since he had left London – unless he had reason not to. *Could he be her lodger, the one she had taken in to help pay for her costs?*

Looking at them now on the quay, he wondered if Bill was more than that.

Goddammit, had his former colleague stolen his old life?

He watched Bill help Agnes into the carriage. Just before she disappeared inside, Bill stopped her and made her turn around and together they viewed something in the distance; from where he stood, they looked like any other loving couple sharing a moment.

For an instant, Frank felt the urge to run down to the carriage and confront them with what he'd discovered, but to his own surprise, the yearning to make them aware of their misconduct towards him was short-lived, like a candle lit near an open window. In a moment of clarity, he knew it hadn't been spurred on by any feeling of jealousy or wanting his old life back. No, instead he wanted them to know he'd seen them, so he could finally start to let go of his guilt. For a long period, he had been walking around with pictures in his head of Agnes's lonely and loveless life, and although seeing her in London had diminished his concern she'd been wasting away, she'd made sure to remind him of his role in her unhappiness.

However, in front of him was a vision of a happy couple, telling him that he no longer needed to be tormented by the images; they weren't required anymore, not just by himself but also not by her.

If England chooses not to fight, let her be beaten.

In the spirit of this year's festivities, nations from around the world have come to England to participate in a celebration of labour and skill, creativity and invention.

We have called upon the nations to share in the promotion of their art and science and in the recognition of the dignity of their labour.

We have urged every foreign ship and carriage, before setting off on their journey to England, to load their hulls and compartments with their products of art and industry as missionaries for the civilization of mankind.

For this, we have set aside the opinion of some that England is a monopolizing country, anxiously withholding from the rest of the world the advantages she enjoys as a manufacturing country.

Instead, we are graciously showing our visitors our latest advancements, in order for them and thus mankind to benefit from the best articles on offer.

As hosts, we were quietly ready to teach our guests a lesson, not acknowledging what lesson could be learned ourselves.

For months now, we have admired, celebrated and marvelled at the products presented to us.

A few we have ridiculed and scoffed at, assuming the more austere and practical articles on display were of an inferior value.

Though subsequently realising their immense significance for the working man and woman, we have had to repent until, finally, we were ready to learn the ultimate lesson as a great Empire: that there is in other nations, as well as our own, something to be admired.

And with that knowledge and an acquired feeling of

brotherhood, we can now confidently predict that further industrial discoveries have been and will be made to help our economies flourish and workers work.

We predict that soon there will be more farm appliances such as the reaping machine, invented to help to feed us all.

And we predict that medical inventions will be created, to help us live longer.

Before long, and inspired by this amicable contest to increase the comforts and enjoyments of life, the day will present itself to us, in which more young and energetic talent will arise from not only these shores but from afar, to bequeath us with yet more of their creations.

Not unlike the maritime craft created by our American cousins.

But how will we know if we are looking at progress in the world of naval architecture?

How will we know if the American builder has put together a swifter vessel than any of the English yachts around, if we choose not to race her?

Let that not be because of our doing, because without a trial, we are not only in danger of losing a cup, we will be certain to lose a favourable public opinion towards yachting, and we will, moreover, be forever associated with a lack of sportsmanship and courage.

But more importantly, we are in danger of depriving our children, the inventors of our future, of seeing possible innovation in maritime design.

I therefore call upon all parents to show your support for this wonderful cause and to show your children how courage should be met by courage, by bringing them to visit this wonderful object of bravery on the Isle of Wight.

And I call upon the men in charge: let her race, and let us all learn from the occasion. Have the courage to accept that, in the pursuit of naval pre-eminence, we might be second. Because if we do not choose to accept the fight, we will deny us all the opportunity to be first.

Frank read the piece a couple of times; despite the turmoil he felt after seeing Bill and Agnes, the article managed to lift his spirits. Seeing his own work in print always had that effect. The night he had written it, there had been an alternative version. The official narrative was sent to McIlroy the next day and, with a degree of childish pleasure, he remembered what he had done with the others. Under the cover of darkness, he had dropped one off at the Squadron's clubhouse for the attention of Commodore Wilton. But the other, the one where he had substituted 'England' in the title for 'America', he had left at the hotel of Commodore Stevens. Worry that the American syndicate would change their mind after all and would decide to send the yacht back to the United States without a race had been sufficient encouragement to make the late-night delivery.

Frank retained the copy he had picked up and started to walk towards the promenade in Cowes. It was getting busier by the minute. Near the Castle, he ran into Archie, who had been helping a friend at the Royal Yacht Squadron ferrying provisions over to the American yacht.

'Can't they feed themselves?'

Archie laughed. 'Judging by the quality of the interior decor, there is no shortage of money for food. For such a racing machine, the decks below are magnificent.'

'I'm sure you took your time to have a good look.'

'I did indeed; today's guests are members of the Squadron who went out to observe the race for the Prince Albert's Cup. I promised to wait around until they return and help the guests disembark.'

'Did they mention the race on Friday? Do you think the Squadron will allow them to participate?'

'I'm sure they will; I can't believe they would risk any more criticism. They only have to waive the one-owner rule, and I'm convinced they're willing to do that. By the way, why don't you stay around a bit longer? Maybe I can get you to help unloading goods so you'll get a chance to have a look for yourself.' He pointed in the direction of the Castle. 'Perfect timing.' Around the corner *America* had come into sight; on the jetty people were getting several rowing boats ready.

'Can you row?' Archie indicated to one of the empty rowboats.

'Row?' Frank answered slightly too loudly.

'I guess not.' Archie smiled. 'You go with him; he's picking up the Duke of Aylesbury and will be dropping you off. Once on board, you need to find the galley and organise with the American cook what needs to come ashore. Ignore the French cook, he can't speak a word of English. You have time enough to get that done while all the guests are ferried back to shore. There will probably be some dishes and cutlery, empty wine bottles and the like.'

Everything went so fast after that that Frank had no time to get nervous about the idea of climbing onto the very unstable-looking rowing boat. And before any thoughts of impending doom could form in his head, they'd arrived at the sleek yacht. The guests had congregated near one side of the boat, merrily conversing with one another.

'We'll go around, where I'll drop you off first.' Frank's companion rowed to the other side and hovered near the stern, waiting for Frank to disembark. The stern of the ship was higher than he expected; he had no clue how to get on board without making a fool of himself.

'Grab that!' The command from Frank's rower sounded impatient and not very helpful; Frank had risen to his feet, but the sudden movement of the boat forced him to sit down again.

'Who would like permission to come aboard?' A resonant voice not far from his head came bearing down. Frank looked up and recognised the stern face of the American captain appearing over the side of the ship; he wasn't sure if the man was making a joke. Should he ask for permission? There was no time to mull it over as the Captain instructed one of his men, 'John, help this man, will you?'

'Ay ay, Sir.'

A handsome man leaned over the side and stuck his hand out

to Frank.

'If you take my hand and put your foot over there, you'll be on board in a flash.'

With a little tug from John and a push from inside the rowing boat, Frank arrived safely aboard. He suppressed the urge to let out a sigh of relief; he wasn't sure if he would ever get used to boats, big or small. He turned around to look for the Captain to thank him for his hospitality, but he'd disappeared. He was left with the man called John. The two of them stood in silence, quietly sizing each other up.

Frank knew he was being scrutinised, but he was getting used to it; most seamen seemed to look at him with suspicion. 'Good afternoon, I'm Frank Grundy, I was asked to help unload goods that were brought by your guests this morning.'

'You'll find them down there. Follow me. Mind your head.' John walked in front. 'I must apologise for my Captain; normally he has more time for new guests to his ship.'

'That's all right.' Frank followed John through the round cockpit and towards the stairs leading down below. He stopped for a moment to have a good look at the ship's long masts and sleek deck; although crowded with people, one could see why they had called her empty; there were hardly any structures to impede the wind from flowing freely into the big sails.

'Sir, down here,' John called from below decks.

Frank carefully made his way down the stairs. He entered the main cabin of the ship and almost immediately forgot that he was on one; this felt more like a pocket-sized stately home. It was difficult to believe that this graceful abode had managed to cross the Atlantic.

'Sir, the galley is this way.'

'Isn't there another way in and out of the kitchen?' asked Frank, wondering if he might have taken the wrong entrance. Hesitantly, he crossed the room.

'Not on this ship; another entrance would mean another hatch catching wind.' John smiled at Frank. 'No back door for any of us;

we all enter the same way.'

'I'm glad you get treated in similar fashion.' Frank smiled back.

'Ah, I didn't say that.' John moved towards the galley. 'Jesse here will help you to get the things together that need to go back to shore.'

Frank recognised the kitchen area. He watched the few people in the small space with amazement; they operated like a well-oiled machine. They cleared, cleaned and reorganised without being in each other's way for one moment. Living and working on a ship seemed to comprise the freedom to go anywhere in the world but an inability to escape your immediate surroundings.

John disappeared through a door and Frank wished he could follow suit instead of having to collect blankets, surplus bottles of wine and other possessions of English guests.

'Let me help you get these on deck.' The seaman called Jesse started to move the goods towards the galley door. 'If we make a chain, we'll be done faster.'

They passed the goods down from one to the other, from the galley to the door, through the main cabin and up on deck. Another seaman helped them out and in a short time they were done, leaving Frank wondering if anybody would notice if he had a walk around. It would be at least another half an hour before all the guests had departed and he could be rowed back, so time was on his side. Moreover, nobody seemed to be worried about his presence there; John had vanished and the grumpy Captain was nowhere to be seen.

There were several doors leading off the main cabin and Frank wavered, unsure if he should open one. As the only noises were the muffled thuds of feet on the boards above him, he slowly opened one of the doors, ready to close it quickly if necessary. The room was empty. To his surprise, he spotted a water closet in what looked like a washroom. *How civilised!* The second door he opened was a pantry, stuffed with provisions, linen and dishes. Maybe life on the ocean wasn't as uncomfortable as he'd previously thought – well, at least not on this side of the ship. He knew that the crew's berths were towards the bow, accessible through the galley, which meant some of the doors here gave access to cabins of the Commodore and the other guests.

One more door. He pulled it a little ajar; it was a private cabin with walls clad with a lovely dark wood and a freshly made bed. He expected the other berths not to be as luxurious. These men were all in the same boat, but it was clear to see they weren't in the same situation.

He pushed the door wide open and with a jolt he recognised John in the corner. 'Oh, I'm sorry, erm, I was looking for you.' Frank couldn't think of anything else to say and stared in embarrassment at the man on his knees on the floor.

John turned around. 'I'm sorry, I didn't hear you knock.' He put down his tool and tested a locker door to make sure it stayed closed properly. 'That should do it.'

Frank felt foolish; he hadn't knocked. 'I didn't think you were a sailor,' he said, looking at the carpentry tools on the floor next to John.

'That makes two of us; I didn't think you were one either. Or an errand-boy.' John collected his tools. 'Tell me, did someone send you over to inspect her?'

'I was sent over to help unload, but you are correct, that's not what I normally do. I haven't been on many yachts in my life, especially not one like this.' There was no need to tell John he was a reporter.

'So you're not one of those members of an English sailing club who sit behind the window of their clubhouse, staring at us through their telescope? And then row over to have a look and be courteous with their compliments, but don't dare to bet on a challenge?'

'No, I'm not one of those.'

'Sorry. We have all been in better moods. Today we are a bit off-colour, with the brothers leaving us.'

Frank was unprepared for John's sudden candour; they hadn't changed their minds, then, even with a race approaching.

'And what do you think of her?'

'She's astonishing: not only a racing machine, but elegant at the same time. Did you work on her?'

'Yes, as a matter of fact, I did, for one long cold winter.'

'And you also sailed over in her?'

'The whole twenty-one days.'

'Why?' Frank said the word with such disbelief that it made John laugh.

'I guess you don't like sailing?' John asked amusedly.

'I don't particularly like the sea. I assume you do.'

'It's not that straightforward, but I've always been fascinated by it, so to speak. It's more a case of accepting one has to cross it in order to go somewhere new. And I'm not afraid to get wet.'

'And was it worth it?'

'The trip or the destination itself? To tell you the truth, neither has been what I expected.'

Frank watched John go red in the face; he looked extremely uncomfortable and Frank wished he hadn't asked the personal question. 'At least you can rest assured that where one journey ends a new one begins,' he said encouragingly. 'Will you consider another sailing trip?'

'Not sure.'

'Back home to your old carpentry job then?'

'Maybe. We'll see. Sailing teaches you to take each day as it comes, you know, with the wind and all of that.'

'Good for you,' Frank said, feeling a twinge of envy; gone were the days when one thought to have all the time in the world and nobody to answer for. He looked at the young man with the strong physique and the handsome face; it was difficult to believe he had nobody waiting for him at home. But whatever his constraints were in America, clearly they had not held him back. How things were different for him; his already compact world had become even smaller over the years, recently culminating in just a square mile around Cowes. The thought made Frank smile: he didn't mind.

'And you?'

Frank looked puzzled. 'Sorry?'

'You said you didn't like the sea, but here you are, arrived by rowing boat.'

'Ah, that. I've never looked for adventure in travelling far distances, especially not by boat. I guess the time was right to face that old demon; I'm not sure how many chances I'll get to visit a yacht like this.'

'And was it worth it?' John wanted to know.

Frank wasn't sure if he was being mocked or if John was sincerely interested in his efforts. 'The journey or the end destination?' he retorted.

'Both.' John smiled; he was starting to like Frank's sense of humour.

'Well, as I said, she's beautiful; just as I hoped she would be. So, yes, even the crossing in the rowing boat has had its use; what better than a little fear to redeem oneself?'

John laughed out loud: 'I'm glad you say that, because you still need to get back.'

There was a sudden knock on the door Frank was leaning against.

'Sorry, gentlemen, have I come at a bad moment?'

Frank opened the door fully to see the surprised face of George.

'Mr Grundy, what brings you here?'

'I've been asked to help to ferry some goods back to shore.'

'You?'

'Yes, my colleague knows some club members and, well, it's complicated, but I couldn't let the chance pass by.'

'I thought you disliked the sea? The things you reporters do to get a story.' George gave Frank a friendly tap on the shoulder. 'Do excuse me, I need to get some of my stuff out of the room.' He pointed to a canvas bag on a table near John. 'I almost forgot – if you're done here, can you let the Captain know whether you're joining us ashore for a last drink?'

'Yes, Sir.' John handed George the bag and squeezed past the two men. 'I'll let the Captain know right away, I could do with a drink.'

Frank wasn't sure what to make of the glance John threw at him as he walked by; he should probably have come clean on his profession. He watched George gather his possessions together.

'You're really leaving then?'

'Yes, it's time to say goodbye.'

'Even though she has been entered for the race on the twenty-second?'

'Now, don't you start writing that I'm leaving a sinking ship or any of that nonsense.' George raised a warning finger. 'I trust Captain Brown will get the best out of her now the syndicate has finally made their decision. When I told you not that long ago my work here is done, I meant to say I completed the task I had set out to do. Making fast, reliable boats is my unique contribution to life. Some would call it a duty.' He closed his bag with a firm hand. 'Anyway, I'm planning on building many more boats in the future, therefore I need to be on my way. Now, if you'll excuse me, I have a parting drink to go to. Besides, when the news of our victory arrives in New York, I want to be there to receive all the praise.' George gave a knowing wink.

Chapter 26

Frank watched George and James disappear into a tavern with the Captain and his men. Over the past months, he'd secretly admired the Americans' unwavering belief they would succeed. He used to be like them. *Did their impending departure allude to a diminishing belief in a satisfactory outcome of the race?* Just like his own confidence had been eroded over time until he couldn't even ask a woman out. He scolded himself; how difficult could it be? All the way back from Cowes, he mulled over how to ask Josephine out, but he arrived at the cottage without a plan. He had contemplated asking her to join him in watching the race at the end of the week, but perhaps inviting her to watch boats was an insensitive idea.

He returned to his room to get dressed for supper. When he caught sight of his reflection in a mirror, he didn't recognise the mature man with a nervous smile glancing back at him. He needed to regain his composure.

Seeing her warm smile when he entered the dining room had been the encouragement he needed; he had done it – he had asked her out.

Luckily, she had made it easy for him. After she had recovered from the initial surprise, she had suggested a walk, perhaps to watch the ladies and gentlemen arrive for the annual ball of the Squadron.

The food that evening had never tasted so good.

'Let's turn away from the road and cut through here.'

Frank followed Josephine into a tree-lined lane, although one could hardly call it a lane; it was more like a forest path with tree roots coming through the soil, making it uneven and sometimes slippery. But he didn't care where he was going; he hadn't felt this light and happy in ages. He looked at the woman in front of him who didn't seem to have any difficulties navigating the rougher terrain.

Although they'd only been walking for a short while, it was as if they'd entered a new world; away from the constant presence of the sea, they'd arrived in the cool protective surroundings of the woods. They walked in silence for some time; the mud underneath their feet and the bark of the trees muffled the sounds of their steps. The light that filtered through the green leaves with little bursts made Frank unsteady and he stopped for a moment to recover his balance.

'Maybe we could have a little rest?' His voice cut through the silence and Josephine slowed to a halt. Frank pointed to an area where a few fallen trees had formed a seating arrangement in an open space.

'Are we tired already?' Josephine asked teasingly.

Frank grinned. 'You're walking too fast for this old man. Allow me.' He indicated to one of the bigger tree trunks. 'Please have this lovely solid seat made from the finest English oak.'

Josephine laughed.

'You know this area very well.' Frank sat down on another tree trunk, far away enough not to invade her space, but close enough to see her face. She seemed at ease in his company.

'Yes, I like coming here; it's a different world, one that is hidden from everything else. When I come here, I think of nothing.' She looked up into the trees and slowly filled her lungs with air. 'It smells so different here, don't you think?'

'Do you bring your children?'

'No, this is my own hiding place; it's where I go, away from the sea, if I have some time for myself.' She closed her eyes and leaned back against the tree.

Avoiding the sea: he recognised that. 'Do you like living on the Island?'

'I do now. At first, I didn't care much; I was just glad my sister could offer us a refuge. But then I was given some money.' She paused for a moment, lost in her own thoughts. 'That's another story, not for now.' She sounded apologetic. 'The money meant I could stay longer and help my sister open the lodging house. That has been a blessing. I realise of late that being new somewhere can have its advantages; there's no one to remind you what is expected. I'm sorry, I must be talking no sense to you.' She had opened her eyes and was looking at him slightly embarrassedly.

'Not at all.' It had meaning to him, although it had taken him much longer than her to realise. A fresh start, reminding you of who you were and what needed to be done differently.

Until recently, his thoughts had revolved around making amends with Agnes. And not even the passing of time had changed the way he felt. Instead, it had made it worse, as if his emotions were trapped in a pothole that was slowly collecting stagnant, foul-smelling water.

But the pothole had sprung a narrow leak and the water was gradually disappearing in a quiet swirl. He couldn't point his finger to the exact source of the hole, but he suspected the cause to be some unrelated and seemingly insignificant happenings. Like following Harold onto a boat for the first time in his life, or seeing the young girl made out of white marble. Or seeing Agnes with Bill.

Frank smiled. He knew that on the bottom of the pothole, just visible under the dirt, lay what men wiser than him would call his own cause worth pursuing. The only thing that needed to be done now was not to lose sight of it.

He looked at the beautiful woman sitting close to him; he admired her resolve.

'I'm glad you are here with me, because I would have probably got lost.'

'That's impossible, you're on an island,' she declared dryly.

'Of course. Anyway, thank you for coming along on this walk with me. I'm aware I'm practically a stranger to you.'

'You don't feel like a stranger.' Before Frank could react to that, Josephine rose to her feet and started walking. 'If we go this way, we'll eventually arrive back at the Esplanade; maybe we could do some sightseeing.'

'That's a marvellous idea. Maybe we can catch a glimpse of the guests attending the Ball.' He followed her down the narrow path.

'Shouldn't you be there? I thought you were here for the sailing? Although, if I may say so, you don't look like most of the sailors I know.'

Frank laughed. 'You're right about that, it's a long story.'

'I'm listening, I like stories.' Her light feet skipped over the trail.

'I'm glad you do, because I write stories for a living.'

'Oh, do you write books?'

'No, my tales for the paper are much shorter and more temporary: often forgotten the next day.'

'Tell me something about the stories you've been working on.'

'You wouldn't want to hear some of them, I can promise you.' He regretted it immediately. 'I mean, they can be terribly boring, unless you're interested in who won the best sponge-cake prize at the local country fair.'

'Maybe you could tell me about your own; how does one go from writing about cakes to writing about sailing?'

'How does one get to write about cakes in the first place would be the better question,' Frank mumbled.

'Was there a life before cakes?'

Josephine had stopped walking. They'd arrived back at the edge of the woods and surrounding fields. Frank squeezed his eyes; the sudden bright light temporarily blinded him.

Josephine chortled. 'Let me guide you.' She grabbed his hand and pulled him along a path that cut through the meadow; he smelled the sea before he could see it.

'I get the impression your previous life didn't take place in the countryside?'

They'd come out on the other side of the field and she gently let go of his hand.

'You've guessed well – very observant. I'm a London boy.'

'Who no longer lives in London?'

'No, but in a sleepy village on the south coast.'

'Oh, look at them!' Josephine's excited voice signalled their arrival at the Castle, where the crowds were thickening with people dressed for the ball.

He followed her gaze in the direction of a few women gathered near the railings at the harbour wall. Josephine sighed at the sight of the beautiful dresses. She had come to a halt in the middle of the walkway, staring at the women in admiration. 'Look at those feathers on her hat; what bird would carry those colours?'

Frank smiled at her childlike awe; he took her elbow and tenderly guided her out of the way of the promenading people. 'Let's take a seat on this bench, shall we?' He beckoned to a wooden seat, set slightly away from the concourse and from the crowds strolling past.

'We've been so busy at the cottage that I haven't had the time to come outside.'

They watched the play of people happy to be seen, while commenting on their choice of dress and the company they kept.

'I'm glad we men have it much easier; I'll stick with the grey tails and the black –' Frank stopped in the middle of the sentence; his eyes narrowed and for a moment he stopped breathing. In amongst the growing crowd, he caught sight of first Bill and then Agnes. It shouldn't have taken him by surprise as it did.

'You could have a colourful tie to brighten it up, couldn't you? Are you all right?' She had seen the worried look on his face.

'Yes, I'm fine, I just saw a… what should I call it…,' he wavered. 'A ghost from the past?'

'Really?' Josephine examined the crowds. 'Scary enough to want to leave? Or do you want me to seek it out and chase it away?'

'Thanks for the offer, but no, let's stay.' He tenderly squeezed her arm.

'Frank?! Is that you?'

He slowly averted his gaze from Josephine to face Bill and Agnes's arrival.

'Bill. Agnes.' Frank rose to his feet, pretending it was as much a surprise for him as it was to them. Seeing Agnes's face, he could tell they hadn't meant to make their advances; she looked terribly uncomfortable and gave him a little nod as if to warn him not to make a scene. They weren't on their own but in the company of two other men.

'Frank, what brings you here? I didn't think you would want to visit an island.' Bill sounded deceptively jovial and didn't wait for Frank's reply; 'Oh, I'm sorry, I didn't mean to be discourteous – let me introduce you to Mr Darlingden-Frence and his son and… well, you know Agnes.'

Did he derive pleasure from introducing her to him? But before Frank had a chance to show his grievance, both father and son extended hands to Frank. He turned to them, wondering where he'd seen the older gentleman before.

'How thoughtless of me,' Bill interjected. 'You two have probably already met. Mr Darlingden-Frence owns the newspaper I work for.'

Frank stared at Bill. Was he trying to be tactful on his behalf, or didn't he want to remind the owner who he was? Because now Frank recognised the name: it was the same name that had adorned his termination letter. The older man must have been in his sixties and Frank vaguely remembered seeing him in the office on at least one occasion. He shook the man's hand, almost feeling relieved that the old man didn't seem to recognise him as a previous employee he'd fired a few years ago. Remembering every document he put his signature on was unlikely. Next, Frank took the extended hand of the son. He looked like a younger version of his father, dressed equally smartly, with a similar sharp nose and the same straight hair that kept falling into his eyes. The way he kept sweeping it to one side gave the impression of a man with a nervous disposition, but his piercing eyes showed otherwise; he glanced at Frank briefly and then turned to focus his attention on

Josephine. Subconsciously, Frank moved closer to Josephine until he was lightly touching her shoulder. By this time, all four were looking at Josephine, who had followed the introductions with curiosity.

Before Frank could say anything, she stepped forward and said in a clear voice, 'I'm happy to make your acquaintance.' She acknowledged each of the four strangers with a little bow of the head and added, 'As a friend of Frank's, I'm pleased to meet some of his old acquaintances.' With a simple gesture, she eased the situation, as if she'd instinctively known that it had been awkward for Frank.

Bill and the older Darlingden-Frence tipped their hats in salute, but the younger man stepped closer to Josephine. He took her hand and kissed it delicately, while holding her gaze. The gesture made the hair on Frank's neck stand up; the demeanour of this man and the way he'd taken her hand was far too seedy for his liking. But whatever Josephine was thinking, she didn't let anything show; she smiled back at him pleasantly.

Frank saw that Josephine had failed to notice the look on Agnes's face. After regaining her composure, Agnes had turned her attention to Josephine and had scrutinized her from top to bottom. Frank recognised the absurdity of the situation; here he was with the woman he was officially married to but hadn't lived with for more than two years, who'd appeared on the arm of a former colleague – a man whom Frank had considered a friend – and also with Josephine, a delightful woman, who had captivated him in the space of a couple of days. He couldn't discern what was going on in Agnes's head, but her eyes looked gloomy.

'And what brings you here to the Island, Bill. You're not working, I assume?' Frank gestured at their fancy dress; he wasn't really interested in the answer, but his curiosity got the better of him.

'Mr Darlingden-Frence here has a keen interest in sailing, so he invited us – me,' he quickly corrected himself, 'to come over to the Island as gratitude for all the hard work I have been doing lately, isn't that so?'

'Are you fishing for a compliment, Bill?' the older man wanted to know. He directed his attention to Frank. 'Only because he had to do two jobs for a while, after he took over from the editor. He thinks he needs to keep reminding me of how hard he has worked; as if it isn't enough he got a promotion and an invitation for him and his good lady to the Annual Ball at the Squadron.'

Frank remembered Bill telling him he'd been promoted to Lewis's job, just as Lewis himself had been promoted. Since when did Bill get this close to the owner? But there was no time to give it much thought; Darlingden-Frence calling Agnes Bill's "good lady" had diverted his attention. From the looks on her and Bill's faces, he gathered he wasn't the only one who had heard; Agnes bent her head down with blushing cheeks and Bill started to speak loudly.

'Talking about the ball, we'd better get going. It was lovely to meet you, Mrs Wickes, and you, Frank, good to see you looking well. Maybe we'll see each other again some time.' He grabbed Agnes's elbow and started to leave.

'It was my utmost pleasure to meet you.' The younger Darlingden-Frence spoke slowly while looking intently at Josephine. 'Next time you're visiting London, please come around, because we like to treat Bill's friends the best we can.' Out of the inner pocket of his coat, he took a calling card and gave it to Frank. They walked away; Agnes hadn't even said goodbye.

'She looked so pretty in that purple dress,' Josephine sighed. 'It must be exciting to go to the ball tonight. I wish I could hide in a room somewhere and watch the festivities.'

'Mmm.'

'Who were these people?'

'Mmm.'

'Frank?'

'Yes?' Josephine's inquisitive eyes were willing him to answer.

'You mentioned a ghost from your past: which one was it?'

It took some time before it dawned on him what she was referring to.

'Ah, yes, of course. Well, Bill was an old colleague of mine from my time as a reporter in London and the older man was the owner of that paper.' He checked whether they were gone, but they were no longer to be seen; the masses had absorbed them. 'The younger one was apparently his son, but I've never met him before.'

'Such a funny name. I wasn't too impressed with the son, if I'm honest. And did you know the lady?'

'Funny name?' Frank asked suspiciously, alerted by her remark.

'Yes, it sounded like a nickname –'

But Frank was no longer listening; he tapped his pockets like a mad man for the card he had been given. Finding it in the last pocket, he turned it over impatiently and stared at the initials printed on it. The card was all too familiar to him, an exact copy of the one given to him by Scarlet.

His breathing became heavy and, with every exhalation, he groaned more and more loudly. 'Of course, of course! No, could it? That's it, it has to be, yes!'

'Frank, what's wrong? Are you all right?'

He threw his arms in the air and started to hop from one leg to the other; a rolling laughter started at the bottom of his lungs and ended in a full crescendo. 'I've got it, finally I've got it!' Passionately, he flung his arms around Josephine and hugged her tightly. 'Thank you so much!'

Josephine giggled and with her head pressed up against his chest, she just managed to speak. 'I can hardly breathe, don't squeeze too hard, please!'

'I'm sorry, I didn't realise.' Frank let her go. 'Did I hurt you? I'm terribly sorry!'

'No, I'm fine, don't worry. But what has made you that happy? It can't be me, I didn't do anything.'

'Yes, you have, you have no idea how happy you've made me!'

She looked puzzled but pleased at the same time. 'Would you care to explain?'

'Yes, but not now, it's a long story; you could say it concerns my ghost from the past and therefore it has no place on this lovely evening! Because a beautiful evening it is!' Frank grinned from ear to ear; he felt ecstatic and the card in his hand felt like a piece of a large unfinished dissected puzzle. On its own it had no meaning, but he knew it to be the key to the overall picture, one he had started to build up a long time ago.

He joyfully grabbed Josephine's hand. 'Let's walk a bit more and enjoy each other's company before I take you home.'

'All right, you crazy man.' She smiled and squeezed his hand lightly. 'I'm glad the ghost is gone.'

'Yes, he's flying away as we speak.' He looked down at her appreciatively, thinking how perceptive she was.

'He? Thus not the pregnant lady?'

'Pregnant lady? Sorry, what lady?'

'You know, the wife of your friend Bill.'

Frank came to an abrupt halt; his jaw dropped. 'What makes you say that?' His question sounded like a demand. 'I'm not sure if I can take more excitement,' he exclaimed.

Josephine wavered; her eyes darted from Frank's upset face to the cobbles, as if she was ready to make a run for it.

'I shouldn't have spoken, I'm sorry, I didn't realise the news would have this effect on you.' She sounded despondent.

His reaction must have seemed quite dramatic to Josephine, but he couldn't contain himself; his head had been spinning with the news that the sleazy young man he'd just met appeared to be one of the men who had been visiting Scarlet and Rose. He was slowly starting to understand the implications of that knowledge; the fact that his father owned the newspaper must explain the resistance he'd met trying to get the story out. *Had Lewis played a role in that? And what about Bill?*

Frank was glad that Josephine couldn't read his mind; he didn't want to have to explain to her about the suspicions he had carried since working in London. But now, at this very moment, she'd managed to throw some more surprising news at him.

'Why did you call her pregnant?' He ignored her remark, irritated he had failed to spot the signs; *hadn't he recognised Scarlet's situation not that long ago? Or was this too close to home?*

'Little things; her glowing face and the pigmented skin on her forehead and cheeks…' Her voice trailed off, and she sounded increasingly embarrassed. 'I don't think it's appropriate for me to talk to you about this, let's forget about it. I could be wrong. Perhaps she has had children before, which would make sense because she did look a little older.'

He stood in silence, conflicted by the news. Here he was, in the company of a woman with whom he had just spent a lovely afternoon and who had given him hope for the future – but who had also reminded him painfully of his past.

Frank saw disappointment in Josephine's eyes; he knew he had to explain something to her, otherwise this delicate friendship would end before it had started.

'Let's walk home.'

Leaving the busy streets of Cowes behind them, Josephine became completely silent. She walked in front of him with quick steps; she'd been so cheerful earlier, but now she was subdued, perhaps even angry.

All he wanted was to tell her was how he admired her courage and how he would do anything to earn her respect. But what he needed to explain to her instead was about his life with Agnes and the lies he used to tell her, leading to their separation.

The fact she might be with child gave him a strange sense of relief; slowly but surely, he was being liberated from the grip of his old life. Finally, he could stop worrying about Agnes. And stop worrying about the worry.

They were getting closer to the cottage. Frank had to make up his mind quickly; he didn't want the new life he could start living to begin with a lie.

'Josephine?'

'Mmm.'

'Please, could you slow down for a moment, I need to tell you something.'

He sped up until he was close enough for her to hear him clearly.

'You are the most courageous, optimistic, beautiful human being I've met. You probably think I'm an old fool, but I'm willing to take that risk as long as you hear me out.' He pronounced every word deliberately and it had the desired effect; Josephine slowed to a halt. He gently touched her arm, urging her to turn around. He sighed with relief when she did, looking at him in a puzzled way but not unkindly. He had to do this right; it felt like a last chance and he had to take the gamble that she would understand. He had no choice; walking away instead of going for the battle was no longer an option.

'I would like us to get to know each other better. That's if you would like that too.' He didn't wait for a reaction, worried he would change his mind. 'But there are some things you need to know first; after that you can decide what you do with them.'

Chapter 27

22 August, 1851, Race day

Frank didn't care about anything anymore; the only thing he wanted was to lie down. He felt like dying. Would anybody notice if he found himself a place to hide? At least he wouldn't be in anybody's way.

Another wave of nausea hit him and with all the strength he could muster, he scrambled down the small steps leading below deck. He needed to find a place to lie flat as soon as possible. Crawling into the main area of the yacht, he found space on a bench, and tried hard to avoid being sick another time. He wished with all his body and mind he was somewhere else.

Struggling to ignore the movements of the yacht, he imagined land under his feet: the sturdy, dried-out soil of the Island, fields of grass, the vegetable garden, anything. Eventually, his stomach calmed down to the point where he could stop worrying about throwing up at any moment, but he didn't dare move an inch.

He hoped nobody would come into the cabin; he didn't want to be seen as this pathetic excuse of a man. What a fool he had been, thinking he could endure a whole day of sailing. But he was mainly angry for being so weak and useless, unable to rise above the physical discomfort he felt. He had to be firm with himself, he thought feebly; he'd waited long enough for this race, surely there was a way to enjoy it, as all the others seemed to do.

The day had started excitingly enough. Full of anticipation, he'd met Archie at the agreed place not far from Cowes Harbour.

'Isn't it magnificent, all these good folk out already and it's still the early morning!' An elated Archie greeted him with a firm handshake and a broad smile. He told Frank to follow him towards the quay. 'You must be feeling quite a sense of pride, old chap,' he added above the noise.

'Me?'

'*If England chooses not to fight:* your eloquent call to arms to the men in charge not to reject such a heroic challenge. As you can see for yourself, it has drawn the attention of more than just sailing enthusiasts.'

'Could that really be?'

'How else can one explain the multitude of our fellow citizens gathered here? Some of them only arrived this morning by boat from across the Solent.'

They were nearing Cowes Castle. 'And you haven't yet been able to observe the magnificent spectacle on the water,' Archie added mysteriously.

'That is quite astonishing!' The sight took Frank's breath away: an array of masts, sails and hulls all merrily bobbing on the water, too many to count or identify. Every possible type of buoyant device carried eager spectators geared up for a day on the sea.

'I don't think any man could have imagined such a scene,' Archie agreed. 'We anticipated being joined by the usual onlookers, but it seems that they have been joined by those who would wish to see the Yankees being given a good thrashing.'

'Will they be?'

'Most certainly! With so many English yachts participating, the odds are clearly in our favour.'

'I think some of these people might wonder whether it is the Establishment that will be taught a lesson.'

'Well, whatever the outcome, you will be there to witness it.' Triumphantly, Archie guided Frank towards a waiting rowing boat. 'Mr Ratsey has been so kind as to arrange a place for you on *Aurora*, one of the competing yachts, so let's get going, she's waiting.'

Frank knew instantly that he couldn't complain about the privilege, so he kept his mouth shut as Archie rowed him out to *Aurora*, explaining that the one-masted cutter had been built some thirteen years earlier by Michael Ratsey. The vessel was much smaller than *America* and straightaway he began worrying that he would be a burden to the crew by interfering with their work. But Archie had introduced him to the Captain and the crew as the reporter who wanted a firsthand account and they didn't seem to take much notice of his presence. They had been far too busy getting ready for the race.

He had tried to relax a little and watched the men preparing lines and checking sails. This was done with a quiet ease compared to the chaos and noise around them. All the yachts participating in the race were lying anchored in two starting lines stretching out from Cowes Castle. On the yachts nearest to them, Frank saw the other crews busying themselves in similar fashion. In between the forest of masts, in the back row, Frank spotted the smooth-looking *America*; he could only guess how the atmosphere on the American yacht was.

After the initial shock of finding out he was going to spend the day on a small yacht, he tried his best to ignore his nerves. The numerous spectator yachts on the water gave him some distraction, as did the thought that the crew clearly knew what they were doing. He felt for his notebook in the pocket of his jacket; he'd come prepared. There was nothing else he could do except sit back and try to enjoy the occasion.

There was still time before the race started at ten o'clock. The skipper of *Aurora* took the opportunity to tell his men in encouraging words what was expected of them that day, all the while keeping an eye on the sky and on his pocket watch. There hadn't been much wind most of the morning and looking out over the Solent, Frank wondered if the overcast sky further down portended more wind around the Island. Over to the other side, towards the shore, he saw the tide steadily rising and out of nowhere he felt the breeze getting stronger. The mist that had draped the coastline like a velvety curtain slowly rose with the warming sun, revealing the cleanly washed horizon.

The calm with which the yachts waited patiently for the first gun at five to ten couldn't conceal the feverish excitement felt by each and every man on board *Aurora*.

Seemingly without warning, the skipper shouted a command to his crew and on *Aurora*, just as on the other yachts, they stood to attention. Behind them, near the Castle, was a flash of light and the crackle of the cannon rumbled nearer, smoke drifting along; the first gun had been fired. The men began to raise their foresail and jib, encouraged by loud cheers from the crowds.

It seemed barely a minute before the second gun sounded. The main sail was hoisted and Frank heard the sailor responsible for weighing the anchor cry out that he was having difficulties getting it up.

Sheets of canvas came alive on the entire racing fleet around them, unfurled from their sleepy state to flutter into action. The race had begun.

Frank worried how they were going to manoeuvre *Aurora* past the flotilla of onlooker boats around them; it was bound to be quite a scuffle and someone was likely going to be hit in the action. With the incessant noise of the crowd, the flapping of the sails and the explosion of commands, Frank's uneasiness started to intensify; the sense of control he had experienced earlier had quickly turned into chaos.

He tried so hard not to be in anyone's way that he had completely forgotten about *America*. He searched the horizon for her, past the yachts in front, but she was nowhere to be seen. Puzzled, he looked around him; *had something happened?* With a mixture of relief and dismay, he finally spotted her at the back of the fleet. Her sails were still flapping wildly in the wind. He had no idea what had happened, but she had clearly been the last to leave, which didn't bode well. She would have to catch the rest of them who were now running towards Ryde before the wind, which was light, something the Americans dreaded because their large sails had trouble filling.

It crossed Frank's mind that the sleek-looking yacht might get a beating from one of the older British yachts after all. But this notion didn't last long; when he looked back a couple of minutes later, he saw that *America* had worked her way towards the rest of the yachts and that she had already caught one of them. It was thrilling to see her come closer. The men on *Aurora* worked as hard as they could, but after some more minutes, they had been chased and caught by the Americans as well. *America* glided past like a proud swan, efficiently paddling its big feet to create a smooth forward propelling movement with no water unnecessarily spilled. As they coasted past, Frank saw the faces of the men on board, including the carpenter John. Aside from the large crew he detected some guests, standing upright in their fancy suits, confident in the ability of their specially built vessel. Finally, Frank saw the Captain at the stern, a beacon of calmness, with the English pilot standing next to him.

It still struck him as odd that the Americans were relying on the information of someone who could be seen as competition to get safely around the Island. But that's what sportsmanship was about, he'd been told several times by Harold and his friends.

It was unclear how the crowds on shore were reacting to the advances *America* was making down the fleet as their roars drifted in from across the water. He wondered if they could feel the wind building, just as he did sitting at the back of *Aurora*: these were weather circumstances that were preferred by the Americans.

The Captain of *Aurora* grunted. 'Don't know why they allow her to boom out.'

Frank strained to see what he'd been looking at; slightly ahead of him, he saw *America* with her sails set wide open to the sides in an attempt to catch every bit of the breeze.

'Is that normally not allowed?'

'No, the Squadron rules don't permit it, but they apparently have waived that rule for the Americans. Just as they did with the one-owner rule.'

Frank smiled to himself; he knew the Squadron couldn't risk them not racing. *Finally, a wise decision.*

'But have no fear, we should make good speed further around the Island.'

There was a determination in his voice that made Frank wonder if he really thought he stood a chance against *America*. They were the smallest yacht in the fleet and although his knowledge of sailing was limited, Frank thought it to be highly unlikely.

For the first hour or so that they moved east along the coastline, Frank had managed to settle into the rhythm of the sailing and had enjoyed watching the unhurried changing of their surroundings. After the spectators on the shore had thinned out, he'd noticed with curiosity how the shoreline had altered; it was the first time in his life that he'd been able to look back at the land from the sea without being overcome by a feeling of panic and an overwhelming desire to feel his feet on solid ground. It had become hard to fathom which part of the Island he was looking at; earlier it had been simple to recognise Osborne House in a dip between the greenery, and passing Ryde had given him a good impression of how far they had come after almost an hour of sailing. He couldn't figure out who was in front of the fleet; up until the moment of passing Ryde, it had seemed like a cat and mouse game, with changing figureheads, but from the Captain's remarks, he understood that they, along with some of the other smaller entries to the race, weren't doing that badly at all. He watched *America* being passed by a fine-lined cutter of similar size to *Aurora*.

'Who is that?' Frank wanted to know.

'*Volante*,' the Captain said cheerfully. 'They need to keep an eye on her; the wind just fell away, and look at the consequences. It could be to our advantage as well today.'

It was easy to see who the common enemy was that day: the whole fleet was against the Americans.

They'd been approaching the first visible mark of the course, a buoy called *Noman's Land*, when Frank saw with his own eyes that *Volante* sailed around it first. Onlookers on a steamship nearby had seen the same thing; the men on board waved their hats in celebration.

Aurora was near the leading group and the implication started to dawn on Frank. *What if the small yacht he was sailing on could actually beat the Americans? Would it change his commitment to the cause?* It would definitely be unexpected and he would have a good story to tell his friends, he thought, grinning from ear to ear.

After that it went downhill rapidly; just after rounding the buoy, the wind increased slightly. The waves became more prominent with foamy, angry heads, and the rhythm of the yacht changed drastically; their boat started to get more of a battering and sprays of cold seawater flew over the bow. Before he knew what had hit him, his stomach was churning and he'd started to feel nauseous and clammy. All the blood had drained out of his face.

'When did you last eat?' Thomas, one of the older crewmembers asked him.

Food? How could this man talk about food?

Thomas shook his head in pity. 'Keep your eyes on the horizon.'

Frank was sure that the man meant well and he wished he'd been able to thank him, but he had to concentrate, more and more worried that he could no longer contain himself.

'You might wish to move to the stern, Sir, it's easier.'

It was only a matter of minutes before Frank found out what he'd meant; leaning over the back of the boat he was sick for the first time without doing too much damage to himself, although he soon stopped caring about those details. It had been the first time of many and Frank had felt the pitiful looks of the men around him, so after a while he'd decided to find himself a place to lie down, where he slowly started to feel less ill, but extremely weak nevertheless.

What was he going to report about the day: lessons to be learned for landlubbers – like trust your instincts, and stay away from water? The only thing intact was his sense of irony, he thought. He heard the noises above his head; how could these men operate without any problems?

'Here, take one of these.' Without warning Thomas stood next to him, holding a tin in his hand. 'Dry crackers.' The tall man tried awkwardly to hold himself up straight in the small yacht and Frank hesitantly took the flat biscuit tin, not sure what to do with it as he wasn't able to eat anything.

'Trust me, eating a few will help settle your stomach.'

'Thank you. Damned nuisance, this.'

'It can catch you any time.' Thomas spoke with a gentle West Country drawl and tried to reassure Frank. 'Even the most experienced fishermen will succumb to a bout of seasickness, so I wouldn't concern yourself about it too much.' He smiled wryly. 'But do come back up when you can; you'll fare much better in the fresh air. Besides, our passage will become smoother when we round St. Catherine's Point and there might be some excitement you would be disappointed to miss,' he added cryptically while leaving.

Frank gazed at the tin for some time before deciding to put his trust in Thomas and to eat a couple of biscuits; they were extremely dry in his mouth and difficult to swallow. After a while, he noticed that, for the first time in a couple of hours, the constant feeling of queasiness had started to fade. Maybe it was possible to go on deck without embarrassing himself. He rose to his feet, steadying himself with one hand against the hull.

He could hear that there was a commotion up on deck; men cursing and hurrying to one side of the yacht. Something had happened and the only way to find out was to leave the relative safety of the cabin. Frank took a deep breath, pursed his lips and made his way little by little up and out on deck.

The instant the fresh air hit his face, he knew he was going to be all right; it filled his lungs and swept the stale and nauseating particles right out of his body. And with every breath he took, his sense of relief grew, as he realised that he wasn't going to be sick for the rest of the journey. The men had congregated at the midpoint of the ship and were arguing loudly while looking out to sea.

'She looks out of control.'

'Indeed, she seems to be drifting; do you think we should stand by in case she needs our assistance?'

Frank spotted two of the other smaller yachts of the fleet; one was sailing in the same direction as they were, but the other gave the impression of not being steered at all, sail flapping in the wind, bow pointing in the wrong direction.

'If they can get the damaged jib boom out of the way, they should be able to sail her on just the main sail.' *Aurora*'s skipper sounded disappointed. 'Another rival gone, most unfortunate.'

The yacht that had suffered the damage was *Volante*, the one that had been doing so well earlier that morning.

'Gentlemen, that leaves us to follow her around. I suggest we return to our stations, there's nothing we can do for them.'

Frank followed the skipper's gaze; in the not too far distance he caught sight of the easily recognisable shape of *America* as she slowly but surely disappeared on the horizon.

'I'm hoping that these shifting winds will wane once we've rounded the most southerly point and with luck it will remain that way, which will most definitely be to our advantage.'

The men murmured words of agreement and returned to work.

'I see you're back among the living,' the Captain said almost kindly, acknowledging Frank's presence.

'Yes, thank goodness, I hope my resurrection will last.'

'There's no reason that it shouldn't. I hope so, because we have some way still to go.'

They were sailing close under the cliffs and Frank recognised they were somewhere to the most south-westerly part of the Island, gradually making their way towards the western part, the Needles, after which the course continued through the Solent, past Hurst Castle on the mainland and back to the finish line at

Cowes. "Some way" sounded quite the understatement.

It didn't take long before there was no other contender in sight. *America* was nowhere to be seen and the other boats that had accompanied them, like *Freak*, had also disappeared from view. There were the odd spectator steamers sailing close to the coast, which meant some distraction from scenery that was otherwise hardly changing. Looking away from the coastline, Frank imagined the immense stretch of water between England and America. Being out of reach of the mainland would have petrified him not that long ago, but as swimming back was no option, his only choice was to enjoy the trip as an experience in itself. He sat back; there was something about the solitude that forced one to appreciate the sea for what it was.

He watched the men at work; nobody had time to talk as the Captain continually pushed them on, accepting no idleness, relentlessly giving commands to tighten or loosen a sail. They were so far behind the leader of the fleet that Frank queried the Captain's decision to drive his men this hard; wasn't it time he started to enjoy a day of sailing as well? He glanced at the man on the tiller; he clearly had a different idea. Eyes scrutinizing the elements around him, the Captain was giving it his all, albeit in pursuit of an unattainable goal.

'May I ask you something?' Frank moved closer to the Captain.

'Please do. Gather the foresail, can't you hear the sail slacking?' the Captain bellowed to one of the crew who jumped up. 'We will be approaching the Needles shortly, so I shall require all hands on deck.'

Again, this optimism in the Captain's voice, as if he was expecting a miracle on the last leg of the race. 'Have you been sailing long?'

'All my life. There is little else to gainfully occupy a man on an island.'

'Do you do a lot of sailing for pleasure – I mean, for sport?'

'Yes, a couple of weeks per year I get asked to command some yachts. But I do get paid for it – no, tighten the jib a bit more!' he called out. 'And I'm competitive,' he continued in a normal voice, 'so this type of racing suits me well.'

'So, you won't mind me asking how you manage not to get discouraged at this point in a race?'

'What do you mean?'

Frank had to think for a moment; how could he say there didn't seem to be any use in continuing the pursuit of *America* or even the finish line?

'Well, I have observed you still pushing your men very hard and I was wondering why, as the likelihood of us catching the leading yacht seems quite remote.'

'What makes you say that?'

'I thought that, considering we haven't seen *America* for some time and with a long way still to go...' Frank didn't finish his sentence; he wasn't sure if the look on the Captain's face was one of disappointment or amusement.

The Captain looked up towards the top of the mast. 'You see that little strip of cloth, flying horizontally along the sail?' He pointed roughly a third of the way up. 'You keep an eye on that; once we've rounded the Needles you'll see it'll start to flutter and shake and that's when we are going to strike.'

Frank wasn't sure what he meant; what was so important at the Needles?

'*America* will have passed them by now and she'll be drifting in lighter winds that will barely be able to move her. She's a hundred and seventy tons, much heavier than our own forty-seven.' He looked straight at Frank: 'I would never abandon a race while we still have a fighting chance.'

'But how do you decide you still have a chance?'

'Years of experience and instinct. The race won't be won until at least one vessel has crossed the finish line.' His hand gripped the tiller tightly. 'I've never understood men who don't see something through to the end.'

Frank felt he was talking directly to him – someone who had

given up several times in life and who always ended up walking away.

'What's your instinct telling you on this day?' Frank cleared his throat.

A quick smile flashed over the Captain's face. 'So, you'd like to learn about the tactics of fighting a lost cause?'

Frank grinned self-consciously. 'Wouldn't we all?'

'Because no handicap applies in this race, we're at somewhat of a disadvantage. But their strength, being the heavier boat, could at the same time be their weakness. When the wind lightens, they'll slow down, yet we will find small breezes to propel us forward and if we're patient and keep pushing it, we might be able to gain several miles in a few hours.'

'That almost sounds easy.'

'It never is. You need good fortune and a willingness to take risks: better a wrong decision than none at all. We sometimes gamble on the best route across and we end up finding no wind, but that's part of the game.'

'That probably applies to a lot in life,' Frank murmured.

It didn't seem long before they arrived at the Needles; the white chalky cliffs sticking out of the water like rugged icebergs were pink in the slowly disappearing daylight. He could see the sharp and grim-looking edge of the ridge of each of them that must have given them their name. They passed the formation of three steep stacks of chalk closer than Frank liked; he couldn't help but anticipate a collision at any time. He looked towards the shore, wondering if he would manage to reach it by trying somehow to stay afloat.

'There are several high-rise rock faces around here, but also several shingle banks, so we have to carefully plan our course around them.' The Captain seemed to have read his mind. 'If you don't want to go the same way as the wrecks that lie off here, you'd better read your sea charts carefully before you set out. Another valuable lesson for every sailor: be prepared for the risks that hide under the surface. There you go.' His voice was suddenly triumphant.

Frank felt it as well; he looked up at the strip of cloth, which drooped for a brief moment, before the Captain raised his voice and commanded the men to adjust the sails. The wind had faded significantly, although Frank couldn't tell how much it had slowed *Aurora* down. He glanced at the shoreline; they seemed to be moving at the same speed. There were still some people on top of the colourful sea cliffs of what he knew to be Alum Bay; he could hear them cheering and he wondered how long they'd been waiting for their arrival after *America* had passed them presumably some time ago.

'If we can find a good breeze now, it won't be that long before we reach the narrow entrance to the Solent and after that the last stretch towards the finish line.'

'Let's do this!'

'Let's chase her down!'

'Let's take her home!'

Loud cheers of encouragement travelled through the slowly darkening evening. The men pumped their fists and slapped each other on the shoulders. If races were won based on camaraderie and mutual encouragement, this crew would definitely win today, Frank thought; they clearly shared the same belief in doing the impossible.

Sailing had the ability to eat chunks out of time and make you lose all sense of it; not just when you were flat on your back in the belly of a ship, feeling sorry for yourself, but also on deck, seeing wave after wave pass by.

It seemed that not long after rounding the Needles, they'd reached the narrow entrance to the Solent; they sailed through the middle of the gap where the channel was at its deepest, with the coastline of Hampshire on one side and on the other the Island.

Aurora had found a good breeze and it felt as if they were flying the last stretch home; it was getting late and Frank wondered if they would make it back before dark and in time for the fireworks display organised by the Squadron in Cowes. He'd hoped he would get to take Josephine, but that prospect was becoming less likely by the minute.

His thoughts drifted to her; he realised she came from the same stock as these men: hard-working, eternally optimistic, making the best out of a dire situation and never giving up. He wondered why she'd decided to spend time with him as he felt he wasn't like any of them and he wasn't convinced it was possible to change. Could he win a battle in which the contenders were much bigger than him?

With a determined look on his face he rose to his feet; it was time he explored the ship he'd been a guest on all day. The bow seemed far away from where he was standing, but what could happen as long as he held on and made sure the boom wasn't going to hit him unexpectedly? He'd done it before. He stepped up on deck, making sure he kept his balance.

'Careful now.' It was Thomas, who was busy clearing lines.

'May I have a look around?'

'Of course, just mind where you're going; we have no time for the man-overboard manoeuvre.'

'I'll do my utmost to remain on board; I've had enough drama today.' He tried to anticipate the movement of the ship instead of fighting it, while keeping his eyes on the fading horizon. There weren't many points of recognition left, but in the distance he detected another sailing ship, going in the same direction as they were. It had to be bigger than theirs, for he was able to see it. They hadn't seen a sailing ship for some time and Frank wondered where they'd set sail from at this late hour.

Thomas joined him at the bow: 'Curious to see that you'd made it.' He grinned.

'Thomas, what do you think about that?' A thought had formed in Frank's head, but he didn't want to sound any more of a layman than he already had. Thomas followed the direction of his finger and Frank watched him do what he'd done himself just before; he squeezed his eyes, moved his head as if to have a closer look and then opened his mouth a little as if not believing what he saw.

'Could that be –?' Frank tried to remember what she looked like from afar.

'Aye yes, no doubt about it!' Thomas started to wave his hands frantically at the Captain. 'Sails straight ahead, two points off starboard bow!'

The other men rushed towards them, one by one confirming it had to be *America*. But instead of the expected exuberant behaviour they'd displayed earlier that day at the thought of catching her, they were eerily quiet, merely watching the ship in the distance, each with their own thoughts. The air was heavy with the inevitable question of whether they still had a chance.

Frank grabbed Thomas by the arm. 'Are you telling me that *America* hasn't finished yet?'

'Not yet. The finish line is off Cowes and looking at her, I guess she could be somewhere near Thorney Bay.'

'Really?'

'Which by my reckoning means she has been running very slowly over the last few miles, whereas we've been gaining distance continually and if this continues,' his voice dropped to a whisper, 'this could be close, very close indeed.'

'Don't just stand there.' The voice of the Captain roared through the air. 'Work as you've never done before.' After all these hours on the water, mostly without another yacht in sight, was there still a possibility they could overtake *America* and win? Frank felt disbelief, but also an unexpected feeling of jubilation; even in the final hour, an outcome could be turned around completely, transforming this miserable day into something extraordinary. *Aurora* had been second for a very long time and the notion that they had an opportunity to change that role was immensely thrilling.

Somehow, the ending of the race echoed their progress throughout most of the day. First of all, it was painfully slow;

Frank became increasingly frustrated by their apparent failure to advance towards the other yacht, even though the men around him worked as hard as they could. But then, all of a sudden, *America* was close enough to be clearly recognisable, low against the dark water with her long masts carrying sails that struggled with the wind.

He tried to figure out how long it would take them to get sufficiently close to identify the men on board. Half an hour? Twenty minutes? Even sooner than that?

There was no mistaking the pressure the crew was under; after sailing for one long day, they were now within reaching distance of the number one in the fleet. Even Frank understood that as long as they had enough miles to the finish line, they would eventually catch up. Briefly he let his mind wander to the eventuality of that happening, but an overriding feeling of betrayal stopped him; whatever the outcome was, he felt as if he would be letting someone down.

Although the Americans were still some distance away, it seemed that the approach of *Aurora* had set her crew into action. Snippets of commands could be heard over the ever-diminishing amount of water between them.

Frank wished he knew how much further they had to go. The last familiar bit of coastline they'd passed had been the mouth of Newtown River some time back, yet from the Captain's intensifying commands it was obvious that it wasn't that much longer to Cowes.

He thought he'd recognised the wooded area in which he'd walked with Josephine, not that far from to the west of the town. He knew what that meant. The Castle was near and their progress was taking too much time; only a miracle gust of wind in their sails would make a victory possible. The crew kept their heads down, concentrating on what was expected of them, pushing the yacht forwards. But *America* seemed to make a last spurt towards the end goal and if there had been any doubt, the sound of the guns going off made it all too clear; the first yacht had crossed the finish line; it was all over.

Frank sat down in the cockpit, exhausted and out of breath. How cruel to get so close in the end; to be given the hope they could actually win the race but to find it had been a hard day's work for nothing.

Over the quiet water came the sound of cheers from a crowd; that must be for *America*, Frank thought with torn emotions. Although they'd lost, the English clearly hadn't lost their sense of sportsmanship and were showing their support for the American victory.

He looked around the yacht; the men were still working hard; somehow he'd expected them to slow down or even stop altogether given that they'd come second, but they carried on. It was now almost dark as the Castle came into sight and with it, the lights and the people on shore. That's how close they'd managed to get to *America* in the end, Frank thought as he pulled his watch from his jacket pocket: about seven minutes had passed since he had heard the guns.

As they glided teasingly slowly through the water towards the finish line, everything around them was silent: no gunshots, no cheers from the shore, the men on board voiceless. Suffering defeat was a lonely affair. But it didn't take long before the spectators realised another boat had finished and soon an appreciative cheer burst out.

Against the lit quay, Frank saw the people who had probably only arrived to watch the firework display and had no inkling about the achievement of the small yacht that they'd seen arrive in the dark. Within no time, they were back anchored at almost the exact same spot where they'd started some twelve hours before. Frank felt worn out and empty; he thanked the Captain for the opportunity and promised him a copy of the story he'd write about the race. The Captain was polite and even managed a joke about a happy ending.

When Frank finally felt the solid ground under his feet he thought he'd be more thrilled about it; earlier that day he'd envisioned lowering himself to his knees and kissing the ground while vowing never ever to leave land again. But he couldn't care much about being back on land except for the sudden empty feeling in his stomach; with wonder, he realised that the overriding feeling after such an exhausting day could be one of hunger.

Chapter 28

'How dare he?' Commodore Stevens slammed the cabin door shut. The muffled sound of the angry conversation with Hamilton continued behind closed doors.

John and the other men on the yacht were astounded to hear their displeasure. They were still recovering from their state of euphoria which had started after they had finished in Cowes the previous evening and had continued long into the night and early morning.

They had celebrated their victorious win with everyone who had been willing to share in their joy. And there had been many. As soon as the signal of their victory had reverberated around the quays of Cowes and they had set foot on shore to the tunes of a band playing Yankee Doodle, they had been welcomed as the heroes of the day. Not one of the English had shown anything but sincere delight in their success. Theirs had been a convincing win and everybody seemed to agree.

And this was the case even with the Captain of the little cutter *Aurora* that had surprised them by sneaking up in the last hour. Straight after anchoring her, he had come over and shown his respect. *Aurora* had come close in the end, but every member of the American yacht had known she stood no chance.

The way they had been treated with such generosity of spirit made the Commodore's suggestion of unsportsmanlike conduct all the more peculiar. His words before retreating below decks hung around John and the men like a dark cloud raining on their delight.

'I don't get it, most of the gentlemen of the Squadron I met last night, however mortified at being beaten, never manifested the slightest indication of displeasure. On the contrary, they were courteous and their expressions of congratulations to us were most remarkable.' Hamilton sounded equally disbelieving. 'Who was this man, you said?'

'One of the English yacht owners. How dare he suggest we in effect won a cup, but in fact lost the race because we didn't comply with the rules? He was heard to say that if the Americans choose to cheat, they should consider themselves lamentably beaten. What a disgrace; is he trying to steal the wind out of our sails after the event? We have beaten them on land and now at sea as well; let them accept that even in yachting Britannia is no longer the mistress of the seas!'

On deck, the men were left wondering what the accusation specifically entailed.

'Mr Ackers, the owner of the schooner *Brilliant*, has logged an official complaint. Something about not following the right racing course around the Nab lightship,' Captain Brown mumbled with a furious look on his face. Evidently not every Englishman had accepted the outcome.

John knew immediately what Captain Brown was referring to; he remembered each segment of the race down to the finest detail. Mainly because the nerve-racking situation at the start of the race had left him in a heightened state of anxiety and with a sharpened memory.

After the guns had fired from the clubhouse battery and before the smoke had lifted, the rest of the fleet had been fully sheeted with canvas and on their way. But Captain Brown seemed to have a different idea; he had taken his time and ordered for the sails not to be hoisted until the others were out of the way. It had been the longest few minutes of John's life. As a result, they had to chase the other yachts from last position in the field.

Eventually they had started to overtake the rest of the fleet. John clearly recalled the exhilarating feeling of effortlessly gaining distance and gliding past the other yachts one by one. The men worked as a team; nobody could have guessed that almost half of the crew at work were volunteering English seamen who had joined them recently.

But the smaller yachts of the fleet were keeping up with them and it had been a close race until No Man's Land Buoy, just after Ryde, which was rounded first by the cutter *Volante*, the second smallest boat in the race and then by another three of the English boats before *America* could catch up. It was after they had turned the buoy that the wind had freshened to about six knots and *America* had found her speed and had overtaken *Volante*.

Not long after that, they had noticed that some of the yachts were running a different course to them; they were sailing away from the coast towards the north, which had seemed to John like a longer way around. The Captain and the pilot Underwood had been having an intense conversation until the Commodore demanded their attention.

'Captain, what course are we sailing?' Commodore Stevens's voice rose above the increasing wind while he viewed the other yachts through his telescope.

'Sir, this is what we discussed earlier. That's the Nab lightship over there. In regattas, they usually round it to the east, but our sailing instructions didn't specify such a course. Mr Underwood here says the tide is just right for us to head inside instead.'

'I like the sound of that, Captain. Underwood, are you sure we have enough time and water to do that?'

'Ay, Sir, if we make sure we keep her well outside the white and black marker buoys to our west. It will save us plenty of ground.'

'If you say the risk isn't too great, let's take her inside.' Stevens grinned contentedly. 'Why are the others not doing the same?'

'Sir, I don't know. Perhaps they don't dare to divert from the route they are used to. I suggest we take the shortest route.'

'Underwood, you're a man after my own heart.'

The rest of the race had passed without too many incidents. Apart from the jib boom breaking off, which could have been a disaster but had pleased the Captain enormously, they seemed to have left their rivals behind. Briefly, they had seen *Aurora*, *Freak* and *Volante* as a little squadron in the distance, but the wind had freshened again and for hours theirs were the only sails on the horizon.

The wind falling away on several occasions during the day had worried John, but as far as he could see, it had no one else. Seeing the Royal steam-yacht at Alum Bay after they had rounded the Needles late in the afternoon had lifted every man's spirit. They had offered their respect to the Queen by taking off their hats and dipping their flags. Not even the dying wind had spoiled that moment.

It had taken them another two and a half hours after that to get to Cowes. Seeing *Aurora*'s sails rapidly approaching in the last stretch to the finish line had been as surprising as the Commodore's news that somebody didn't want them to win the Cup for which they had fought so hard, not just during the regatta, but over the previous weeks.

The men gathered around the cockpit; some of them looked the worse for wear but all of them were lost for words, as they worriedly contemplated what would happen next.

Suddenly, the Commodore stormed out of the stateroom with Hamilton in tow, brusquely informing the Captain that they were off to the Clubhouse to hear the outcome of the protest and to receive that 'damned Cup'.

When Comstock returned from dropping them off on the quay, he handed John a leaflet and whispered that 'lucky the Commodore never wanted a piece of metal'. John looked at what he had given him; in his hand was a printed programme of the race they had won outright. Or so they thought. He scanned the text impatiently until his eyes fell on the words 'race to be round the Isle of Wight, inside Noman's Buoy and Sandhead Buoy and outside the Nab'.

Comstock shrugged his shoulders as if he couldn't care less, but John knew he was just as upset as he was. They huddled together - *was their reward going to be denied them after all?*

'At least we left them with something to think about.' Comstock sounded like an older brother trying to offer comfort, making John wonder if he looked like someone in need of comforting.

'When I dropped them off, there were some men on the quay discussing where they were going wrong with their own designs. They were already considering the improvements they could make to their hulls and sails.'

'Oh.'

'The Englishman who is willing to learn from us. That's a big compliment, isn't it?'

'Sure.'

'Although one suggested buying *America*, which would save them some time building a new one.' Comstock grinned foolishly, knowing his attempt to lighten the mood had fallen flat. 'What will you do after we're done here?'

John looked blankly at Comstock; he hadn't thought about it for a long time. He wished he knew.

'You're spoilt for choice now: a carpenter who can sail! I'm sure you'll be in demand anywhere you go.' He gave John an encouraging tap on the shoulder.

Before he could admit to Comstock that sailing wasn't for him, and that from now on the only travel on a boat would be to get somewhere, Comstock said grimly, 'Here they come.'

After what felt like ages, the Commodore and Hamilton signalled their arrival on the harbour wall. The men tried to read their faces to determine the result of the meeting, but the distance was too great.

As they climbed aboard, the Commodore smiled broadly and said, 'We've done it; we've won! The Squadron has made it official by dismissing the protest.'

There was a sigh of relief amongst the crew, but the Captain grumbled. 'We already knew, what took them so long?'

'Calm down, Captain, they acknowledged the sailing instructions they gave us contained no guidance on rounding the

Nab. The fact that a number of the other participants chose the same course must have helped; they had no choice.' The Commodore turned to the men, 'Gentlemen, let me take this opportunity to thank you for your endeavours and your unfaltering commitment to this cause. In the contest of speed organised by John Bull we've shown that little Brother Jonathan has produced the faster sailing boat. And we not only outran them, we've gone so far ahead of the entire English fleet that nobody else was left in sight! I might add that our victorious yacht has done more to humble the pride of England than anything else since the war of 1812!'

'Hear, hear.'

'It won't be long before we will be presented with a trophy and return home to tell our people every practical success of the Exhibition belongs to the Americans. As a young nation, not yet a century old, we can hold up our heads proudly and stand tall in the knowledge that we can achieve more than our ancestors give us credit for. From now on, we stand on an equal footing with our forefathers. Britannia no longer rules the waves!'

'Well done, let's drink to that!'

'Harkness, let's see if the liquor store has something to offer and let's have a drink to us: courageous men who, against the odds, have achieved the unthinkable because of our willingness to forge ahead; here's to genius and perseverance.'

The men filled their mugs and raised them in a toast. Comstock grinned and turned to John. 'Here's to us and what we do best!'

John smiled back. He had asked himself that question numerous times; *what was he best at?*

'I bet that by next August every vessel of the Squadron will be trimmed to the very image of *America*!' mused Comstock, waiving in the direction of the Island.

John looked at Cowes in the background and the green hills in the distance; could it be that the answer was closer by than he had considered?

Chapter 29

Frank woke up in the middle of a dream with a feeling of immense guilt. He lay motionless on his bed, wondering what had stirred him from his nightmare. There were a few faint noises, but it seemed as though everyone in the cottage was still in a deep sleep. He recalled the disappointed faces of the crewmembers of the yacht he had been travelling on before he'd fallen overboard. He could even remember the shock of the cold water, but most of all, he remembered the feeling of being to blame for just missing out on a victory, because they'd had to turn back to fetch him from the sea. It wasn't apparent which boat he had been sailing on, nor which race it was, but the shame of being responsible for their defeat was as clear and chilling as the water he had plunged into. They didn't even have his drowning as a reason for their loss, he thought wryly – whoever *they* were.

It was still too early to get up and so he rolled onto his side, pushing the pillow further under his head. He thought about the actual race of Friday; he'd played no role in the event, so he didn't believe that the outcome of that battle could have been the reason for his dream. What had happened that day should have pleased him no matter what; he'd been fantasizing about it for such a long time that he should have been contented it had finally taken place. But now that it was over and done with, he felt oddly deflated.

To see the happy faces of the crew of *America* when they'd met on the quay of Cowes had generated a brief sense of pride, as he'd always proclaimed theirs was the faster yacht. But thinking of what *Aurora* had almost managed to achieve had created disappointment nevertheless. The crew of *Aurora* had been graceful in defeat and he'd wondered how they managed it, having come so close to a victory. Maybe he wasn't the sportsman they were; he didn't like the idea that somebody had to be second. But Archie had cryptically reminded him there was no point in becoming first if there was no second.

On the day after the race, when he had returned to the anchor site of *Aurora*, he had met Archie and the crew to discuss how well she had sailed.

Archie shook the hand of one of the men and said encouragingly, 'Next time you'll do it.'

'I'm of the opinion they already did.' Another man had joined their group.

'What makes you say that?'

'Haven't you heard? *America* rounded the Nab lightship on the inside, not like you and most of the rest of the fleet; that must have saved her about ten minutes.' He nodded knowingly. 'Do your calculations, gentlemen; you arrived eight minutes later.'

It had taken Frank a brief moment to realise that it must have happened while he had been sick below deck.

'Why didn't you follow her, like some of the others?'

The Captain of *Aurora* shrugged his shoulders. 'We always round the lightship to the east. I didn't see any reason to do it differently; I couldn't take the chance and get us disqualified. No use crying over spilt milk,' he mumbled.

'But their pilot should have known; after all he was English!' a young crewmember exclaimed.

The group fell silent; the sense of injustice felt by some hung in the air.

The house was slowly waking up; the floors creaked as people moved around, and a soft murmur of voices could be heard. Frank didn't feel like getting out of bed; he had a thumping head and a heavy heart. His eyes fell on his half-packed travel bag and he knew he couldn't delay his journey back home much longer.

He swung his legs over the side of the bed, pausing for a moment on the edge; how different things would have been if they'd had rounded the Nab lightship in the same way as the Americans had done. Or if they had sailed with a time allowance for tonnage.

In the end, the Royal Yacht Squadron had treated the Americans well. They had allowed them to boom out against the rules and they had waved the one-owner rule. And now they had dismissed the complaint. The decision made by the English pilot, however, remained intriguing; he should have known better.

He sat looking at his feet and bare legs: the limbs of a man getting on in life. He didn't like the way they had changed, how they were losing their strength. And he didn't like where they had been when, driven by his ambition for recognition and gratification, they had taken him to a desolate place which he had been desperate to leave.

However, there was no more time for regret and self-pity. Instead, the time had come to put pen to paper. Writing was what he was good at, but he had been in need of a reminder as it had become more of a curse than a gift. Didn't George call it one's "unique contribution"?

Frank smiled at the thought of George; he would return home to the news of a victory which he'd never doubted. But for Frank, going home wasn't that straightforward.

He rose from the bed, walked over to the windows and threw open the curtains; he stared out over the garden towards the sea. He knew it had been a dream, but they hadn't let him drown; he'd been found and dragged back on board, cold and wet but relieved. They had been defeated, but it had been suffered with grace. There were no sore losers. Perhaps their defeat was seen as temporary, until the next chance to win presented itself. He himself needed to prepare for that next chance. He owed it to the people behind his stories.

And even if he could no longer walk, he could still write.

The garden below was slowly being lit by the early August sun. He'd already seen a change in the colour and the angle of the light, with the shadows starting to elongate as the sun crept lower. Soon the autumn chill would arrive. A different worry crept back into his mind: he had to say goodbye to Josephine. He didn't want it to be a definite farewell but not knowing what she felt about him was troubling. She had given him the impression she was enjoying his company as much as he did hers. But after his decision to tell her of his suspicion that several of the people they'd run into had taken part in buying and selling young girls, he didn't know what to expect. And when he had gathered up the courage to explain his failed marriage to Agnes, and the breakdown of his life afterwards, Josephine had turned completely silent.

He desperately wanted to explain his decision to tell her, but as Josephine had been busy with the guests in their fully booked cottage, they had only managed looks at each other from across a crowded dining room.

He felt such an idiot; he had made no plan as to how he was going to say goodbye and how to convey his feelings towards her; he was an indecisive fool in love.

When he'd finally got dressed and fully packed, he walked past the busy dining room as he had no appetite for breakfast.

The option to sneak out was tempting; he couldn't think of anything to say to Josephine. With his bags in one hand and his coat and hat in the other, he walked into the hallway. On the little table, he scribbled down his name in the guestbook and looked for a separate piece of paper. Maybe he could leave Josephine a message; writing was so much easier.

'You weren't going to leave without saying goodbye, were you?'

Josephine's voice came out of nowhere. He turned around to see her standing in the half dark of the corridor, hands on hips, with a stern face. *Was she angry?*

'I, erm, couldn't find you.' He sounded apologetic and stepped awkwardly in her direction. This was what he'd been trying to avoid: the disappointment he would feel after finding out she rejected him.

'Really?' Her voice sounded less forbidding. 'You didn't look that hard.'

Frank wondered how long she'd been standing there. He should have known better; she saw through his lies already.

'I didn't know what to say.'

'So you decided to leave without saying anything?' She stepped out from the darkness, her inquiring eyes insisting on a straight answer.

Was there sadness in her eyes? Her candour encouraged him to be truthful and in a hoarse voice he said, 'Don't ask me if I'm leaving or in what manner; ask me when I'll be back.'

'Will you come back?' she asked forthrightly.

He sensed the vulnerability of someone strong enough to take care of themselves, but willing to allow another into their lives. 'Yes, I will.' He took one more step until he was as close to her as he dared. Gently, he put his hand to her face and lifted her chin. 'I hope you'll let me back in.' He watched her face intently, trying to read her mind. The biggest heart-warming smile he'd ever seen crossed the face in front of him and if he'd had any doubts about her feelings for him, they had just evaporated into thin air.

'When will you be back?' She cupped her hands around his.

'I've got one more thing to resolve.' He had difficulties refraining from pulling her into his arms and he concentrated as hard as he could on what he was about to say. 'In London.'

'You're not talking about Agnes.'

Frank looked at her in surprise. 'No, I'm not, she no longer needs me.'

'Will you be careful?'

It had never crossed his mind that what he had been working on could be dangerous; he had no intention of getting himself into trouble. 'I'll be back as soon as I can.'

'Even if that means crossing the water?'

'I no longer care,' he said, while his heart skipped a beat.

Chapter 30

A seagull shrieked; it struggled with the bitter winds, flapping its wings, seemingly out of control.

Just out of reach of the frothy waves, it steadied itself and continued with speed along the surface.

Frank watched the scene in front of him, his shoulders hunched against the cold, the collar of his warm jacket turned up. The air was biting; winter was not yet forgotten.

The boats bounced patiently on the water, as they had done for months now, idle and forlorn, waiting for the change of season and for the men who would take them out once more.

Not only were the boats abandoned; the whole place was. Most sensible human beings avoided the outdoors on a chilly day like this. Except for one other person who sat on a bench, also wrapped in a thick coat and scarf, similarly attracted to the rough seas.

They both caught sight of the seagull passing them swiftly overhead, marvelling at its ability to master the unpredictable winds.

Frank was automatically drawn to the stranger, not least due to the fact that the man was sitting in the most sheltered part of the harbour. When he drew near, he realised the man wasn't overly interested in the view; he was trying to read a newspaper, albeit with great difficulty. Such was his immersion in the story that he was unconcerned about the horizontal sprays of water and also Frank's presence.

He watched him for a while, admiring how he managed to read something as clumsy as a paper by folding it into small manageable pieces.

'That must be one hell of a story.'

The other man was taken by surprise. He turned and acknowledged Frank with a brief nod. The two men studied each other with interest, each wondering why the other, underneath the layers of clothing, seemed familiar.

'Any space on your bench for a rambler who's chilled to the bone?'

'Please, go ahead.'

He sat down on the wooden seat; he had expected to hear the other man's American accent. He smiled and pointed at the newspaper. 'Anything interesting in there?'

The younger man looked at the paper in his hand. 'Well, I'm not sure, I've only managed to read the first page and the last; I should have known better than to take it out.'

'You're the first person I've encountered attempting to read a newspaper in force eight winds.'

'I was reading an article in here about that sailing race last summer.'

'Ah, the one in which the Americans took away a cup and left us with a lesson learned? What about it?'

'That's the one.' The other man smiled. 'I was just reminded of how easily it could have been a different result: not as humiliating for the English as the American newspapers have made it out to be. They keep repeating the phrase that there was "no second that day" but I know for a fact that *Aurora* finished only minutes after *America*.'

'Ah, but there's no honour to be had in being second nor any prize to be won; perhaps they're referring to that. Or...,' he turned to the man next to him, 'it could be they're alluding to the Cup that was won; I've been told the engraver left out *Aurora*.'

'Really?'

'Yes, all boats participating that day are mentioned, except for the one that came second.' Frank smiled. 'Can I take the opportunity to compliment you and your fellow countrymen on your deserved win? That yacht was a creation of someone's dreams and I salute the man whose dream it was; he should have all the credit.'

'Funny you bring that up. If you are referring to the designer, I have to disappoint you; this newspaper mentions that George Steers did not get the recognition back in New York for the part he played.' The younger man pushed the paper inside his coat.

'You sound annoyed.' Frank felt slightly like a fraud since he well knew what was in the article.

'Well, it says here how they celebrated their victory with a special dinner in New York and unveiled the cup they'd won, but that it was in honour of the owners of the yacht, not of Steers.'

'Really?'

'Steers wasn't even invited to the dinner, apparently. What a disgrace.' The American pulled up his collar.

'Don't despair. If you read on, you'll see that he has received a lot of attention over here. He's inspired people on to innovations in the shipbuilding industry. Even on this island.'

'He should have stayed in his native country,' the younger man murmured under his breath.

'Excuse me?' Had the other man referred to Steers's place of birth, something Steers seemed to keep mostly to himself?

'Never mind.'

They sat in silence for a while, watching some rubbish being lifted up by a little twist of wind, before it got blown higher in the air.

'I met him once last summer. He had a lot of expectations resting on his shoulders.' Frank paused before continuing. 'We ourselves met during that important sailing week, don't you remember?'

'I knew you looked familiar.'

'Why did you come back to the Island?' Frank wanted to know.

'I never left.'

'Really? Similar to me. What a coincidence. I moved here not long after that race. Only I didn't have to travel as far as you.' He hesitated. 'May I ask where home is? Or should I say "was"?'

'New York. Manhattan to be more precise.'

'You've travelled all that way from one island to come and live on another much smaller one? Why?' Frank was pleased to see a smile flash across the other man's face.

'I wanted something new, but if you put it like that, I haven't quite managed it, have I?' The smile was now full of self-mockery. 'I considered living in London briefly, but I guess I prefer a smaller place.'

He pulled the newspaper from his coat and showed Frank the front page. 'Here, another reason for not wanting to live in a big city with its debauchery.' He sounded flustered once more. 'Did you hear about it – the scandal emerging about some high-ranking people involved in selling young English girls into…' He faltered. 'Some sort of slave trade? These girls were very young, some only as old as ten.'

Frank watched the man's agitation and just nodded.

'They treated these girls as dispensable goods. I just read that they were sold abroad, never to be seen again.'

'Awful story.'

'The person who discovered the crimes spent years figuring out these girls hadn't just walked away from home, but were the victims of men with a perverse interest.'

'Years?'

'Yes, he had to pretend he was one of these men himself; some say it ruined him. Especially when he discovered that the son of a respected member of society was involved, and everyone turned against him; he was on his own.'

'And who is this man?'

'Nobody knows; his letters are anonymous and we haven't had all the instalments yet. Some think he could be a policeman as he discovered that the police were involved in avoiding raids on certain brothels, protecting specific prostitutes and with that the men who visited them.'

'Police officer? Instalments? Couldn't that just be a trick by the newspaper: come up with an exciting story and have the reader pay for extra editions?'

'Maybe, but the paper printing it would take an enormous risk, don't you think?'

'What do you mean?'

'The anonymous letter-writer is implicating the owner and family members of a rival paper, which would suggest that the evidence had to be checked thoroughly, otherwise they'd be in trouble, wouldn't they?' He suddenly turned to Frank. 'I thought you were a reporter, you should know.'

'I guess so.'

The American became quiet and stared vacantly in front of him. 'Think about those poor girls' families; they will now find out about their awful fate. I think they're better off not knowing what happened to them.'

'You think so? Because I think living with uncertainty is worse.'

'I'm not so sure about that. Nor is the letter-writer; unearthing the truth almost killed him. The rumour has it that he got arrested and subsequently lost his job. They say that it took so much out of him, he'll never work again and has gone into hiding.'

'Is that true? Interesting.' The irony didn't escape him; supposedly he'd had to stop working to finally get noticed. Maybe there was some truth in it; writing for the Island paper and helping to run a lodging house probably wouldn't be seen as fitting work for a reporter who had once worked for the best newspaper in the country. However, standing on the sidelines and being an 'activist letter writer', as Josephine kept calling him, suited him perfectly, even if it meant he would no longer be able receive recognition for the things he achieved.

And as far as the gossip about his hideout was concerned: it wasn't as if he'd gone to a place where he could waste away the time he'd left. It was more like he'd arrived in the safety of the harbour after enduring a storm at sea.

'I suppose some of us seek refuge by looking for a place to hide, and others keep on moving.' He glanced quickly at the American, adding, 'As long as one feels at home wherever one ends up. I hope the Islanders have made you feel welcome.'

'Yes, they have. And what about you?'

'The same for me; they've embraced me – literally, so to speak.' He gave the American a wink.

'Ah, a lady brought you here?'

He felt the eyes of the younger man on him: he thought he could see a surprised look. Most people had reacted the same way when he told them he was going to move again, although Harold said he had known all along; he hadn't stopped smirking, telling everyone in the office it was because of him that Frank had conquered his fear of the sea and had found love on the way. Harold had been the first friend to visit them at the cottage.

'No American lady has joined you here?' He immediately regretted his question when he saw the sadness in the younger man's eyes. 'I didn't mean to pry, I do apologise.'

'That's all right, I don't mind you asking. There was a lady back home.' He paused, as if trying to find the words. 'It's a long story. We met in very unfortunate circumstances and we kept reminding one another of sad times; I don't think we were right for each other.'

'So you left.'

'I didn't want to end up hurting her.'

'Or get hurt by her.'

The American opened his mouth to react, but nothing came out. Frank felt bad for being so direct, but the younger man's evasive demeanour had hit a nerve with him; he recognised it all too well.

'I hope you don't mind me saying, but no matter how much running you do, it will catch up with you one day. I only found that out recently.'

'And what did you find out?' The American's question wasn't without mockery.

'That it is possible to live on an island, although not that long ago I feared the sea with every fibre in my body. What about that?' He laughed out loud and with a sense of relief he saw the

American smile.

'I remember now. What changed?'

'Good friends of mine urged me onto unstable boats until I got so seasick I stopped caring about my fear,' he said with irony. 'Truthfully, I was lucky enough to be reminded of what I do best.'

'Which is?'

'My writing.' He pointed his finger at the newspaper the younger man was still holding. 'That article, the one that says George Steers should be honoured, I wrote that. Although I'm sure George himself would feel no need for it. And the other one, the one referring to the anonymous letter-writer who disclosed the horrendous fate of the girls? That's my story as well.' He paused and continued. 'It's taken me a long time to get that done; for most of the time they weren't the proudest years of my life, but in the end, I realised that the significance lies in what you do, not in what you avoid.' He pulled his collar up and looked at the American. 'What will you do?'

'For now, I'll stay. I thought you could do with some help.' Suddenly he grinned mischievously. 'I've gotten myself a job at Ratsey's shipyard in Cowes.'

Frank laughed. 'Good for you; I'm sure we could benefit from your knowledge.' He got up and stretched his legs, shivering slightly; then he said in a voice loud enough to be heard over the wind, 'By the way, the cup they awarded – Steers couldn't care less about it. Fundamentally he wanted his design acknowledged and nothing else. That we both know that Steers was born in England, which technically makes him an Englishman who has beaten the English with an American yacht of which half the crew was English, doesn't change a thing; in the end, the victory was his.'

The American looked up at him in astonishment; his mouth wide open, his eyes almost popping out of his head. 'What did you just say?'

'I thought you knew as well, didn't you?' He looked at the surprised American and wondered if he had misunderstood him earlier when he had been referring to Steers's nationality. They stared at each other for some time, until the younger man broke the silence. 'How did you find out?'

'He told me. I don't think at the time he knew I was a reporter. What about you?'

'He told me as well. Remind me, when does something stop being a secret – if more than two people know?' He smiled and leapt up. 'In your article, you had a chance to mention it; why didn't you?'

'I didn't want to distract from the significance of the American win as I believe the accomplishment transcends the futile question of Steers's nationality. I didn't want to give anybody an excuse to challenge who the glory belonged to.'

'Maybe you're right.' He shook his head thoughtfully. 'But what about you: what about your name? After all the work you did for those girls, don't you want people to know?'

'Getting the story told was more important than who was doing the telling. I decided that this story didn't need a name.'

'I see.' He extended his hand with a playful smile. 'It's been a pleasure meeting you again and; I'm glad to see it hasn't ruined you as was claimed.'

Frank smiled back and took the young man's hand. 'On the contrary, I've finally taken charge of my own life. I'll keep an eye out for you, John.' He squeezed his hand lightly and turned to walk away.

'Shame your stories are only featured in the local paper, though,' were the last words he could hear the younger man say, before the wind picked up once more.

But they're my stories, he replied without words. *What will yours be?*

The End

of this book,
the beginning of the America's Cup

298

Advertisement in The Times

23 August 1851

Timber for sale – A great quantity of Planks, Sticks, Masts, and Spars, to be had cheap – Inquire at the Royal Yacht Club House, Cowes

Birth place of George Steers

Early on during the research for this book, we came across the following Passenger's List, showing arrivals on 11 July 1821 in the District of Norfolk and Portsmouth, United States:

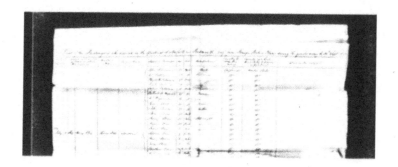

The list mentions George travelling with his family from England, "the country to which they belong", to the United States, the country "of which they intend to become inhabitants". (Note that the family name was originally spelled without the second 's').

Curious as to why we had seen information elsewhere stating that George was born in the United States, we decided to investigate his birth further. The information below is a summary of what we discovered.

In the newspapers that refer to a birth in the United States, dates and places of birth differ - New York is mentioned (and the year 1823), but mostly Washington D.C. (in 1820). The latter is repeated by family members, such as his brother James R. Steers (in a journal written before his death in 1869) and by a son of George (in a newspaper interview in 1896), information that seems to have found its way into other literature.

Other newspapers refer to George as being an Englishman, born either in Devon or Bow (in London) before he emigrated with his parents to the United States. In addition, a number of newspapers in 1851 and during the years thereafter allude to a rumour that George might have been born in England.

Until this day, we have not managed to find a birth certificate (or record of baptism) to confirm which is correct, although this isn't unusual given registering of births only became law in later years.

However, George's grave stone in Greenwood Cemetery, Manhattan states *"to the memory of my husband George Steers who died on 25 September 1856 aged 37 years, 1 month, 10 days"*, which makes his date of birth 15 August 1819.

Although this date doesn't correspond with George's age on the passenger's list (which indicates late 1818 or early 1819), a birth date in 1820 seems out of the question. Even more so given his sister Caroline is recorded as being 8 months old in July 1821 and hence likely to have been born (and conceived) in 1820.

This leaves the question as to whether it is possible that George could have been born in the United States and then returned to England with (part of) the family, before taking another ship to the United States in 1821 with the whole family.

During our research, we found a suggestion that George's father, Henry, travelled to the United States (Washington naval yard) around 1819 following the recommendation of an old colleague from Devon called John Thomas, who was already working there.

If this is correct, wife Ann (and their children at the time) must have travelled with Henry for George to have been born in the United States. It also implies that, sometime after George's birth, the whole family returned to England, either together or else separately, only to return to the United States in July 1821.

Considering the practical challenges of transatlantic travel under sail in those days, such as the cost of passage, the poor conditions aboard and duration (crossings in favourable winds could take on average 6 weeks and unfavourable significantly longer), this seems highly unlikely. Furthermore, the fact that Caroline was conceived and born in 1820 would have further complicated such a travel scenario for the family.

In addition, whilst we have found evidence of John Thomas working at the Washington Naval Yard in 1819 and 1820 (in the workbook and payroll records), Henry Steers isn't mentioned until 1822, when he is listed in a Washington DC street directory (as is John Thomas, albeit at a different address). Henry is mentioned in the payroll records of 1823.

My conclusion.

Although my research has not found concrete evidence to a birth in either country, I am of the view that George was born in England in 1819 and that the family travelled together to the United States for the first time in 1821.

I should however note that, in the 1855 Census of New York City, a few years after the £100 Cup had been won, George is recorded as being 36 years of age (supporting a birth year of 1819) and having been born in "Columbia Co(unty)" (New York State).

Given what I have learned about the man and the way he was celebrated for his achievements only a few years earlier, I believe that this shows that he saw himself at that time to be a true American. Just like the victory in the 1851 race became more than just a symbol of sailing supremacy, as it had restored the American pride, George himself had come to represent the American dream; the "boy from the shipyard" who had "advanced the flag of his native land". His funeral, only a year later in 1856, confirmed the high esteem in which George was at the time as he was mourned by the whole City and his death "regarded as a public calamity".

George chose in 1855 to give something to the country he grew up in; he was feted by; and he was proud of: his nationality, as for him, being an American had started long before his success as the designer of *America* and it had no relation to the country he was born in. This, I believe, reflects the true American identity even more.

May this spirit long continue.

Map of Race Course

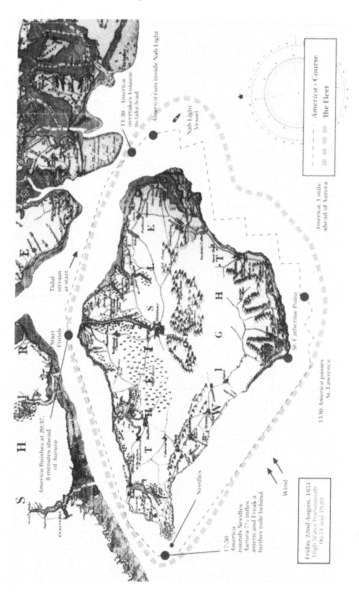

11.30 America overtakes Volante to take lead

America cuts inside Nab Light

Nab Light Vessel

America 1 mile ahead of Aurora

St. Catherine Point

13.30 America passes St. Lawrence

America's Course
The Fleet

25 26 29 30

Tidal stream at start

Start
Finish

America finishes at 20.37, 8 minutes ahead of Aurora

Needles

17.50 America rounds Needles Aurora 7½ miles astern and Freak a further mile behind

Wind

Friday 22nd August, 1851
High Water Portsmouth
06.24 and 19.03

Acknowledgements

By now you will have read (or not yet: if you're like my mother-in-law, you read the end first), this novel about a race that almost didn't happen for a trophy that was nearly melted down. Because that's what the winning Americans contemplated doing; having the silver cup turned into medals to be given to each member of the syndicate, as the trophy had sat without use in a cabinet, in need of a polish.

I'm glad they didn't; the Cup has since become the oldest perpetual international sporting trophy, still vehemently fought over until this day. Having said that, some might disagree, many fortunes could have been saved over the years!

I dare to state that there are similarities with the writing of this novel. It has been a work in progress for many years; fought over, and against, by myself (but never alone).

We first heard about the America's Cup in 2001 (the 150th Anniversary celebration on the Isle of Wight, in which the breathtakingly beautiful three remaining original J Class yachts also participated). Our curiosity about the Cup's origin has taken us on a long and wondrous journey - to Museums and shipyards throughout Old and New England, and to wonderful institutions such as Royal Yacht Squadron and the New York Yacht Club.

Many years, thus many people I'm grateful to. Finally, the time has come to thank you!

Ian Walker, for introducing us to the Royal Yacht Squadron after which we were permitted to visit the New York Yacht Club, as well as the Commodores at the time, who were most generous in allowing us to spend several days in their libraries.

The readers, for some of whom the manuscript was still twice the size and therefore required much determination; you gave me faith to continue, so thank you Chris Horton, Julia and John Hamilton, Jackie Shepherd, Elizabeth Bickham, Pippa Fawcett, Nicky Hudson, Roger Gascoigne and Julian Metherell.

The professionals who have assisted me: Leslie McDowell

from The Literary Consultancy, Sarah Quigley at Cornerstones, and above all her colleague Nicola Doherty who helped me cut my manuscript in half with a smile. Caroline Teagle in New York, who creatively and patiently designed the wonderful cover. Payam Azadi from Action Graphics, Barry Pickthall from PPL Media and Georgina Aldridge from Clays.

Others who have kindly given their time and shared their knowledge and family history with us: Rupert Paget, brother of the current Marquess of Anglesey; Rod Hingston, the former senior silversmith at Garrard who had repaired the trophy after it was damaged in 1997; David Hughes, honorary historian at the RYS, and John Sharp, who explained the history of the Washington naval yard civilian workforce in the 19th century.

Friends, all of you – you know who you are - who teased me for taking so long but at the same time continued to show a sincere interest and, in the end, never doubted it would become a book. And especially the friend who convinced me to come sailing for many years: Frans van der Zee, may your sailing 'on the other side' be as good as those years. We miss you.

New friends, who spontaneously showed – and keep showing – their enthusiasm for this project; I hope you realise who you are; holidaymakers in Bermuda and boat-enthusiasts in the Netherlands, the UK and US.

My family. My English parents-in-law and sister-in-law Joanna who was always willing to share her knowledge with us. And, of course, my dear, dear mother and two sisters; they embody creativity and inspiration. I wish for everyone to have examples like you. I love you.

And, to Rob, because whenever I mention 'us', I mean him: we come as a team. How wonderful it is to be loved unconditionally and wholeheartedly. My biggest support (and of many others!) and the love of my life. Actually, very similar to the love our dog Boots(ie) gives me; she takes after him.

Leaves me with this: may your 'sparrowhawk', whatever it is, not paralyse you, but spur you on!

Sources

I have searched through countless newspapers, books, websites and other indispensable resources for information and inspiration for this work. Below is an attempt to list them all.

For historical facts and information on the few real persons that appear in this book, I am immensely grateful to the following:

Historical newspapers and other periodicals - and those wonderful people who have digitised them over the years - such as: The Times (of London), New York Daily Times and Tribune, The Illustrated London News, London Examiner, Morning Courier, Harper's Monthly, Isle of Wight Observer, Bell's Life in London, Punch Magazine and many others.

The private libraries of the Royal Yacht Squadron and New York Yacht Club which gave us access to – amongst other things – letters and other documents, such as: the diary of James Rich Steers, containing the "Log of Yacht America"; the James Hamilton collection of papers; and the George Schuyler papers.

Other libraries and institutions in the UK, such as: the British Library, Guildhall, Victoria & Albert, British Museum, Priaulx Library Guernsey, Hyde Park Family History Centre - Church of Jesus Christ of Latter-day Saints, National Archives, Society of Genealogists.

And those outside the UK, such as in the USA: New York Historical Society, New York State Archives, Old York Library, Fire Museum of New York, City Island Nautical Museum and Historical Society, Mystic Seaport Museum, New York City Department of Records and Information Services; and Sweden: Swedish National Maritime Museums.

As more and more information gets digitised, I've rummaged through numerous websites, impossible to do them all justice, but I'll mention a few. Family history sites, such as Ancestry.co.uk, Rootsweb.com, Familysearch.org, newyorkroots.org, and sites with information on the America's Cup, such as Yves Gary's beautiful website "america-scoop.com".

And finally, I have consulted the following books:

Boswell, Charles. *The America; The Story of the World's Most Famous Yacht*: David McKay Company Inc., 1967

Coffin, Captain Roland F. *The America's Cup. How it was won by the yacht America in 1851 and has been since defended.*

Fisher, Bob. *An Absorbing Interest; The America's Cup – A History 1851 - 2003*: John Wiley & Sons Limited, 2007

Linwood Snow, Ralph and Lee, Captain Douglas K. *A Shipyard in Maine – Percy & Small and the Great Schooners*: Tilbury House Publishers, 1999

Morrison, John Harrison. *History of New York shipyards*: 1909

Rayner, Ranulf. *The Story of the America's Cup 1851 - 2000*: David Bateman, 2000

Rodgers, Charles T. *American Superiority at the World's Fair*: 1852

Rousmaniere, John. *The Low Black Schooner: Yacht America 1851 – 1945*: Mystic Conn.1986

Shaw, David W. *America's Victory*: The Free Press, 2002

Thompson, Winfield M., Stephens, William P. and Swan, William U. *The Yacht "America", A History Written*: Martin, Hopkinson & Company Limited, 1925

Thompson, Winfield M. and Lawson, Thomas W. *The Lawson History of the America's Cup*: Ashford Press Publishing, 1986

With regard to the fictional characters, Frank and John, and the story that connects them; that part is completely made up. I've tried to be as historically accurate as I could, but any inaccuracies in their story are due to my imagination alone…